Originally from South Manchester, Stephen Galbraith moved to Sheffield in 1994 and still lives in the city with his wife and daughters. After working in senior management in several business sectors, he sold his company and embarked upon a Creative Writing MA at Manchester Metropolitan University, graduating with Distinction. *The Wythenshawe Dandy* is his debut crime novel.

S. J. GALBRAITH

THE WYTHENSHAWE DANDY

CROMER

PUBLISHED BY SALT PUBLISHING 2026

2 4 6 8 10 9 7 5 3 1

First published in Great Britain in 2026 by
Salt Publishing Ltd
12 Norwich Road, Cromer NR27 0AX United Kingdom

www.saltpublishing.com

Salt Publishing Limited Reg. No. 5293401

A CIP catalogue record for this book is available from the British Library

ISBN 978 1 78463 382 0 (Paperback edition)
ISBN 978 1 78463 383 7 (Electronic edition)

Typeset in Neacademia by Salt Publishing

Printed and bound in Great Britain by Clays Ltd, Elcograf S.p.A

THE WYTHENSHAWE DANDY

1

EDINBURGH BUS STATION

GEMMA GRANT GLANCED at the station clock and inspected her ticket, all the while wondering if the man who had once tried to kill her still wanted her dead.

It would be fine, she told herself. Two years had passed, and she had long ceased to be any sort of threat to him. Had he not loved her, loved her with a passion, before that terrible day? He had; she was sure of it. Gemma smiled as she remembered the good times: playing footsie under the table at Nona's Bistro, walking hand in hand through the gardens at Chatsworth, endless kisses by the fallen oak in Whitely Woods.

She checked the clock again, checked the departure time on her ticket again, checked her phone again. Heart pounding, legs jiggling, Gemma stuffed the phone and the ticket back into her coat pocket and stared into space.

At nine o'clock, the 547 to Sheffield rumbled into the bus station, spewing diesel fumes into a blustery Edinburgh evening. She got up and brushed the creases out of her coat. There was snow in the air – thick flakes gathered and swirled with every passing bus; they stung Gemma's nose and cheeks as she stepped outside. The tiny wheels on her holdall couldn't cope with the kerb, so she grabbed the strap and hoisted it over her shoulder, taking care not to snag the manila envelope that she had tucked under her arm. It was a large envelope – the stiff sort, with a cardboard back, designed for certificates or photographs. After turning it through 360 degrees, checking the corners for damage, and testing the rigidity of the all-important cardboard back, Gemma slipped it under her coat. With her envelope safe from the snow, and the holdall's shoulder strap digging deep into her collar bone, she waddled across three lanes of slippery tarmac to the boarding point.

This was to be a new beginning. Gemma Jane Grant's story would start where she wanted it to start; and she wanted it to start today – on her eighteenth birthday – at Edinburgh bus station, with all her worldly goods in a full-to-bursting holdall slung over an aching shoulder. She deserved a fresh start, of course she did. And, after all *he* had suffered, poor Flynn deserved a fresh start too. But Flynn's emails had been curt and matter of fact – downright cold, actually. It was as if he'd had his secretary write them. And he didn't even have a secretary. Or did he?

No, no secretary.

It was just that things were a bit awkward between them right now – of course they were. But still, she'd expected something more than platitudes; something more than 'Okay' or 'Yes, I'll be around'; something more than the promise of a taxi waiting at the station.

Perhaps he'd been busy – too busy to chat; or perhaps he thought she'd prefer to keep things business-like for the time being; or perhaps it was simply that Flynn was as nervous and as apprehensive as she was.

Gemma watched the coach driver sling her holdall into the luggage compartment. She straightened the strap on her handbag and pressed the big manila envelope tight to her chest.

Perhaps she should stop speculating and get on the bloody coach.

SNAKE PASS, PEAK DISTRICT

If, at the age of thirty-five, you can look back on life and regret only the things you *didn't* do, then you're a smug bastard and you've probably never killed anyone.

Flynn tore *the Guardian* in half and tossed it into the kindling basket. He wasn't sure what annoyed him most: the bullshit article, the columnist's name (Sebastian Montagu-Fiennes), or the accompanying photograph of a sparsely bearded man wearing hipster glasses. He reached for the bottle by his feet and poured himself a large one.

Flynn's musings were interrupted by the bleep of a text message from someone asking if he'd ever been injured at work. He smiled, very nearly laughed out loud.

It was nine o'clock. Nine o'clock exactly – he watched the digits on his phone slip from 8:59 p.m. to 9:00 p.m. Too early for bed, but too late for . . .

Too late for what, exactly?

Too late for a night out at the theatre? Too late for a game of five-a-side with the crowd from The King's Head? Too late to head into Sheffield for dinner at some well-reviewed restaurant?

Flynn sighed and poured himself another measure – he hadn't gone out on the town for ages, not since what had happened on the Snake Pass that cold December night.

He'd stuck to his exercise regime at least. Exercise kept him sane, just about. He needed his exercise – needed it as much now as he'd needed it in the old days, if for very different reasons. Press-ups in the yard, rain or shine, preferably rain. Sit-ups in front of the stove, the hotter the better. Pull-ups on the eleventh tread of his wrought-iron staircase. Long runs across the Pennine moors – or along the Snake Pass when there wasn't too much traffic – all the way to the south-western fringes of the city. Exercise was good. Exercise kept his demons shackled.

But Flynn hadn't exercised for the last few weeks, not since the two-year anniversary brought it all back. Over the last couple of weeks his hangovers had got so bad that he just couldn't. He was disgusted with himself.

Now, he whiled away the hours writing a novel that he knew was crap. Now, he spent his days thinking thoughts that made him miserable. Now, his demons were loosed.

❧

THE ROYAL OAK, PITSMOOR, NORTH EAST SHEFFIELD

On any other Thursday evening, Sean Mulligan would have grabbed the thieving little bugger by his hair and smashed his face into the table. He'd have flipped open the trusty Zippo, sparked up, and held the flame under the gormless chuff's earlobe. He'd have held it there until the skin blistered and turned purple.

Mulligan was sitting opposite Trevor Murray in the back room of The Royal Oak, staring at a pile of bank notes. Trevor's numbers were a complete fiction of course, but it wasn't something Mulligan wanted to deal with on this particular Thursday evening. No, he couldn't allow himself to be distracted – the job he was planning for tomorrow morning was far too important. A risky venture, for sure, but by Friday teatime, if everything went to plan, he'd have tied up the loose end that had been haunting him these last two years.

Trevor continued to catalogue a collection of gripes and excuses: rival dealers, unprecedented police activity on his patch, a dodgy car battery, inclement weather. He went on and on and on.

Mulligan put the cash into his briefcase without comment,

looked at his wristwatch (it was 9:00 p.m.) and held up a hand. 'We're out of time, Trev.'

Trevor scowled, grabbed his beer, walked away.

A lorryload of whimpering Romanian girls, Mulligan reckoned, would be easier to manage than that cocky little gobshite. Which reminded him: when tomorrow's business was done, he'd need to talk to Gary about planning for next month's shipment. Not that Gary needed his dad's help these days – Gary was a natural, especially with the young ones.

Mulligan scanned the three mobile phones he had lined up on the table: one red, one white, one blue. The blue one was vibrating. He picked it up, read the text, and shook his head. 'Pervy Yank bastard!'

Carl and Gary were keeping an eye on things from the other side of the bar. Mulligan beckoned them.

Carl was carrying an army surplus duffle bag; Gary had brought his mum's cabin case (the one she'd bought for that long weekend in Benidorm last month). They put down their luggage and sat at the table.

'Good,' Mulligan said, nodding at the bags, 'you got my message then.'

'Yes.' Gary screwed up his face and folded his arms.

Mulligan rolled his eyes. 'I've booked us rooms at The Snake Pass Inn.'

'But why do we have to stay overnight?' Carl asked. 'You said the job wasn't till tomorrow morning, and The Snake Pass Inn can't be much more than a half-hour drive.'

'They're forecasting snow,' Mulligan said. 'We're taking no chances.'

Carl sank back into his chair. 'We'd be all right in the Range Rover, surely?'

Mulligan snorted a noisy breath. He resisted the temptation to tell them to shut up and do as they were bloody well told, and stared at the tabletop instead. This was no time to provoke another interminable argument with Gary.

Gary sighed and shook his head. 'Go on then, Dad. Tell us what's happening.'

From his jacket pocket, Mulligan produced an envelope, and, from the envelope, two photographs – two head and shoulder shots. He laid them side-by-side on the table.

'James Flynn,' Mulligan said, left hand shielding his mouth, right hand nudging the first picture forward. It was a photograph of a strikingly handsome man in his mid-thirties – black hair, blue eyes, broad shoulders.

Then he turned his attention to the second picture, a photograph of a fair-haired young woman – porcelain skin, peony lips, pretty. 'Gemma Grant,' he said, from behind a tightly clenched fist.

Carl raised an eyebrow. 'I don't recognise this Flynn bloke, but Gemma Grant . . . isn't she the one . . . it must have been two years ago, but isn't she the girl who—'

'Yes,' Mulligan said, squeezing his fist even tighter.

Gary frowned.

'Now then, lads,' Mulligan leaned in and lowered his voice, 'which one of you is up for a spot of blackmail?'

2

WITH ONLY A dozen or so passengers boarding the coach at Edinburgh, Gemma managed to bag a pair of seats all to herself. She sat by the aisle, which left the window seat free for her stuff: handbag, phone, Pringles, Pepsi Max, big manila envelope. The Pringles tube and the bottle of Pepsi Max were clamped upright between the handbag and the armrest to stop them rolling about. The envelope, wedged under the bag because it wouldn't quite fit inside, was going nowhere either. She propped her phone in the coils of her handbag's shoulder strap so that she could read any incoming message without having to rummage around in the dark.

Smiling at her own ingenuity, a handful of Pringles scattered on her lap, Gemma pulled her headphones back over her ears and settled down to Stephen Fry reading *Harry Potter and the Philosopher's Stone.*

❧

At one minute past nine on the morning of Friday, 10 January, Gemma Grant stepped off the coach at Sheffield Bus Station. She checked her phone to see if Flynn had replied to any of her texts. She'd sent one to warn him that she'd be late, another joking about the misery of sitting in stationary traffic for three hours, and another about all the rubberneckers she'd seen driving past a burned-out lorry on the M1.

He hadn't responded to any of them.

She desperately wanted to ring him to let him know she'd arrived, but there was little point – he never answered his phone. Even when she left a voicemail (older men responded best to voicemails – or maybe just *her* voicemails), Flynn responded by text. Gemma sent yet another text before setting off across the road to the railway station.

The station concourse was heaving. Gemma walked briskly past the bustling tables outside Café Ritazza and on towards the toilets. Distracted by a little girl carrying a hot chocolate loaded with whipped cream and marshmallows, Gemma tripped over a toppled suitcase and stumbled. The big manila envelope slipped from under her arm and slid easily across the polished tiles, coming to a halt only inches from a pool of spilt coffee.

Gemma decided to put the envelope into her holdall. She unzipped the top flap and squashed everything down, but the bag was too small and too flimsy and too rammed with clothes. If she tried to squeeze the envelope in, it would get bent out of shape. So she gave up and tucked it back under her arm.

It would have been nice to shower and change before going to Flynn's place, but all the station toilets had to offer were tiny wash basins with those annoying taps that you have to keep pushing. And besides, her clothes were so horribly crumpled that it wouldn't be worth it. She rifled her handbag, digging out a pack of cleansing wipes, a lipstick, her fancy mascara from John Lewis, and an eyeliner pencil from Superdrug.

Gemma enjoyed doing her makeup, enjoyed looking at herself in the mirror. She knew that vanity was a bad thing (well, everyone said it was), but she couldn't resist looking at herself at every opportunity. And why not? She was young and she was pretty. Why shouldn't she take full advantage of that?

'Because you're a wee girl of eighteen, dear: *only just an adult.*' That's what the old lady had said. 'Stay in Edinburgh a while longer, get yourself an education, there's plenty of time for all that later.'

Only just an adult as far as drinking and smoking and voting go, Gemma thought, as she applied her lipstick – but she'd felt like a woman for years. And she'd passed for a woman for years: from the age of fifteen, she recalled – around the time she'd found herself all alone in the world. And then she remembered that cold December night when it all went so horribly wrong.

No. She would stop thinking about the past and focus on the here and now. Gemma hated her pale skin and dense copper locks. But she didn't have freckles (thank God!), and since she dyed her hair and tinted her eyebrows, nobody would guess she was a ginger. She studied her hair in the mirror, stepping back to check the position of the parting, leaning in to assess the colour. She had tried for the 'dark ash blonde' promised on the colour chart, but it hadn't quite worked out. It never quite worked out: natural ginger outshines chemical blonde every time, so she always ended up auburn. A girl can't escape her genes, she thought, or her *roots*. Gemma smiled as she put the make-up back into her handbag. She smiled again as she took one last look at herself in the mirror. Auburn would do just fine.

A text came through from Flynn:

> sent taxi 2 collect u
> be w8ing in pick up zone at 9:45
> blue vauxhall insignia

Gemma tutted. 'Thanks,' she said out loud. 'Can't wait to see you, either.'

❧

The driver of the blue Vauxhall Insignia was a fat, sweaty man with thinning hair and tattooed knuckles. He didn't bother to wind down his window when Gemma approached. He looked hard at her, then back to his phone, then hard at her again. He nodded at her holdall and thumbed towards the boot. The tailgate hissed as it rose.

Gemma put her hands on her hips and stared at him.

He lowered the window to eye level.

'Taxi for Gemma Grant?' she said.

He gave a perfunctory nod and buzzed the window back up.

'Charming,' she said under her breath, shoving the holdall into the boot. The tailgate hummed back down without warning, narrowly missing her head. 'Charming,' she said again, this time loud enough for him to hear.

'I take it you know where you're going?' Gemma said, fumbling for the seatbelt.

He glanced at her in the rear-view mirror and nodded.

She glared back.

The shops and bars and restaurants they passed on the Ecclesall Road sparked happy memories. She'd had a whale of a time back then.

She'd misled him, of course. And there had been consequences. Little lies, she'd thought at the time – just a bit of fun. She gripped the door handle tight and tried to think more positive thoughts. The old lady had told her she was wrong to blame herself – she'd been adamant about that. But what did she know?

Soon, they were out of the city. The Ecclesall Road became the Hathersage Road. Suburbs faded into countryside. Pasture gave way to woods and moorland. Now, there was snow by the side of the road. As they drove higher, the snow got thicker. From time to time it was piled so high that Gemma couldn't see past.

On they drove, through Hathersage and Bamford and along the western fringes of the Ladybower Reservoir. She recognised the bridge that spanned the tip of the lake, and the tall traffic lights at the end, and the sign: SNAKE PASS – OPEN. They turned left onto the Snake Pass and drove east along the northern shore. Water to her left, woods to her right. There had been snow on the ground two years ago. Not quite as much back then, she recalled, but there had certainly been snow.

3

FLYNN WOKE EARLY, racked with remorse. He went downstairs and sat at the dining table with a glass of water and his last two paracetamol; he studied his reflection in the window a while before turning off the light. For the briefest of moments, Flynn pictured his wife sitting beside him – he pictured her as she was the day they met.

Flynn's recollection of that day was not, he understood, what others would consider a typical sort of memory. It was no vague succession of patchy visions, biting emotions, amplified sensations. Flynn's memory was as solid as a scene from a movie – it was as if that first encounter with the girl who would become his wife had been captured on acetate.

He closed his eyes and played the reel in his head. It had become a habit: something he did when he was feeling low. It was a bad habit. But each time he replayed that scene he would spot some fresh nuance in the leading lady's dialogue, observe a new detail about the setting, notice something that he had never noticed before. He had played the reel so many times that he now remembered more about that brief episode, back in 1998, than he could possibly have taken in on the day he'd acted his part in that scene for real.

❧

13 JULY 1998

Sheffield was spookily quiet with most of the students gone for the summer. He had James Joyce in his rucksack, and the idea that a cool pint of Moonshine would help the *Ulysses* go down. She was in the beer garden of The Porter Brook, sipping Chianti and reading Dostoyevsky. A soft black dress hugged the contours of her braless breasts. He found himself staring.

'Can I help you?' she said, letting her hair fall over her face. Auburn hair. Hair the colour of honeyed oak. She tossed it back with a practised flick.

Posh accent, very posh indeed.

And so confident.

Intimidating eyes. If he'd had to guess the colour, he'd have guessed green – dark green with a hint of indigo. Eyes the colour of the North Sea in February.

Slowly, deliberately, shamelessly, she looked him up and down.

'No,' he said. 'I—'

'What then?'

'I was looking at your book.' He swallowed hard. '*Crime and Punishment* – Dostoyevsky. I—'

'Really?'

'Yes.'

'Oh.' She frowned – made a bit of a show of it. 'Well, if it's only the book you're interested in . . .'

'No, I—'

'You're a *big* bastard, aren't you,' she said. 'How did you get like that? Pumping iron à la Arnold Schwarzenegger, was it? But why would you bother? You're big anyway, naturally big, born to be big. What are you – six foot eight? And not bad looking, in a *big* sort of a way. So why would you make all that effort?'

'I—'

'Vanity, is it?'

'No.'

He waited for her to interrupt again.

She didn't.

'Rugby,' he said at last. 'I used to work out for strength, but I don't play anymore.'

'Shame.' She sniffed and looked into her glass. 'I like a man in shorts.'

She patted the seat of the chair beside her.

He sat down.

'So, remind me,' she said, in a lippy whisper, 'what was it you were looking at?'

He cleared his throat and took a deep breath. 'You. I was looking at you. I thought you looked . . . nice.'

'Nice?'

'I mean, you know . . .'

'Well, darling,' she said, looking hard into his eyes, 'I'm afraid I'm a very long way from *nice*.'

'No, I'm sure—'

She held up a hand and shook her head. 'What's your name?'

He tried to hold her gaze but couldn't. He looked down: down at the sun-silvered table top, down at the dappled shadows cast by the trees on the riverbank. But soon he found himself staring at the soft black dress that clung to her slim thighs, found himself staring at her porcelain-perfect calves and her flip-flopped feet and her coral-pink toenails. He looked away, looked up at slate roofs and weed-infested gutters, looked up into the cloudless sky.

'If you told me, would you have to kill me?' she asked, pressing an index finger to her chin.

'What?'

'I only asked your name!'

'Sorry. My name's Flynn.'

'Flynn?'

'Yes.'

'No first name?'

'Everyone calls me *Flynn*, just that, just *Flynn*. You know, like at school.'

She nodded. 'I like *Flynn*. It's a solid name, an honest name, the sort of name you can rely on. My name is Parker, but,' she coughed a laugh, 'it makes me sound like a chauffeur, doesn't it!'

'No, not at all. I—'

'I've got it, *Flynn!*' She slapped his knee hard, then patted it gently, then squeezed. 'Why don't you call me *Sarah*, just that, just *Sarah*.'

❧

Flynn opened his eyes to a dark January morning in 2014.

Sarah was dead. He should have got used to it by now.

He hadn't. Not completely. Especially not when he woke up and rolled over and reached across and—

No, he hadn't got over Sarah.

Sarah once told him that she took up smoking at fourteen and gave up at fifteen, only a few months later, 'but it took two bloody years for the cravings to die!'

Two years after her death, his cravings for Sarah hadn't even *begun* to die. The past had a powerful hold on Flynn. His history defined him. And no matter what all those comfy-shoed therapists might think, it always would. They could say that none of it was his fault. They could dismiss his teenage years as some sort of botched prologue or false beginning. They could prattle on about him being the author of his own story – a story that could start now, if he wanted. Or later today. Or tomorrow. Or whenever he chose.

But what they said was, and would always be, complete bollocks.

As if you can choose your own beginning! Wherever his story

might end, the beginning was fixed – fixed in his own unfortunate history. And if—

'Stop!' Flynn said out loud. He groaned and stretched and breathed in through his nose and out through his mouth.

'Hot bath,' he decided. Things never seem quite so bad when you're in a hot bath.

The phone started to ring. He ignored it.

'Anyway . . .'

He'd said *anyway* out loud. He was talking to himself again. The sound of his empty little words echoing round his empty little house made his head hurt.

Flynn's house was in the Peak District, half an hour's drive out of Sheffield. He remembered the day he came to see it for the very first time. It was hidden amongst the trees and heather and boulders at the end of a rocky and rutted track. The track wound uphill, steeply, from an unsigned turn-off on a wooded stretch of the Snake Pass. Your average four-wheel drive wouldn't be able to cope with that track, but Sarah had bought them an ex-Forestry Commission Land Rover with oversized wheels. Sarah sometimes used to—

He tried to fight it (used every technique, every distraction, every ruse), but memories, sharp as needles, began to prick. Sometimes they came to him as images or sound bites; sometimes as nothing more than vague feelings; sometimes as suffocating, gut-tightening passions. Often though, his memories came to him as narrative – like a story he'd crafted over so many drafts that, by the final edit, he couldn't remember how the thing had started out.

She hadn't let him see their little Snake Pass retreat until the builders were finished. Wanted it to be a surprise for him, she'd said. It was small, but big enough for a weekend getaway. It was open plan. It was heated by a cast-iron stove that she'd chosen because of its nice big window. There was a kitchen at one end, a big comfy sofa at the other, and an ancient oak table with mismatched chairs in the middle. The slope of the roof made the mezzanine bedroom awkward for a man of Flynn's size, but Sarah's architect had managed to squeeze in a king-size bed and a comfortable bathroom. The day she brought him here for the first time, Sarah had made him close his eyes until—

'Enough!'

Flynn wrapped his arms around his head and roared.

The brooding had to stop. The self-pity had to stop. The drinking had to stop. His father had pissed his life away after Mum died, and he was well on the way to doing the same. It was a blessing, actually, that he and Sarah had never had children. And—

'Stop! Stop! Stop!'

The phone stopped ringing. It was bound to have been Lizzie McDonald. Flynn felt a pang of guilt. He knew it would have been Lizzie because no one else rang the landline, and he felt guilty because he knew that she worried about him. But recently she'd begun to nag him about moving on. No, not 'nag', that wasn't fair. She was trying to persuade him to 'reboot' his life – and she was right, of course she was. But Lizzie McDonald had also appointed herself chief matchmaker. This was one of the reasons he hadn't turned up at the McDonalds' house for Christmas or New Year, and now he was feeling guilty about that too.

It wasn't that he didn't want a new relationship, it was just that Lizzie's matches were never quite right. He found himself thinking of Sarah again. That first meeting. The black dress, the porcelain skin, those eyes – eyes the colour of the North Sea in February.

I'm a very long way from nice.

Yes, Lizzie's matches were a bit too *nice* for Flynn. Now he was thinking of Cassie. Lizzie would never try to fix him up with someone like Cassie. Never in a million years. Cassie May was self-obsessed, high maintenance, paranoid, unpredictable, sharp-tongued, and too clever for her own good. Cassie May was perfect. And she was single now – had been since Marco ran off to

London last year. And he *did* need to 'reboot' his life. If he asked Cassie out it would certainly get Lizzie off his back. So why not? Yes, he'd go for it. He'd telephone Cassie and ask her out. He'd been thinking about it for weeks. Today he would actually do it.

It was utterly dark outside. No moon and no stars meant heavy cloud, which might mean snow. He stared out at the blackness, wondering if it had snowed, wondering if the snowploughs and the gritters had been out, wondering if the Snake Pass would be open or passable at least. He looked at the clock on the microwave – 9:00 a.m.

Ten o'clock, he decided, was a more respectable hour to ask a lady out to dinner. In the meantime, he would have a nice soaky bath, get dressed, and get lively. Because, if she said yes, there'd be provisions to buy and a meal to prepare.

Coffee. He needed coffee.

❧

In the end, Flynn needed more than coffee. He downed a couple of measures of whisky before making the call.

'Okay, yes,' Cassie said, at one minute past ten. 'That would be lovely.'

'Just the two of us, I mean.' Flynn held the phone tight to his ear and grabbed his car keys from the hook by the door.

She breathed out, heavily. 'Yes.'

'It would be, you know,' he searched for a word that didn't sound too American but couldn't think of one. 'It would be a *date*,' he said at last, gripping his car keys tight.

'I get it, Flynn. How many more times do you want me to say *yes*?'

4

SEAN MULLIGAN, GARY and Carl huddled round the table furthest from the bar, and nearest to the fire, at The Snake Pass Inn. Mulligan had his three phones lined up. As he stared at them, their clocks shifted, simultaneously, from 9:00 a.m. to 9:01 a.m.

A young woman in a tight black T-shirt came over to clear their breakfast things. 'Everything all right for you, gentlemen?' she said, loading her tray.

Carl had been watching her for some time. 'Fantastic, luv.'

The others nodded.

'More tea?' she asked.

Sean Mulligan shook his head.

'No thanks, luv,' Carl said.

The girl took the tray back into the kitchen. When the swing door finally stopped swinging, Carl got up. 'I'm going outside for a smoke,' he said, and walked off.

Mulligan grunted. 'Best be quick,' he called out after him. Then he turned to Gary: 'Now you're sure you know what you're doing, you and Carl?'

'Yes, Dad. But . . .'

'But what?'

Gary shook his head. 'These fuckers could hurt us, Dad. Or hurt the business. Or both.'

'Yes, they could. And that's precisely why we're doing this. In a day or two it'll all be sorted.'

Gary held his head in his hands. 'Either that or we'll be well and truly fucked.'

'Oh, for Christ's sake, Gary!' Mulligan said. 'You're such an old woman sometimes.'

'Think about it, Dad! That girl turns up after all this time. Turns up while *he*'s in town, for fuck's sake!'

'Coincidence, Gary. And they're hardly likely to meet, are they? Not if we keep on top of things.' Mulligan leaned back and folded his arms. 'He's here on business, that's all. Still trying to buy himself a fucking football club.'

'And the girl?' Gary said. 'Why'd she come back?'

'Does it matter? She was bound to turn up eventually. And it suits us now, anyway. All that matters is that we're on top of things.'

Gary sighed. 'Maybe.' Then he turned back to his father. 'But fucking hell, Dad, I can see all this turning to shit, really I can. If that fucking American—'

The blue phone began to vibrate. 'Speak of the Devil,' Mulligan said. He took a deep breath and picked up the phone. '. . . Yes . . . Yes, it's all in hand . . . Yes . . . No . . . Yes, I'll sort it.'

Mulligan put the phone back down with the others and turned to Gary. 'He wasn't happy with the girl you fixed him up with last night. You know what he wants.'

Gary pressed the heel of his hand into his forehead. 'I know exactly what he wants, but Jesus Christ, Dad, it's risky. I swear that American fucker's going to drop us in the shit one of these days.'

'Just sort it, Gary. One last time.'

Gary looked away and nodded.

10:15 a.m. Another buzzing phone, the white one this time. Mulligan snatched it up and pressed it to his ear.

'She's on her way, is she?' he said. 'In the cab, yeah . . . Good, right . . . What? . . . Fucking hell, Dave. What do you mean, *Flynn's just driven off*? You told me he never goes out in the mornings; you told me he was a total pisshead and . . . What? Where's that? . . . And you're sure he'll be there? . . . Yeah, well you'd better be fucking sure. And how long till the girl gets here? . . . Right. Stay put, and make sure you get some decent footage?'

After a moment of silence, Mulligan, knuckles white, put his phone down.

'I told you, didn't I,' Gary said. 'I told you we couldn't trust Dave Roland, I told you he was a twat. I even said—'

Mulligan drew rapid, snorting, nasal breaths. He tensed, half closed his eyes, and wagged a finger.

Gary stopped talking.

Mulligan breathed out, and then in again. He rested his hands, palms down, fingers splayed, on the table. 'We can still pull this off,' he said. 'Now here's what we're going to do . . .'

5

FLYNN WAS GIDDY as a schoolboy. Cassie was coming to dinner! His city centre flat was empty (or 'between tenants', as his useless estate agent would have it), so he thought he might as well make use of it. He couldn't expect her to drive out to his place in the sticks, and he couldn't afford a restaurant in town, so it made perfect sense.

A memory of Sarah surfaced. Her lips, warm and wet; champagne breath hot in his mouth. Flynn felt a lump rise in his throat. But he knew that if he didn't look forward, if he didn't force himself to forge a new life, then, one way or another, he wouldn't have a life to reboot.

'Sarah would have wanted you to be happy,' Lizzie had said. But Lizzie didn't know Sarah the way he knew Sarah.

At 10:15 a.m., Flynn set off for Glossop with a list of ingredients for Jamie Oliver's scallops with fennel, orange and almond salad, and Delia Smith's lasagne al forno. By 1:00 p.m. he was back in his kitchen chopping onions. By 2:00 p.m. he was in the shower, applying the hair conditioner he'd found at the back of the bathroom cabinet. By 3:00 p.m. he was in his car and ready for his first proper date with Cassie. He'd planned the dinner conversation, the seduction, the courtship, the proposal, the wedding, the children, and the long and happy lives they would lead together.

Another pang of guilt. But Sarah would never have understood what he was feeling right now. She'd have laughed at him, she'd have said, 'How can you be unfaithful to a corpse?'

Sarah wasn't like other people.

❧

As Flynn deposited his cool bag on the kitchen worktop in the city flat, he spotted the time on the oven clock – 5:00 p.m. – and was struck by an intense feeling of déjà vu. Then came a moment of overwhelming and inexplicable panic. The panic dissipated as quickly as it had come on, but when he checked his watch, wondering how it could possibly be five o'clock already, a lump rose in his throat. He was confused now, and anxious, and his head hurt. Maybe it was because he was behind schedule, or because this was his first *first date* in years. Yes, that was probably it.

He unpacked the cool bag. Half a dozen hand-dived scallops, fresh salad, home-made lasagne, two Gü chocolate mousses, a bottle of Bollinger that some idiot newspaper editor had sent Sarah for New Year's Eve a few weeks back.

Cassie wouldn't be arriving for a couple of hours, but already his stomach was tight. Had the cleaners laid out fresh linen in the bedroom? Would it even come to that? He walked over to the bedroom door, twisted the knob, and went in. Yes, he thought to himself, even if she didn't stay the night, she might . . . they might—

A young woman lay naked on the bed. Her head, shoulders and upper torso were propped up on well-plumped pillows. Eyes closed. Arms crossed neatly over her chest. Dense auburn hair. Alabaster skin. She looked like a Pre-Raphaelite painter's muse.

And she was dead. Flynn just knew.

It is natural to want to touch, to feel for warmth, to check for life. He ached to lay a hand on her wrist, just to be sure, but he couldn't bring himself to touch the dead. Flynn's windpipe tightened. Dismay overwhelmed him. He forgot who he was, where he was, why he was. Some primordial part of his brain had taken control: cut him off from himself; cut him off from all memory, and all reason, and all knowledge of the world.

Flynn made for the window, pressed his hands against the glass, and stared out. The night was all darkness and stars. No, not stars – lights: street lights, car lights, lights in windows. From the 13th floor he could see most of south-west Sheffield, but the windows were triple glazed so he couldn't make out any sound from the city below. He strained to hear the buses on the ring road, strained to hear the breathing of the young woman on the bed behind him. Nothing was as it should have been. He fell to his knees and covered his eyes.

Slowly, Flynn returned to himself. It was a piecemeal process but, bit by bit, things began to fall into place. He looked at his watch expecting hours to have passed. Actually, it had taken him only a minute to recover his wits – although he wasn't sure that the process was complete, wasn't sure that every piece had fallen back into place. Flynn tried to remember the events of the day – minute by minute, hour by hour – but everything was jumbled and uncertain. It was like trying to reconstruct a dream. He wished he hadn't needed quite so much Dutch courage to ring Cassie that morning, and he definitely shouldn't have bought that sneaky half-bottle in Glossop.

Deep breaths. In through the nose, out through the mouth. What to do? He had to do something. After forcing a dry and painful swallow, Flynn steeled himself and approached the bed. He scanned the girl's body for some sign of injury: a wound, a bruise, a puncture mark? There was nothing obvious. But she looked familiar, so familiar that he felt that pang of nostalgia one feels when looking at an old photograph of a long dead friend. He turned away but still he could see her, like a waxwork rendering. Not alive, but not quite dead either.

He looked again. Her hair and her arms and her legs had been carefully laid out, but aside from her pale and naked body, there was nothing else of her in the flat. No clothes, no bag, no coat, no shoes.

No shoes.

Flynn's breathing quickened. He began to implement the techniques he'd learned to suppress bad memories, but the memories came too quickly. An image flashed into his mind, an image from long ago.

Red shoes.

Shiny red shoes.

Brand new, shiny red shoes.

Shame and remorse tore through his gut. His heart began to race, and his breathing followed. Soon Flynn was bent double, clutching his chest and snatching air in short, rapid gasps. He staggered back into the kitchen, pulling the bedroom door closed behind him, and steadied himself against the island unit. After a minute or two his breathing returned to normal, but he felt sick and his head ached.

Flynn went to the sink and splashed water on his face. A modicum of calm returned. He knew he should dial 999, but instead he dialled another number. She answered after five rings.

'Hi,' he said. It came out a little too brightly. He cleared his throat. 'It's—'

'I know who it is, Flynn.' Cassie let out an exasperated gasp. 'Are you bailing out on me?'

'What?'

'I mean tonight. I mean our date.'

'No. But . . .'

'What then?' Now, she sounded properly cross.

'Cassie,' Flynn began, offering her an opportunity to interrupt again.

She didn't take it, so he went on: 'Well . . .' Now he was willing her to interrupt because he couldn't think what to say.

Again, she didn't oblige.

'Something's come up, Cassie,' Flynn said at last.

6

FLYNN WAITED BY the front door, as far from the dead girl as he could get without leaving the flat. He wanted to go outside, breathe the cold January air, feel the damp chill of the coming snow on his cheeks. He opened the door, looked out into the hall, and watched the numbers scroll ever higher on the display above the lift door. But he couldn't bring himself to step outside and leave that poor girl all alone.

The lift pinged, and a posse wearing blue overalls emerged. DI Cassie May led, a furry-hooded parka over her arm and a phone in her hand. She folded the coat and put it down on the hall carpet by the lift door. One of the sleeves was twisted and wouldn't lie flat. She picked it up, shook it out, refolded it, and put it back down on the carpet. She looked ever so stern. He found himself thinking of Sarah.

'*Something's come up?*' Cassie hissed. 'Shit, Flynn!'

'I—'

'And you're absolutely sure you don't know who she is?'

Flynn shook his head. 'I'm sure.'

'Where is she?'

He led her to the bedroom door.

'Ok,' Cassie said, 'you'd better go downstairs. Constable Davies is waiting to take your statement in the lobby.'

Flynn watched Cassie pull on a pair of latex gloves and push open the door. Even in overalls, she shone – like Marilyn Monroe in a badly fitting jumpsuit. She moved around the bed with the sure and graceful steps of a dancer. Lush black hair, gentle Latin nose, large sensuous mouth, big brown eyes – DI Cassie May was as beautiful as Flynn imagined a woman could be.

The big brown eyes narrowed. 'Flynn, I asked you to wait downstairs.'

'I . . .' Flynn felt himself blush. 'I—'

'Any news on the doc?' Cassie was looking straight past him.

'On his way, parking-up,' a woman replied.

Flynn turned to see who was speaking. Tall and slim, with brutally short-cropped hair, she nodded at him: 'Detective Sergeant Harper. I'm afraid I'm going to have to insist that you wait downstairs. Constable Davies is expecting you.'

'Found any clothes, Meg?' Cassie asked.

Meg Harper shook her head. 'Not in the flat.'

'Right then, we need to set up a search for this girl's clothes. Now. I don't want to risk anything being touched before we get to it. Start with the common areas, and the bins for this block, then radiate outwards. She's young, thin, small. But I want any clothes at all, even if they don't look like they'd be hers. Okay?'

'Yes, Ma'am,' Harper said.

Cassie glared at her.

Harper bit her lip. 'Sorry. *Cassie.*'

'And when you've organised that,' Cassie said, 'I need you back here. I need you to get a good look at the body in situ before they take her away – photos are never enough.'

Harper scurried off, and Cassie – suddenly pale-faced – turned back to Flynn.

'Are you all right?' Flynn said.

'What do *you* think? She's only a girl for God's sake. It's horrible. I feel sick. How do you expect me to feel?'

'I—'

'Wait downstairs, Flynn. You can't be up here. How many times do I have to tell you?'

'I'm going, I promise, it's just . . .'

'What, you thought that after a couple of years doing this job, I'd be immune to it, did you? I work in South Yorkshire, Flynn. It's hardly an everyday thing, especially not . . .' Cassie shook her head and growled. 'This isn't bloody Cape Town, you know!'

'Sorry, I just . . .'

'Davies is waiting downstairs,' she said. 'He'll take your statement.'

❧

Constable Davies was one of that growing tribe of middle-aged men who have spent most of their lives sitting – he was, at once, slight and flabby. Having jotted down a brief statement, and having reminded Flynn (twice) to come to the station to sign it once it was properly typed up, he assumed a position of importance and authority on a fold-up chair by the main door.

From the window of the first-floor lobby at Bessemer Towers, Flynn watched the traffic go by and tried to shake from his mind the image of the dead girl, with her pale skin and auburn hair. He picked out a face from the street below – a complete stranger – and invented a family for him, and a house, and a job. He imagined this man to be an accountant on his way home (a mock-Tudor semi in Fulwood) to be derided by his wife (a sociology lecturer at the University of Sheffield) and ignored by two teenage daughters (Charlotte and Sophie).

It had worked for him before, retuning the mind to block out unwelcome memories, but not this time. When Flynn's accountant went upstairs to change out of his suit, he found a dead girl with alabaster skin and golden hair lying on his bed.

Try again.

Two party girls, young and pretty, in a brand-new S-Class Mercedes, waiting at the traffic lights. The driver was chattering away while the passenger, oblivious, attended to her phone. When the traffic lights turned green, the Mercedes drove on and out of sight.

Flynn was staring after them, concocting a story that might explain what they were doing in the sort of Mercedes that you'd expect to be driven by a middle-aged sales director, when he caught Constable Davies watching him watch.

'Nice,' Davies said.

Flynn shrugged. 'A bit young for either of us, I reckon – barely out of their teens. Footballers' WAGs, maybe?'

'I was talking about the car,' Davies said, with a puritanical look of disapproval that Flynn hadn't thought existed outside Sunday evening period dramas.

❧

When the lift doors hissed open, Cassie found Flynn and Davies standing awkwardly in the lobby staring out of the window. She acknowledged the constable with a sympathetic smile. 'You can get off now, Simon. I don't think there's much more you or I can achieve here tonight. Meg Harper will manage things.'

Davies grabbed his coat. 'Right you are, Cassie.' The big glass front door swung shut behind him, rocked on its hinges a couple of times, then settled.

'I saw all the food, Flynn,' Cassie said. 'You'd gone to so much trouble. I really didn't expect . . . and now . . .'

'Somebody should have been looking out for that girl,' Flynn said. 'It's too easy to make mistakes when you're young and all alone.'

'What do you mean, *all alone*? And what mistakes?' She fixed on him. 'Flynn?'

He turned away. 'I don't know,' he said, shaking his head. 'I just mean she shouldn't have ended up, you know . . .'

'No, I don't. What mistakes?' Cassie waited for him to turn back to her.

He didn't.

They both stared out at the road.

Cassie nudged Flynn's elbow. 'I'm sorry I snapped at you. You didn't deserve it.'

'So, I'm not going to be arrested then?'

'What is it with you, Flynn? You were like this when Sarah . . .' She blew a long and laboured breath. 'Do you think we arrest everyone who calls in a suspicious death?'

'No, but . . .' He hung his head.

'But what? Are you guilty of something? Is that what you're trying to say?'

He looked up but said nothing.

'Well, then,' she said, 'we have your statement. That'll do for now.'

'I'm sorry, Cassie. I just feel a bit . . . I don't know.'

She frowned. 'Look, you and I talking like this, alone, after what's happened. It isn't, you know, . . .'

'*Appropriate?*'

She nodded. 'Why don't you give Angus a ring? It's Quiz Night at The King's Head, isn't it? You could meet him there.'

'Maybe. It's a bit awkward. I didn't turn up at Christmas or New Year, and I haven't returned any of his calls.'

'So call him.'

'I will. But not tonight.'

Cassie shook her head. 'By the way, was the door to the flat locked when you arrived this afternoon? Only there's no sign of a break in.'

'Yes, but . . .' Flynn grimaced. 'There was a spare key in the plant pot by the door. It was for the cleaners.'

Cassie pulled a phone from her pocket and dialled. 'Meg, would you check the plant pot outside the flat for a key . . . Thanks . . . Yes, I know . . . Yes, Mr Flynn *is* an idiot.'

He made to speak but she held up a finger.

'No,' she said to Meg. 'He doesn't live here, he rents it out . . . Nobody currently . . . Yes, I know . . .' she looked him up and down '. . . Not judging by his clothes . . . No, I don't think Primark would do his size . . . Not quite, more like six foot five, I reckon . . . Oh, yes – and he knows it . . . Okay, thanks, Meg.'

Cassie put the phone back in her pocket and ran her fingers through her hair, tucking it behind her ears and smoothing it flat over her shoulders.

Flynn nodded upwards. 'So what do you think about . . . you know?'

'I can't discuss that.' She looked right through him.

'But she *was* murdered?'

'It's a suspicious death.'

He rolled his eyes.

'Flynn, please!'

He shrugged, walked over to the sleet-speckled windows, and looked out.

'Okay then, yes,' Cassie said. 'It looks very much like she *was* murdered. Unless she walked in off the street completely naked, took the lift to the top floor, broke into your flat, had a nap on your bed, and then died, spontaneously, on your duvet. We'll know more after the post-mortem, but, whatever the cause of death, it seems pretty clear that someone else was involved.'

'Why my flat? Do you think it has something to do with the last tenant?'

Cassie ignored the question. 'Where will you stay tonight?'

'I'll go home,' Flynn said, 'unless you can think of someone who could put me up in town.'

She looked at her feet. 'Why do you refuse to ring Angus? I thought he was your best friend.'

'I will. It's just that . . .' Now, it was Flynn's turn to look at his feet. 'You see . . . Angus lent me some money, and I haven't been able to pay him back yet.'

'Yes, but Angus and Lizzie wouldn't . . .' She shook her head. 'How much do you owe him?'

'Three and a half thousand.'

'But that's nothing to Angus!' Cassie huffed a laugh. 'I bet Lizzie would spend more than that on a handbag without even blinking. And I'm sure he isn't bothered about when you pay him back.'

'No, he's made it clear that he isn't bothered about me paying him back at all.' Flynn shook his head. 'I'm the one who's bothered.'

She fished her phone from her coat pocket. 'I'll book you a room at the Travelodge.'

'Don't be daft,' he said. 'I'm going home. I *want* to go home. What I need now is a nice fire and a large whisky.'

'But they're forecasting more snow, Flynn! It'll be bad up there, it always is when it snows. You might get stuck.'

'The tyres on my Land Rover are like something off a tractor. I couldn't live up there if I wasn't prepared for a bit of snow.'

'I know, but . . .'

He was already heading for the door.

'Flynn,' she called after him.

He stopped.

'I,' she began; then faltered.

He raised his eyebrows.

She looked down at her feet again. 'I need you in for interview first thing tomorrow.'

'I see,' Flynn said. 'So all this concern about me driving home tonight was—'

'No!'

He turned and walked away. 'See you in the morning.'

Cassie scanned the lobby for onlookers and, satisfied that she wouldn't be seen, caught him up, grabbed his hand, and kissed him on the cheek. 'I'm sorry,' she whispered. 'Sorry for being . . . you know. It's just that I was looking forward to tonight, and *he* used to cancel on me at the last minute, and then . . . well . . . well, you know what happened. And now I'm always angry, always expecting the worst, always biting people's heads off for no good reason.'

Flynn squeezed her hand. 'No, it's me. You've got a job to do, and I'm being a pain in the arse.'

'Oh, I wouldn't go that far,' Cassie said, head tilted, eyes closed. 'Well, maybe a little!' She stepped back a pace and nodded towards the lift. 'By the way, the dead girl – don't you think she looks a bit . . . ?'

She couldn't bring herself to finish the question. She shouldn't have started it. It was insensitive, thoughtless. Sometimes she hated herself. Often, actually.

'A bit what?' Flynn asked.

'And you're sure you don't know her?' Cassie said. 'Absolutely sure?'

Flynn nodded. 'A bit what?'

She found herself avoiding his eyes.

'A bit what, Cassie?' he said again.

She forced a smile. 'See you in the morning, eh. Nine o'clock, sharp.'

7

PARKED-UP IN HIS Land Rover, engine running, old memories played across Flynn's inward eye. He tried to shake them, tried to replace them with recollections of Cassie - plum lips brushing his cheek, ruby red fingernails sliding through sumptuous dark locks, olive skin shimmering gold in Christmas candlelight. But the older memories persisted. They played like a news reel - with Flynn as subject, narrator, and audience.

A girl, a bed, a bedroom. Christmas Eve. Eighteen Christmases ago. The Christmas after he turned sixteen. It had been a quiet night - so Flynn had spent most of his shift writing an essay on the nature versus nurture theme in Shakespeare's *The Tempest*.

He remembered a tiny tinsel Christmas tree on a table in the corner. She was wearing her best party frock and brand-new shoes - red patent leather, soles that had never seen the street. She was lying on a bare and heavily stained mattress, thumb in her mouth like a sleeping infant. A syringe, the needle still plunged deep into the pale skin of her left foot, was wedged between her toes. Her name was Maria.

'Terrible waste,' Scotty said after examining the paper wrap Flynn recovered from under the little Christmas tree. 'If only she'd come to *us* for her gear. We might not be the cheapest, but at least you know what you're getting.'

Flynn sat beside her on the bed, put a hand on her slim, cold wrist, and wept.

Scotty patted Flynn's shoulder. 'Never get involved,' he said. 'That's the golden rule when it comes to keeping whores.'

Flynn had always liked Maria. She wore a tight red dress most nights, which suited her Spanish looks. She was pretty and funny and clever, and, he suspected, she was the same age as him. They all lied about their age in that place – one way or another. If he had been born a girl, Flynn mused, he'd most likely have ended up like Maria. And if, as a boy, he hadn't grown quite so big, and quite so handy with his fists, God knows what would have become of him.

Three nights before, face contorted with yearning and shame, Maria had pleaded for a wrap. He made her promise that this would be the last she'd ask him for. And she'd kept her promise – she went elsewhere for her final fix.

Flynn wrapped Maria's body in a sheet and carried her down to the Transit van in the yard. He didn't ask where the van was going.

No one had ever come looking for Maria. No one cared. No one except Flynn: eighteen years had passed and still he'd wake in the early hours and find himself calling her name in the dark.

And now, again, Flynn found himself amongst the dead. His heart was racing. He wound down the window and forced his eyes to blur in the sharp light from the street lamps, but still they came. He turned on the radio, revved the engine hard, but he couldn't shake the visions. Contorted faces, darkened blood on pallid skin, the stench of soulless bodies. Not at peace, not resting, not sleeping – Flynn's dead raged against a life cut short. The murdered girl with the auburn hair and alabaster skin opened her eyes and mouthed strange words in an alien tongue. No, not alien. Familiar. A language once known but long forgotten. And it wasn't the girl anymore. It was Sarah. It was his long dead wife come back to haunt him. Sarah sat up, clapped her hands, and vanished.

He slammed the gearstick into first and roared out of the car park. But he didn't get far. The roads were jam packed. Engines rumbled and whined, fumes swirled, no one was getting anywhere. The Land Rover was suddenly becalmed, and Flynn too. He found comfort in this helplessness – he felt the tension in his core dissipate, and the pressure at his temples ease. Fifteen minutes later, for no apparent reason, the traffic began to move again.

On the Ecclesall Road, he relaxed his grip on the wheel and peered through misted windows into the bars and restaurants that held happier memories. Beyond Hunters Bar roundabout, the road began its steady climb into the hills to the south-west of the city. Bars and restaurants gave way to shops and cafés, which gave way to suburban housing. Flynn parked outside a double-bay-windowed pub in the middle of a Victorian terrace. From behind him there came a squeaking of brakes and a bellowing of horns: a Mini had darted into a parking space that a growly-engined Subaru had been about to take.

When the shouting had subsided, and the Subaru had driven off, Flynn got out of his car. He counted the loose change in his pocket and looked up at the stars. The longer he looked, the less certain he became.

Thick grey smoke rose from the pub's tallest chimney, dissipating as it caught an easterly breeze. For a conspicuous while, Flynn stood by his car wondering if he should go in. He hadn't planned to stop, and if there hadn't been a parking space he would have driven straight home. Probably.

It was odd, he thought, that the Mini driver, who had been in such a hurry to park, hadn't yet got out of the car. But no odder, he had to admit, than a man getting out of his car, on a freezing January evening, and staring at a pub's front door for longer than could ever be justified. The door was black and shiny and intimidatingly new. The bay windows were still yellowed and peeling just as he remembered them; and condensation (which dribbled into murky pools in the rotting sill) obscured the view in, as it always had this time of year. It didn't matter – he knew what he would find inside. Friday night was quiz night at The King's Head.

Flynn glanced back at the Mini – headlights still on, engine still running – before locking up the Land Rover and going in.

❧

The King's Head was an ordinary sort of pub, neither obviously shabby nor spankingly new. It must have been redecorated more than once over the last forty years, but no one could remember when, or what it looked like before. If you were lucky, on a cold January night, you would find yourself at a table by the fire.

As Flynn stepped over the threshold, memories surged – happy memories, youthful memories, carefree memories. For more than a decade, he'd been part of the most successful quiz team The King's Head had ever seen: Flynn, Angus McDonald and Marco Walters. They had met as students. Marco was a medic. Angus was doing a PhD in applied mathematics, which he was incapable of explaining without recourse to equations. They used to rib him mercilessly about that – scarcely an evening went by without one or the other turning to Angus at some point and saying, 'So, Angus, explain your PhD to us again.' It took Angus the best part of a year to work out that they were taking the piss.

But Angus McDonald was the cleverest man Flynn knew, and the richest. How Angus had made so much money was a mystery. Flynn had never asked, of course, but Marco reckoned Angus had made his millions selling some clever computer code to the MOD. Marco also claimed Cassie had once let slip that Angus worked for the security services – for GCHQ or MI5 or MI6 or something like that. Angus, for his part, only ever talked about working for merchant banks. Flynn didn't care how Angus made his money. He'd come to the King's Head because his mind was buzzing, because he needed to talk, because he needed a friend.

Angus was also a good friend of Cassie's (her confidant, by her own account). Flynn assured himself that this had nothing whatsoever to do with his visiting the King's Head, on a quiz night, out of the blue.

He scanned the tables. Marco wouldn't be there of course – he'd recently bagged a prestigious cardiac consultant post and moved down to London. Angus was there though, at a table by the fire with a newspaper on his lap.

'A one-man quiz team!' Flynn said, taking the free chair.

Angus smiled and offered a sinewy climber's hand. 'I don't mind being on my own. Sometimes it's nice to be on your own . . . it's calming. Sometimes.'

'Yes,' Flynn said. 'I know what you mean.'

Angus ran a finger along the sharp bridge of his nose. 'Sorry, that was a thoughtless thing to say. I just meant . . .' He picked up his beer mat and then put it back down. 'We worry about you, that's all. You've lived like a recluse since . . .' He shook his head. 'Christ, Lizzie wept when you didn't turn up for Christmas. She couldn't bear to think of the big man all on his own, out there in the middle of nowhere. And now she says you won't even take her calls.'

Flynn grimaced. 'Tell her I'm sorry, and tell her, you know, . . .'

'Hmmm,' Angus said, rolling his eyes. Then, a little too cheerfully, 'So, written any new stories?'

Flynn shook his head.

Angus folded his newspaper and stuffed it into his jacket pocket. 'My round then. Usual, is it?'

Flynn nodded.

'The quiz starts in a couple of hours,' Angus said. 'Will you be staying?'

'I . . .' Flynn scratched his head. 'It's been a long day.'

'Okay, well . . .' Angus picked up his glass and stretched his back. 'It'll be Burns Night in a couple of weeks – the 25th, a Saturday. I've ordered the haggis, a McLay's Chieftain like last year. You'll come, won't you?'

'Wouldn't miss it!'

Angus raised his eyebrows but said nothing and made for the bar.

Flynn wondered if Cassie would be going to Angus's Burns Night supper. She'd been there the previous year, but that was with Marco. Maybe this year . . .

Maybe not.

In any case, *Dr Angus McDonald of the Clan McDonald* would sit at the head of the table and deliver Rabbie Burns' 'Address to the Haggis' – it had become a tradition. The after-dinner entertainment had become a tradition too: Lizzie would light candles all around the drawing room, turn out the lights and call for everyone to gather by the fire. Those who couldn't find room on armchairs or sofas would lounge on the thick Persian rug in the middle of the room. Flynn would get the wing-back in the corner by the fire, the story teller's chair. One year, he remembered—

But other memories, long suppressed memories, elbowed their way in (a bare mattress in a dead room; Victoria's wide fixed eyes; Ryan Gallagher's shattered face), they swooped down on him, pecking like ravenous gulls.

Angus arrived with the drinks. 'So, what can I do for you? Are you all right for money?'

'That's not why I came,' Flynn said. 'I just came to see you, to have a chat, like old times.'

'Oh?'

Flynn couldn't think what to say. He wanted to talk about the events of the day – about the dead girl on the bed, about the date with Cassie – but not yet.

Angus, too, seemed to be struggling for conversation.

The girl from the bar offered a shy smile and squeezed by to tend the fire. She poked at the embers a bit, slung a fresh log on top, and left.

Distraction over, the silence became unbearable.

Angus looked like he was about to say something. But, after he'd cleared his throat, and sipped his beer, he just sat back and frowned.

'So,' Flynn said, 'how are the kids?'

'Fine! A joy and a burden. You know how it is.'

Flynn nodded.

Angus squirmed.

Flynn shook his head. 'Don't be daft!'

'Sorry,' Angus said, 'I—'

'Forget it.'

Angus drummed his fingers on the table for a few seconds before asking, 'How are the properties doing? Any luck with the empty shop?'

'Actually, yes!' Flynn said, brightly. 'Oxfam is taking it. Should be in by March, then I'll be able to pay—'

'Oxfam! Fantastic! That'll be a weight off your mind.'

'Yes. Yes, it will.'

'Good. Great news. I'm relieved for you.'

They supped their ale in silence for a very long minute.

Angus put down his glass and resumed the finger drumming.

Flynn took a large gulp before clearing his throat and leaning in over the table. 'I found a dead girl in the flat at Bessemer Towers this afternoon,' he said.

Angus raised his eyebrows.

'It all started this morning,' Flynn said. He wouldn't mention Cassie by name, he'd decided. Not yet. 'It all started with a phone call . . .'

Angus squeezed his fingers into a fist. He knew that Flynn loved stories – reading them, writing them, telling them. And he was good at it, no doubt about that. But Flynn had an annoying habit of transforming what should be a simple account of real-life events into the sort of yarn designed to entertain more than inform. This was fine when the subject matter was amusing and of no real import – Angus *did* get jokes, whatever people might think – but Flynn would tinker with important stuff too.

Ironically, the thing Angus loved about Flynn's short stories was that they sounded so real. And here was the problem: how can you ever be sure, with Flynn, what is real and what is not. Angus bit his lip, folded his arms, and leaned heavily on the table.

Flynn's account had a beginning, a middle, and an end. The narrative was chronological, but Angus suspected the timeline may have been tweaked in places for dramatic effect. There were a few carefully timed pauses, one cunningly crafted simile, and a few colourful characterisations.

Flynn reached for his beer, which signalled *The End*.

'No clothes in the flat,' Angus said. 'Nothing at all?'

Flynn shook his head. 'No.'

'And you're sure you didn't know her?'

Flynn nodded.

Angus drummed the table with his fingers.

'And Cassie reckoned it had to be murder,' Flynn said. 'She was a bit coy at first, but she said as much in the end.'

'So,' Angus said, pressing his palms together and fixing on his old friend, 'who *was* this mystery woman you invited round for dinner?'

Flynn sipped his beer and savoured the moment.

Angus folded his arms. Another dramatic bloody pause. Why wouldn't he just—

'Actually,' Flynn said, slowly enunciating each syllable, 'it was Cassie.'

❧

Cassie was weary and miserable and needed a shoulder to cry on. She needed a friend. She needed a confidant. She needed Angus. And then Flynn had turned up. She couldn't face Flynn, not tonight, so she'd waited outside The King's Head until he left.

It took nearly an hour of waiting.

Flynn's Land Rover disappeared into a fug of tail lights and exhaust fumes. Her Mini was new, so Cassie was sure Flynn wouldn't have recognised it. And it was dark, so he wouldn't have seen her face.

She shouldn't have kissed his cheek; she shouldn't even have talked to him. This was a murder enquiry, for Christ's sake – what was she thinking? Cassie had always found comfort in procedure, in rules, in doing things correctly. What was it about this man?

Hollywood handsome (with impossibly blue eyes)?

Intelligent, articulate, thoughtful (someone who actually cared about her opinion)?

Ebony hair (thick, with a hint of grey at the temples)?

Funny (sometimes, when he wanted to be)?

Big and strong (gosh, ever so – he could probably pick her up and . . .)?

Yeah, yeah, all of that. But even so . . .

She wiped her eyes with the soft cuff of her coat and pulled down the visor to check her face in the vanity mirror. Not too bad: nothing that couldn't be tidied up with fingertips and a licked tissue.

As she got out of her car it began to snow.

❧

'You've just missed the big man,' Angus said, without smiling. 'He didn't mention that you'd be coming here tonight.'

Cassie took off her coat and sat in the chair opposite. 'So, he's told you, has he?'

'Yes,' he said. 'And he also told me about the dead girl in his flat. Any leads?'

She stiffened and folded her arms.

'Sorry. I shouldn't be asking, should I?' Angus said. 'Police business, I expect.'

'Go on then, Angus!' Cassie unfolded then refolded her arms. 'Say what you're dying to say.'

'What?' He didn't look up from his pint.

'I'm a needy, paranoid cow,' she said, 'and you don't like the idea of me going out with Flynn! Well, I'm sorry but—'

'No, Cassie, I just think—'

'You think I'm no good for him, don't you? That's not fair. It was Marco who walked out on me, remember. He's the bastard – I've never walked out on anybody. And if everybody did the right thing, and played by the bloody rules, nobody would ever get hurt.'

Angus shuffled his chair towards hers and put an arm around her.

She let her head rest on his shoulder.

'People are always going to get hurt,' Angus said. 'If you're not getting hurt, you're probably doing the hurting. And believe me, feeling hurt is better than feeling guilty.'

'What would *you* know?' she mumbled into his collar before sitting up straight and fixing on him with half closed eyes.

Angus tilted back his head, breathed a quiet sigh, and stared up at the nicotine-stained ceiling. He swallowed and cleared his throat.

'And anyway,' Cassie said, 'what's wrong with me and Flynn getting together?'

'You're on the rebound, that's all, you *and* Flynn.'

'Jesus Christ, Angus!' She pulled away. 'You really hate me, don't you?'

'Oh, for God's sake, Cassie. Stop it, please.'

Cassie squeezed shut her eyes. 'Sorry,' she said, then punched his arm. 'Go and get me a glass of wine and tub of Pringles, will you, I deserve it.'

Angus smiled. 'I don't blame you for falling for Flynn, you know. I'm sure I would, if I were a woman.' He stood up and gave Cassie a knowing nod.

'It's not about his looks,' Cassie snapped. 'Marco fucking Walters was a good-looking bastard and we all know where that got me.'

'I know it's not just his looks, Cassie,' Angus said gently. 'Christ, I'm a little in love with Flynn myself. He has that effect on everyone, I think. Or used to – before Sarah died.'

Cassie sighed ostentatiously. 'Yes, well, even Marco had a bit of man-crush on Flynn, I reckon. He used to say . . .' She threw back her head and growled. 'Oh, who gives a fuck what Marco thought.'

'Well he did say that Sarah was "trouble waiting to happen",' Angus offered, looking at the floor. 'He told me that in his medical opinion, she was a psychopath. And he wasn't kidding around – he really meant it.'

'Will you please stop going on about Sarah Flynn. Honestly, Angus, sometimes I think you and Marco were just as obsessed with that awful woman as Flynn used to be.'

'But I think he's *still* obsessed, Cassie. That's why—'

'Oh, shut up and get me my wine.'

Angus turned and made for the bar.

'And don't forget the Pringles,' Cassie shouted after him. Then she sat up straight, took a deep breath, and promised herself that she wouldn't turn maudlin. She wouldn't rake up the past. She wouldn't talk about Marco. She would look forward. She would think about Flynn.

The way Flynn doted on his late wife had always been a mystery to Cassie. Love might be blind – people have been saying it for centuries, so it must be true – but Sarah, by *every* account Cassie heard, had been a nasty piece of work. She found herself thinking back to her investigation of Sarah Flynn's car crash, her first case after moving up north – two years ago almost to the day.

Cassie had driven up to that notorious bend on the Snake Pass; she'd seen Sarah Flynn's fancy old Mercedes at the bottom of a rocky ravine. It was surprisingly intact, she remembered. The coroner had said that it would be a comfort to loved ones to know that she'd died on impact.

Sarah Flynn was a scandal-hungry freelance investigative journalist. The best anyone had to say about her was that she was highly intelligent, hard-nosed, and good at her job. And everyone said that sort of thing, so Cassie took it as read. The worst was, 'complete and utter bitch'. This, too, Cassie was happy to take as read.

Even Angus's wife, Lizzie, who seemed to have been the closest thing Sarah had to a friend, had refused to be drawn on her character during the investigation. All she'd said at interview was that Sarah was 'very pretty – body like a supermodel', and, 'she sounded ever so posh – like royalty'.

Cassie remembered trawling the BBC radio archives online and listening to some interviews that Sarah Flynn had given on *Woman's Hour*. Her voice *had been* nauseatingly posh, that much was true, but she had sometimes lapsed into coarse Americanisms, which pleased Cassie more than it should.

Angus was back with the crisps. He was talking about Burns' Night or something (would she be coming?). She wasn't really listening.

'Cassie?' he said, banging the tub of Pringles down on the table. 'Burns Night. Can you come or not?'

She ignored the question.

'The dead girl,' she said, 'the one we found in Flynn's flat.' Cassie was staring at the mirror above the fireplace, trying to recall the pictures. 'And I know I'm only going by photographs, because I never met the woman . . .'

'What photographs?' Angus asked. 'What woman?'

Cassie shifted in her seat. She looked first at Angus and then at her ruby red fingernails. 'Sarah Flynn,' she said.

Angus sat down. 'What about her?'

'The dead girl we found in Flynn's flat was the spitting image of Sarah Flynn. Younger, of course. In her late teens, I'd say. But still, it's uncanny.'

8

FLYNN SPENT THE journey home trying to shut his mind to those old images that leaked, periodically, into his consciousness. A dead face, a bare mattress, mottled skin, the rusty back door of a Transit van. He tried disassociation: he imagined the scenes as if they were being witnessed by that pretty pathologist from the TV show. It might have worked if he were at home, if he were able to close his eyes and put all his energy into the task – but he was in a snowstorm, windscreen wipers squeaking and clacking at a hundred beats per minute. He caught a few withering stares as his Land Rover ploughed on past a dozen or so stranded cars. But he couldn't rescue them all.

And he couldn't stop himself remembering. He remembered life-battered girls crawling, insensible, through existence. Abused girls, neglected girls, charge-by-the-half-hour girls. Girls who snorted or smoked or injected everything they earned. He'd offered what protection he could, but most of them were beyond rescuing.

Around the time Flynn turned seventeen, Scotty Deakin went upmarket and set up a nice little members-only club in Sale. It was open only in the evenings on weekdays, so it fitted nicely around his sixth-form timetable. These girls charged by the night and expected to be wined and dined into the bargain; they drove nice German cars (one of them, Victoria, had given him his first driving lesson in her BMW 3 series); and Sasha, a post-grad student, helped him with his A-level revision on quiet Sunday afternoons. These girls, like Flynn, had an exit plan.

Scotty Deakin had issued the security team with Italian suits and white shirts for this new venture. He'd said he couldn't trust them to dress decently by themselves; he'd said he wanted them to blend in with the better class of punter. No, not punter: *customer.*

One day – after a bit of trouble – Scotty decided that they blended in a little *too* well. 'Even posh punters need to see that there's paid muscle on hand,' he'd said, bitterly. After that, to make them stand out, security staff were given pale chinos and navy-blue T-shirts.

'Do *I* have to wear this stuff?' Flynn said. 'I liked the suit.'

'Yes,' Deakin snapped back, 'you do.'

'But look at me, Scotty, I'm too big for this sort of outfit. I look like a thug when I wear a T-shirt. I'll make myself stand out some other way, I promise.'

'How?'

'I'll think of something.'

❧

A silver people carrier, with its hazard warning lights flashing, brought Flynn back to the present. It had skidded into a snow drift by the side of the road and a woman in a long coat was trying to dig it out with a lever arch file.

Overwhelmed by a sudden urge to rescue someone, and desperate to distract himself from the long shadows of his past, Flynn stopped the Land Rover and got out. The woman's eyes were wet and puffy. There were three little girls in the back of her car. The youngest (four years old, perhaps) was crying; the eldest (ten or eleven) was stony faced, the middle child was asleep. The woman waved her phone. 'No signal,' she said, and then burst into tears.

'There's a pub a few miles up the road.' Flynn pointed into the darkness. 'They have a payphone. I'll take you.'

The woman looked him up and down and turned back to the

car. The middle child was now wide awake, and all three were staring at Flynn.

'Okay,' she said.

He enjoyed having the car full. The mother did little more than nod at his attempts to make conversation, but that was fine. He looked into the rear-view mirror and pulled silly faces at the children. Two bashful smiles. The older girl refused to acknowledge him. Flynn pictured Cassie sitting beside him. Small, slender hands with soft olive skin and fingers that narrowed gently from knuckle to tip. Nails painted ruby red. Her hand resting on his.

He dropped the family off at The Snake Pass Inn and went home.

❧

Flynn had just finished setting a fire in the stove when the phone rang. He stared at the flames until the ringing stopped. On the big table, its power cable strewn across a pile of unopened mail, sat Sarah's old MacBook Pro. Top of the range when she bought it, she'd passed it on to him when she upgraded to a newer model not long before she died. His friend, Angus, had certainly been impressed – bits and bobs made by Apple, Flynn remembered, were what Angus and Sarah had talked about when they found themselves forced to make awkward conversation.

Angus always seemed intimidated by Sarah. Even Sarah noticed it, which was not like her. 'He hates me, Flynn,' she once said, 'I just know he does.'

Sarah always got on with Marco though. But then Marco got on with everyone. 'Particularly women,' Flynn said out loud, 'especially the pretty ones!'

He shook his head – 'So we're talking to ourselves again, are we?' – and sat down in front of his hand-me-down computer. It was the only thing of hers that he'd kept. In the aftermath of her death, he'd wanted rid of everything that might remind him of her, but he'd needed the computer to write, and he hadn't had the money for a new one.

'Still don't!' he said out loud.

She'd be furious if she saw it now: battered and scuffed with its broken power thingy gaffer-taped to the side. He lifted the lid and waited for it to wake.

Six hundred pages into his first novel, Flynn realised that it would never be read by another soul – it was for him alone. It was a roman à clef. It was his penance. It was self-indulgent crap. He feared he might never get to the end, but perhaps that was the point of it.

The phone rang again. Flynn grabbed a bottle of whisky, poured himself a large one, and began to type.

9

8 DEVONSHIRE RISE was a grand Victorian gentleman's residence that Sean Mulligan had bought for a song in the early nineties. Gary Mulligan stepped back from the window when a stretch limo appeared at the end of the drive. From the shadows, he watched the limo pull up, watched the burly chauffeur open the rear door, watched the passenger step out and straighten his overcoat. It was the American. It was Brett McRoss. McRoss was short and slight with ice white hair, ginger eyebrows and a pasty pink complexion. One day, Gary would tell him that only gangster rappers, hen parties, and complete twats drove around in stretched Chryslers. But today was not that day.

The doorbell rang.

Gary counted to twenty then let him in.

Neither man spoke as Gary led McRoss across the hall and into a dimly lit butler's pantry. The walls were lined with cabinets and shelves – floor to ceiling, dark oak worn smooth with age. Gary locked the door behind them and readied a second key. He guided McRoss to a set of small cutlery drawers by the window. There was a shiny brass escutcheon on the front of the topmost drawer. When Gary inserted his key and turned it ninety degrees, a door-sized section of cabinetry swung open to reveal a stone staircase down to the cellars.

'Hope I'm not going to be disappointed,' McRoss said, stepping through.

Gary didn't reply. He followed the American inside, stopping at the top of the stairs to pull the cabinetry back into position. The lock clicked home.

10

'YOU WANTED TO see me, sir?' Cassie was tired. She'd left the pub before the quiz started in order to get to bed early, but that poor girl they'd found in Flynn's flat had played on her mind all night and she'd barely slept.

Deputy Chief Constable Bernie Muxlow looked up from his desk and greeted her with a smile so big and so false that Cassie was tempted to reciprocate. She thought better of it, closed the door behind her, and sat down. Muxlow snapped his laptop shut and slid it into a drawer. He scanned his desk (clear but for a telephone) and used the pressed handkerchief from his top pocket to buff out a finger mark he spotted on the mahogany. 'Sorry to drag you here at the crack of dawn. How are you, Cassie?'

'Fine, sir. But DCI Foster won't like it when he finds out you sent for me. He's very much for observing the chain of command, I think.'

'Charlie Foster thinks you want his job.'

'I *do* want his job.'

Muxlow spotted another finger mark, brought out his handkerchief, and attended to it. 'I want to talk to you about this business at Bessemer Towers,' he said. 'The suspect, James Flynn,' he sniffed and glanced sideways, 'he's known to you, is he?'

'Not a suspect, sir. A witness.'

'Didn't you interview him about his wife's death a couple of years ago?'

Cassie folded her arms and stared at her knees. 'Yes, but that was the first time I ever met him. And he wasn't a suspect then, either.'

'He was *the husband*,' Muxlow said, raising his eyebrows. 'And anyway, it was *you* who insisted on treating Sarah Flynn's death as suspicious. Everyone else had it down as a road traffic accident – she wasn't the first to come to grief on the Snake Pass, and she won't be the last.'

Cassie looked up and found Muxlow staring at her. She held his eyes for as long as she could bear, then turned her attention to the reflection of his bald patch in the window behind him. 'Well, that investigation came to nothing,' she said. 'And as far as this one is concerned, we've no reason to suspect Mr. Flynn of any wrongdoing.'

'That's not how Charlie Foster sees it.'

'Charlie Foster!' Cassie's voice rose a full octave. She collected herself. 'DCI Foster hasn't been fully briefed yet. I was told you needed to see me immediately. I'd only just walked through the door. I'll brief him when—'

'Your new Sergeant is very good. Harper, is it? Fast track, like you. Just passed her inspector's exam. Very keen. I hear she was up all night writing the preliminary report. I look forward to getting a copy when she's done.'

Cassie nodded slowly. 'Yes, Meg Harper is good. I hope it doesn't hold her back.'

'Now, now, Cassie.' Muxlow folded his arms. 'You *turned down* a promotion not long ago.'

'That's not fair, sir. I couldn't just up sticks and move to London, not then, I had . . .' she glanced up at the ceiling, 'I had personal commitments.'

Muxlow squeezed a shallow smile. 'We all have to make choices, Cassie. I must say, your decision surprised me. I do hope he was worth it.'

She looked away. Everyone at the station knew that Marco had dumped her. And they probably knew that *he* had moved down to London to advance *his* career. She didn't know how they knew all this stuff, but they knew. And Muxlow would know too. Muxlow made a point of knowing all the station tittle-tattle.

'In any case,' he said, 'we are where we are.'

'Yes,' she said without looking at him.

'And now there's this business with your *new* man.'

'My what?' Cassie blushed, she felt her blood rising. 'What are you trying to say?'

Muxlow leaned back in his chair and folded his arms. 'Of course, your personal relationships are none of my business . . .'

'But?' Cassie offered. She had never felt this uncomfortable with Muxlow before. She didn't like the man, and she didn't trust him, but—

'But,' Muxlow began. He unfolded his arms and found another fingerprint to polish out.

There was something different about Muxlow today. The Muxlow Cassie knew was the epitome of politeness. He had no qualms about shafting anyone who stood in his way, of course, and he didn't do favours. But he didn't do sarcasm either, or make snide remarks, or—

'You know perfectly well what I'm going to say, Cassie.' He leaned in when she blanked him. 'Cassie?'

She didn't like the way he said her name. She let her vision blur so that he was out of focus. 'Yes, sir.'

'You're too closely involved with this James Flynn character. I've instructed DCI Foster to take you off the case. He'll run it himself while you're on leave.'

Cassie lay her hands on her lap and dug in her nails. Muxlow didn't have to take her off the case. Not yet. The rules afforded him discretion: he could easily argue, for example, that—

'Good, that's settled then.' Muxlow retrieved his laptop from the drawer and arranged it on the desk in front of him. Cassie understood this to mean that their meeting was over.

'How long?' she asked.

'A couple of weeks, I expect. It'll be a nice break for you.'

❧

She got back to her office to find Detective Chief Inspector Foster sitting at her desk.

He stood up and offered a smug smile.

'Have you moved anything?' Cassie said. She grabbed her coat from the stand and scanned the office.

'Like what?'

She walked round to look under the desk. 'An archive box.'

'No.'

Meg Harper was waiting by the door, her eyes heavy. 'Meg,' Cassie said. 'Have you moved an archive box out of my office?'

Meg shook her head and followed Cassie into the incident room. They both jumped when Foster slammed the door behind them.

'Where is everyone?' Cassie asked.

'Foster's got half of them doing house to house, and the other half searching for the clothes.'

'Still nothing then?'

'Not yet. But we have daylight now, so . . .' Meg ruffled her hair. 'Ma'am, I'm ever so sorry about this morning. I was tired. I didn't mean to . . .' She puffed out her cheeks. 'Foster's just told me that you're off the case.'

'Forget it, it's not your fault.' Cassie was pacing the incident room, looking under desks. 'You look knackered, Meg,' she said. 'Why don't you go home and get some sleep? I'll clear it with Foster.'

'But I had to tell the Deputy Chief, didn't I?' Meg said. 'He asked. What else could I do?'

Cassie smiled. Meg followed the rules – Cassie liked rules: if Cassie didn't approve of a rule she would change it, or work around it, but never break it. There were rules for policing; there were rules for life. She turned back to Meg. '*What* did you have to tell the Deputy Chief Constable?'

'About you and James Flynn.'

Cassie stopped walking. '*What* about me and Flynn?'

'Only what you told me: that you were the intended dinner guest, you know, at the murder scene.'

'Oh,' Cassie said, and went back to checking under desks.

'I'm sorry, ma'am, I—'

'Where are they?' Cassie turned to Meg. 'Where are the Sarah Flynn case files?'

Meg shrugged. 'If I'd known it would cause you trouble, ma'am, me talking to the Deputy Chief. Oh, I don't know. He put me on the spot – he's the Deputy Chief, what else could I do?'

Cassie pulled out a chair by Meg's desk, sat down, and took a deep breath. 'What are you going on about, Meg? Muxlow already knew it was me that Flynn was expecting for dinner – I had no choice but to disclose. And will you please stop calling me *ma'am*?'

'So you *had* told the Deputy Chief.' Meg sat down beside Cassie and rubbed her eyes.

'No,' Cassie said, 'but good old DCI Foster must have been straight onto Muxlow when he got the email I sent him last night. Any opportunity to stick the knife in. The only surprise is that the lazy bugger checked his email outside of office hours. I didn't think he would – I was planning to tell him about me and Flynn this morning, face to face. I only sent the email to cover my back.'

'But . . .' Meg pulled herself upright and leaned forward. 'But Foster knew nothing about it until he heard it from me. Did you copy-in the DCC when you emailed Foster?'

'God, no. Foster's very sensitive about chain of command

– especially with me.' Cassie patted Meg's knee. 'Forget it. It doesn't matter.'

'But . . .' Meg stood up. 'I hadn't even sent out the preliminary report. I wanted to run it past you first. So how did the Deputy Chief find out? He and Foster turned up here at six in the morning, expecting to find the place deserted, I reckon. The Deputy Chief asked what I knew about your romantic relationship with James Flynn, and I, well . . .'

'It doesn't matter, Meg, really. Forget about Muxlow.'

'It matters to me. I feel like I've been played.'

'Forget it and go home.'

'But Foster went ballistic. It was clearly the first he'd heard of it. No way had he read your email.'

Cassie put a hand on her shoulder. 'I need to sort out this hand-over before I go on leave, but *you* need to sleep. Please, go home.'

'I'm going,' Meg said grabbing her coat. 'But if I'm the only one you told about the dinner with Flynn, and if *he* hadn't mentioned it to anyone . . .' Meg scratched her chin. 'How could the Deputy Chief have possibly known anything about your relationship with him? He wasn't fishing, you see, he was asking me to confirm something he already knew, I'm sure of it.' She slung a leather satchel over her shoulder and started towards the door.

'Meg,' Cassie said. 'Did they go into my office? Could either of them have taken my Sarah Flynn case files?'

Meg shrugged. 'Don't know. I kept my head down after Foster lost it over you and Flynn.'

11

FLYNN HAD SET the alarm earlier than usual in order to make his nine o'clock meeting with Cassie. He was grateful for the dark. The bedsheets were damp with sweat, his hair was wet, his pillow was sodden, his left cheek was sore.

He tried to imagine Cassie sleeping peacefully beside him, tried to imagine reaching over and stroking her hair, tried to imagine the warm skin of her cheek under his fingertips. But another image lingered in his head, one that would not be shaken.

It was an image from long ago. A memory. It was the day after his thirteenth birthday. It was Paddy Riley, his old boxing coach. Small black eyes, white-spittle-cornered mouth, saggy pink cheeks. Paddy was staring at him from the safe side of the ropes.

Flynn was remembering their first ever conversation. No, more than *remembering*: Flynn was *reliving* it, face down on the canvas, cheek grazed and sore. He could taste blood in his mouth, feel the sting of sweat in his eyes.

'How old are you, laddie?' Paddy said.

'Just turned thirteen, sir.'

'Why d'you come here today?'

'To learn.'

'Well, you certainly know how to take it, and that's something no bugger can be taught.'

'Yeah, but I've had enough of *taking it*, sir.'

Paddy Riley wiped the spittle from the corners of his mouth

with the back of his hand. 'Will you train hard, lad? Do you even know what training hard means?'

'Yes, sir. I train hard for the rugby team at school, I'm the Number 8.'

Paddy Riley sneered and screwed up his face. 'Alright then, *Number 8*, let's see if we can't make a boxer out of you.'

Last night's whisky bottle was on the floor by the sofa; he swigged the last gulp. Half-bottles from now on. He wished he'd never logged on to Facebook, wished he'd never found out that Cassie and Marco had split, wished he'd never made that phone call and asked her to dinner. He had no right to dream that he and Cassie could ever . . .

She was so . . .

And *he* was, well . . .

Folly!

And he should never have been in that flat, staring at a dead girl with alabaster skin and auburn hair, and remembering the sorts of things he had spent his entire adult life trying to forget. He should have been at home. He should have been writing the next maudlin chapter of his novel, or staring at the flames in the stove, or contemplating the silhouette of the larch plantation from his kitchen window. He should have been wallowing in a whisky-fuelled trance of boredom, loneliness and self-recrimination. He should have been wondering when he would muster the courage to throw his novel onto the fire and begin something that someone might someday want to read.

❧

The morning sun, filtered through woodland and mist, was still soft. While the Land Rover warmed up, Flynn cleared the snow from the windscreen and fetched fuel for the stove. The coal bunker was under a foot of snow – too much, surely, for the rusty old frame. No time now, though; he'd clear it tomorrow.

He turned back to his house. Snow lay thick on the roof, and on the ground it had drifted up to window level in places. From a distance, he fancied, you might easily mistake it for one of the hundred or so house-sized boulders that littered this part of the Derwent Valley. An easy mistake to make on a day like today, but even in the summer – even amidst the damp green hues of a wet Pennine July – this building, with its stone walls and stone roof, sat quietly in the landscape, like a lioness in the long grass of the Serengeti.

There was no traffic on the Snake Pass. Last night's snowfall must have been sufficient to close it. The trees were heavy with the clingy sort of snow that hangs on the underside of branches; the sky was a deep, clear blue.

His spirits lifted. Only this sort of day, or this sort of landscape, or a hot bath on a cold night, or the thought of Cassie's hand in his, could have such an effect.

❧

The door bounced back on its hinges and clipped her elbow as Cassie stormed out of South Yorkshire Police Head Quarters.

She saw Flynn walking across the car park. There was much to like about Flynn: she liked that he had nothing bad to say about anybody; she liked that he listened to her – really listened; and she liked that he was a bear of a man – so much bigger than that bastard nurse shagger, Marco.

But he was late. She walked straight past him.

Flynn called out.

She stopped but didn't turn around. 'You promised. Nine o'clock.'

'I know. I'm sorry. But I'm here now. Interview, statement, whatever you need. I'm all yours.'

'Forget it.'

'But . . .'

She turned to face him. 'I'm off the case, Flynn. If Foster wants to interview you, he can sort it out himself.'

'Who's Foster?'

'Doesn't matter.'

No one said anything for a little too long. It had stopped snowing but the skies were threatening. Cassie spotted Charlie Foster watching from her office on the seventh floor. Foster stepped back from the window. Not far enough though, she could still see him.

'Let's go to back to your place,' she said.

'I thought you were off the case? And won't there be a constable on the door?'

'Not the flat – your barn place. I've always wanted to see it.'

'Right,' Flynn said, as slowly as it was possible to enunciate a single-syllable word. He looked curiously incurious.

'On second thoughts,' Cassie looked up at the miserable grey sky, 'I've better things to do with my day.' She hoisted her handbag over her shoulder.

'Wait!' Flynn said. 'I'd love to show you the barn.'

'You weren't so keen a moment ago,' Cassie said, looking at the ground.

'I was . . . I just . . . Yesterday, you said it was inappropriate for us to be talking outside of an interview room.'

She looked up, tilted her head, and fixed on his eyes. 'Yesterday, it was,' she said. 'And maybe it still is. Maybe—'

'No!'

'No?'

❧

It happened while they were still in their boots, standing on the big coir mat by Flynn's front door. The barn was warm, and he was telling her all about his stove.

Cassie wasn't listening. Her life was shit. If she'd been at home, she'd have thrown herself onto the bed and sobbed for an hour.

Instead, she pulled Flynn close and kissed him. She slid a hand under his jumper, and dug her nails into the warm, taut flesh below his ribcage.

His big hands fumbled past her coat and under her cardigan; he tugged down the zip on the side of her dress and touched the skin below her bra clasp; he stroked the curve of her spine with soft fingertips.

Cassie squeezed him tighter, kissed him deeper. A bead of sweat landed on her nose. It tickled. 'You're melting,' she said and pulled away. 'And I'm melting, too.' She made for the sofa, pulling her parka off as she went. 'Sorry about, you know, *that*.'

'Why would you be sorry?'

'Because . . . I don't know.' She reached back and zipped up her dress.

'I'm not sorry,' Flynn said. 'You made me feel . . .' he closed his eyes '. . . good.'

Cassie cupped her face with clammy hands and rubbed her eyes. 'I'm having a bad day, and . . . oh, I don't know.'

He took her coat, hung it on a peg by the door, and smiled. 'Lizzie says—'

Cassie growled, and sat on the sofa, and crossed her legs. 'What the fuck does Lizzie McDonald know about *my* life!'

'Not you, Cassie. Me.' Flynn sat down beside her. 'She keeps telling me I need to move on.'

'Yes, well . . . I'm sorry. Lizzie's right – of course she is. She's always right. And she's a much a nicer person than me. Perhaps you need to find yourself someone more like Lizzie McDonald.'

'I don't think so.' Flynn put a hand on her shoulder and

squeezed. 'Lizzie says – and I know it sounds trite, but she has a point so I'll say it anyway – Lizzie says people should focus on what's good about themselves.' He let go of her shoulder when he felt her flinch. 'She says people should forgive themselves their petty weaknesses. And you can't argue with that, either. It's how *she* gets through life, she says. I think that's why she's so . . . so . . .'

'So *what*, Flynn?'

Flynn frowned and stroked the stubble on his chin with a forefinger. 'So serenely confident,' he said at last.

Cassie scoffed. 'Lizzie McDonald has pin-up good looks and a wardrobe to match. She has a doting millionaire husband, a pair of kids straight out of some TV advert for washing powder, and a house from the centrefold of *Homes and Gardens*. Of course she's serenely fucking confident.'

The fire was dying. Flynn knelt in front of the stove, raked the embers and piled on some fresh coals from the scuttle. When they'd taken, he shut the door and came to sit back down beside her.

He was too close. She got up, made a strenuous show of removing her boots, and then sat back down as far away from him as she could get.

The house phone rang. It rang and rang and rang. Flynn ignored it. He collected their boots and arranged the two pairs neatly by the door, side-by-side.

Cassie shook her head. Her mobile phone rang.

They listened, tight lipped and motionless, until all the ringing had stopped. Then, silently, they sat a while longer.

'Would you like a coffee?' Flynn said at last.

'Yes, please.'

ꕥ

'Cassie,' Flynn began. He had gone over to the sink to fill the kettle.

Cassie was staring at her phone, wondering why her sergeant might have called. Meg Harper would have been told not to make contact, and Meg Harper was a stickler for procedure.

'Cassie,' Flynn called out again.

She looked up from her phone.

'Why did they take you off the case?'

She frowned. 'I had to tell them that the meal you'd prepared was intended for me.'

'But I told them it was just for me,' Flynn said.

Cassie laughed. 'I know! Two sets of crockery? Two sets of cutlery? Two champagne flutes?'

'Yes, but—'

'And candles, Flynn! Come on, it looked like it you'd been planning an evening with *her* – with the dead girl. I had to say something.'

Flynn squeezed his eyes shut and sighed. 'Okay, so I didn't think it through. It was all I could come up with at the time. I was only trying to keep you out of it.'

'I know.' She smiled and then sighed. 'Very gallant.'

Her mobile started ringing again. She got up and paced a few steps towards the sofa.

'Don't mind me,' Flynn said. He set a cup of coffee down in front of her and then went back to his little kitchen – went to the other end of the room. 'Take the call.'

It dawned on Cassie that he was trying to give her some privacy. She wouldn't have done that for him. It would never have occurred to her to do that. She couldn't tolerate secrets. No wonder Marco had fled.

She answered her phone. 'Meg, Hi.'

'Sorry to disturb, ma'am, but I thought you ought to know that the focus of the investigation has shifted back to Flynn.'

'You do surprise me!'

'With good reason, though. We've new evidence that links

Flynn to the victim.'

'What sort of evidence?'

'A video.'

Cassie glanced at Flynn, who was wiping down the worktop by the sink. She lowered her voice. 'The two of them together?'

'No, just her. But she's at the end of his drive, on the Snake Pass. Do you know where I mean?'

'Sort of,' Cassie said, gulping down a sharp intake of breath. 'And?'

'Well, it's a clear picture, high definition, and there's no doubt that it's her. It's Flynn's place, for sure, and there's even a time and date stamp. She was outside his house on the Snake Pass at 10:30 a.m. on the day of the murder.'

Cassie nodded, lengthily. 'Thanks, Meg. I . . .' She felt her stomach churn.

'Ma'am?'

Cassie cleared her throat. 'Where did we find this video?'

'DCC Muxlow got it in the post this morning. On a flash drive. Anonymous.'

Cassie turned and looked at Flynn. He had his back to her and was staring into the sink. She knew nothing about this man. Dead wife, dead parents, no siblings – little more. Born in Manchester, she remembered. Came to Sheffield as a student and never left. Nothing unusual about that – lots of people she knew had come to Sheffield as students and never left. But they all had a back-story. Not Flynn. She remembered how she'd tried to prise things out of him in the aftermath of Sarah's death. He'd been happy enough to talk about their life in Sheffield (Sarah this, Sarah that, Sarah the other), but he'd sidestepped any questions about himself and his life before he met his wife. It was odd, but not that odd. Maybe—

'Odd, don't you think?' Meg said. 'Why send it to Muxlow?'

Cassie wasn't listening. 'Sorry?'

'Why send the video directly to DCC Muxlow? Why not to the *Senior Investigating Officer?* Why not just to *the police?*'

❧

Cassie's first instinct was to challenge Flynn about the video. But how would that help? He'd only say he knew nothing about it. And that was very probably true. In any case, without having seen it herself, and without being able to show it to Flynn, she was in no position to challenge anyone about anything.

Flynn's landline rang out again.

'Don't you think you ought to pick up,' Cassie said.

Flynn sat down beside her again. 'No.'

Cassie got up, went to the big oak table, and perched on the edge. She was tempted to pick up the phone herself – she hated not knowing.

'I've got to go back to the office,' she said. Flynn's phone was still ringing. 'Sorry, but something's come up.'

He didn't respond.

'I'll walk back to my car,' she said. 'No need for you to—'

'Right.' Flynn said. And there was that look again – interested but unimpressed. The ringing had stopped now, but she could hear its echo still.

'Right!' Cassie said, making for the door.

Flynn got up and tried to kiss her cheek.

She dodged him and went for her boots.

'You regret coming here, don't you?' Flynn said.

'No.'

'So?'

Cassie pulled on her boots. 'Bad timing, that's all.'

'Perhaps if we—'

Flynn's landline rang out again. Cassie went for the receiver but hesitated before lifting. She looked at Flynn. 'May I?'

He shrugged.

It was Angus McDonald. 'I'll put him on,' she said.

Cassie passed Flynn the handset, grabbed her coat, and listened.

'Sean Mulligan?' Flynn said. 'No, but I've heard of him. Why do you ask?'

She couldn't hear what Angus was saying.

'Angus wants a word.' Flynn said, holding out the handset.

Cassie took it and turned away. 'Angus?'

'We need to meet,' Angus said. 'Soon as you can, ring me when you're back in town.'

'Okay, give me an hour.' She handed back the phone and watched Flynn untangle the cord. It must be important, Cassie had decided, because Angus didn't do *spontaneous*.

'What?' Flynn said.

Cassie fixed on him like a school mistress. 'What did Angus say to you?'

'He wanted to know if I knew Sean Mulligan.'

'And do you?'

'No! Why would I know someone like that? He's a local villain, isn't he? Drug dealer or something? His name came up a couple of times when Sarah was doing a piece on the cannabis re-classification back in . . .' Flynn sighed. 'What's this about, Cassie? What did he say to you?'

'Nothing.' Cassie made a show of looking out the window to the snow-covered yard. 'Did you know that Angus works for MI6?' She only said it because she was cross with the pair of them. She regretted it immediately.

Flynn raised his eyebrows. 'Angus? MI6?'

'Right. I'm off.' Cassie pulled a woolly hat from her coat pocket and arranged it on her head in the mirror above the sofa.

'Let me drive you down to your car, at least,' Flynn said, opening the back door.

The cold draught stung her eyes.

❧

The short drive along Flynn's track was awkward: he kept looking at her. She was used to men looking at her, and an hour ago she would have been pleased to have Flynn looking at her – but not now. Did she believe Flynn was responsible for that girl's death? Of course not. Flynn wasn't a murderer. Even if he was, he wasn't stupid enough to murder someone in his own flat. And when Cassie tried (hypothetically) to put Flynn into the frame, nothing made sense.

But he did have secrets – she'd convinced herself of that – and she couldn't bear secrets.

'Protecting secrets, I expect,' Flynn said.

'What?'

'Angus. MI6. I know he specialises in computer security, and I know the big merchant banks pay him a small fortune as a consultant. I expect he's involved in cyber espionage – stopping it, I mean. Am I right? Or is he just a highly paid assassin?'

Cassie laughed. She didn't want to – it annoyed her that she did – but she couldn't help herself. 'Probably!' she said.

'Really?' He brought the Land Rover to a slippery halt in the pub car park. 'Angus, a hitman,' he said, 'who'd have thunk it?'

She smiled, gathered her handbag, and opened the door. It squeaked on its hinges and the glass rattled.

'Sarah didn't like MI6 very much,' Flynn said. 'Perhaps that's why she and Angus never got on.'

Cassie puffed out her cheeks. 'I don't think your wife liked anyone very much.' She slammed the door and started back towards her Mini. 'Except for you, of course,' she said under her breath, 'you big bastard!'

❧

When she'd gone, Flynn sat for a while with the engine running, looking out across the road to the far side of the river. The woodland around here was ancient, the Ashop Valley being so steep that no one had ever bothered to clear or cultivate the land. He loved the moors – where what was harsh was beautiful, where what appeared barren was fecund, where what seemed to go on for ever always came to an end. But even more than the moors themselves, he loved the oak and birch woodland that populated the many valleys, gorges and gullies that cut through the moorland – the steep banks had been left untouched since Neolithic farmers began clearing the primordial forest that once covered these hills.

The Romans built the first ever road across the Pennines along this route – along the course of the River Ashop – and Flynn imagined a Centurion (cloaked and sandaled and stamping his feet for warmth) looking out over the very same woodland.

The modern route across the Pennines, the nineteenth-century turnpike, is known as the *Snake Pass*. The road was named after the eighteenth-century *Snake Inn*, Flynn remembered, one of the few buildings on its higher stretches. But at some point over the last few years the *Snake Inn* had been renamed *The Snake Pass Inn* . . . after the nineteenth-century turnpike that had originally been named after the inn! It pleased Flynn to know that old histories – old truths – could die, and that new histories – new truths – could be born.

For the first time in a long while the idea of going back to an empty house filled him with melancholy. He was remembering Sarah, who had loved this place nearly as much as he did. Or perhaps she had loved it more, even, than he did. Or perhaps one should never measure love by degrees.

Sarah had always enjoyed the noisy, crowded bars of the Ecclesall Road, where conversation was close to impossible. He remembered suffering this for an hour or so before moving her on to a restaurant where there might, at the very least, be seats to be had. He thought of Sarah in her Friday night frock and ridiculously high heels. She wore tight dresses in order to squeeze as much woman as she could from her boyish frame. And she wore the heels . . .

'Because I'm short, why else?'

'You're not short, Sarah, you're petite. "Short" makes you sound odd-shaped.'

'Thanks for reminding me: as well as being short, I lack hips and tits!'

But for all her self-deprecation, Sarah knew damn well that she turned heads – knew she was irresistible to men.

The doors to The Snake Pass Inn were open now, and a sign had appeared outside: *Jack Daniels promotion: double-up for free.*

Flynn gave in.

12

THE KING'S HEAD was almost empty, so Cassie could have her pick of tables. She made for the best one – the one by the fire with the big comfy chairs – and sat down to wait for Angus. A few taciturn men sat at the bar supping ale and watching rolling news on the big screen. Cassie wondered what sort of men propped up bars at one o'clock on a Saturday afternoon. Her father, probably, in the old days – he'd have enjoyed obliterating his life in silent company. Perhaps he still did. Perhaps not. These days, she imagined, he got home in time for dinner, got home in time for bedtime stories. No, not bedtime stories: they'd be too old for that. She wondered if Flynn, who liked to write stories, and to read stories out loud, had ever had stories read to him. Flynn was a kind and gentle man. He had nothing to do with the death of the girl found murdered in his flat.

Cassie remembered sipping Pimm's on the lawn at little James McDonald's Christening party and chatting with the most flirtatious vicar she'd ever encountered. 'Doubt is no barrier to faith,' he'd said, with the sort of conviction that comes only after two glasses of champagne and three large Pimm's, 'quite the reverse: doubt is an essential part of faith. There can be no faith, I think, without doubt.'

Flynn had approached, looking even bigger than usual. 'Adonis in a light grey morning suit', was how Lizzie would describe him later that evening. God knows how much she spent having the suit made ('Well, he *is* the Godfather. And you can't get a suit in his size off the peg – not a nice one').

When the vicar spotted Flynn coming over, he made his apologies and withdrew.

'Sorry,' Flynn said. 'Did I frighten him off?'

Cassie smiled politely. 'He had to go and mingle, apparently.'

Flynn turned and watched the vicar stroll towards the summer house. 'Well, he certainly did his fair share of mingling with you, Detective Inspector May.

Cassie blushed and found herself giggling like a school girl. 'It's *Cassie*, please. And, for your information, he was talking to me about faith. All very proper. He said, "Doubt is an essential part of faith – there can be no faith, I think, without doubt". '

Flynn thought about that for a while and shook his head. 'When someone plays with words like that, I tend to stop listening. It's usually politicians, or priests, or sales reps. And they're almost certainly trying to get you to swallow something they don't properly understand, or don't really believe.'

Cassie was taken aback. 'That's a bit rich, coming from a writer!' she said. 'Don't you lot play with words all the time?'

Flynn looked hurt. Flynn was not a man you could offend or rile, but he was, she would come to learn, a man you could very easily hurt.

'I only write stories, Inspector,' he said. 'I don't tell people what to believe or how to think.'

'I'm sorry, Mr Flynn, I didn't mean to suggest . . .' But she couldn't let it go. 'Honestly, though, I do think you're being a bit precious.'

Flynn looked her straight in the eye. 'Fancy another Pimm's?'.

'Only if you stop calling me *Inspector*.'

'I'll stop calling you *Inspector if* you stop calling me *Mister*. Everyone calls me *Flynn*, just that, just *Flynn*.'

❧

'How old is your youngest, Angus?'

Angus sat down and slung his coat and bag over the chair back. 'Just turned two,' he said.

'Hmmm.'

'Why?'

'Oh, I was just thinking about his Christening. About when I first met Flynn. Socially, I mean – the first time we really talked.'

Angus looked at her but didn't say anything.

She busied herself neatening the arrangement of beer mats on the table. 'Coffee?'

'Yes.' Angus turned and made for the bar.

Cassie watched eager flames twist and swirl in the fireplace, and thought about Flynn's little barn. It suited him, which was surprising since he was such a big man and the barn was such a little house. If that girl hadn't turned up dead in Flynn's flat, if last night's dinner had gone as planned, if . . .

No, there was too much she didn't know about Flynn – too much to take on faith.

Angus arrived back at the table. 'Coffee's on its way.'

'Angus,' Cassie said, looking up from the fire.

'Yes.' He put his elbows on the table and leaned in.

'You don't think Flynn had anything to do with that girl's death, do you?'

'No, I don't. Why would you even—'

Cassie held up both hands. 'I know. But how can you be sure? What do you know about him, really? What do you know about him from before he came to Sheffield? Isn't he from Manchester originally?'

'I don't . . .' Angus stalled. 'Look, Cassie, I think I know him well enough to be confident he isn't a murderer.'

'Yes, but they all say that, don't they.'

'Who's *they*?'

'The friends of murders,' she said, making no effort to hide her exasperation, '*that's* who.'

The coffee arrived on a small tray. 'Milk?' the girl asked, setting down the cups and a bowl of sugar cubes.

Cassie shook her head.

Angus looked up and smiled. 'No thanks. We're fine.'

She gave them a disapproving look and stomped back to the bar.

Angus frowned. 'I thought you'd want to help him, that's why I asked you here.'

'Of course I want to help him. But I can't help him if . . .' Cassie closed her eyes and took a deep breath. 'There's new evidence – evidence that suggests he knew the victim.'

Angus took a sip of coffee and dabbed his mouth with a paper napkin. 'I *trust* him, Cassie.'

'Trust!' She slapped the table. Their drinks trembled but didn't spill. 'This has nothing whatsoever to do with trust. This is a murder case: it's about evidence, suspects, witnesses. It's about facts.'

The girl who had just served them was staring now. Angus offered an apologetic shrug, which riled Cassie so much she couldn't speak.

'What's with all this paranoia?' Angus said. 'Why can't you bring yourself to trust anyone?'

Cassie felt her cheeks burning.

Angus stirred a rough cube of brown sugar into his coffee.

'How dare you talk to me like that!' Cassie said, hands clenched into a double fist. 'How dare you!' She turned to the fire and gazed into the angry flames before rounding on him. 'So, my good friend Angus, who spends half his time gawping at my boobs . . .' She raised her eyebrows. 'Oh, did you think I hadn't noticed? Well I have. Now, where was I? Oh yes . . . So, the man who likes nothing better than to spend an entire evening ogling my breasts thinks I have issues with trust. And why do you suppose that might be?'

Angus got up. 'I've changed my mind about the milk.'

Cassie sank back into her chair. 'I'm sorry,' she said. 'Please, I didn't mean it, I—'

Angus held up a hand. 'Back in a minute.'

There were five men propping up the bar that lunchtime, and all five were now looking at Cassie. When they realised that she'd noticed, they turned back to their pint pots, back to their communal silence.

❧

Angus dumped a handful of plastic UHT milk tubs on the table. 'On second thoughts,' he said, 'I think I'll stick with black.'

'I didn't mean it, Angus. Honestly.'

Angus stared into his coffee cup. 'Perhaps you should find yourself some female friends, Cassie.'

'I have plenty of female friends,' she said.

'Like who?'

Cassie watched him stack the little milk pots into a pyramid. She tried to catch his eye but he wouldn't look up. 'Just say what you want to say, Angus, I'm sure I deserve it.'

Angus shook his head and sniffed. 'I'm ashamed, I don't know what to else to say.'

'I'm the one who should be ashamed, Angus. What I said was spiteful and unfair and I'm sorry. You've always been there for me. I'm the one who takes advantage, we both know that.'

Angus stared at the floor and said nothing.

'Please, Angus, look at me.'

Angus looked up and forced a smile.

Cassie beamed back. 'Let's start again. You wanted to meet up, so what's on your mind?'

'Sod the coffee,' Angus said, 'I could do with a pint. How about you?'

'White wine, please, and a tub of Pringles.'

❧

While the landlord changed the barrel, Angus thought things through. Flynn's story about the dead girl on his bed, and Cassie's conviction that the dead girl looked just like Sarah Flynn, had sparked in him a curiosity normally reserved for matters mathematical. He'd wanted to see a picture of this girl for himself. And as much as he'd told himself that it would be an anticlimax – that Cassie didn't know Sarah, and that the dead girl probably didn't look anything like Sarah – he hadn't been able to shake it. He'd tossed and turned for a few hours after getting back from The King's Head the previous night, but at three o'clock in the morning, with no prospect of sleep, Angus crept out of bed, went down to his study, and logged on to his computer.

He checked the local weather forecast. And then he checked the forecast for Mumbai, and for Moscow, and for Singapore, and for Sydney, and for another dozen random places. Once he'd established which would be the warmest and coldest places in the world that day, he checked his credit card account, and his utilities accounts, and his mobile phone account. He scanned the headlines on the BBC. He checked the league positions of Sheffield United and Sheffield Wednesday, and read recent match reports (just so that he'd be able to make football-small-talk with any other dads in the school playground at pick-up time).

The next thing he knew he had logged onto a secure server at GCHQ and was running a communications traffic check on 'James Flynn'.

And it hadn't ended there. Angus had broken a great many rules over the last few hours.

❧

'I've broken a few rules,' Angus said, depositing the drinks and the Pringles on the table in front of Cassie. 'That's why I brought up the *trust* thing. Because I need you to trust me.'

Cassie twirled her glass by the stem and took a sip of wine. 'Do you trust *me*, Angus?'

'Yes.'

'Then tell me what's on your mind.'

'I've been doing some digging,' Angus said. 'This business at Flynn's flat doesn't seem right. If you take the position that Flynn had nothing to do with the death of that girl . . .' (he looked hard at Cassie but she didn't flinch), '. . . then you have to deal with the likelihood that he's being framed for it.'

'Come on, Angus!' Cassie put down her glass and nudged it slightly to the left so that it sat more centrally on the beer mat. 'That's a bit of a leap, isn't it. If Flynn is innocent, it doesn't automatically follow that he's being framed. And if he is being framed, it's a pretty poor job. There really isn't much evidence against him.'

'But there will be soon, I'm convinced of it.'

Cassie stared at Angus.

Angus tried to focus only on her eyes. He felt himself blush.

'I take it your "digging" is unauthorised,' she said.

'Yes.'

'Will you get into trouble?'

'Yes.'

She glanced over her shoulder at the lunchtime regulars.

Angus looked too.

The regulars turned back to their drinks.

The fire was dying – the last log was about to collapse into the embers. Angus found himself looking at Cassie's chest. Had she had undone another button on her blouse? Or had it had just come undone? He thought about the police photos of the dead girl, and about how much she looked like Sarah Flynn. She looked even more like Sarah in the film recorded outside Flynn's place: the way she walked, the way she moved her head and tossed her hair. He couldn't get the bitch out of his head: two years dead and Sarah Flynn was with him still – haunting, taunting.

'Why are you doing all this, Angus?' Cassie said. 'Why not leave it to the police?'

He looked into his coffee. 'I owe it to Flynn to do what I can.'

'You *owe* it to him?'

Angus looked at the floor. 'He's my oldest friend.'

When Angus looked up, Cassie was doing up the button on her blouse. He looked away.

'Honestly, Angus. I told you I didn't mean all that stuff. Please look at me, I'd rather you . . .' She tucked her hair behind her ears. 'I've spoiled everything, haven't I. Oh please, Angus, say something.'

'She's Sarah Flynn's daughter,' he said.

Cassie rubbed her temples. 'What? Who? Hang on, Sarah Flynn didn't have a daughter. What are you on about?'

'The dead girl. The dead girl in Flynn's flat.'

Cassie stiffened. 'What makes you think she's Sarah's daughter?'

'DNA. She's definitely Sarah's daughter.'

'And Flynn's daughter?'

'No,' Angus said. 'Nothing to do with Flynn.'

'He might not be her biological father, Angus,' Cassie leaned in and glared at him, 'but she has everything to do with Flynn, surely?'

Angus shook his head. 'Flynn didn't know about her. She was eighteen, so Sarah must have been fifteen when she had the baby – at least three years before any of us knew her.'

'You can't be sure he didn't know. We all have secrets, don't we, and I'm beginning to think that your mate Flynn has more than his fair share.'

'He didn't know, Cassie.'

'And how did you get hold of her DNA results before the police?'

Angus ignored the question. 'The girl had a record; she was caught shoplifting in Edinburgh when she was fourteen. Her DNA is already in the system, so your lot will soon have an ID. Sarah's DNA is in the system too – *you* put it there, two years ago, after the car crash, along with Flynn's.'

'But how could you even access that sort of data? And how could their DNA have been compared so quickly? It's impossible.'

Angus folded his arms. 'It wasn't done that quickly.'

'What are you saying? The results of the comparison were already in the system?'

Angus nodded.

'But I though Sarah couldn't have children,' Cassie said. 'Flynn told me that once, I'm sure of it.'

Angus lay his hands flat on the table. 'A charade. She lied to him. That's the way she was. I know for a fact that she was on the pill.' He began to drum his fingers.

'How could you possibly know that?' Cassie said, rapping his knuckles with a beer mat. She folded her arms. 'Oh for Christ's sake, Angus, you've hacked into her medical records, haven't you?'

'Don't you want to know the girl's name?' Angus asked.

'Go on then.'

Angus planted his elbows on the table. 'Gemma Jane Grant.'

'Gemma Jane Grant.' Cassie repeated the name, slowly. 'Is that supposed to mean something to me?'

'Does it?'

'No. Does it mean anything to you?'

'No. Her last known address was in Edinburgh, by the way.'

Cassie pushed back her chair and got to her feet. He looked up at her: she was puckering her lips the way she did when she was agitated. She turned to the mirror above the fireplace and straightened her mouth when she saw the reflection. Angus tried to catch her eye but she didn't notice, or else she was ignoring him.

'I'm on leave,' she said, still studying her reflection.

He nodded. 'Good.'

Good because Angus had no idea where to go from here. He could find things out if he knew what he was looking for, he could solve a problem if someone gave him a problem to solve, he could test hypotheses to destruction if they were laid out before him – but right now, he was lost. His tutor at Cambridge once told him that finding the answer isn't enough: 'the mark of a genius is his ability to find the *question*.' Angus lacked imagination: his tutor knew it; he knew it.

'I need you, Cassie,' he said. 'I need a detective.'

She eyed him in the mirror. 'Why were you asking about Sean Mulligan?'

'Flynn's phone records show calls received from a number linked to Sean Mulligan.'

'People like Sean Mulligan don't leave traceable phone records, they use unregistered pay-as-you-go phones.' Cassie shifted her gaze from the mirror and looked Angus straight in the eye. 'Sean Mulligan isn't stupid.'

'Yes, but the number isn't registered under his name, I followed a flag in the data, he wouldn't have known it could be traced back to him.'

'Mulligan's no fool, he knows he's watched.'

'So you don't think Mulligan rang Flynn?'

Cassie frowned. 'Stop playing games with me, Angus. You know all this. That's why you think the whole thing is a frame up.'

'Okay, but why plant a link to Mulligan? I can't find anything that links them before this week, and I can't find a link between Mulligan and Gemma Grant.'

'Gemma Grant,' Cassie said. 'What was the cause of death?'

Angus shrugged. 'Post-mortem report hasn't been uploaded yet.'

'Heroin overdose,' Cassie said, matter-of-factly.

'How do you know that?'

'Well, Sean Mulligan is a dealer.'

'So it's just a guess?' Angus shook his head.

She scowled. 'I'm thinking on my feet here. It's a working theory. Now come on, what else do you know?'

He leaned in. 'Have you seen the video of Gemma Grant outside Flynn's place?'

Cassie's eyes widened: 'Have *you?*'

He pulled a laptop from his bag and opened it up on the table. They stared, for a minute or two, at a loop of the fifteen second video of Gemma Grant wading through deep snow at the end of Flynn's drive.

'Hmmm.' She rubbed her eyes. 'Wobbly – must have been a very long lens – and roughly edited, which makes it all a bit confusing. I don't know, there's something odd about it. Email it to me.'

He nodded.

Cassie's phone rang. 'I'll take this outside,' she said.

Angus snapped shut the laptop and let his eyes close. The long night, the relief of having Cassie on board, the gentle warmth of the fire – they were taking their toll. He wanted to sleep.

The dead girl on the bed appeared to him in a waking dream: more real than the image he had downloaded from the police server – she appeared as clear, and as uncertain, as a memory. The girl eased herself onto her elbows, crossed her legs and sat up. She moved the way people do in dreams – slowly and without effort, like an astronaut in space. He tried not to look, but the harder he tried, the more vivid she became. Her nostrils flared, her lips parted and she started to breathe. Her chest rose and fell with his own. Now her eyes were open. They were bright and emerald green. They were Sarah Flynn's eyes. It *was* Sarah Flynn – naked and gloating and without remorse. She smiled her wicked smile and held out a hand. Angus dreamed himself walking towards her, but no matter how fast he walked, he couldn't get any closer. Sarah looked to her left and scowled. He turned to see who she was looking at—

'Angus, are you asleep?'

He opened his eyes. Cassie was standing over him. 'No,' he said, 'just thinking.'

'Me too.' Cassie sat down. 'I can't get Sarah Flynn out of my head.'

'No?'

'No. Somehow, she has to be at the bottom of this mess.'

'She's dead, Cassie. Long gone.'

'Dead, yes. But I don't think she's gone.' Cassie rubbed her eyes. 'I need to find out what she was working on just before she died. I know she was looking into a procurement scandal at the NHS, but I can't believe that's connected to any of this. And she'd been investigating the trafficking of child prostitutes, but she broke that story months before she died so I don't think that's it either. There must be something else?'

'Did you ask Flynn?' Angus said.

'Yes, but he didn't know. He did admit that she'd been a bit secretive those last few weeks. All Flynn remembered from that time was some story about an American who was over here with plans to buy the big two Sheffield football clubs, but that came to nothing. There must have been something else, and I need *you* to find out what.'

'Me? How? You already trawled everything after she died didn't you: email, phone, laptop? If it's in the cloud, if it's accessible via the internet, I can probably get at it, but I'd have to know what I was looking for.'

Cassie opened her handbag and pulled out a package. 'The hard drive from Sarah's computer. Our guys couldn't get into it back then; it's encrypted and password protected, apparently. I was looking into sending it to the techies at Cyber-Fraud, but Muxlow pulled the plug on the investigation into her death and it's been in my desk drawer ever since.'

'Ah.' Angus affected a pained expression.

'What?'

'It was me who set up her security. If your guys had a go at it,' Angus twisted his mouth 'it'll most probably have been wiped clean.'

Cassie looked crestfallen. 'Well, do what you can. If I knew who she was meeting the day she died, that would be a start. She told Flynn she had a meeting with some MP in Manchester. But she lied. I checked.'

'I think she was at the *Manchester Evening News*,' Angus said.

Cassie's eyes narrowed.

'A couple of months after the crash,' he went on, 'Flynn asked me to go through her mail because he couldn't face it himself. Amongst all the junk, there was a parking ticket – there were several actually – but this one stood out because it was issued the day she died. I looked it up and—'

'The *Manchester Evening News*. You're sure?'

'Well, she was parked outside their offices. And given her line of work, it's got to be a fair bet.'

'Anywhere near the Trafford Shopping Centre?'

'No, the paper's based in Oldham, half an hour from the Trafford Centre on the M60.'

Cassie puffed her cheeks and rubbed her forehead. 'It's just that she spent a small fortune on a credit card at the Trafford Centre the day she died: that's how we knew she'd been in Manchester. I just assumed she'd met someone *there*.'

'Maybe she did meet someone at the Trafford Centre. Maybe she had two meetings.'

'But we didn't find any shopping in or around her car after the crash. That was one of the things that troubled me at the time.'

'Maybe her card was stolen or cloned.'

'Don't think so. We recovered her handbag and her card, and we checked every purchase made that day. All the receipts were for women's clothes. Expensive stuff – and all in her size, too. And no one attempted to use the card after she died, so it's unlikely that it was cloned.' Cassie pulled on her coat. 'Anyway,' she said, shaking her head, 'I'll pay the *Manchester Evening News* a visit, I think. You find out who she was seeing there.'

'What . . . now?'

'I'll be there in couple of hours, so yes. And see what you can do with that hard drive. Oh, and I need to know about her past: Sarah Flynn's life before she came to Sheffield. Maiden name was Parker. Parents dead. No siblings. Went to some posh boarding school, don't know which. That's all Flynn seemed to know. I'd start with the boarding schools if I were you.'

'But that was pre-digital, Cassie. I can't hack into filing cabinets!'

'Try using the phone.'

13

HAD THERE NOT been boxing on TV at The Snake Pass Inn that Saturday lunchtime, Flynn would only have had the one *double up for free* Jack Daniels.

Probably.

But there *was* boxing on TV, so he had another and another and another, until the world became a gentler place – a world where bored men, who had never been punched senseless, didn't pay middlemen to watch other men beat the shit out of each other.

There are many techniques one can be taught to suppress bad memories. Flynn had learned a few, but the method that worked best for him was this: identify the trigger and reprogramme the brain's response to that trigger. Cravats were one such trigger, and he'd reprogrammed his brain to recall the famous Rowan Atkinson scene from *Four Weddings and a Funeral* whenever he saw a man wearing a cravat. Boxing rings were another – when he saw a boxing ring, he would recall Frank Bruno dressed as a pantomime dame.

But that Saturday lunchtime he was tired, and more than a little drunk, and he forgot to remember Frank Bruno as a pantomime dame. Instead, he remembered how a baying crowd suddenly fell silent; he remembered how all eyes turned away from him, and settled on his opponent.

It was Flynn's sixteenth birthday, and he'd been sitting on one of the hay bales that formed the pit, wiping blood from grazed knuckles with a handful of straw – he'd stopped when he noticed the silence, and looked up.

Mike Bolan was standing in front of him, red faced and shaking. 'You'll pay for this, you fucker,' he said.

Flynn got to his feet.

Bolan took a couple of steps back. 'I told you to go down,' he said, pointing a trembling finger. 'And don't think you can—'

Flynn walked straight past him.

Ryan Gallagher was laid out on across two bales: white, acne-scarred skin; ginger stubble smeared with blood; nose crushed and bent to one side; one eye open, the other swollen shut. The referee was frantically pumping his chest with the heel of his right hand.

'But,' Flynn said, still scrubbing at the blood on his fist, 'I only hit him the once, properly I mean.'

No one was listening.

He felt suddenly lightheaded.

A bitter chill, which began in his gut, soon engulfed him.

Scotty Deakin and one of his heavies appeared from nowhere. Scotty was pointing a pistol at someone behind Flynn. Flynn turned and saw Bolan – arms raised, bloodied flick knife in his right hand – glaring at him.

No, it was not a chill he could feel. Not cold but heat. Flynn was burning up – caustic skin scorching muscle, sinew, and bone. He clutched his ribs and felt blood, warm and slick, between his fingers. He dropped to his knees, head spinning, and curled up on the cool concrete floor.

'Don't panic,' Scotty said, stepping over him. 'It's only a scratch.'

The barn was a blur now. Voices all round him, but no words. Flynn slipped into a world of timeless calm – Mum's perfume sweet in his nostrils, her breath warm on his cheek, her lips soft on his forehead.

14

CAFÉ DES POTES was unusually quiet for a Saturday lunchtime. Deakin ignored the barman and walked straight to the table where the old lady was sitting, hunched over her knitting. For a moment he imagined himself strangling her with a length of her own yarn.

'Mr Deakin,' the old lady said, looking up with a broad smile. 'What a pleasant surprise.'

Everything about this woman annoyed him: her prim face, her dowager duchess clothes, her clipped Edinburgh accent. He pulled out a chair, and sat down.

She offered another smile, pensive this time, then asked, 'How long has it been since you were last in Edinburgh? Or the UK, even? Fourteen years? Fifteen? Longer?'

'I'm here because my lad's in trouble,' Deakin said. 'What are you going to do to sort it?'

The old lady held up her knitting, a tiny pink bonnet attached to four knitting needles. 'This is for my youngest great-granddaughter,' she said. 'I had eight at the last count.' She put her knitting into a tote bag by her feet. 'I was under the impression that you were childless, Mr Deakin.'

'You know who I'm talking about.'

'Yes. He's a fully-grown man now, I think.'

'He's being stitched up like a kipper.'

The old lady raised a hand and glanced at the barman. 'Mr Deakin,' she said, 'why have you come all the way up to Edinburgh?'

'Because I want it sorted.'

'But I'm retired.'

'You said that the last time.'

'And it was true. But there were special circumstances.'

'There are always special circumstances where your sort are concerned.'

'Come now, Mr Deakin. Surely you have your own people to sort things out.'

'The police are involved now, so it's delicate.'

The old lady raised her eyebrows. 'I thought you'd have *that* well under control, too.'

'Well, I don't.'

'And what makes you so sure that *your lad* didn't kill the poor girl?'

Deakin closed his eyes and drew a long breath.

The barman arrived with a tray. A measure of Pastis in a tall narrow glass with a long spoon. A jug of water. A bowl of peanuts. He arranged these on the table in front of the old lady, along with a whisky for Deakin.

'I understand you enjoy a single malt, Mr Deakin. Darren assures me this is one of their finest.'

Deakin looked up at Darren and nodded a half-hearted thank you.

Darren executed a barely perceptible bow and left.

'I'm out,' Deakin said. 'That's what I've come here to tell you. To warn you. A courtesy, if you like.' He downed his whisky in one angry gulp.

The old lady filled her glass with water, stirred it, took a sip, and reached for the peanuts. 'Sounds more like a threat than a courtesy, Mr Deakin.'

'No. I'm just being straight with you. I'd rather work through this with Unit 17, of course. But if you won't play ball, if you won't sort things out, I'll have to deal with this in my own way.'

Leaning back a little (so that she could look down her nose, Deakin assumed) the old lady studied him with what he took for mild amusement. 'You mistake me for something I am not,' she said at last. 'You mistake me for someone with influence or power or both. I have neither. I retired a very long time ago. Nowadays, I offer what help and support I can to young women. Young women who happen to be directed my way. I've been little more than a welfare officer – a mentor, if you like – these last twenty-five years.'

Deakin didn't believe a word of it. 'And do they *all* end up dead before their time.'

No reaction. The old lady put a handful of peanuts in her mouth and chewed slowly. When she'd finished, she dabbed her mouth with a paper napkin. 'And how many young women have died under your care, Mr Deakin.'

'Different. Totally different and you know it.' Deakin felt his blood rising. 'My girls were free to go any time they liked.' He rounded on the old lady, pointing a finger. 'And my girls were old enough to decide things for themselves – my girls weren't fucking children.'

Darren turned up at the table with a tray. He set down a fresh glass of whisky, topped up the peanuts, and took the empty glass away.

'If you're a player,' Deakin said, studying his whisky, 'you know the rules. And if you live by those rules then you'd better be prepared to die by them.' He looked up and fixed on the old lady. 'But I've never done harm to innocents. That's the difference between you and me.'

The old lady appeared unmoved. 'I understand an awful lot has been invested in developing those Russian contacts of yours. I understand there are people who would be very disappointed to see all that effort put to waste.'

'I'll stick to business from now on. Why don't you lot stick to politics?'

'Your *business*, Mr Deakin, is crime. And I'm given to understand that you've done very well out of it. Very well indeed. Wouldn't it be a shame to jeopardise all that?'

'And your business,' Deakin said, 'is politics. Christ knows what you get out of it, but you're welcome to it.'

She tilted her head slightly and spoke softly. 'Business, crime, politics: an unholy trinity, but a trinity none the less, especially in Russia.'

'I don't care, I'm out. And if anything happens to me, your entire operation will be exposed. It's all arranged. There are plenty more Sarah Flynns poking their noses into what you lot get up to with taxpayers' money.'

The old lady pressed her fingers together and bowed her head. 'I think you're cutting off your nose to spite your face.'

'No,' Deakin said. 'I'm amputating a leg that's riddled with gangrene.' He frowned and reached for his drink. 'And this latest business. What's that all about?'

'You tell me, Mr Deakin.' The old lady took another sip of pastis, patting her lips dry afterwards. 'Your franchisee: your affair. I assure you, this *business* has nothing to do with Unit 17 or the Russians.'

Deakin downed his second whisky in one go and shook his head. 'Yeah, right. Well, I've said what I came here to say.'

'Don't do anything hasty,' the old lady said. 'In my experience these things often sort themselves out.'

'That's what you said about my Jamie and your little bitch,' Deakin said bitterly.

She rolled her eyes. 'What was I supposed to do?'

'Call her off, that's what.'

'I never quite understood what you had against Sarah.'

Deakin squeezed his eyes shut. 'You. That's what I had against her.'

The old lady sighed and folded her arms. 'This is ancient

history. I let the girl go a long time ago, she was more trouble than she was worth. Maybe, after fifteen years, it's time for you to let *your lad* go too.'

Deakin stared into space.

'I don't know why you're bringing all this up now,' the old lady continued, 'she's dead and gone.'

Darren approached; she waved him away.

'Sarah's come back to haunt him,' Deakin said. 'That's why I'm bringing all this up now. Don't imagine that I don't know what's going on here.'

The old lady threw him a sceptical look. 'I don't believe in ghosts any more than you do.'

'No?' Deakin laughed. 'No. I don't expect you do.' He looked up at the ceiling then down to his empty glass. 'But I take my responsibilities seriously. Something *you* wouldn't understand.'

The old lady fished the half-knitted pink bonnet from her bag and arranged it on her lap. 'Will that be all, Mr Deakin?'

15

THE POLICE WOULD have the DNA results for Gemma by now, so they would know who she was. But they wouldn't know that she was the daughter of their prime suspect's late wife. Cassie could have tipped them off. She didn't. Had Muxlow been right to take her off the case?

She was in unexplored territory now, looking upon an unfamiliar landscape. Right was wrong and wrong was right. She told herself that this had nothing to do with protecting Flynn, and it had everything to do with getting to the truth. Foster would focus all his attention on building a case against Flynn. That was all he knew: form a theory, gather evidence to support it, and dismiss anything that didn't fit. And he would do it within the rules. And his investigatory audit trail would be impeccable.

Muxlow would have his reasons for loosing this monster, reasons that would never be articulated. Justifications would be voiced, of course, but justifications are not the same as reasons. Cassie tensed and writhed and pummelled the steering wheel with her fists. Secrets and lies – endless secrets and lies. Lies had put her into this position – lies and liars. How she loathed Muxlow, and how she loathed all those with the facility to choose to believe in their own rhetoric: politicians, big bosses, union men, PR men, priests . . . and fathers.

This was war! And all's fair in love and war. She slammed the Mini into gear and tore up the freshly gritted Ecclesall Road, spattering parked cars with brown slush as she went.

❧

Flynn's Land Rover was still in the car park when she drove past The Snake Pass Inn. Perhaps it had broken down again, or perhaps he'd decided to walk home.

She remembered her father coming home drunk from the pub one time (lots of times, actually). He would open her bedroom door enough to put his head though and whisper, 'Goodnight, darling. I love you'. He didn't do the same at Mum's door. Cassie wished he would, but he never did. He would stumble up to the attic, lay down on the bed fully dressed (this she knew because it was how she'd find him when she woke him for work the next morning), and begin to snore.

Broken down, probably – Flynn's Land Rover often broke down. Cassie accelerated hard, she wanted to clear the tops before the snow.

It would prove a complete waste of time of course. She was driving all the way to Manchester on the off chance that Angus was right about Sarah Flynn being at the *Manchester Evening News* two years ago. Even if Angus were right, would he be able to find out who Sarah had gone there to meet? And would whoever she'd met still work there? It didn't matter. Cassie needed to do something – anything but sit around and wait. As she approached the first set of traffic lights in Glossop, at the western end of the Snake, she got a text from Angus:

Estelle Middlewood, Editor, MEN. She's expecting you.

16

THE LAND ROVER wouldn't start. Flynn was too drunk to do anything about it so he had no choice but to walk home.

A white van had parked across his drive, and a deliveryman was walking away from the mailbox. With a thumbs up for a thank you, he trudged over to see what it was.

He was fumbling the key into the lock when someone pulled a plastic bag over his head. Flynn spun a wild and speculative back-fist, which caught the attacker full in the chest and floored him.

Now for the bag.

But it was tight and damp and slippery, and his fingers were numb with cold, and he couldn't see a thing, and he could scarcely breathe.

It wouldn't come off.

Then came a blow to his stomach. He reeled sideways, regained his balance, and swung a blind overcut. He missed the head but found a shoulder. A solid contact – the attacker gasped and moaned – and Flynn was sure he'd gone down.

Back to the bag. Flynn was bent almost double, to make it easier to tug the thing off, when something hard glanced the side of his head. He staggered but stayed on his feet. Two of them, had to be. He threw a right hook – he knew where to aim, experience teaches you to know – and it made contact with a chin. Not a perfect contact, but good enough; now both attackers would need a few seconds to recover. Enough time, he persuaded himself, to get the bloody bag off his head. Enough time, surely, to—

❧

The shriek of a van door sliding open brought Flynn round. They dragged him out and onto cold, wet tarmac – hands and feet bound, the plastic bag still tight over his head. There was a hole for his mouth and nose now, so he could breathe properly, but the back of his head ached like hell. He could taste snow in the air and whisky in his mouth. A padlock clunked, chains clanked, a door creaked open. They untied Flynn's legs, hoisted him to his feet and pushed him forwards. Inside, it was echoey, and no warmer than outside. The air tasted stale. Someone yanked the bag off his head.

Flynn was standing in a derelict sports hall. A balding man in a camel coat sat at a desk in the middle. It was an old wooden school desk with liftable lids and dark, empty inkwells. The man eyed Flynn with indifference. 'My old school, is this' he said. 'Used to play five-a-side in here. Remember it like yesterday.'

They were back in Sheffield if this man's accent was anything to go by. And there was still daylight, so it couldn't be more than an hour since he left The Snake Pass Inn. The fire exit they'd come in through was guarded by a young thug with a crew cut and a pistol. The only other way out was through a set of wire-glazed double doors at the far end of the hall. It was dark beyond the glass. There were holes in the walls where gym apparatus had once been attached, and all that was left of the basketball nets were the steel supports. Three badminton courts, each with a tarpaulin laid out in the middle, were marked out in blue tape. The tarpaulins reminded him of groundsheets from sixer tents at cub camp.

The man at the desk waved at the chair opposite. 'Please,' he said, his voice echoing around the hall, 'have a seat.'

Flynn walked slowly towards the desk. The rope around his wrists was beginning to unravel so he pressed his hands into the small of his back to keep it in place.

'My lad came here as well,' the man said, nodding at the thug with the crew cut. 'Of course, this wasn't my first choice of venue for our meeting. I'd planned to have this little chat at your place, yesterday morning. We'd have been much more comfortable there, roaring fire in the stove and all. Would have been a nice little reunion. But you weren't in, so here we are.'

'You should have called ahead,' Flynn said. The tarpaulin crackled when he stepped on it. It sounded louder than it should. 'I'm usually in of a morning.'

The man smiled and sighed and scratched his head. 'So I'm told.'

'Hardly a *reunion*, anyway,' Flynn said. He stopped a couple of paces from the desk. 'I don't think we've ever met.'

The man appeared to give this a good deal of thought. 'No,' he said, eventually, 'we haven't.' He pulled three mobile phones from various pockets and laid them out side-by-side. 'This was always a shit school,' he said, without taking his eyes off Flynn, 'but it took them forty years to shut it down. I'm Sean Mulligan, by the way. I once met your wife. Sarah, I think?'

Flynn eased himself onto the chair and slid back as far as he could so that the loose rope around his wrists wouldn't show. 'Sarah died,' he said.

'So I'm told.' Mulligan fixed on him with watery grey eyes. 'I could have gone to grammar school, you know, just like you.' He leaned back in his chair and folded his arms. 'Passed my eleven plus, I did. Loved learning back then. Loved reading – read anything I would.' He laughed. 'Even enjoyed maths – good at maths, I was. Very good. But Sheffield City Council shut down the grammar schools and sent me to this shit hole instead. Much fairer system, they said. If most kids had to go to shit schools, then all kids should go to shit schools – except the ones with parents who could afford to go private, of course. I'm sure the socialists saw some logic behind their politics, just like religionists see some logic behind their religion. Can't blame the teachers, of course: if you fill a school with scum, what do you expect?' He cast a wistful eye around the sports hall and sighed.

'What can I do for you, Mr Mulligan?' Flynn said.

Mulligan rapped his fingers on the desk, aped a quizzical expression, and rubbed his chin. 'I want the photographs,' he said.

Flynn closed his eyes for a moment. 'You . . . want . . . the . . . photographs.' He enunciated each syllable with care, inserting a pause after each word. It was something Scotty Deakin used to do. It unnerved people. 'What . . . photographs?'

Mulligan stared at Flynn but didn't answer.

Some say you can see a man's soul through his eyes. Not true, Flynn thought. And he had looked enough people in the eye to know. He stared into Mulligan's eyes now – they were small and grey and moist. And that was all.

Mulligan looked down and scanned each of his phones in turn. They were identical models, but each had a different coloured case – one red, one white, one blue. He slid them round, like a bazaar trickster shuffling upturned cups, then turned back to his guest. 'I hope you're not going to disappoint me, Mr Flynn.'

It was coming, Flynn thought to himself – the routine. The sort of routine he'd seen Scotty Deakin perform a hundred times: the dramatisation of a simple message – *if you don't give me what I want, I will hurt you.*

Choosing the right setting is essential: your audience must experience the pang of isolation, the sorrow of abandonment, the anticipation of pain, if it is to feel a proper sense of peril.

And you must exude calm: your audience must understand that you cannot be provoked or persuaded or placated.

Pure theatre, of course. Just like the movies.

Flynn often wondered, in the old days, if Scotty drew from the movies or if movie makers drew from men like Scotty Deakin.

Mulligan lifted a battered Macbook Pro (its power cable still gaffer-taped into position) from a bag by his feet and put it on the desk. It was Flynn's. It was the laptop Sarah had passed on to him: the charging socket had worked loose a year ago and the tape was his clumsy but effective repair.

Mulligan junior approached, noisily, across the tarpaulin. He had Flynn's mobile phone and made a show of scanning the content. He shook his head and put it on the desk by Flynn's computer.

'Password protected, I'm told,' Mulligan said, nodding at the laptop. 'Nowadays, everything ends up on these things, doesn't it. Personally, I prefer an old-fashioned photo album – you know the sort, with those little sticky corner things to hold the pictures in place. And I liked it when everything was black and white. Never took to colour photographs, myself, they're never the colours you remember.'

Flynn stared at his laptop.

Mulligan drew a hunting knife from his coat pocket, unsheathed it, and set it on the desk. 'The photos, please,' he said. 'Now.'

'They're not on there,' Flynn said. 'I can have them for you tomorrow.'

Mulligan drove his knife into the desktop. 'I want them now!'

Flynn shook his head.

'Okay.' Mulligan was suddenly calm. 'Just wanted to be sure. I've already had someone look through your files. I'm told that having your wife's name and birthday as a password is pretty common. Not very secure though, eh.'

Flynn shrugged. 'There's nothing of any value to anyone but me on that computer.'

Mulligan picked up the white phone, dialled, and put it to his ear. 'Carl, bring him in.' Then, to Flynn, 'I want those photos today. My boys will take you wherever you need to go.'

Keeping the loose ropes around his wrists pressed into place, Flynn nodded and made to get up.

'Not just yet,' Mulligan said, waving him down. 'There's someone I'd like you to meet.'

The glass doors at the end of the hall flew open and a man in a disposable white overall and latex gloves (Carl, Flynn presumed) lumbered in, dragging behind him a scrawny youth.

'On your feet, Trevor.' Carl barked the order like a Sergeant Major.

Trevor was a gormless looking kid (early twenties, probably): his lips were too big for his mouth, and his nose too small for his face. Dressed in a long and filthy vest, and jeans that sat low about his haunches, he was shivering and shaking and weeping.

Carl nudged Trevor into the middle of the tarpaulin and folded his arms.

'Trevor, here,' Mulligan said (he had his back to Trevor and was thumbing over his shoulder), 'thought he could have one over on me.'

Trevor shook his head violently; he opened and closed his mouth a few times, but nothing came out.

'Then he got himself pissed and bragged about it in The Wagon and Horses. That was a bit silly, wasn't it, Trev? Of course, I'd have found out anyway. Wouldn't I, Trev? I always find out. Don't I, Trev?'

Trevor had given up protesting; he hung his head, snorting snot in periodic, violent gasps.

'So,' Mulligan finally turned to face the boy, 'where's my money?'

Without looking up, Trevor shook his head. Mulligan nodded at the man in the overalls: 'Go on then, Carl, he's had his chances.'

Fifteen years before, in a long-abandoned Victorian hat factory under the shadows of the Stockport Viaduct, Scotty Deakin had said something very similar to Flynn. A bookmaker from Heald

Green owed Scotty fifteen grand. He was pale and scrawny, with sickly yellow eyes. He was probably someone's granddad. Drunk on gin and fear, the old man wet himself when he saw Flynn take off his jacket and straighten his cravat – the piss pooled and steamed around scuffed brown brogues.

Would Scotty have made him go through with it? Would *he* have *let* Scotty make him go through with it?

It didn't matter. It didn't matter because the old man's heart gave out before he had to decide.

It *did* matter. Why else would he be thinking, now, about the old man in that abandoned hat factory all those years ago?

Carl kicked Trevor's legs from under him and pushed him to the floor. Trevor, with his hands strapped behind his back, landed heavily on his chest. He gasped and wheezed and tried to turn onto his side. When Carl knelt on his shoulders, Trevor stopped moving. With his left hand, Carl prised open Trevor's fist; with his right, he clamped a pair of wire cutters around the boy's little finger. Trevor let out a long and pathetic moan. When the jaws of the wire cutters finally snapped shut, he went quiet again. Blood bloomed on Trevor's vest. It seeped into the fabric, like ink on blotting paper, accumulating at the hem before dripping onto the tarpaulin.

One of the three phones on the desk vibrated – two short bursts. Mulligan scanned the screens. It was the red one. He picked it up, looked at the message, and turned to look at Flynn. It was an odd sort of a look, more questioning than threatening. He pulled the back off the red phone, removed the battery and the sim card, and arranged the bits on his desk.

'Fuck it, I've changed my mind,' Mulligan said. 'No more chances. Finish it now, Carl.'

'But . . .' Carl turned to Gary

'I mean it, Carl,' Mulligan said. 'And hurry up, we're running late.'

Carl produced a Stanley knife. He pulled Trevor's head back by the hair and slashed the boy's throat. Trevor didn't react: didn't resist, didn't squirm, didn't convulse. Carl slipped the knife into the back pocket of Trevor's jeans and stepped away. He ripped off his overall and tossed it over Trevor's body. Mulligan junior went over to help. In a couple of minutes they had wrapped the body in the tarpaulin and secured it with duct tape.

'Carl, I need you out front,' Mulligan said. 'And Gary . . .'

Mulligan junior turned to his father. 'Yes, Dad?'

'Give Carl the gun.'

Mulligan turned back to Carl: 'Keep an eye on the main gate.'

Carl nodded, took the gun, and disappeared through the glazed doors.

'Go on then,' Mulligan said to his son, without taking his eyes off Flynn. 'Put Trevor in the van.'

Gary looked from his father to the bundled tarpaulin to Flynn, and back again. 'You want me to leave you on your own with—'

Mulligan cut him off with a glare, grabbed the hunting knife, and pointed it at Flynn's throat. 'Better make it quick then, Gary, hadn't you!'

If Sean Mulligan hadn't been so determined to stare Flynn out, he might have seen those massive arms shift as the rope around Flynn's wrists unravelled.

If Sean Mulligan hadn't been so determined to stare Flynn out, he might have noticed Flynn's right shoulder twitch when Gary dragged the tarpaulin outside and stepped out of sight.

If Sean Mulligan hadn't been so determined to stare Flynn out, he might have seen the punch coming.

17

THE EDITOR OF the *Manchester Evening News* was not a tidy woman. Cassie distracted herself from the chaos of collapsed cardboard boxes, mounds of papers, chewed biros, and discarded sandwich wrappers by studying the collage on the wall. Dozens of photos had been glued to a sheet of paper torn from a flip chart.

Estelle Middlewood was a smart looking woman of about forty. She had a husband and three children: eldest, a boy; middle child, a girl; youngest, a baby. Estelle lived in a large Victorian semi – somewhere leafy, with a trampoline in the back garden and a people carrier on the front drive. The family had recently holidayed in Tuscany, and in the Lake District, and in Northumberland. They enjoyed weekend walks in the Peaks. Their house was furnished with cheap antiques and Ikea classics. Her son supported Manchester City and got an iPad for Christmas. Their vacuum cleaner was a Dyson. Her daughter was learning ballet and got a pink bike for Christmas. Estelle got a Kenwood bread maker. She had breakfast in bed on Mother's Day. Her kitchen ceiling had recently been replastered – a leak upstairs, perhaps.

'Detective Inspector May,' Estelle said, shutting her office door. 'Have they offered you tea or coffee?' She looked at her watch. 'Christ, it's quarter to four already and I still haven't had my lunch. I'm starving.' She pulled a packet of Hobnobs from her desk drawer and began to eat. 'Would you like one?' she said, tossing the packet across the desk.

'I'm fine, honestly. And it's *Cassie*, please.'

'And I'm *Stella*. For God's sake don't call me Estelle, I only use it on by-lines to please my mother. Hope you haven't been waiting too long. I was busy being told off by some little gobshite from Legal. Honestly, barely out of nappies and she thinks she can tell *me* how to run a bloody paper!'

'I feel like I've known you for years,' Cassie said, nodding at the collage on the wall.

'A Christmas present from my kids. Becca said it's so I don't get lonely when I work late. She's only seven. I cried buckets.' Stella sat behind her desk and grabbed a handful of tissues from her top drawer. 'Oh shit, I'm off again.'

'You have a lovely family.' Cassie glanced back at the collage. 'You're very lucky.'

'I know.' Stella dried her eyes and threw the tissues into an overflowing wastepaper basket. 'So, what can I do for you?'

Cassie crossed her legs. 'Do you remember Sarah Flynn, she came to meet you a couple of years ago?'

'Yes, your colleague said you were looking into her death. Such a shame. Car crash wasn't it? Snake Pass?'

'That's right. I believe she was on her way back home after meeting with you, and I wondered what the meeting was about.'

'Does this have anything to do with her husband?' Stella scratched her head. 'James Flynn, isn't it?'

Cassie gripped the arms of her chair. 'I don't . . . I'm just trying to fill in some gaps.'

'He's a suspect in the Penthouse Murder Case, isn't he? Girl found dead in his flat.'

'The *Penthouse Murder*!' Cassie gulped air then put her hand to her mouth in a vain attempt to stifle a cough. 'I can't say.' She cleared her throat. 'It's early days.'

'I see,' Stella said, without conviction.

'So,' Cassie said. 'Your meeting with Sarah Flynn?'

Stella ignored the question. 'James Flynn,' she said, 'he's a friend of yours, isn't he? Is that why you've been taken off the case?'

Cassie squeezed her eyes shut.

'Come on Cassie,' Stella said, leaning on her elbows, 'let's be straight with each other. If there's a Manchester angle to this story it's my job to make sure this paper covers it.'

Cassie stared at Stella's desk. 'Who've you been talking to?'

'Just a friend, ex-colleague actually, who works in Sheffield – he's covering the story for *The Star*.'

'Look, Stella,' Cassie uncrossed her legs and leaned in, 'I'm on leave for a couple of weeks, and I'm curious about Sarah, that's all. To be honest, this isn't police business, it's . . . personal.'

Stella tapped her chin with the chewed end of a biro. 'Personal?'

'It's important to *me*. The police aren't interested in Sarah.'

'I see.'

Cassie stood up and slung her bag over her shoulder. 'Perhaps I shouldn't have come.' It was a gamble: she was calling Stella's bluff. Surely Stella would rather keep her talking – surely she would choose to invest a little into a relationship that might yet bear fruit.

'I didn't expect you to give up this easily,' Stella said.

Cassie stood tall. 'I'm not the sort of officer who leaks things to the press.'

'I know.' Stella waved her to sit down.

Cassie stood firm.

'I doubt I know anything that would help you,' Stella said, 'but I'll do my best.' She pointed at the biscuits. 'Why don't you sit down and have a Hobnob. I'll go and dig out my old notebooks from the store room.'

Cassie spent the next five minutes studying the photos in the collage. She munched through seven Hobnobs and wondered where her life was going.

Meg would have the search warrant by now; they might already be searching Flynn's home. Would there be evidence of her recent visit? She thought it through: fingerprints, maybe. But that wouldn't prove she'd been there *after* Flynn had been named a suspect.

A sense of hopelessness engulfed her. What could the details of Sarah Flynn's meeting with Stella two years ago possibly tell her? What did it have to do with anything? Right now, she couldn't imagine any information that would help her work out what was going on with Flynn and Gemma Grant. And how was she going to break the news to Flynn that the dead girl was Sarah's daughter? Would Angus have already told him? She should have—

'Right!' Stella came back in and slapped a pile of tatty looking spiral-bound notebooks onto the desk.

'Did you find something?' Cassie asked.

'Let's have a look.' Stella opened the first of the notebooks. 'I don't think it had anything to do with those dodgy sex rings she'd been investigating. It was something else . . .'

'Sex rings? In Manchester?'

'Not here, no,' Stella said. 'You must remember, it was on your patch. Rotherham, wasn't it, a few years ago. She claimed that a gang of taxi drivers were abusing girls from three council-run children's homes. And I bet what she uncovered was only the tip of the iceberg. I bet it's going on everywhere.'

'I hope not,' Cassie said. 'And *yes*, of course I remember.'

Stella looked up from her notes and gave Cassie a sceptical frown. 'It was Sarah Flynn who uncovered evidence that the police knew exactly what was going on. She went to press alleging that they had taken the view that girls like that were asking for it – that they were complicit, not really victims.'

Cassie decided it was time to change the subject: 'So you knew Sarah, before she came to see you that day?'

'Sort of. Not really. Although,' Stella slapped the table. 'Ah ha,' she said, staring at a squiggle of shorthand, 'I think I've got it.'

Cassie leaned in.

'Scott Deakin,' Stella said.

'Scott Deakin?'

'That's who Sarah was asking about. Scott Deakin was a local villain who operated in South Manchester until about fifteen years ago. Usual sort of thing: drugs, prostitution, protection. Big player, by all accounts. Then he vanished without a trace. Ring any bells?'

Cassie did nothing to disguise her disappointment: 'No.'

Stella shrugged. 'And I can't even tell you why she was interested in him . . . or what story she was working on.'

'So what was she hoping to get out of you?'

'Background, rumours, names of people who worked for him – anyone who might talk.'

'And what did you tell her?'

'Not much.' Stella said. 'Scott Deakin was a cut above the usual thug: educated – apparently – and clever. Over the space of ten years he forged quite a little empire for himself. Rumour has it he was killed by a rival gang – him and his minder, Jamie Boreman.'

'They disappeared at the same time?'

'Yes. Although there were also rumours that Jamie Boreman was going to leave him and join another gang. One guy I spoke to reckoned Boreman had killed Deakin and done a runner.'

'Doesn't sound like Sarah's thing, though, does it?' Cassie said. 'Low life villains killing one another?'

'Unless,' Stella wagged a finger, 'and this is pure speculation, unless the police were involved. There was a rumour that Deakin had a senior police officer in his pocket. Maybe this copper thought that Deakin was getting too big for his boots, too powerful to control. Maybe Jamie Boreman was paid to get rid of Deakin.'

With two fingers pressed to her lips, Cassie closed her eyes. If

Sarah had a senior officer from Greater Manchester Police in the frame, there'd certainly have been good reason to poke around the Deakin disappearance. But . . .

Cassie slumped in her chair and wondered what on earth it was that she had hoped Stella might be able to tell her? It was only because Sarah had concealed her meeting with Stella from Flynn that Cassie had attached any importance to it. And she didn't know for sure that Sarah *had* concealed it; perhaps she'd forgotten to tell Flynn; perhaps she *had* told Flynn and Flynn had forgotten; perhaps it had no significance whatsoever. And why would Sarah have concealed a meeting with a newspaper editor? She was a freelance journalist – meeting newspaper editors was her bread and butter, surely?

'Thanks, Stella,' Cassie said. 'You've been very helpful.'

'Really?' Stella's forehead creased.

'And I promise you'll be the first to know if anything interesting comes of it.'

Stella smiled. 'Thank you, Cassie.'

Cassie picked up her coat and bag.

'I'll walk you out,' Stella said.

❧

It was already dark. Cassie hated driving at night, and if there was snow she would struggle to get home by the Snake. Rain in Manchester meant snow over the Pennines. She shook Stella's hand and thanked her.

'Shame really,' Stella said. 'Kev says that he was a lovely lad. Scared the bejesus out of him when he first saw him, of course. Six foot ten and built like Arnold Schwarzenegger!'

'Who? Cassie said, absently. She put her handbag on the floor and got into her winter coat.

'Jamie Boreman – he was in the sixth form at Sale Grammar

School, where my husband got his first teaching job. Kev's still there, Head of English now, bless him. He'd have been twenty-three or twenty-four back then, not much older than Jamie when you think about it. I put a lot of effort into researching that story, fancied a by-line in the 'Society' section of *the Guardian*, but it came to nothing. It was the year we met, my final year at university. I might have done a bit better in my exams if—'

'What!' Cassie's eyes narrowed. 'Scotty Deakin's minder was a sixth former? A grammar school boy?'

Stella nodded. 'Yep. *Part-time* minder of course, on account of his A-level studies! But it's true: *Deakin's Dandy* was only eighteen when he disappeared.'

'Deakin's Dandy?'

'That's what they called him. Because he wore expensive suits . . . and a cravat, would you believe!'

'A cravat?'

'Famous for it, apparently. And he talked like a toff.'

'Like a toff?'

'Well, the people who said that would think that anyone who could construct a sentence without using the word "*fuck*" talked like a toff.'

'And you're sure it was the same boy.'

Stella nodded. 'Social Services had known about him for years: Jamie lived with his dad in a council house in Wythenshawe.'

'Wythenshawe? Where's that?'

'Just down the road from Sale, where he went to school. But a world apart. You'd struggle to find an area of Manchester rougher than Wythenshawe, especially back then: biggest council estate in Europe, mass unemployment, drugs, gangs, knives, guns. Jamie Boreman's dad was a drunk, and his mother was dead, so he looked after himself the only way he knew how. Social Services were too scared to get involved, I expect, because he mixed with some very dangerous men.' Stella sighed. She rested her chin on the back of her hand and stared into space.

Cassie resisted the temptation to interrupt, or to push, or to do any of the things she normally did when she was feeling impatient.

Eventually, Stella continued: 'I bet they were relieved when he turned eighteen and they could wash their hands of him, social services I mean. Bit of a cliff edge for kids like that – turning eighteen.'

Cassie nodded along.

Stella went quiet again.

Cassie waited.

Stella sat up straight and tapped the desk with her index finger. 'I've just remembered something.' She flicked through her notebooks and examined the loose cuttings and photos that had been stapled in. 'No, it's not in here. But I'll have it somewhere.'

Cassie mustered her best calm-but-interested expression. 'What isn't in there, Stella? What are you looking for?'

'Not long after he and Deakin disappeared,' Stella said, 'I showed a photo of Jamie, from the school yearbook, to a contact of mine on the estates. That's how I know that Deakin's Dandy was definitely Jamie Boreman, the lad from my Kev's A-level English class. To be fair, you don't get too many seven-foot, besuited, cravat-wearing Conan the Barbarian types roaming Wythenshawe. He stood out!'

'But you've lost it, this photo?'

'Oh, I'm sure I'll have it somewhere. And if not, Kev still has all the old year books in our loft.'

Cassie pulled a notebook from her bag, wrote down her personal email address, tore out the page, and handed it to Stella. 'Please, Stella. Please send me that photo?'

18

FLYNN FOUND HIMSELF leaning over the balustrade of the brightly painted bridge that crosses the weir at Kelham Island. He had no idea how he came to be there. He closed his eyes and listened to the river rush by. Slowly, he began to remember. Flynn slid his hand into his coat pocket to check. Yes, it was still there.

A courting couple ambled by, arm in arm. They stopped briefly outside The Milestone to look at the menu; they stopped lengthily at the end of the street for a snog; when they were done, they turned left onto Green Lane.

Flynn guessed they were heading for The Fat Cat on Alma Street. He fancied a drink himself – craved a drink – but it would have to wait. He scanned the streets for onlookers and, satisfied that there were none, pulled the knife from his coat pocket and dropped it over the railings and into the river.

White foam frothed and fizzed at the bottom of the weir, but at the top, directly under the bridge, the water was black and still and deep. Mulligan's hunting knife made barely a ripple when it hit the surface. It seemed to float, if only for a split second, before sinking silently into the depths. Flynn fancied he saw the water turn red where it landed.

How had it come to this? Flynn put his head in his hands and stared hopelessly into the dark waters. When had it all started?

A double-decker bus rumbled by. He looked up and saw a boy of eleven or twelve watching him from the brightness of an otherwise empty top deck. The boy stared at Flynn without shame, the way children do.

Then Flynn remembered. He remembered exactly when it had all started. Back in October 1991. Back when he was a boy of twelve. Back when people still called him Jamie.

❧

13 OCTOBER 1991

It took two buses to get home to Wythenshawe.

The first bus was packed with other kids from his school.

The second bus wasn't.

The first bus cruised along smart streets with meticulously mown grass verges. It passed neat suburban houses, clipped privet hedges, shiny Ford Sierras.

The second bus took a left at the end of Brooklands Road – soon it was clattering past overgrown front lawns littered with rotting settees and rusting fridges.

Jamie had already rung the bell for his stop when he spotted three scallies sitting on the bus shelter roof. The driver had seen him ring the bell, so if he didn't get off at this stop he'd get a right bollocking.

Two of the scallies were throwing stones and bottles at the still-smouldering remains of a burned-out Austin Allegro. The third was watching – smoking a needle-thin roll-up and drinking Tizer from a can. Jamie got off the bus and gave them as wide a berth as possible. He kept his head down, making sure not to look at them.

'What the fuck are you looking at?'

Ginger-haired, pizza-faced, and mean-looking, the youngest of the scallies jumped down first, spliff smouldering between thumb and index finger. The others followed.

Jamie turned and made to cross the road but the two bigger lads (older than Ginger — fifteen, maybe) blocked his path.

'Don't they learn you any fuckin manners at that poncey fuckin school?' Ginger said. 'I asked you what you were looking at.'

He was good five inches shorter than Jamie, but heavily built. Ginger spoke with his head cocked, like a nurse talking to a patient lying on a hospital bed. The wisps of copper on his cheeks and chin and above his top lip did little to conceal the rampant acne. Perhaps it wasn't supposed to, Jamie thought, perhaps it was just that all those spots made shaving impossible.

Ginger was pointing now. 'Oi, I'm talking to you, y'fuckin wanker.'

'Sorry, I didn't realise,' Jamie said. He knew he sounded like a prat.

Ginger pulled a face and started scratching his crotch. 'I shagged your mam last night.'

'My mum's dead.'

'You calling me a fuckin liar?'

'No.'

'You saying I shag fuckin corpses?'

'No.'

Ginger's spliff had burned down almost to the roach. He blew on the end to get it glowing then threw it at Jamie's chest.

It took several flicks for Jamie to dislodge the embers from the stitching around the badge on his blazer. Mum had wept with pride as she sewed it onto his top pocket that summer. 'My clever boy,' she'd said, 'Grammar School! Who'd have thunk it?'

It had become harder, of late, to picture her face, but sometimes the smallest of things would trigger the most vivid of memories. The rub of the clumsy stitches around his school badge was the trigger that day. He remembered watching her sew it on. He could see her face, taut with concentration. He could hear her voice, her soft Cork accent, 'I'm not a natural with a needle, of course.' He could see freckles on the bridge of her nose, mascara clumped on a long and curling lash, laughter lines (five discrete wrinkles for each eye – one short, three long, one short). He could see more now, he thought, than he'd ever noticed when she was alive.

Jamie didn't see the punch coming. It landed square on his left cheek. He fell backwards but Ginger's mates caught him and pushed him into the bus shelter. Ears ringing, vision blurred, head throbbing, Jamie had never felt quite so alone.

Ginger took off his Kappa cagoule. He hung it neatly on a bolt that had once fixed a timetable to the plexiglass at the back of the bus shelter. The two older lads yanked Jamie's blazer off him, and slung it onto the grass verge.

'Come on y'fucker,' Ginger said. 'I'm cock of the first year at Moorlands High. They say you're cock of the first year at Sale poncey wankers fuckin Grammar School for benders.'

'No, I'm not. I've never even—'

'Yeah, well, you're a big bastard aren't you. Biggest fuckin twelve-year-old *I've* ever seen. What are you, six foot? They say that no fuckin first year's ever dared take you on. Well, I've shat on bigger fuckers than you. Much fuckin bigger. So come on!'

Jamie's vision had cleared but his ears were still ringing. 'No. I need to get home, my Dad'll be waiting.'

'That fuckin pisshead!' Ginger turned to his mates and laughed. 'We've all seen him, you know, too trolleyed to walk straight. He'll be asleep in front of the telly by now. Pissed his kecks, probably.' He tapped his chin. 'Go on then. Have a fuckin go. I'll give you one free swing on account of you being such a fuckin bender.'

Jamie shook his head.

Ginger spat in his face.

Jamie threw his best punch.

Ginger – coolly, and with only the slightest movement of his shoulders – dodged it. As Jamie gathered himself, Ginger began to bounce like Mohammed Ali. He was up on his toes, feet apart, elbows tight, fists high, head low.

For every jab that Jamie blocked, Ginger landed a good one: stomach . . . right eye . . . stomach . . . ribs. Jamie managed to ride the first few blows, but then came a punch to his left kidney — it hurt so much he thought he would die. He clutched his middle, reeling, gasping, retching. A right hook, square on the jaw, floored him.

A girl with a pushchair ambled by. Jamie hadn't the strength to lift his head, but he could make out blue wheels, pink ankles, lilac carpet slippers. She stopped for a moment, dropped a crushed Coke can onto the kerb by the dustbin, and then moved on - wheels rattling, heels scuffing - at the same languid pace.

Ginger squatted in Jamie's sight line, lit a cigarette, and blew smoke into his face.

Jamie's head was spinning. He felt sick. Every inch of his torso throbbed. He must have lost consciousness for a moment, for the next thing he knew there was something sharp in his back. No, not sharp: burning. Something burning right between his shoulder blades.

He tried to jerk himself up, tried twisting and writhing and kicking out, but his arms and legs were pinned down fast.

Then the cigarette was burning the small of his back. It might have been only a few seconds; it might have been more like a minute. Then the laughing resumed; then there was a cheer; then his arms and legs were free

He heard it before he felt it - the dull spatter of piss on his back.

'Mi mam says running water's the best thing for burns,' Ginger said, matter-of-factly.

The three boys moved away, but Jamie stayed down - he saw them pick up his school blazer from the grass verge, heard shuffling by the dustbin, heard liquid being poured in, heard a match being struck, heard the whoosh of flames, heard them cheer and laugh and run away.

Mum's eyes had been blue, like his. Blue like the badge on his blazer. Blue like the sky on the day of her funeral. Blue like the sky on the day that Ryan Gallagher had beaten him up, branded his back with a cigarette, burned his school blazer in a dustbin, pissed all over him.

Mum's eyes smiled down on him now; soft lips kissed his forehead. 'It's over,' she said, holding him tight in her arms.

Jamie knew it wasn't over, but he didn't let on.

19

DETECTIVE SERGEANT MEG Harper wasn't happy. It was not that she didn't agree that Flynn was a suspect worthy of investigation (the evidence, though largely circumstantial, was compelling), it had to do with DCI Foster's purpose in all of this. Foster, she reflected, was motivated by the glory of getting the big conviction, while DI Cassie May – who was as careerist as the next man – was driven by a hunger to solve crimes. There was a difference, and it mattered.

The sun had set. The windows of the incident room, which looked west over the snow dusted trees, houses, and hills beyond the ring road, were now as mirrors. No matter how hard she strained, she couldn't see out. Meg turned back to her computer and found herself thinking about her boyfriend. She'd had her doubts about Graham for a while now, but a day under the direct command of DCI Foster had sparked an epiphany.

Graham worked in the Management Consultancy division of a big accountancy firm. He'd risen rapidly through the ranks without ever having actually managed any sort of business himself. Now she saw him for what he really was. He was no better than an upmarket version of DCI Foster. He was a career careerist: *being seen* to be doing a good job was far more important than actually *doing* a good job.

No, she wouldn't be driving down to his tiny, million-pound, one-bed flat in Notting Hill this weekend. He could come up north for a change!

But he wouldn't. He'd have wangled a table at some restaurant he wanted to be seen in. He'd tell her there was a six-month waiting list. He'd have invited close friends who couldn't be let down because he wanted their business. She'd relent. He'd introduce her to his goggle-eyed companions as Detective Sergeant Harper. They'd laugh and crack the usual jokes. He'd explain that she'd had her head shaved for charity. The Hoorah Henriettas – who wore £500 Jimmy Choos to work – would coo earnestly and tell her how they'd adopted an AIDS orphaned child in Sudan: '*Sixty quid a month by direct debit . . . Yah, right, you'd pay more than that for a decent bottle of wine on a Friday night! . . . Yah, sixty quid a month buys a kid a bed in a Sudanese children's home . . . and food . . . and schooling . . . and everything.*'

This time she would speak out. She'd tell them that Graham's charity head shave story was complete bollocks. She'd tell them she'd hacked off her own hair with a pair of kitchen scissors after drinking two bottles of £4.99 Cava. She'd tell them she couldn't remember why she did it, but it probably had something to do with having a complete wanker for a boyfriend.

She hated Graham and everything he stood for. She—

'Any joy getting hold of Flynn?'

It was Foster, back from Flynn's place.

'No, sir,' Meg said. She wondered how long he had been standing there. 'I've been trying his mobile every half hour all day long but he doesn't answer. I think his battery's gone flat. Either that or he's turned it off.'

'He's scarpered,' Foster said, 'but he left this.' He held up a plastic bag containing a smart phone. 'The pay-as-you-go he used to communicate with our victim, Gemma Grant – hidden in his toilet cistern. According to the text messages, she'd come all the way down from Edinburgh to see him.'

'Edinburgh?' Meg said. 'But Social Services told us she'd left Edinburgh a couple of years ago. I'll check with Missing Persons.

If someone's reported her missing, we might at least be able to identify next of kin.'

Foster grunted.

'But about Flynn, sir,' Meg said. 'What makes you think he's gone on the run?'

'His place has been cleared out. Every cupboard and drawer left wide open, hardly anything left. He's been back to collect his stuff and done one. *And* he's had help.'

Meg sat up straight. 'Had help, sir? Why do you say that?'

'Because he left his car at the pub. Someone must have picked him up. Apart from Flynn's place, there's nothing within walking distance of The Snake Pass Inn.'

'Any CCTV?'

'Don't be soft, Harper. This is The Snake Pass Inn we're talking about. Middle of nowhere.'

Meg glared at Foster. 'Precisely. That's why—'

'Well there isn't!' Foster sat down heavily in a chair by Meg's desk.

'Perhaps I should ring DI May,' Meg said. 'She might know who his friends are, or where he would go. But I really can't see why he'd have done a runner – he'd have had no reason to think we were on to him.'

'Unless May tipped him off.'

'But . . .' Meg hesitated. She'd told Cassie about the video, hadn't she – told her that Foster was going after Flynn.

Foster leaned over the desk and stared at her. 'But what, Harper?'

'DI May,' she said, folding her arms, '*would not* tip him off. And don't you think it's a bit odd that Flynn cleared out and cleared off, but left a phone that might incriminate him? Or that this incriminating secret phone had no password protection? I take it that's why you were able to get at the text messages so quickly?'

Foster leaned back in his chair and scowled. 'I want DI May here. Now. You phone her. And mind you tell her nothing. Understand? Just get her here.'

'Yes, sir.'

'And when you've done that, get authorisation to trace Flynn's other mobile, the one he doesn't hide in toilet cisterns.'

'Will do,' Meg said.

'Ah ha!' Foster had spotted DCC Muxlow coming through the main doors. 'Perfect timing.'

Muxlow crossed the office. His stride, usually long and purposeful, was, today, squirrel-like. He wavered by a filing cabinet and appeared to take great interest in an old coffee stain on the carpet.

Foster stood to greet Muxlow. 'I'll need your authorisation to track Flynn's phone – he's done a bunk.'

Muxlow reached into his trouser pocket, retrieved a crumpled yellow post-it note, and passed it to Foster. 'I've already had Flynn's phone tracked: that's where he was half an hour ago. Nothing after that – he must have turned it off.'

'Parkgate School?' Foster said, reading the note. 'Didn't they close that place down?'

'Three years ago,' Meg said. 'Should have been demolished that summer, but the developer—'

'Whatever.' Foster scanned the room. 'Vic, Charlie – you're with me.' He turned back to Muxlow: 'Thank you, Sir.'

Muxlow nodded, gravely.

Meg pulled on her coat.

'No, Harper – you stay here,' Foster said. 'Get hold of DI May. I want her in this office when I get back. And remember . . .' Foster gestured a zip being pulled across his mouth '. . . understood?'

Meg squeezed her eyes shut and nodded. By the time she opened them again, Foster, Vic and Charlie were on their way out.

Muxlow pointed to Cassie's office. 'Could you spare me a moment, Sergeant Harper.'

❧

The lights were out in Cassie's office. Meg stood at the window and watched Foster, Vic and Charlie striding across the car park towards Foster's flash looking Audi. 'Fire up the Quattro,' she said under her breath. And he did. And then they wheel spun onto the road in a swirling blue cloud of steam, exhaust fumes and grit salt. Graham had the same car – well, similar. A DCI's package wouldn't stretch to Graham's £60,000 specced-up Audi S4 (supercharged V6, 18 inch rims, Quattro four wheel drive, most of the extras list). Why did she even know all that stuff about Graham's car? Because Graham was a boring twat, and a show off, that's why.

Meg turned away and winced. As she sat down at Cassie's desk, her foot hit a cardboard archive box. Meg leaned down to read the label, but it was too dark under the desk so she pulled it out a little to see.

Sarah Flynn 15/12/2012

Meg was kicking the box back under the desk when the door creaked open.

'In the dark, Harper?' Muxlow said, setting two mugs on the Sheffield United coasters that Foster had smuggled into Cassie's office.

'Just admiring the view, sir.'

On a moonlit night, covered in snow, the city was monochrome – like a sepia photograph – except for the orange streetlights, and the red tail lights, which looked like they'd been added with a felt tip pen.

The office lights came on and the outside world was suddenly gone. Meg closed her eyes against the brightness. When she opened them, Muxlow was sitting stiffly in front of her. There was a reflection of his balding crown in the window behind.

'Have you changed your hair recently, Harper?'

'Yes, sir. Cut it all off for charity. To build an orphanage in Sudan for kids with HIV. If you're interested, you can sponsor a child for £60 a month.'

Muxlow brought his hands together. 'I think it suits you.'

Meg looked at her reflection in the window: her hairdresser had done a decent enough rescue job, but she hated how it looked.

'Harper,' Muxlow said, leaning in, 'have you been in contact with DI May?'

Meg sat back. 'I left a message on her mobile, five minutes ago. Asked her to come in.'

'I mean since she went on leave this morning.'

Meg shifted in her seat. 'Only to gather information for the investigation.'

'And you understand that it would be . . .' Muxlow rubbed his hands together ' . . . inappropriate to discuss this investigation with her.'

'I understand,' Meg said, still staring over his shoulder at her own reflection in the window.

Muxlow picked up his mug and took a sip.

Meg crossed her legs and glanced down at the *Sarah Flynn* archive box that Cassie had been looking for. Inconceivable that she could have missed it – so it must have been moved out, and then moved back in later. Foster wasn't interested in Sarah Flynn: he hadn't even known who she was until Meg mentioned her in passing. So who took it, then brought it back?' Meg watched Muxlow take another sip of coffee: his Adam's apple was pronounced – she could see the skin stretch as he swallowed. And how could Muxlow have known about the relationship between Cassie and Flynn? And why trace Flynn's mobile without telling his SIO . . . and before anyone knew that Flynn was missing?

Muxlow put down his mug. 'DI May was seen leaving with Flynn this morning. Any idea where they went?'

'Leaving where, sir?'

'Leaving here. Leaving these premises. Leaving this bloody Police Station!'

Meg uncrossed then re-crossed her legs. 'I don't know where either of them are.'

Muxlow folded his arms. 'Thought it might come to this, that's why I had his phone tracked. Just a hunch though, that's why I didn't bother DCI Foster with it. A precautionary measure, if you will.'

Meg nodded, lengthily, wondering why Muxlow had felt the need to explain himself to her.

'Tell me, sir,' she said, 'was there anything in particular that led to your *hunch* about Flynn doing a runner?'

Muxlow's small eyes narrowed and his mouth tightened.

Meg bit her bottom lip.

'Twenty-seven years in the job,' he said at last, 'that's where my *hunches* come from.'

20

'IT'S BEEN A long day, Meg. What does Foster want? And why are you standing in my office in the dark?'

Detective Sergeant Meg Harper turned from the window and shook her head. 'Sorry, Ma'am, things have been a bit frantic here today.'

'Really?' Cassie looked over her shoulder at the deserted office.

'They'll be back soon. I'm having a quiet moment.'

Cassie went to join Meg by the window. 'I grumbled a bit when they put us on the seventh floor. But actually . . .'

'Yes.' Meg tilted her head to one side. 'It helps me to think, this view, especially at night. Everything moves so slowly when you watch from up here, and so silently'

'And what are you thinking about?'

Meg shrugged. 'My life has become complicated.'

Cassie pressed her forehead against the glass and watched a circle of mist form as she breathed a long, slow sigh. 'Are you going to tell me what's going on, Meg?'

'I've been told to keep my mouth shut where you're concerned.'

'Right.'

'Muxlow and Foster think you're helping Flynn. Are you helping Flynn?'

'Depends what you mean by *helping*?'

'And they suspect I'm feeding you information about the investigation.'

Cassie stepped back from the window. 'Are you feeding me information?'

'Depends what you mean by *feeding you information*.' Meg nodded at the archive box under the desk. 'I'll go and get us a couple of coffees,' she said. 'Back in five.' She turned on the lights as she left.

Cassie rifled through the Sarah Flynn files, photographed what she was looking for, then put everything back.

'Thank you,' she said, when Meg came back with their drinks.

Meg sat down beside Cassie. 'So, why the interest in Sarah Flynn? What can she possibly have to do with this investigation?'

'I don't know. Probably nothing.'

Meg crossed her legs.

'Honestly, Meg. It's just a feeling.'

'Just a feeling?' Meg folded her arms. 'Funny, that. The DCC said something similar about Flynn.'

'Muxlow doesn't have feelings, Meg. He has agendas.'

'And Foster?'

Cassie laughed. 'He's just a prick.'

'Yes, well,' Meg went over to the window, 'the prick's pulling into the car park as we speak. They tracked Flynn's phone to Parkgate school. He wasn't there, but they found three bodies. Two with their throats cut, one with a gunshot wound. Sean Mulligan, Trevor Murray, and Carl Yates.'

Cassie's mouth fell open.

'Quite,' Meg said.

Cassie began to pace the office. She stopped by the window and watched Foster light a cigarette in the car park below. 'Maybe Trevor Murray stole Flynn's phone, he's got form for that sort of thing.'

'He's got form for mugging school kids and old ladies,' Meg said, 'I can't imagine him taking on Flynn.'

'Maybe,' Cassie said. She was still watching Foster smoking

in the carpark – he took two more drags then tossed the cigarette into the shadows. 'Or maybe Flynn dropped his phone in the street, or left it in a café.'

Meg shook her head. 'And why did Muxlow order the trace before we knew Flynn was missing?'

'*Missing?*' Cassie spun round.

'Please, don't let on that you know any of this,' Meg said, in a whisper.

Cassie nodded. 'But—'

Meg shook her head. 'Foster will be here any minute. I'd best get back to my desk.'

❧

Foster paused at the door then went over to Meg's desk, pulled up a chair, and sat down.

She glanced up at him – his face was pale – and carried on typing.

Foster just sat there.

'I've circulated a mugshot of Gary Mulligan,' Meg said, when she could bear the silence no longer, 'but nobody knows where he is.'

Foster didn't react.

'His father's had his throat cut,' she said, 'and his best mate's had his head shot off. So *where is* Gary Mulligan? Two possibilities: either he's dead in a ditch or he's in hiding.' Meg waited for some sort of response but none came. 'I'm working on the assumption that the killer – or *killers* more likely – are a rival gang.'

Foster nodded.

'And Detective Inspector May is waiting in her office. Sorry: *your* office.'

'You don't like me much, do you, Harper?'

Meg leaned back and folded her arms. 'You've gone out of your way to make sure that I don't, haven't you, sir?'

'It's easy for the likes of you and May – with your degrees, and your posh way of talking.' Foster puffed his cheeks and blew a long breath. 'For someone like me, who was in uniform and getting spat at by drunks while you were reading each other's poems in student bars, it's much harder.'

'I did a chemistry degree.' Meg folded her arms. 'No poems.'

Foster grunted. 'I'm trying to make my way the only way I know how. I'm not a sweet talker, and I'm no intellectual – I can't compete with your lot when it comes to all that shite. So I'm a dog with a bone. It's the only way for the likes of me.'

Meg couldn't think how to respond. 'I thought you wanted to talk to DI May,' she said, lightly.

'Do I need to?'

'What do you mean?'

'I might not have a degree in chemistry,' Foster said, 'but I'm not a chuffing idiot. She won't tell me anything she hasn't already told you, will she?' He sat back in his chair and frowned. No snarly-lipped, narrow-eyed aggression. No patronisingly cocked head. No resentment. No anger. Nothing.

Meg unfolded her arms and pressed her hands together. 'I asked her if she knew where Flynn was, or where he might be, and she said she didn't.'

Foster scratched his neck.

'Honestly, Sir, she doesn't know where James Flynn is.' Meg lay her palms flat on the desk and looked him in the eye. 'I'm sure of it.'

'Anything else?' he said.

'No, sir.'

'Right then, I'm off home. It's been a shite day and I need a drink.' Foster got up and pulled his coat collars tight about his neck. 'Four murders in two days! The press are like pigs in shit.

Muxlow's all over this like a rash now. And he's got every excuse he needs to take direct control of the investigation.'

'But . . .'

'But what?'

'But why would he want to take direct control of this investigation? Why would he want to get his hands dirty?'

Foster sniffed. 'Fuck knows.'

'Come on, sir,' Meg said. 'You can't fool me with all that *I'm only a simple copper* crap. You're a shrewd bastard. Nothing gets past you, and you understand the politics of this bear pit better than . . . well . . . better than me.'

There was a long silence.

Foster fixed on Meg with an indulgent smile, and, after what seemed to her like a bout of serious consideration, he said, 'Goodnight, Sergeant Harper', and walked away. He hesitated when he got to the door, and turned back to Meg. 'Look, Harper. I really don't know why Muxlow is so *interested*. But let's focus on James Flynn, eh. Let's keep our heads down and get the job done. Best for all concerned, I reckon.'

❧

'I thought you handled him well,' Cassie said. And she meant it.

'I shouldn't have said anything.' Meg shook her head. 'He'll be on his guard now.'

Cassie was zipping up her parka. 'He's always on his guard. And don't imagine *he* has some sort of hidden agenda like Muxlow. He doesn't. It's pure pretence. Men like him want you to think that they have hidden agendas because while you're busy trying to work out what that agenda is you'll miss the obvious.'

'And what *is* the obvious?'

'That they're idiots.'

Meg frowned. 'Maybe.'

'Definitely.' Cassie slung her bag over her shoulder. 'We're in this together, now, whether we like it or not.'

'Yes.' Meg held the door open to let Cassie pass. 'And I don't like it.'

Cassie sighed. 'Do you know what I was thinking on the way up here. I was thinking of packing it all in – the job, the career, everything. Leave it all to the likes of Muxlow and Foster, I thought. Marry a millionaire and live like Lizzie McDonald.'

'Who's Lizzie McDonald?'

'It doesn't matter,' Cassie said, 'The point is, I'm beginning to feel like a priest who's lost his faith.'

'But you still have faith in Flynn, don't you?'

Cassie looked at her feet.

'Well, you'd better bloody well have faith in him! After all this shit.'

Cassie looked Meg in the eye. 'Flynn's no murderer.'

'No, Ma'am.' Meg said it in a way that made Cassie feel dirty.

'Right then,' Cassie said. 'And please stop calling me *Ma'am*.'

21

IT WAS MID-AFTERNOON on a drizzly day in September 1998. Flynn had gone to The No 7 Gentleman's Club to return his keys and suits. He remembered finding Scotty Deakin and Victoria Bramley in high spirits at the bar. They were the only ones in the club that afternoon, and they were drinking champagne.

'Hello, handsome,' Victoria said. 'We're celebrating Scotty's *deal of the century* – he won't tell me what it *is*, but hey!' She raised her glass. 'Fancy a drop of fizz?'

'No thanks, I just popped in to drop off some things.'

Victoria wagged a finger. 'Shouldn't you be in Sheffield? At University? At Fresher's week?'

'Tomorrow. I wanted to return this lot before I left.' He handed his keys to Deakin and draped three freshly dry-cleaned suits, complete with shirts and cravats, still in their white plastic covers, over a bar stool.

Deakin slapped the keys down on the bar and pointed at the clothes. 'Keep them. What am I going to do with them?'

'They came with the job, and I know they were expensive, so—'

'They were expensive because you can't buy off the peg clothes for someone your size! No one else is going to wear them.'

'I know, but . . .' He patted the pile of clothes.

Deakin turned to Victoria and sighed. 'What do *you* think he should do?'

'I think you should keep them, handsome. I'll be moving

on, one day, just like you – and I'll sure as hell be keeping my wardrobe!'

'Quite right,' Deakin said. 'And one day, Jamie, maybe years from now, you might find you have need of them again.'

Flynn remembered blushing and looking down at his feet. As much as he'd wanted to escape that life, and as much as he'd hated what Scotty Deakin was, he'd felt guilty about leaving this surrogate family. And he admired Scotty Deakin. More than that: he liked the man.

He was still looking at his feet when the Bolan twins came crashing in through the double doors wielding shotguns.

❧

The memory of this shock brought Flynn back to the present. He found himself standing in Sheaf Square, by the Railway Station, heart pounding, fists clenched. He had a vague memory of running, and then walking, and there was a gunshot (or was it two gunshots), and then he was running again, and there was a river, and a knife. He rubbed his neck, first with his fingers, then with the Velcro on the cuff of his coat, but nothing could shake the memory of the cold muzzle of Mike Bolan's gun pressed to his throat. Only now he saw Sean Mulligan holding the gun; a sneering Sean Mulligan with blood-scumbled teeth and a gaping wound in his throat. Mulligan was standing in a puddle of his own blood — hollow eyes, pallid lips, ghostly white skin.

Flynn squeezed his eyes shut and thought of Cassie. He remembered the smell of her hair, the taste of her lipstick, the warmth of her skin. He had her in his arms, they were kissing, then she was gone.

He opened his eyes. Mulligan was gone too.

There were plenty of taxis around, but he had only a twenty-pound note, which wasn't quite enough for the twenty-mile ride home. And besides, he couldn't go home, not today. The last time he'd been in this sort of fix, back in '98, it was easy: new name, new city, new life, and a hold-all stuffed with cash. Not running away: running *to*. All planned. Scotty Deakin had promised him that nobody would come looking, and nobody ever did. Now, people *would* come looking: Mulligan Junior, the Police, Cassie, Angus. He felt the cold creeping into his bones. Part of him wanted to let the frigid air do its worst, but he was won over by a stronger yearning.

The Sheffield Tap was warm and busy with Saturday shoppers. Spirits were *double up for free* between five and seven. It was half past five. He calculated that he could have a couple of large ones here and still have enough left to buy a cheap bottle of blended at *Pop's Mini Market* in Nether Edge. This would leave nothing for a taxi across town, but it was only a half-hour walk to the empty shop that would soon be an Oxfam. He would spend the night there.

❧

Brincliffe Edge Road marks the southern boundary of Nether Edge: stone walled and slate roofed houses on one side, dense woodland on the other.

Flynn found himself standing outside a neat Victorian terraced house – his first home with Sarah a dozen or more years ago. The house was more than most final year students could afford. At first the landlord wasn't keen on renting to students, but Sarah's upper-crust charm (and a year's rent, upfront, in cash) soon mollified him.

He had no idea how Sarah managed to fund the clothes and the restaurants and the convertible red Mercedes. She never talked about her life before Sheffield, never mentioned parents or family or school friends. And *he* never asked. She had spent some time in America, he thought: she sometimes used idioms that jarred with her Sloane Square accent. But maybe not.

And Sarah knew nothing about *his* life before Sheffield. She must have wondered how he came up with his half of the rent, and half of all those restaurant bills. She must have wondered how he'd found the money to buy a Land Rover Discovery immediately he passed his driving test. If she did, she never asked.

Their relationship was founded on a tacit understanding that their respective pasts were not a subject for discussion. It was as if their lives had begun the day they met. Occasionally – when the mood took them, and the night was clear, and they found themselves hand in hand looking across the city from their bedroom window – they spoke of the future. Sarah wanted to buy the biggest house on the road (a few doors down); *he* would turn the attic into a study with windows looking south over the woods, and north over the city, and write the great modern novel. But these were rare, wine-fuelled moments. Mostly, they discussed the matters of the day. Always, they rounded off the night with tender and wordless sex.

Sarah *would* buy the biggest house on the road a few years later, and Flynn *did* get his attic study.

He walked on to the big house, their old house, and looked up at the dormer window in the roof. Someone had installed curtains.

And the garage doors had been painted a muted shade of olive, which he rather liked.

He began to cry. It felt good.

By the time he got to the shops he was dry eyed and sober. At *Pop's Mini Market*, he grabbed a cheap bottle of whisky and large bag of crisps. He was seven pence short. Mr Ali let him off.

22

ANGUS WANTED EVERYTHING to be just right for Cassie. The Chinese takeaway was on its way, the Zinfandel was open and breathing, there was a bottle of Pinot Grigio in the fridge, there was a bottle of Baileys in the pantry. He poured himself a small malt and mulled over what Smythe-Browne had told him that afternoon, wondering how to break the news to Cassie.

❧

Cassie turned down the offer of a drink and she said she wasn't hungry.

'Where are Lizzie and the kids?' she asked, sharply.

Angus led her into the dining room. 'At her mum's,' he said. 'Her heart this time. Palpitations. And low blood pressure. Or was it high?'

'Is it serious?' Cassie looked at him properly for the first time since she'd arrived.

He took a seat directly opposite her at the dining table. 'I don't know. But she's recovered from three or four terminal illnesses over the last ten years, so we're not too worried.'

'Right.' Cassie opened up her computer. 'Yes, I remember Lizzie telling me that her mother was a bit of a hypochondriac.'

'She's not a hypochondriac, she's just a selfish, attention-seeking, old woman.'

Cassie glared at him.

Angus wondered what raw nerve he had touched this time. 'I'm going to make a start on the red,' he said. 'And I'll fetch you a glass, just in case.'

She slumped back in her chair. 'Angus, is everything all right between you and Lizzie?'

Angus shrugged.

'What's happened?' she asked.

'Nothing. Like I said, she's just spending a week with her sick mother.'

'And she's taken the kids, too? Come on, Angus, tell me what's happened.'

Angus didn't answer.

'Angus?' Cassie sat up and folded her arms.

'Her mother gets *plenty* of attention,' he said, 'more attention than me, that's for sure. This place is her second home.'

Cassie opened her mouth to speak, but Angus got in first.

'We might have had words,' he said. 'About her mother. And about . . . oh, I don't know. Look, the bottom line is this: Lizzie married me for my money. If I hadn't been driving a Porsche she wouldn't have given me a second look. I'm not in her league, am I? I know that. I don't ask much, but I don't expect to play second fiddle to her bloody mother.'

'You don't really believe that, surely? You must know that she loves you – I mean *really* loves you. It's bloody obvious to everyone else.'

Angus looked up at the ceiling.

'Christ, Angus. Please tell me you haven't spouted all that shit about the Porsche and the money to Lizzie.'

He went over to the sideboard and grabbed the Zinfandel and a couple of glasses. 'All the attention in the world won't cure you of loneliness, will it?'

'No,' Cassie said, quietly. 'But Angus—'

'She'll be back when she's maxed out the credit cards.' He sat down beside her and poured the wine. 'She'll be back when she has a use for me.'

Cassie drew a long breath. 'Just a small one for me, I'm driving'. Then she turned back to her computer.

Angus watched those gentle brown eyes of hers dart this way and that. Her eyelashes were thick and black, and when she blinked he could see the flaws and smudges in the burnished gold eye shadow she'd favoured for as long as he'd known her.

'Expecting an email?' he asked.

Cassie ignored his question. 'Do you know where Flynn is?'

Angus shrugged, 'I expect he's at home, where else would he be? But I don't think we should involve him just yet. He's still a bit . . . you know.'

'He's missing, Angus, that's what he is. The police went over to his place this afternoon. No sign of him, and he's not answering his phone.'

'But he never answers his phone,' Angus said.

'Anyway, Foster thinks he's done a runner.'

'A runner?' Angus took a sip of wine and swallowed it awkwardly. 'Where would he go?'

'I don't know. Do you?'

'No, why would I?'

She waved her hand. 'It doesn't matter, let's get on.'

'I'm sure he's fine.' Angus smiled and rolled the stem of the glass between his fingers. 'Probably in a pub somewhere. What makes them think he's done a runner?'

'In a pub? Why would you say that?'

He rubbed his nose with the back of his hand. 'No reason. Just trying to make light of it – you seem worried.'

Cassie's eyes narrowed.

'Anyway,' he said, brightly. 'Did you find out anything in Manchester?'

'Maybe, I don't know.' Cassie appeared to be thinking about

something else. 'So, what do you have for me?' she asked, eventually. 'Did you find out anything about Sarah Flynn's history? Did you take a look at that hard drive of hers?'

Angus put his elbows on the table and rubbed his palms together. 'The hard drive has been wiped clean, as I expected. But, knowing her, she'd have made a backup of anything important. If it was at their old house in Nether Edge, it's probably lost for ever. But she might have hidden it at the barn, at Flynn's place. Could be an SD card, though, or even a microSD card, tiny enough to hide anywhere – so I don't know how we'd find it.'

'Perhaps we ought to have a look round Flynn's place,' Cassie said.

'Yes. He might have an idea where she kept stuff like that.'

'What else, Angus? Did you find out anything about Sarah?'

Angus went over to the fireplace and leaned on the mantlepiece like a country squire posing for a portrait. 'Her maiden name was *Fitzroy*-Parker, not just plain old *Parker.* Daughter of a Baronet, Sir Richard Fitzroy-Parker, and the sixties socialite, Clara Brown. Parents own Hedmere Hall, in Cheshire, but lived mostly in New York and Washington DC.'

He looked hard at Cassie for some show of appreciation, or surprise, or anything. Cassie just stared back, so he went on:

'Sarah boarded at St Winifred's Catholic Girls School, in Hampshire, until the first term of the fifth form, when she left under some sort of a cloud. She disappears off the radar for about a year, then turns up at Hazelmere Academy in Wilmslow, another boarding school, in Cheshire, just outside Manchester. Leaves with four A Levels (straight As) and goes up to the University of Sheffield to study English Literature. This gives us something to work with, I think.'

'Yes,' Cassie frowned. 'Parents not dead then. Interesting. But why Sheffield? I know it's a decent University, Russell Group and all that, but what would attract a posh girl like that to Sheffield?'

'Angus shrugged. Don't you want to know how I got all that, given that I started with the wrong date of birth.'

'Wrong date of birth?'

'She was born on 3rd April, not 4th March. Simple transposition error: 03/04 to 04/03 – or a simple way of hiding her in the system so that it will look like a simple transposition error if ever it were to be discovered. She's a month younger than the police records show.'

'Do we have contact details for the parents?' Cassie asked.

'Yes, but they're in South Africa for the winter. Back in April, or so the housekeeper says. She also said that they had no contact with Sarah after she left school.'

Cassie puffed her cheeks and scratched her head. 'Anything else?'

'Don't you want to know how I traced her?'

'Don't worry, Angus, I know you've been fiendishly clever.'

'And how would you know that?'

'Because you *are* fiendishly clever.'

Angus shook his head.

Cassie smiled. 'And because I tried to build up a background for her two years ago – had a team of three working on it for a week, in fact – and came up with sod all. It was as if she didn't exist before she turned up in Sheffield.'

'Well she didn't – not the Sarah you were looking for. It was only when I—'

'Anything else?'

Angus rolled his eyes. 'Yes, there is. The summer vacation after her A Levels, she did a work experience placement at the *Manchester Evening News*.'

'The *Manchester Evening News*,' Cassie repeated, slowly. 'Interesting. I wonder if Stella Middlewood was around back then. Will you check for me.'

'Why don't you just ring her up and ask?'

Cassie shook her head. 'Because I want to already know the answer when I look her in the eye and ask the question.'

'Yes,' Angus said, idly, 'I expect you do.' He sat down beside her. 'Cassie,' he began . . .

She closed her computer and looked up at him.

Angus stared at Cassie's long, slim fingers and the immaculate red nail polish. She wore no rings, which gave her hands a girlish look, and—

'Go on, Angus. For Christ's sake!'

He got up, went back over to the fireplace, and resumed his squirely pose.

Cassie got up too. She folded her arms and looked down her nose at him like a school teacher eyeing a naughty little boy.

'We're firmly behind Flynn, aren't we?' Angus said at last.

'Don't play games with me, Angus.'

'I'm not.'

'I don't think I'm the one with the trust issues right now,' she said. 'If you have something to say, just say it.'

The doorbell rang.

'That'll be the Chinese,' Angus said, making for the door.

He looked over his shoulder and saw Cassie follow him into the hall where he paid the delivery man. He could see her out of the corner of his eye, watching, arms folded. He took the bag of food into the kitchen and loaded the foil containers into the oven to keep warm. Cassie followed him. He could see her reflection in the french doors that led onto the patio. She propped herself, legs crossed, arms still folded, against the island units. He decided that now was not the best time to tell her about Smythe-Brown.

'Come back into the dining room,' he said. 'Let's eat some dim sum, drink some wine, and decide what to do.'

'Sorry, Angus. Sounds lovely but I should really go home. I'm tired. And I'm in the car, anyway, so I can't have any more wine.'

'Right.' Angus found himself looking at Cassie's chest. He looked away.

'So,' she put her hands on her hips, 'what were you going to tell me?'

'Nothing.'

Cassie ran both hands through her hair.

'I was going to ask you to stay the night,' Angus said. 'I'd be glad of the company. Honestly, Cassie, I—'

She shot him one of her looks. 'Shall I phone your wife and ask her if *she* minds me keeping you company overnight?'

He winced. 'You know that's not what I meant.'

She looked down at the marble floor tiles, rocking on her heels.

'You're never going to let it go, are you?' he said, his voice close to cracking.

Cassie pulled him towards her and gave him a hug. With her cheek still pressed into his shoulder she whispered, 'Can I have that room at the top of the house again, the one that looks over woods at the back? Everything looks so lovely in the snow.'

'Of course you can. And there's a lock on the door, so—'

She squeezed him tighter and dug her knuckles into his ribs. 'Stop it. You know I didn't really mean it. And you know I'm sorry – very sorry.' Cassie sighed. 'I'm always sorry.'

'I know,' Angus said. 'Now, will you tell me what you found out in Manchester?'

She pecked him on the cheek and pushed him away. 'Where's my supper?'

23

IT WAS FREEZING in the flat above the shop. Flynn lit the Calor Gas heater and sat cross-legged in front of it. The air above the burners swirled and glowed blue. He thought of Cassie, and then of Sarah, and then of Cassie again.

When he'd warmed up a bit, Flynn went over to window and wiped away the condensation with the flat of his hand. Tears formed on the glass. They trickled all the way down to the timber frame which was black with mould. He cracked open his bottle and took a swig.

When he'd told Scotty Deakin, all those years ago, that he'd be leaving to go off to university, Scotty had slapped him on the back and grinned.

'Perhaps, it's for the best,' he said. 'You're a bright lad, and ambitious, and that's good. If you stay round here much longer I'll probably end up having to kill you, or worse: you'll end up having to kill me!'

'I'm not a killer, Scotty,' Flynn said.

Deakin had nodded. 'Neither am I.'

❧

From the window, he could see a light in the attic bedsit across the road. That very bedsit had been his first home as a student. He remembered the day he moved in. Not for him a Volvo estate stuffed with boxes and suitcases and pillows and duvets and kettles and toasters. No groaning dad, and fretting mum, ferrying life's requisites from car to student digs. No good luck cards. No hugs at the door. No teary-eyed goodbyes. Flynn had arrived in a taxi with a brown leather suitcase full of clothes and a large adidas holdall stuffed with twenty pound notes. Both gifts from Scotty Deakin. He thought two hundred thousand pounds would last forever. By the time he married Sarah, six years later, the bulk of it was spent. Sarah said she had enough money for the both of them. She insisted he keep whatever he had put by for himself. He should invest it, she said. She organised for a man he didn't know, from a bank he'd never heard of, to advise him on the stock market. He invested in property instead. He invested in what he could see and touch.

As he looked across the road, through the sleepy night air, through the frosty glass of the bedsit window and into the warm glow of a three-bar electric fire, he remembered and remembered and remembered.

He remembered the first bed he'd ever shared with Sarah in their student house. It was a king size, but his feet always hung over the end so that when she pulled the duvet up over her ears – as was her habit – his toes would freeze. One night he tried to wear his rugby socks to bed, but she refused to sleep with a man wearing socks. There was no point arguing.

It was in that bed, one winter, huddled in the foetal position to keep his feet under the covers, that he suffered his first night terror. He went to the doctor for sleeping pills. The doctor prescribed therapy. The therapist concluded that Flynn's problems stemmed from his past. Genius!

The first story Flynn ever wrote was composed when he was twenty, as part of a programme devised by his genius therapist. If he fictionalised his past, she said, if he turned it all into a story, it would be easier to detach himself from that past – easier to distance himself from the source of the nightmares. Five years later this text would become the embryo of his first short story, *The Wythenshawe Dandy*, which won a prize and was published in a collection entitled *Tough Love*. Vanity had got the better of him back then.

Now Flynn regretted writing the thing, regretted allowing his story to see the light of day. Some things, it turns out, are not so simple as therapists would have you believe.

Now he was dozing on a damp sofa.

Now he could hear the crackle of New Year fireworks outside, and Pulp's '*Disco 2000*' playing too loud on a radio.

Now Sarah was in the room. She was dancing, naked but for a paper crown and a seductive smile. She was beautiful. Blonde bob bobbing. Arms high above her head. Bottle of Bolly in one hand, champagne flute in the other.

He held that memory, held that dream, for as long as he could.

❧

Outside, a maroon Bentley pulled up on the far side of the road. A man with a shaven head slipped out of the shadows by Café No. 9 and got into the passenger seat.

Scott Deakin turned off the ignition. 'Everything sorted?' he asked.

'Getting there,' the man said. 'I've only been in town a few hours.'

Deakin looked up at the flat above the shop. 'Does anyone know he's here?'

'Only me. And anyway, from what I've seen your lad can handle himself.'

Deakin grabbed the steering wheel and squeezed. 'But he shouldn't have to *handle himself*, not anymore. Everyone should have the right to choose.'

'And you *did* let him choose, Scotty. So what's all this is about.'

Deakin grunted. 'Unit 17, that's what it's about.'

The man chuckled. 'Queen and country, eh?'

'Yeah well,' Deakin said. 'I got that wrong.'

'Been there,' the man said, 'got the bloody T-shirt!' He sighed and shook his head. 'Well, the beret, actually. And the medals. And the leg full of shrapnel.'

Deakin rubbed his thigh. 'Yes, well, Unit 17 is my leg full of shrapnel.'

The man in the passenger seat raised his eyebrows. 'So, are you going to tell me?'

Deakin studied the backs of his hands for a while, then nodded. 'When he came to Sheffield,' he said, 'I'd just started with the unit. And while I was spying for them, they were spying on *me*.' He nodded up at the window of Flynn's flat. 'And they assumed he was still on my payroll, so they set that little bitch on him.'

'What little bitch?'

'Sarah Fitzroy fucking Parker.'

'Ah.' The shaven headed man nodded, slowly. 'I'd never have guessed she was—'

'Well she *was*, and he fell for her, didn't he?'

'And *she* fell for him, surely.'

'Maybe,' Deakin said.

'She married him, Scotty! And by then the unit would have known for sure that he'd had nothing to do with you for years.'

'Maybe.' Deakin rubbed his chin.

'Definitely,' the other man said.

Deakin shook his head. 'When you've worked with that lot for as long as I have, you come to understand that anything's possible.'

The other man shrugged. 'Well she's gone now. Dead and gone.'

'Maybe,' Deakin said. 'But maybe it's not as simple as that.'

24

CASSIE PULLED BACK the curtains and looked out. Lizzie McDonald was a fortunate woman indeed. Rich husband, pretty children, big house with an orchard and woods. It had snowed heavily overnight, a good six inches, but the sky was crisp and cloudless now. She looked deep into the woods. Dark trunks, silvered branches, white snow, blue sky. She loved the woods - they spoke of a world long lost, a simpler world.

She picked up her phone and opened the email Stella Middlewood had sent her late last night. The photo was conclusive. The serious looking schoolboy in the picture was Flynn. He was Jamie Boreman, he was Deakin's Dandy, he was the Grammar School boy turned gangster's hired muscle. He was *their* Flynn.

Angus hadn't seemed so sure - he said it was too grainy to tell - but he'd drunk a lot of wine. Then Cassie remembered what Angus had told her about Sarah Flynn doing work experience at the *Manchester Evening News*. Stella had been at that paper for ever. Had she met Sarah there all those years ago? Had she known Sarah before—

A knock at the door. 'Are you up?'

Cassie pulled the borrowed dressing gown tight about her. 'Yes.'

'Are you decent?'

'Yes! What is it, Angus?'

Angus came in waving an iPad. 'I've found the birth certificate. You were right about Jamie Boreman.'

Cassie scanned the screen. 'Jamie Boreman, 9 September 1980. Father: James Boreman. Mother: Theresa Flynn.' She forced a laugh: 'Not very imaginative.'

'I expect he wanted to keep their memory alive.'

'Bastard.'

'Cassie, come on. We don't know—'

'And *are* they dead, his parents?'

'Yes, I checked. Mother died of a brain tumour suddenly, in August '91; father died two years later - drank himself to death according to the coroner's report.'

Cassie growled and walked back over to the window. 'Or maybe not. Maybe *they* changed their names too.'

Angus sighed. 'I think you're being a little—'

'I don't like being deceived, Angus, that's all. And I don't think that's unreasonable.'

He went to join her by the window and put a hand on her shoulder.

She shrugged him off.

'I think we should talk to him before we jump to any conclusions,' he said. 'He had it pretty tough as a kid.'

❧

Cassie's winter boots clunked on the wrought iron treads as she squeezed back down the spiral staircase at Flynn's barn. 'Foster was right,' she said. 'Looks like he's packed up his things and cleared out. They haven't even bothered to leave a uniform outside - Foster must have convinced himself that Flynn isn't coming back. A few years ago we wouldn't have taken that sort of chance. But I suppose, with resources as they are . . .'

Angus was sitting at the dining table staring through the window, he glanced round the room and shrugged. 'Except for his computer,' he said. 'I can't see that anything's missing. Do you think the police would have taken the computer?'

'Probably.' Cassie frowned. 'There must be stuff missing: nearly all the cupboards down here are empty. And it's the same story upstairs: a few clothes in a chest of drawers a whole wall of empty wardrobes.'

'I know, I know. But that's how he's lived since Sarah died. He cleared out anything that reminded him of her, even all the clothes she'd bought for him – which amounted to pretty much all his clothes.'

'*All* his clothes?'

'Yep. He bought a few new things – the basics – but not much.'

Cassie sat on the big oak table and swung her legs like a bored schoolgirl. 'I didn't notice it so much when I was here the other day, but this place really does feels like a holiday cottage – like nobody actually lives here.' She scanned the room one last time and clapped her hands. 'Come on, let's go.'

❧

The roads were quiet because of the snow but Angus was forced to mount the verge a couple of times to get past stranded cars.

'Glad I fitted those winter tyres,' he said.

Cassie had her iPad balanced on her knees; she was watching the video of Gemma Grant at the end of Flynn's drive. She'd played it over and over, looking for something – anything. She'd found nothing so far.

'And Flynn's very proud of the tractor tyres on *his* car,' she said. 'What is it with men and wheels?'

'What is it with you and that video of Gemma Grant? It was sent because it implicates Flynn – I can't believe there's anything more to it than that. And it isn't difficult to fix the time stamps on a video. It could have been filmed anytime.'

Cassie shook her head. 'There was no reason to fix the time

stamp: the connection between Flynn and Gemma is all that matters. But the fresh snow on the ground fits with the time and date, so I think it's probably right. There are two close ups: one of Gemma Grant's face, one of Flynn's mail box. Flynn says he didn't know the girl – this video says he did. The mail box is the clincher, it even has his name on it – his and Sarah's; otherwise, with all that snow, we wouldn't have a clue where this this was filmed.'

'I suppose,' Angus said. 'But it's hardly conclusive.'

'Well, it doesn't *look* good – for Flynn, I mean – and that's enough.'

'Odd thing is . . .' Angus broke off as he squeezed the Range Rover past an abandoned BMW that hadn't made it up the last incline, ' . . . I must have been up to that place a dozen times since Sarah died, and I don't think I ever noticed the mail box before. Not obvious, is it? Buried, almost, in that big hawthorn hedge. Daft place to put it. If it were down to me, I'd have—'

'Shush.' Cassie was watching the video again. 'There, that's it. I knew there was something.'

'What?'

Cassie paused the video. 'She was carrying an envelope, a big one. It's only in shot for a fraction of a second, but it's there. And now,' she tapped the screen, 'no envelope. And the snow on the ground around the mail box is pristine, so she didn't put it in there.'

Angus pulled over and stopped the car. 'Show me.'

She angled the screen so that he could see.

'Right,' Angus said, sceptically, after the fourth loop. 'And I suppose you noticed the jump in the time stamp.'

'A thirty-minute gap: she must have walked up the drive and delivered the thing by hand.'

Angus accelerated hard to get over the lip of the verge and back onto the road. 'Or someone else met her there, by the road, and she passed it on.'

'No. She went up the drive, you can see her footprints in the snow.'

'You can see *someone's* footprints, Cassie. Or maybe she just put it in her handbag.'

'It's too big for her handbag.'

'Not if she folded it in half.'

Cassie persisted: 'If she was going to fold it in half,' she said, 'she'd have folded it in half and put it in her handbag before she set off for Flynn's house. No, I think it's one of those stiff-backed envelopes for photographs. You wouldn't fold photographs, would you?'

Angus didn't bother to argue, which annoyed her immensely. She bit her tongue, closed her eyes, and replayed the video in her head. 'Does she remind you of Sarah?'

He shrugged.

'Well, *I* think she looks just like her.'

'If she took after her mother,' Angus said, slowing down to manoeuvre past a stranded people carrier and an abandoned lever arch file, 'the world's probably a better place without her.'

It took Cassie a moment to process what Angus had just said. She turned to face him. He was staring, tight jawed, out at the road.

'Good God, Angus!' She waited for him to glance her way but he didn't. 'That's a horrible thing to say. What did she ever do to you?'

Angus put his foot down hard on the accelerator. The engine roared. Cassie held the armrest tight and stiffened. When they were back up to speed, Angus eased off the throttle. 'I think I know where Flynn might be holed-up,' he said.

Cassie turned to face him. 'Where?' she asked, in as calm a voice as she could manage.

'He's completely skint, you know,' Angus said. 'Overdraft and credit cards maxed out. I lent him another couple of hundred quid the other day just to get him through the week . . .'

'Where is he, Angus?'
'. . . so he can't afford to go far.'
'Bloody hell, Angus! Just tell me.'

25

THE GAS FIRE had been on all night, and the room was unbearably hot. Flynn woke, fists clenched, teary eyed, sweat streaming down his face. The curtains were open, and the room was painfully bright. He tore off his coat, jumper, and shirt. He bumped into his laptop on the way to the window, nearly knocking it off a makeshift coffee table. The hard drive whirred, and the screen sprang to life, but Flynn didn't look back. He pushed up the bottom section of the sash window and stood in the cold draught. Across the street, in his old bedsit, a young woman was hunched at her desk in the dormer window.

He remembered sitting where she now sat – writing, and looking out across the roofs. He remembered watching mums with pushchairs, and pensioners with string shopping bags, go about their blameless business. He had written the first draft of *The Wythenshawe Dandy* at that very desk.

❧

Cassie let them into the empty shop with a spare key she'd borrowed from the woman who ran the café next door.

'I think he'd have let us in if he were here,' Angus said.

Cassie shook her head. 'He's here. Look, the door's been opened – all the post has been brushed to one side. And then there's that open window upstairs, the woman said it was closed when she opened up the café this morning.'

'Burglars, maybe?'

Cassie waved Angus up the stairs. 'You go first, then.'

The door at the top of the stairs was unlocked. Angus went in and Cassie followed. At the window, naked from the waist up, and with his back to them, stood Flynn. Even in silhouette, Flynn's massive frame was unmistakeable.

'Are you all right?' Angus said.

Flynn didn't answer.

'Maybe . . .' Angus spotted Flynn's computer open on a cardboard box in front of the sofa. There appeared to be a video playing. He leaned in to get a better look.

'Maybe what?' Cassie said.

'Maybe I should wait in the car.' Angus barged past an open-mouthed Cassie and stormed out.

'Angus? What?'

He was already gone. She turned to the computer, but a starburst screensaver kicked in before she could get a proper look. 'That draught is freezing, Flynn.'

He closed the window and drew the heavy brown curtains. It took a second or two for Cassie's eyes to adjust to the darkness. She found a switch by the door and turned on the light, an energy saver that took a while to warm up. There was a pile of clothes on the floor beside an empty whisky bottle.

'Flynn, are you drunk?'

He didn't answer.

With the window closed, the stench of booze and sweat was overwhelming. She was reminded of her father. Her insides began to spasm. She clutched her belly. She wanted to cry. But crying never did any good – if anything, it made things worse. No, she must hold it in and get on with things. Tidy up, get him cleaned and dressed, make everything right, make sure—

No. No. No. That was another life. She would never go back to that.

'Are you drunk?' Cassie asked again. 'Because if you are, I—'

The bulb had reached full brightness, and now she could see Flynn's broad and powerful back. Scars, dozens of them - dull and dark and purple - disfigured his pale skin. Some were long and thick, like lash scars from a flogging; others were old knife wounds; a few looked more like burns. One of them (small and round and right between his shoulder blades) was certainly a cigarette burn.

Flynn spoke without turning: 'Please, Cassie, just go.'

'Where's your phone?'

He didn't answer.

'Where, Flynn?'

'Coat pocket, probably. Battery's flat.'

She went to check. His coat pockets were empty. 'It isn't there Flynn,' she said. 'So where is it?'

'Home? Car? Don't know.'

'Three men were killed at Park Gate School yesterday,' she said. 'Do you know anything about that?'

He turned; his chest and lower abdomen bore yet more scars, but they were less obvious under the hair. His eyes narrowed. 'Three?' he said, and folded his arms.

She folded hers. 'Well?'

He shook his head.

'Your phone was at the scene.'

Flynn held his huge arms aloft, like a priest delivering mass.

Outside a lorry was reversing. There was a diesel roar, then the hiss and pop of air brakes, then the clunk and squeak of doors opening. Business as usual.

Cassie approached Flynn and ran a finger along a thick scar just below his ribs. He flinched. She withdrew. 'Does it hurt?'

'No.'

'But you don't like me touching?'

He was looking straight past her, eyes half closed. 'Sarah used to touch my scars, stroke them.'

Her chest tightened. 'Well I'm sorry I'm not your precious bloody Sarah.' She regretted saying it even before she'd finished speaking.

'Please,' Flynn said. 'Give me a few hours. Then we can talk.'

There were more scars on his arms. She realised that this must be the first time she'd seen him without long sleeves. 'And will you tell me about the scars?' she said.

But Flynn had already side-stepped her and was picking through the pile of clothes in the middle of the floor. He pushed aside the sweat sodden shirt and jumper, and put on his coat.

'But I have to know, Flynn.' She squeezed her eyes shut. 'There can't be secrets, there just can't.'

'Sarah never asked.'

Cassie clenched her fists. 'Fuck Sarah!' There, she'd said it. And she'd meant it. And now she was sorry for saying it.

Flynn walked over to the far side of the room.

Cassie pulled back one of the curtains and looked out. Angus was sitting in his car. 'I'm jealous of Sarah,' she said. 'Jealous of a dead woman! And I'm sure Angus has told you what a needy, self-absorbed cow I can be. And he's right, of course.'

Why was she telling him all this? Perhaps because she knew he could lift her, as most men might lift a skinny wretch like Kate Moss. Perhaps she wanted Flynn to lift her high into the air, spin her round, and cuddle her like a doll – like her father used to do when she was little. Before the drink. Before he left.

She turned from the window and sat on the sofa in front of Flynn's laptop. What was it Angus had seen? What had made him bolt? Cassie leaned forward and reached for the keyboard.

'No,' Flynn said. 'Please don't.'

But she'd already tapped the space bar.

It was a short video, no more than ten seconds, playing on a loop. There was no sound.

She looked up at Flynn, eyes wide.

'She wouldn't have done it to hurt me,' Flynn said. 'It wouldn't have occurred to her.'

Cassie opened her mouth to speak but could think of nothing to say.

'Tell him I'm not angry,' Flynn said. 'Really, I'm not. I know it wasn't his fault. And I know he'll have paid a price.'

Cassie turned back to the screen. She knew it was wrong, but she kept watching. The same loop: once, twice, thrice – again and again and again.

'She liked to be naked,' Flynn said. 'She spent most of her time naked when it was just the two of us at home. Me too, sometimes.'

He reached over and closed the laptop.

Cassie got up and paced the room. Eventually she stopped by the window and looked out again. Angus was still sitting in his car.

'Your wife, Flynn,' she said, '. . . and Angus. The bastard. The absolute bastard.'

Flynn shook his head. 'No,' he said. 'That's not fair.'

'Not fair! He was screwing your wife!' Cassie blew out a long breath. 'How long have you had this?'

'Came last night. Don't know who sent it – the email address looks like a bunch of random letters.'

Cassie glanced at the empty whisky bottle.

'And not so much of a shock as all that,' he said. 'Not really. I knew what she was capable of. Perhaps that's why I loved her. Because with me, and only with me, she was different.'

Cassie put her hands on her hips. 'Different how, Flynn?'

'She loved me, Cassie. I know she did.'

'Yeah, right.' Cassie pointed at the computer. 'So what was that then?'

'It doesn't change anything, not really.'

'You're drunk, Flynn, and you're talking like a drunk.' She shook her head. 'Your best friend! I could never forgive *that*.'

Flynn grimaced. 'I know. But you're . . .'

'What?' Cassie turned to face him, forced him to look at her. 'Not the forgiving type?'

'That's not what I meant,' Flynn said, sitting down on the sofa.

Cassie waited.

Flynn's blue eyes darted around the room before settling on her. 'I've done things I wish I hadn't. I know what it's like. Angus will be feeling bad enough about this without me making it harder for him. Besides, she probably went with lots of men. She'd do anything to get what she wanted. I knew that about her.'

'And what about you?' Cassie screwed up her face. 'Were you ever unfaithful to Sarah?'

'No.'

She went to kiss him on the mouth, but the reek of stale whisky on his breath made her recoil.

Flynn's eyes filled with shame.

She tried again – went for an innocent peck on the cheek this time.

Flynn dodged her and heaved himself off the sofa. 'I want to be alone now.'

'You still love her, don't you?' Cassie said. 'In spite of everything?'

He didn't answer.

'I wish I could forgive as easily as you,' she said.

'You don't *need* to forgive, Cassie. People who want to be forgiven, they're the ones who *need* to forgive.'

She shook her head. 'Why do you think so badly of yourself, Flynn? No one else does.'

'I want to go home,' Flynn said.

Cassie put her hands into her coat pockets. 'They might go looking for you there.'

'I don't care.'

'Well you should.'

Flynn looked down at his feet. 'Cassie . . .' he said.
'What?' she snapped back.
' . . . would you lend me twenty-five quid for a taxi home?'

26

BY FOUR THAT afternoon, Cassie was back home and staring blankly out of her kitchen window. She was furious with Angus, and with Flynn, and with herself. But her back yard looked ever so pretty under all that snow. Silent and calm and glistening, even in the meagre light from the house.

Then Stella rang. For some reason she was putting on a comedy cockney accent – something akin to Dick van Dyke in *Mary Poppins*.

'I understand you are desirous to speak with me, m'lady,' Stella said.

'Yes,' Cassie said cautiously. 'Can I come and see you tomorrow? It won't take long?'

'As you command, Madame May.'

'Stella, have I done something to piss you off?'

'No, Madame. You'd never do no such thing, I'm sure.'

Cassie heard a roar of laughter in the background. 'Where are you?'

'In a public house, Madame. A public house called by the name the Sheffield Tap.'

'You're in Sheffield?'

'Yes, Madame, but if that displeases Madame I can get on the next train home.'

'Stay put,' Cassie said. 'I'll be there in fifteen minutes.'

Cassie was barely through the door of the Sheffield Tap when Stella greeted her with a bear hug and a wet kiss on the cheek.

'You've just missed Katherine,' Stella said. 'She couldn't stay. Had to pick up Frankie from football or ballet or dogging or something.' She staggered sideways into a table taking Cassie with her. 'Sorry. I think I'm a bit squiffy.'

Cassie wriggled out of Stella's arms and stepped back to look at her. 'You're pissed as a fart, Stella. And its only half past four.'

'Kev's left me.'

'The bastard,' Cassie said. 'What happened?'

'I kneed him in the balls. I didn't mean to hurt him. The hospital said he'd be all right.'

'Hospital! Bloody hell, Stella.'

'That was last night. And he's still not talking to me. He's taken the kids and gone to stay with his mother. And it's all your fault.'

'How's it my fault!'

'Because you got me thinking about Sarah Fitzroy fucking Parker. And I was telling Kev what a slag she was.'

'I thought you didn't know her that well.'

'I didn't, but I knew her when she was a teenager.'

Cassie clapped her hands. 'From the work experience she did after her A-Levels?'

'I need a drink, Cassie. I need a Gin & Tonic'

'I'll go,' Cassie said, guiding Stella towards an empty table. 'You sit down.'

Cassie's phone rang. Angus. She rejected the call and ordered a Chianti for herself and a gin-free tonic water for Stella.

'Tell me about Sarah Fitzroy-Parker,' Cassie said, handing Stella her drink.

'I don't want to talk about her.'

'Please, Stella. I really need your help.'

Stella downed half the tonic water in one swig. 'I met her at her parent's big house in the country,' she said. 'I was covering some charity dinner for the paper. The house was like a stately home. There were parties there every weekend in July – posh parties for A-listers.'

'A-listers? Like who?'

Stella shrugged.

'Think, Stella,' Cassie said. 'Are we talking politicians? Or business tycoons? Or pop stars?'

'Everybody!' Stella drew a circle with her arms. 'TV people, business people, Hollywood stars, footballers. The American ambassador was a regular, apparently.'

Cassie nodded encouragement.

Stella sighed. 'There were even rumours that Bill Clinton was there one weekend in '95.'

'Really?' Cassie said.

Stella shrugged. 'Sarah's mother, Clara Brown, was a super model in the sixties, you see. A proper A-lister. She was the one who got the Hollywood stars to come up to Manchester.'

Stella's eyes were closed now, and she began to sway. Cassie took the glass from her hand and set it on the table. 'Stella?' she said quietly, squeezing her arm. 'Stella, are you all right?'

'Just tired,' she said, half opening her eyes. She grabbed her glass and downed what was left. 'Another G & T might help – I'm gasping.'

❧

By the time Cassie got back to the table with a tonic water and a packet of crisps, Stella seemed to have got her second wind. She looked almost sober.

'So,' Cassie said, 'how did Sarah end up working on the paper that summer?'

Stella screwed up her face. 'The little witch scammed me, didn't she.'

'How?'

'She said that if I could fix it for her to get a placement at the paper, she'd get me into all the VIP parties at her parents' house. She said I'd get interviews with all the celebs.' Stella stared into her tonic water.

'And . . .' Cassie said, leaning in.

Stella harumphed. 'After I got the little cow her placement she told me her mother had put the kibosh on our deal. Mother, apparently, had decided that there were already too many press-types around.'

'And you think she'd known that from the start?' Cassie took a sip of wine and licked her lips. 'You're sure it wasn't a genuine mistake?'

'Of course I'm sure. The little bitch ended up doing all the celebrity interviews herself, didn't she!' Stella offered a wistful smile. 'Slept with half the men she interviewed, probably. Maybe even some of the women. She even managed to get her own column on the paper for the summer party season. I'd been there nearly two years, and I was lucky to get a bloody by-line.'

Cassie nodded. 'Yes,' she said, 'that *would* piss anyone off.' She selected a small crisp from the packet and chewed it slowly. 'But yesterday you gave me the impression you hardly knew her.'

Stella groaned. 'I was being discreet. Acting the professional. After all, she turned out to be a fucking good journalist in the end. She broke that big child sexual exploitation story on your patch, didn't she?' Stella shovelled a handful of crisps into her mouth, chewed them thoroughly, then wiped her lips with the back of her hand. 'Went national, that one did. And it wasn't her first big splash in the nationals. She broke a lot of stories . . .' Stella snorted a laugh '. . . and a lot of rules, too!'

'And was she really that promiscuous?' Cassie asked, still struggling to shake the image of Sarah and Angus, *at it*, in Flynn's little barn.

'Yes,' Stella said, rubbing her eyes. 'Oh, I don't know. Maybe I'm exaggerating a bit. But around men, even much older men, she wasn't your typical shy and awkward teenager. She was slick and confident and clever.' Stella shook her head. 'And they lapped it up – the way they looked at her was . . . oh, I don't know. She wasn't overtly sexual, she was just . . .' Stella held up her hands, spilling her tonic water. 'I can't describe it.'

'I think I understand,' Cassie said. 'You're not the first to describe her like that.'

Stella looked suddenly forlorn. 'I'm not being very professional now, I suppose.' She took a deep breath. 'But it's Sunday, and we were supposed to be out walking in Castleton today – as a family.'

Cassie patted Stella's knee. 'So why did you come here?'

'Well Kev's in no condition for hiking up Mam Tor, is he, not with his bruised fucking balls.' Stella rubbed her eyes.

'But why come here,' Cassie said. 'Why come to Sheffield?'

Stella shrugged. 'My old mate Katherine lives here; I thought she might cheer me up. And I thought she might give me the latest on your Penthouse Murder case.'

Cassie leaned back and crossed her legs. 'And did she?'

'Oh, yes.' Stella giggled. 'She certainly cheered me up. Or maybe it was the gin.'

'I meant the murder case,' Cassie said. 'Did she have anything for you about the murder case.'

'Nah. She knew bugger all. All Katherine wanted to talk about was some squillionaire American who's going to pour gazillions of dollars into Sheffield United and get them back up to the Premier League. I thinks that's why I ended up having one too many gin and tonics.' Stella pressed the flat of her hand to her forehead for a few seconds, leaving a thin line of soggy crisp crumbs just above her eyebrows. 'She's a boring old cow when she gets going about football. And I bet it'll never happen anyway. She's been on about this Brett McRoss character for the last couple of years.'

Stella reached for her glass and missed; Cassie guided it into her hand. 'Anyway, when he wanted to buy Sheffield Wednesday he was a wanker. When he wanted to merge Wednesday and United he was tosser. But now that he just wants to buy United he's a bloody hero.'

'Brett McRoss,' Cassie said slowly, 'that name rings a bell.' She grabbed a tonic sodden paper napkin from the table and cleaned up Stella's forehead.

Stella didn't seem to mind, or even notice. 'Yeah, well,' she went on, 'he's headline news in the sports pages.'

'No, I remember it from a couple of years ago. It was to do with Sarah. That's right, Flynn told me he thought she was researching him just before she died.'

'No surprise there.'

'Why?'

'Because two years ago Brett McRoss was over here proposing to buy the two Sheffield clubs and merge them. It was just before Christmas when the news broke. I remember because I was here, in Sheffield, out on the razzle with Katherine. There was uproar.' Stella coughed a laugh. 'I'm surprised the man got out of Sheffield alive. That's Americans for you: no sense of history or tradition. Anyway, he's back now with Plan C.'

'Yeah, but . . .' Cassie thought it odd that Sarah Flynn would have been interested in a story about sport. She folded up the sodden napkin and slipped it into the empty crisp packet. Then she folded up the crisp packet, pressed it flat, and set it down neatly under a beer mat in the middle of the table.

Stella was giggling again now, but her giggles soon turned to tears. 'Poor Kev, I didn't mean to knee him that hard, really I didn't.'

'He'll be fine,' Cassie said. 'So what happened, anyway?'

'He said I was jealous! Jealous of that little witch.' Stella wiped her eyes with her fingertips. 'Well not in so many words, maybe, but that's not the point. I was telling him about Sarah Flynn – Fitzroy-Parker as she was back then – and that summer when she was doing work experience at the paper. The men in the office were like flies round shit, and she definitely slept with a couple of them. But not the ones you'd expect – not the young guns – she went for the editor and the deputy editor, both fat and married and pushing fifty. She went for power.'

'Why am I not surprised?' Cassie said. 'It's women like that . . .' she shook her head. 'Anyway, what exactly *did* Kev say to deserve a knee in the nuts?'

Stella closed her eyes for a moment. 'It wasn't what he said so much as the way he said it.'

'Right.' Cassie narrowed her eyes.

Stella lifted her head defiantly. 'It was what he was thinking.'

'Ok, but what did he say?'

Stella didn't answer.

'He didn't say anything, did he, Stella?'

'It was the way he looked at her,' Stella said. 'All those years ago. That time he came to pick me up from work. I wasn't jealous of *her* – Sarah Fitzroy-Parker was an evil little bitch – I was jealous of the way Kev looked at her. He's never looked at me like that. Never.'

Cassie said nothing for a while.

Stella stared into her tonic water.

'Stella,' Cassie said at last, 'why did you agree to see Sarah if you hated her that much?'

Stella looked up and pressed a palm to her forehead. 'Curiosity? Or professional courtesy, maybe. I don't know. She remembered I'd been researching gang related crime in South Manchester while she was working at the paper. She'd even dug out a couple of my pieces from back then. She flattered me, I suppose. And we both pretended nothing had ever happened between us.'

Cassie took a few slow sips of wine, twirling the glass with her fingertips between each sip. 'If only I knew why Sarah Flynn was asking about Scott Deakin two years ago. Something tells me if I knew that, I'd know everything.'

'Maybe,' Stella said, rubbing her temples with the heels of her hands. 'Or maybe it's a red herring.'

'And I still think it's odd that she should choose to come to study in Sheffield,' Cassie said. 'Why Sheffield? I wonder if she knew people here.'

'Perhaps she liked rock climbing,' Stella said. 'That's why my mate Katherine came here, for the rock climbing.'

'Rock climbing?'

'Yes. Our Sarah was a toff, wasn't she? And rock climbing's always been a bit of a toff's sport. And Sheffield's the rock-climbing capital of England, didn't you know?'

'No,' Cassie said, her brow creased.

'Well, if you live in Sheffield you're bound to know someone who's into rock climbing.' Stella looked Cassie in the eye. 'Don't *you*?'

Cassie swigged down the last of her Chianti. Yes, she did know someone: Angus.

27

NEXT MORNING, CASSIE made a few resolutions:

1. She would leave the murder investigation to Foster and break off all contact with Flynn. Flynn didn't need her help. The police didn't have enough evidence to take the case to the CPS – they didn't even have a motive. Flynn was a girlish infatuation that could lead only to disappointment and misery. He was damaged.
2. She would forgive Angus. It was against her nature to blame the proverbial wicked temptress of a woman, but in the case of Sarah Flynn she was willing to make an exception.
3. She would go back to London. She wouldn't wait for a promotion, she'd ask for a transfer. In any case, the prospects for promotion were better down there. And in London, she might find a man over thirty who wasn't married with kids. In Yorkshire, it seemed, if a man over thirty wasn't married with kids, there was a bloody good reason.

A pang of guilt rose from her latent feminist core. But she wanted a family; she wanted to love and to be loved; she wanted what she'd never had. And for this, *she* needed a man. Nowt wrong with that.

Nowt! She'd gone native on top of everything else – time to go back to London. But right now she needed a long walk in the cold winter air. Cassie put on her hat and coat. The door bell chimed while she was checking her pockets for gloves. It was Meg Harper.

'Meg! What's wrong?'

'Sorry, ma'am.' Meg's eyes were red from crying; she sniffed and cleared her throat. 'You're on your way out. It's nothing. I shouldn't have come.'

'Come in.'

'But—'

Cassie pulled Meg over the threshold and shut the front door. 'Do you fancy a hot chocolate? And when I say hot chocolate I mean a *proper* hot chocolate. I mean a bar of Bournville melted into just enough milk to make it pourable.'

❧

Meg talked. Cassie listened. They polished off their hot chocolates.

'You're better off without him,' Cassie said.

Meg sighed and ruffled her boyish hair.

'And the haircut?' Cassie said. I wanted to ask, but . . .'

Meg sighed. 'I'd gone platinum blonde. All for the posh Christmas bash that his firm throws every year. Claridge's, don't you know! Last year he said I looked frumpy – and he was probably right, the shit. They were all laughing at me, those bitches. So this Christmas I made a real effort. Didn't want to let myself down in front of the Chelsea brigade. I wanted to look . . . you know . . .

'Bought a posh frock – the classic *little black dress*. Paid for a boutique hairdo and a makeover. Cost me a fortune.' She forced a smile. 'I thought it would be like that scene in *Pretty Woman* where Julia Roberts walks back into that hotel looking like something out of *Vogue* and . . .' Meg rubbed her eyes and looked up.

Cassie offered a knowing nod.

'I imagined heads turning for *me*,' Meg said. 'I imagined him kissing my hand, I imagined him opening doors and pulling out chairs.' She shook her head. 'I got there a bit late. Only twenty minutes, for Christ's sake, but he was furious. He said I looked like a prostitute and refused to speak to me for the rest of the evening.'

'Bastard!'

'I didn't look like a prostitute. I know I didn't.'

'Of course you didn't.'

'I cut my hair off with the kitchen scissors when I got home. I'd drunk a bit too much and it seemed . . . oh, I don't know. I don't know if I did it to punish him or to punish myself. I knew he'd hate me with hair this short. Christ, *I* hate me with hair this short!

Cassie cleared away the empty mugs. 'It gets better, you know, with time.'

Meg nodded. 'It'll grow back. Of course it will.'

'That's not what I meant. I meant—'

'I know what you meant!' Meg snorted and put her head in hands. 'Does it really get better?'

Cassie was loading the dishwasher now. She slammed the door shut. 'Yes. Of course it does.'

'Really?'

Cassie sighed. 'Okay then. No!'

They both laughed. When they stopped laughing they looked at each other, broke down, and started laughing all over again.

Cassie hadn't seen Meg like this before: hadn't noticed how pretty she was; hadn't noticed her ever-so-slightly protruding teeth, nor the dimples in her cheeks, nor her sky blue eyes; hadn't noticed her at all, really, not as a person, not as a woman. At work, Meg wore shapeless trouser suits, but Cassie suspected a catwalk-perfect figure lurked underneath. She tried to imagine Meg in a little black dress and long blonde hair. She would have looked gorgeous.

Meg coughed. 'I feel better for having got it off my chest.'

Cassie smiled. She was rather pleased to be playing the agony aunt for the second time in two days. It wasn't a role she was used to. People didn't come to her with their problems; she wasn't the sort of person people came to with their problems; she wasn't the sort of person—

'My friends wouldn't understand,' Meg said. 'They're all married with kids – or good as. Fiona was the only one left, but she announced that she was pregnant on New Year's Eve, and she's been with Nick since uni, so . . .'

'So I'm the last resort?'

Meg's face fell. 'No, honestly, it's not like that.'

Cassie held up her hands. 'Ignore me. I say these things but I don't mean them.' Outside, the sky had cleared and the sun was shining. Cassie needed space: she wanted to be a speck on the landscape, not the elephant in the room. 'Do you fancy a walk, Meg?'

❧

Cassie paused at the bookshop opposite the Hunter's Bar entrance to Endcliffe Park, and peered through the window at this week's display. Children's books – bright and colourful and full of joy. Meg leaned in to look for herself, but Cassie ushered her towards the pedestrian crossing before she had a chance to see.

The park was quiet at ten o'clock on a snowy weekday morning and peopled mostly by women with pushchairs.

'They should rent them out,' Meg said, '. . . babies and pushchairs!'

Cassie laughed. 'Let's get away from them – let's go off-road!'

Beyond the playground, they risked the stepping stones to cross the Porter Brook for the woodland on the far bank. Cassie led them along a high track through bare trees and thorny shrubs and rotting windfall branches. They didn't speak for the first ten minutes, walking in easy silence, frosted leaves crunching with every stride, until they'd crossed Rustlings Road and were making their way along the bridleway through Whitely Woods.

'They've identified the dead girl from Flynn's flat,' Meg said. 'Gemma Jane Grant, eighteen, from Edinburgh.'

Cassie sensed Meg's eyes upon her. She looked straight ahead and kept her stride, acknowledging what she'd just been told with a polite nod.

The Porter Brook, swollen from the previous day's brief thaw, crashed through exposed roots along the banks. Its roar drowned out their footsteps and made conversation impossible. Eventually, the path drifted away from the brook.

'DNA tests show that she was Sarah Flynn's daughter,' Meg said, matter-of-factly.

Cassie toyed with the idea of feigning surprise. But by the time she'd thought it through it was too late to act surprised. Instead, she went for stoney indifference.

Meg continued: 'James Flynn is not the father. He didn't meet Sarah until a few years after the baby was born. She must have been fifteen, Sarah, when she gave birth.'

The path widened, and a middle-aged man in Lycra overtook them on a mountain bike. 'Thank you, ladies!' he called back over his shoulder. There was a note of sarcasm in his voice. Cassie wondered how long he'd been waiting to pass.

'We found a mobile phone,' Meg said, 'at Flynn's place, hidden in the toilet cistern, sealed in a freezer bag.'

'What phone? When?'

'An untraceable pay-as-you-go. Yesterday, during the search.'

Nobody spoke for the next twenty yards.

'Seriously though?' Cassie said at last. 'Flynn decided to hide a mobile phone in the favourite hiding place of every TV villain since the TV cop show was invented. What moron would buy that?'

Meg didn't speak for four or five paces.

Cassie grabbed Meg's hand and squeezed. 'Sorry. I'm frustrated, that's all.'

'Okay,' Meg said. 'It looks like Flynn used this phone to arrange a rendez-vous with Gemma. It's been used to send emails from a Hotmail account in the name of "jflynn1966", and there are text messages too.'

'And you think it's Flynn's? Did it occur to you that it might have been planted by somebody pretending to be Flynn?'

Meg rolled her eyes. 'Of course it did. But Flynn's done a runner, hasn't he, so Foster's going with it.'

Cassie nodded but didn't comment.

'I thought you should know,' Meg said. 'It's yet another link to James Flynn, and now Foster's like a dog with a bone.'

'But what do *you* think, Meg?'

Meg groaned and held her hands up. 'The email address can't be traced back to him. The techies have tried and drawn a blank. So unless they find Flynn's DNA on the phone, there's no proof that it was ever his.'

'And the texts and emails, what do they say?'

Meg cast her eyes about the bare-branched oaks and sycamores, as if scanning for eavesdroppers. 'Well,' she said, looking over her shoulder, 'they tell us Gemma came by coach, overnight, from Edinburgh, and that she was delayed on the M1. They tell us that she arrived in Sheffield at nine in the morning on the day she died, and that Flynn, or *somebody*, ordered a taxi for her, a blue Vauxhall Insignia.'

'And have you . . .' Cassie checked herself. 'Sorry, go on.'

'A stolen blue Vauxhall Insignia turned up, last night, completely burned-out. That same car was picked up by traffic cameras leaving the station at 9:48 a.m. on the Friday in question, presumably with Gemma inside. We tracked it all the way to the Snake Pass. And then all the way back into the city near where it was burned out. We can be pretty sure that it dropped her off at Flynn's place, because we've got the video of her at the end of his drive, and because the timings are right. But we've nothing else. No forensics, and no ID on the driver.'

'And Flynn's alibied for that morning, isn't he? He was in Glossop. There are witnesses, surely, and CCTV.'

'I'm on it, Cassie, but it's far from watertight.'

They had reached Ivy Lane bridge. 'Do you fancy a coffee or something?' Cassie said. 'It'd be nice to sit somewhere warm.'

❧

Forge Dam Café was a large timber shed with uPVC windows and a tin roof. Aesthetically, the building benefited hugely from the thick covering of snow. They served butties, and things that go with chips. Meg had a chip butty ('Because I deserve it!'). Cassie stuck to black coffee ('On account of the size of my arse!').

'Don't be daft,' Meg said, 'I'd love to have a figure like yours.'

Cassie poached a chip from Meg's plate. 'Well, you're going the right way about it.'

'Cassie . . .' Meg finished chewing, wiped her lips with the back of her hand and put her elbows on the table, ' . . . how well do you know Deputy Chief Constable Muxlow?'

'Not very well,' Cassie said. 'He wants to be Chief Constable – somewhere, someday. That's all I know, all I need to know.'

Meg ruffled her hair. 'I think he's controlling our investigation.'

'A Deputy Chief Constable's prerogative, I suppose.' Cassie fixed on Meg, studied her face, her hands, her eyes. Meg was going to say something that she thought she shouldn't.

'I'm sure he's holding something back,' Meg said, 'and then there's all that business about you being taken off the case and put on leave.'

'Muxlow's cautious.' Cassie twisted her mouth and ran a thumbnail along her top lip. 'Like I said, he wants to be a Chief Constable someday. If this case were to collapse because of me, he'd be the one held to account.'

'It's not that, Cassie. It's that he knew about you and Flynn before he could possibly have known about you and Flynn – before you'd even had a first date. Just like he knew that Flynn was missing before he could have known that Flynn was missing. And then there's the trace he put on Flynn's phone: it turns out the location was pinpointed a good half hour before he passed the information to Foster. And the more I think about that, the more I think that he had no intention of passing on the information – not until Foster asked him to authorise a location trace, which left him with no choice. And now there's the problem with the DNA match.'

'What problem?'

'Gemma Grant's DNA was already in the system,' Meg said. 'But why was it cross-checked with Sarah Flynn's DNA? Who would have thought of doing that? No one on the team, I can tell you that for nothing, and certainly not Foster. That leaves Muxlow. And if I ask him what made him think of doing it, he'll just tap his nose and tell me it was intuition – *"fifty years in the job"* – or some such bollocks, that's what he said about tracking Flynn's phone before we even knew the man was missing.'

Meg went back to her chip butty. She licked the ketchup that had dribbled over her fingers before taking another huge bite.

'And your theory?' Cassie said. 'You wouldn't tell me all this if you didn't have some sort of theory to explain it.'

It took Meg a full minute to finish chewing – and Cassie knew that it wasn't just the chip butty that Meg was chewing over; she didn't dare interrupt.

'James Flynn was under surveillance when the girl was murdered,' Meg said, at last. 'And he probably still is. Perhaps it's the National Crime Agency, or Special Branch, or even MI5. Whoever it is, Muxlow must be involved, or at least acting as liaison.' She wiped her mouth with her fingers. 'And another thing: Flynn and Gemma Grant wouldn't have found themselves together in that flat by accident. So either *they*, or someone else, *arranged* it.' She winked. 'Why would Flynn arrange that when he had a hot date lined up with you?'

Cassie put down her coffee and turned it slowly through 360 degrees. 'What if Gemma went looking for him, what if he wasn't expecting her and there was an argument, and, you know . . .' It was far-fetched: killing someone with a heroin overdose is not a spontaneous sort of a crime. And then she remembered that she didn't know for certain that it was a heroin overdose that had killed Gemma. 'What was the cause of death, by the way?'

Meg put down her butty and reached for the ketchup. 'Not the gunshot wound to the back of the head.'

'Gunshot wound?' Cassie leaned forward and lowered her voice. 'What are you talking about Meg, there was no—'

'Historic injury; happened years ago. Miracle she survived, apparently.'

'But how . . .' Cassie began. She pressed her fingertips, still warm from the coffee cup, to her temples. 'Come on, Meg, just tell me what killed her.'

'Heroin overdose,' Meg said, with a sneer. 'And indications that it was forcibly administered. Surprising choice of murder weapon for a man with no record of using drugs. And besides, why would he need a murder weapon? Flynn's the sort of man who could snap you in two with his bare hands. He could have wrung her neck between his thumb and index finger, probably – she was such a tiny little thing. A man like Flynn could have folded her in two, wrapped her body in his coat, tucked her under his arm like a Sunday newspaper, and left the building, waving cheerfully at the other residents as he passed.'

Cassie raised her eyebrows.

'Alright, I'm exaggerating!' Meg said. 'My point is, he could have easily moved her body and disposed of her somewhere she might never be found. His Land Rover was in the car park, remember. Why would he undress her, pose her on the bed, hide all her clothes? Why call the police and hang around for them to arrive and find him holding the proverbial smoking gun? No, whoever killed her wanted her to be found, and wanted her to be found *in that flat*. I've thought it through every which way – it's obvious he's being framed!'

Cassie drew a long breath. 'And since neither me nor Flynn had told anyone that we were meeting at the flat that evening . . .'

'He's under surveillance,' Meg said, with a knowing nod. 'His phone, or his home, or both, must have been bugged somehow. Someone was listening-in when you and he arranged to meet at the flat – it's the only explanation.'

'Okay.' Cassie could see the logic in what Meg was saying; it answered many of the *hows*, and it was the best theory anyone had come up with so far. 'But *why, Meg?*'

Meg closed her eyes and pinched the bridge of her nose. 'I don't know. And it's driving me mad, that's why I called in sick this morning.'

'I thought it was because you broke up with whatshisname.'

'Oh, that too,' Meg said, looking lost in thought. 'And another thing: some solicitor's being dragged up from London this afternoon – a bloke called Smythe-Brown. He's Gemma Grant's next of kin since she has no living relatives. Who traced him? Not me. Not anyone on *our* investigation. Muxlow organised it himself, didn't he. And how did he manage to track down this solicitor guy within minutes of getting Gemma's ID from the lab? Do you see what I mean?'

Cassie watched the last feeble wisps of steam rise from her coffee cup. They faded as they rose, eventually dissipating – along with all the resolutions she'd made that morning – into the rafters.

28

THE TRACK UP to Flynn's house was long and arduous in the snow. But Cassie had a good pair of boots, and the sun was out and the sky was blue. She would take it slowly - think about what she should say to him. Either side of the track, the woods were thick with birch - tall, spindly, leafless. White bark and snowy ground conspired to make the woods appear transparent. Convinced, for a moment, that she might be able to see all the way through to Flynn's Barn, Cassie strained to focus on what lay beyond ever more distant trees. She gave up when her eyes began to ache. There would always be too many trees to see past, Cassie conceded. Always.

Now, she began to hope that Flynn wouldn't be in. Now, she wished the track longer than she remembered it - endless, in fact.

There came the low rumble of a diesel engine: a Land Rover with over-sized tyres heading back towards the Snake Pass, Flynn's unmistakeable bulk in the driver's seat, and a passenger beside him. The car slowed to a crawl. Flynn wound the window down a couple of inches and called out, 'Back in ten minutes.' Cassie felt her guts twist into a knot. She tried to see past him, tried to get a look at the passenger, but Flynn was not an easy man to see past.

❧

Angus was sitting at Flynn's dining table with his laptop.

'What the hell are *you* doing here?' Cassie said. 'And why's Flynn still here? Hasn't he told you the police are after him for three more murders?'

'Yes.' Angus shrugged. 'But they've been here already, haven't they? Been and gone.' He kept his eyes low, squeezing his palms between his thighs. 'And if you're so surprised to find him here, why did you come in the first place?'

Cassie stared at him but didn't speak.

'Look, Cassie,' Angus said, 'I have no idea what to do next.'

Cassie knew exactly what *she* should do next. Her fingers closed round the phone in her coat pocket. She should ring Meg and tell her where Flynn was, that's what she should do.

But she didn't.

The stove was blazing. She took off her coat . . . and then her scarf . . . and then her gloves – to give herself something to do, and time to think, as much as to make herself comfortable – and arranged them, fussily, on the coat pegs.

'I didn't see your car at the pub,' she said eventually.

Angus didn't look up. 'You wouldn't have recognised it. I've got a new one, picked it up this morning.'

'You bought yourself a new car!' Cassie folded her arms. 'Christ, Angus. And there was me thinking you'd have other things on your mind, like, hmmm, let me think, oh yes: your best friend is wanted for four murders. Oh, and wasn't there something else? Hmmm, what was it? Oh yes, he's just found out that you were shagging his wife.'

Angus closed his computer. 'I ordered the car months ago. And the dealer had a buyer lined up for my trade-in – I didn't want to let anyone down.'

'Didn't want to let anyone down!' Cassie forced a laugh. 'What's that, a new year's resolution?'

He hung his head and closed his eyes.

In spite of the resolutions *she'd* made that morning, Cassie found herself unable to forgive Angus. He had a wife. He had children. His betrayal was unpardonable. She hated him.

'Go on then,' she said. 'Start explaining.'

Angus didn't look up. 'Flynn and I have drawn a line under the whole thing. It's forgotten.'

'Not by *me*, Angus.' Cassie puffed out her cheeks and shook her head. 'How will I ever be able to sit at a table with Lizzie, knowing what I know?'

The mention of his wife had the impact Cassie wanted. He looked up like a frightened child. 'Please, Cassie. You wouldn't?'

'And if Lizzie were shagging Flynn? Would you want me to keep *that* from *you*?'

'Cassie, please!' Angus looked on the verge of tears, which was not what she'd intended. Or maybe it was.

'But it won't be a problem,' she said. 'I shan't have to look Lizzie in the eye ever again because I'm leaving Sheffield and moving back to London.'

Angus rubbed his eyes. 'What, because of me?'

'Don't flatter yourself!'

The phone rang. They both turned, let it ring, sat it out.

'Who was in the car with Flynn?' Cassie pulled out a chair, noisily, and sat down.

'A solicitor. Smythe-Brown. I was about to send you an email.'

'And?'

'Cassie, we'*ll* be all right, won't we, you and me? I know you're angry now, but . . .'

Cassie didn't answer. Mostly she was angry with herself: angry for being so pleased that Sarah Flynn had been exposed, pleased that Sarah Flynn had turned out to be a complete and utter bitch. She turned away from Angus and towards the stove. She stared deep into its furious flames.

'Sarah was using me,' Angus said. 'I made a mistake.'

Cassie scoffed. 'Oh right! So if she hadn't been *using you* it would have been all right, would it? It wouldn't have been a mistake?'

'That's not what I meant.' His hands dropped back onto his lap.

She let him stew.

Eventually, Angus spoke: 'You and Marco, Flynn and Sarah, and Lizzie too . . . you were all so bloody good looking. I saw the way people looked at you, all of you. Nobody ever looked at me that way, not even Lizzie. We're all a bit vain, aren't we – we all want to be fancied. Well, Sarah knew exactly how to play me. She flattered me.' Angus glanced up at Cassie.

Cassie looked away.

'It doesn't matter,' Angus said. 'It was wrong. I knew it was wrong, but I couldn't resist.'

'But *why?*' she asked, without looking up.

'Like I said. Honestly, I just couldn't resist.'

'No, Angus. I know why *you* did it, you complete shit. Why did *she* do it?'

A log stirred in the stove and tumbled against the glass in a flurry of sparks. Angus went over to deal with it.

Cassie waited.

'She knew,' Angus said. 'I don't know how, but she knew . . .' He closed the stove door, rehung the tongues and the poker, and sat cross legged in front of the hearth. 'She knew I had access to stuff. She asked me to pull the records on some people she was looking into. I told her I wouldn't do it, told her it could be traced. She said someone as clever as me would find a way.'

'Who?' Cassie said. 'Whose records did she want to see?'

Angus shook his head. 'I can't remember the names.'

Cassie pressed her fingers to her temples and looked away.

Angus got up and returned to his place at the table. 'It didn't matter in the end,' he said. 'This happened the day before she died.'

'And *would* you have done it for her?' Cassie asked. 'If she hadn't died, would you have given her what she wanted?'

Angus leaned back and folded his arms. 'Yes, Cassie, I probably would. Like I said, I couldn't resist her.' He looked away. 'And still I hate her, even now that she's dead. Why? Because if she came to me tomorrow, came to me to seduce me, after all I've been through, knowing everything I know, I'm still not sure that I'd be able to resist.'

Cassie couldn't bring herself to look at him. She was disgusted by his weakness. And then she thought of all those battered women who went back to their husbands and partners. That was different, of course. Those women weren't weak; they were controlled and coerced and abused. No, Angus wasn't controlled or coerced – he just couldn't keep his dick in his trousers.

'The day before she died,' Angus went on, 'Sarah came round to my house, on some pretext or other. It was awful. We were all in the kitchen and she started joking with Lizzie about some celebrity's affair that was all over the red tops. She was taunting me, threatening me, reminding me of the power she had over me. She was a bully. I'd been a fool, of course I had. I'd always known what she was like, but I still let her seduce me. I'm utterly ashamed, Cassie. If you want to punish me more, if it makes you feel better, there's nothing I can do to stop you. But please don't punish Lizzie and the kids.'

Cassie rubbed her forehead with the heel of her hand. 'Fuck you, Angus. How dare you make this about me?'

'No,' Angus said. 'I'm not . . . I . . . I'm trying to . . .' He covered his face with his hands. 'I'm just desperate, Cassie.'

'Really!' Cassie threw her head back and forced an unconvincing laugh.

Angus got up, stood for a while – rocking on his heels and fidgeting like a child waiting for permission to leave the dinner table – then sat down again.

Cassie collected herself. Now was not the time for this discussion. And anyway, this whole business still didn't make sense to her. 'Are you trying to tell me that Sarah slept with you so that she could blackmail you?' she said. 'Because that sounds ridiculous – *she* had as much to lose as you. She might have been a complete bitch, but everyone agrees that she doted on Flynn.'

'In her own way, yes.' Angus thought for a moment. 'But that didn't stop her doing whatever it took to get what she wanted. And I'm sure Flynn knew exactly what she was capable of.'

'What are you saying? You think he'd have forgiven her?'

'Probably.' Angus shrugged.

Cassie shook her head. She didn't know what to believe anymore. 'Just give me the names, Angus,' she said. 'Whose records was she after?'

A gust of wind shrieked through the trees and blew a broken branch against the window. They both flinched.

'Weather's breaking,' Angus said. 'More snow to come, I think.'

Cassie brushed her hair behind her ears. 'You'd shag *me* wouldn't you, if you got half a chance? If I got too drunk, or if you found me miserable and vulnerable and a little too desperate for attention?'

'That's not fair!' Angus stood up, turned his back on her, folded his arms.

She put her hands on her hips. 'Wouldn't you?'

She watched his reflection in the window.

'You have a cruel streak in you, Cassie,' Angus said. Sometimes you remind me of her, remind me of Sarah. Maybe that's what attracts Flynn.'

'Well, I know exactly what attracts *you*, don't I.' Cassie could feel the veins in her temple throbbing. 'Maybe Lizzie knows too. Maybe that's why she's run off to her mother's. Maybe I should phone her. Maybe—'

'Vincent and Michael Bolan,' Angus said. 'That's who Sarah

was interested in. Just a couple of thugs from Manchester as far as I could make out. Both dead. Died years ago – 1998, I think. According to the papers the Bolan brothers got into a fight over a woman and ended up shooting each other dead. Case closed.'

The squeak and rumble of Flynn's Land Rover pulling up outside startled them both.

❧

'Has he told you?'

There was something about Flynn's voice that made Cassie uncomfortable. No more the placid, deferential, soft-spoken man – here was a Flynn who knew he was the hardest kid in the playground. Aggression made the big man bigger. Fear (and there was no mistaking the fear etched across that handsome face) . . . fear made him intimidating.

'Yes,' Cassie said. 'Unbelievable! All forgiven and forgotten. Very mature. Very sensible. Personally, I—'

'No!' Flynn roared. He pulled off his coat, yanked it over a peg, and rounded on Angus.

'I haven't told her yet,' Angus said.

Flynn started up the spiral staircase but paused after a couple of steps. His face softened. 'I need a shower and a change of clothes,' he said. 'I'm sorry I shouted, but . . .' He tapped the handrail, thoughtfully, then trudged upstairs.

Cassie turned to Angus, eyes narrow.

'He probably thought you were here to arrest him,' Angus said.

'Why?' she snapped. 'And what is it you haven't told me yet?'

Angus sat down. 'The man you saw in the Land Rover was Smythe-Brown, a solicitor from London. Sarah's solicitor, and now Flynn's solicitor.'

'Okay,' Cassie said stiffly. 'Well, it's good that he has a solicitor.'

Angus took a deep breath. 'You know you said the police

couldn't build much of a case against Flynn because they didn't have a motive?'

The uncanny silence of the barn, which Cassie hadn't noticed until now, was suddenly broken by the sound of the shower upstairs, and a very noisy extractor fan.

'Yes,' she said.

'Well, very soon they'll have one.' Angus frowned and pressed his palms together. 'Sarah had a trust fund. It paid her a very generous allowance until she turned twenty-one. After that she got complete control of the capital. On her twenty-first birthday she took half for herself and put the other half into a trust fund for her daughter. Back then she didn't know where Gemma was – didn't even know what name she'd taken after the adoption – but all that had changed by the time she made her most recent will, which makes James Flynn sole trustee of Gemma Grant's trust fund in the event of Sarah's death.'

Cassie's eyes opened wide. She sat down. 'So he knew! Flynn knew. The bastard knew exactly who Gemma was. He's played us like idiots, Angus.'

'No, Cassie! No.'

Cassie covered her face with her hands. 'I'm a fool, Angus. A bloody fool.' She looked up at him. 'Why did you talk me into all this.'

'He didn't know!' Angus took her hands and squeezed them gently. 'Flynn knew only what Sarah's solicitor told him after probate – that Gemma Grant was family, that Sarah was sole trustee of her trust fund, and that the job of trustee passed to him upon Sarah's death. Flynn never met the girl, he didn't even know she existed until after Sarah died, and he certainly didn't know she was Sarah's daughter.'

'But how could he not have met her, if he was the trustee?' Cassie became aware that Angus was holding her hand across the table. She pulled away and marched over to the stove. The glass glowed amber. Flames that once bobbed and darted like merry dancers had merged into a solid sheet of angry fire. 'And I don't see why this gives him a motive to kill Gemma Grant', she said, 'unless you're telling me he's been stealing money from the trust fund.'

'No, of course not,' Angus said. 'Smythe-Brown never managed to trace Gemma, and the trust fund hasn't been touched by anyone.'

'So where's the motive?'

Upstairs, the shower and the extractor fan went quiet. There were footsteps on the mezzanine and the sound of a drawer being opened and closed. Angus lowered his voice to a whisper. 'Look, Sarah died broke. God knows what happened to all her money – she left Flynn with nothing but the barn and a pile of debts. But when Gemma's trust fund is wound up, Flynn will inherit the lot – not far short of five million pounds.'

29

A ROOM AT the Edinburgh Sheraton was an extravagance – but what a view! Frosty rooftops, snow-covered lawns, the floodlit castle on the hill. Cassie leaned on the windowsill and gazed out across the city. She'd glimpsed a side of Flynn that she'd never before encountered. She'd seen him cornered, afraid, aggressive. She'd seen the heave of his chest, the lupine snarl, a flash of magenta in those oh-so-blue eyes. She'd seen all this, and she couldn't unsee it.

What did it mean? Nothing, probably. He might have grown up in the midst of violence, but it didn't have to follow that he was a violent man.

People can change, of course they can. But Cassie couldn't think of anyone who had.

And then there was Angus and Sarah Flynn! The day before she died, Sarah had turned up at Angus's house and all but threatened to expose their affair to his wife. Back then, Cassie had her suspicions about Sarah's death. But, back then, there was no clear evidence of foul play, and no suspect, and no motive.

Now she had a suspect and a motive. But *Angus?* Really? And why, two years after Sarah's death, had someone sent a video of Angus and Sarah, shagging, to Flynn?

There were two possibilities. The first, was to implicate Angus in the death of Sarah Flynn. But why implicate a man two years after the fact? The second possibility was that someone wanted to drive a wedge between Angus and Flynn. But again, why? To stop Angus digging into Sarah's past? What on earth was he likely to uncover?

Meg's conspiracy theory was outrageously speculative, but Cassie couldn't shake the idea. And it was Angus who gave it credibility – Angus and his links to the Security Services. According to Angus, Sarah Flynn had seduced him to get hold of the files MI5 had on the Bolan brothers, a pair of long dead Manchester gangsters. But he couldn't explain why MI5 should have any interest in a pair of petty criminals. According to Stella Middlewood at the *Manchester Evening News*, Sarah met with her only hours before she died to find out about Scott Deakin. And Scott Deakin was a contemporary of the Bolan brothers in gangland Manchester. And Scott Deakin led straight back to Flynn.

The Parkgate School massacre, according to the *Sheffield Star* website, was a gang related incident that left three dead, including Sean Mulligan. Probably true. There was, of course, no mention that the police had only discovered the carnage because they were tracking Flynn's mobile phone. Could the location of Flynn's phone be pure coincidence? Had Flynn's phone been stolen only to end up in the wrong place at the wrong time? Perhaps, but even if the phone had found its way there without its owner, there was certainly a link between Flynn and Sean Mulligan – according to Flynn's phone records, according to Angus.

Why had she stormed out of Flynn's place without asking all these questions? What had she been afraid of? Afraid of Angus? Afraid of Flynn? Or just afraid of the answers? Cassie pressed her face against the cold window and closed her eyes. She was getting nowhere.

Bed.

❧

Morning had not quite broken when Cassie's taxi drew up outside the grand Georgian terrace that housed Leith police station.

Sergeant Grierson darted from desk to filing cabinet to whiteboard, long blonde hair swishing so that it was difficult to see her eyes. She was sorting, searching, organising. Hers was a neglected role, and under-resourced, so she really didn't have time to . . .

Cassie nodded or shook her head as befitted each grievance.

'I barely have time to think,' Grierson said as she searched her desk (awash with scattered files and papers) and scanned the bezel of her computer screen (plastered with Post-it notes). 'If I'm not preparing for court, I'm writing reports. They gave me two constables, but I ask you, what am I supposed to do with that pair of giggling girlies? They've no experience of juveniles, you know. Some bright spark upstairs must have decided that it takes juveniles to deal with juveniles. I've no time to train them, have I – so I still end up doing everything myself, while that pair gawp like idiots.'

Beyond the glass partition, two serious looking young women were working silently at their computers. They faced each other across a tidy desk, each sneaking the occasional peek into their sergeant's office.

'I think that's everything,' Grierson said to herself, bundling an armful of files and ring binders into a large shopping bag. 'Need to drop these off and brief the barrister. Back in half an hour, if you've time to wait, though how anyone would have time to sit around waiting for half an hour I don't know. Perhaps it's different in Yorkshire.' She looked at her watch and grimaced. 'Right,' she said, kicking open the door to the adjoining office. 'Grace, you'll have to drive me to court, I'll not have time to park.' Grace nodded, grabbed her handbag, and made for the coat stand in the corner. Grierson groaned. 'Come on, lassie, you'll not be needing your coat!'

Grace's colleague was dark haired and dark eyed, and she looked pleased when Cassie sat herself at Grace's desk.

'My name's Cassie. I've come up from Sheffield.' She offered her hand.

The young woman shook it enthusiastically. 'PC Helen Burley,' she said. 'Pleasure to meet you, DI May.'

Cassie smiled. 'So I *was* expected.'

'Oh yes, ma'am. Sergeant Grierson mustn't have had time to check the diary this morning . . . or yesterday afternoon.'

'Busy woman!'

Helen nodded, uncertainly. 'You're here about Gemma Grant?'

'Yes.'

There was something reassuring about Helen: she reminded Cassie a little of Meg; she had the air of being on top of things.

Helen pulled a folder from the middle tier of her stacker tray. 'I dug this out yesterday when we got the call from Detective Superintendent James. He asked us to do everything we could to help, spoke very highly of you.'

Cassie felt herself blush. 'He was my boss when we worked down in London, years ago. I rang him to ask for his help on a death I'm looking into. I wasn't sure he'd even remember me.'

Helen raised a sceptical eyebrow. 'Oh, he remembered you all right, ma'am.'

'*Cassie*, please. I hate all that *ma'am* business. So, what do you have for me?'

'Not much, I'm afraid. Is it true the poor girl was murdered?'

'Yes,' Cassie said. 'And we know precious little about her, that's why I'm here.'

'Punter, was it?'

'Punter?'

'Client, you know . . .'

Cassie's eyes narrowed.

Helen looked confused. 'I thought you'd be from the Child Sexual Exploitation Unit. With all that trouble in Rotherham, and Gemma's history, I just assumed . . .'

'No, I . . .'

It had never occurred to Cassie that Gemma might have worked as a prostitute. This changed everything – opened up new possibilities, new motives, new scenarios. What sort of men used prostitutes? Men who saw women as sex objects? Men with low self-esteem? Men with confidence issues? Dirty old men who wanted sex with young women? Married men looking for easy thrills? Lonely men? Lonely men whose wives had died? Lonely men like Flynn? Suddenly, Gemma's likeness to Sarah took on new significance.

'There was nothing on her record about soliciting or prostitution,' Cassie said. 'As far as I knew she was only in the system because she was convicted of shoplifting.'

Helen nodded. 'That's right. Everything else on her file is just background information, informal local intelligence. She was under sixteen so if there'd been anything solid we'd have gone after the punters for unlawful sex. But there never was.' Helen opened the file, which contained little more than a photograph of the girl and a bundle of handwritten notes. 'She was moved-on a dozen or so times, from bars in posh hotels. It was obvious what she was up to – but there was never any firm evidence. Seems to have happened regularly over a period of about four months, then nothing. No record of her since she was last arrested two and half years ago. She spent a night in the cells but wasn't charged.'

Helen slid an envelope across the desk. 'I made a copy for you. I'm sorry there isn't more to go on.'

'Thanks,' Cassie said. 'You said she spent a night in the cells. What was she arrested for?'

Helen flicked through her file. 'Oh, yes, I see. She was ID'd in a pub. Random check. We do a sweep every few months to keep licensees on their toes. She was arrested for assault when she threw red wine in an officer's face. But like I said, she was never charged.'

At the bottom of the pile of photocopies that Cassie pulled

from the envelope was a list of the contents of Gemma's handbag, nothing unusual until the last item: a business card for David Roland, of David Roland Associates, Sheffield. 'Interesting,' Cassie said showing the entry to Helen.

Helen was suddenly animated. 'Yes, I noticed the Sheffield connection too. So last night I googled David Roland Associates. They're a firm of private investigators. That's got to be a good lead, surely.'

'Hmmm,' Cassie said. 'Could well be.'

Morning light broke through the Edinburgh cloud, casting stripes across the far wall.

Helen sat back in her chair and brushed out the creases in her skirt.

'Doesn't anyone do anything for these girls?' Cassie asked, staring at a photograph of Gemma stapled to the inside cover of her file.

Helen shook her head. 'By the time we have anything to do with them it's too late. By then we're the enemy.'

'Yes, I suppose so.'

'And,' Helen went on, 'it pisses me off when people blame the girls. As if a fifteen-year-old is going to come up with the idea of going on the game all by herself! No, these girls are groomed. They're flattered and given attention – affection even – probably for the first time in their sad little lives. Then it's drink, then it's drugs, then they have to earn their keep, then there's no way out.'

Cassie looked up. 'And you think it was like that for Gemma?'

'Gemma was a bit different,' Helen said. 'She was educated, articulate, dressed older than her age.'

'So you met her?' Cassie tapped the picture of Gemma with her index finger.

Helen shook her head. 'Before my time. But yesterday, out of curiosity, I spoke to her social worker. Apparently, Gemma wasn't like the other girls: posh background, you see – knew how to present herself as the sophisticated young woman about town.'

'She'd have had no idea,' Cassie said. 'You think you know everything when you're fifteen.'

'Aye,' Helen said ruefully, 'you do indeed. By the way, I arranged for you to meet the social worker. Did you get the message?'

It was the venetian blinds at the window, or perhaps the angry fifteen-year-old in the photograph, that took Cassie back to the faded front room at her old house in Epping Forest, back to her fifteenth birthday.

Mum was asleep on the sofa as usual. When she wasn't asleep, she was hunched over photograph albums, or watching black and white movies, or reading old letters.

Outside, tapping at the window and peering through the blinds, stood her father. She would ignore him as she always did. Or perhaps, if he lingered too long, tell him to fuck off back to his new family.

He would telephone, later, as he always did. He would say that he loved her and that she could have a better life with him (as if one can choose one's life!). Sometimes she would put the phone down immediately she knew it was him; sometimes she would listen a while, crying silent tears. He had made his choice, and she had made hers. And if *he* wasn't prepared to live up to his responsibilities, then *she* would take them on. What right did he have to think he could have it both ways? What right did he have to pick and choose which parts of his family he would keep, and which he would replace?

Sometimes she felt sorry for him, pitied him even. Always, she missed him. But she wouldn't speak to him. He was weak and cowardly and selfish. He had done a wrong thing – he'd left them – and Cassie didn't have it in her to forgive him.

As she looked at that picture of a fifteen-year-old Gemma Grant, red-lipped and golden-eyed and sneering at life, Cassie began to sense her father's pain.

'DI May,' Helen said, 'are you okay?'

Cassie sat up straight. 'Sorry, just trying to get my head round everything.'

'But you got my message about the meeting I fixed up with that social worker?'

'Yes, yes. Thank you. Thank you for everything.'

'No problem, ma'am. Glad I could help, only . . .' Helen looked a bit sheepish.

'Yes, Helen.'

'I wouldn't want to get anyone into trouble or anything.'

'Go on – don't worry about that.'

'Only, I went through this file with one of your colleagues a couple of years ago. I remember it well because it was my first day on the job here.' Helen tapped her copy of the file. 'I made a note – 22 September 2011.'

Cassie's eye's narrowed. 'That was before I moved up to Sheffield. Who was it?'

Helen looked down at her notes. 'Detective Chief Inspector Charlie Foster.'

'Charlie Foster? Why was he interested in Gemma?'

'I don't know really. But it was a *she*, not a *he*. Definitely a woman. She rang the office looking for background information on Gemma Grant.'

'A woman? A *woman* called Charlie Foster?'

'Yes. I expect she was a *Charlotte*. Sounded like a Charlotte all right, spoke with a plum in her mouth. Really posh, I remember that. Graduate fast-track, I expect. She'll probably be Head of the Met before I make Sergeant.'

'Sarah *bloody* Flynn,' Cassie said under her breath.

Helen cupped her ear. 'Sorry, ma'am?'

'Before my time,' Cassie said. 'I didn't start in Sheffield until the December.'

30

EDINBURGH WAS A beautiful city indeed: in the half-hour it took to walk to the bar where she was to meet Céline Douglas, Gemma's social worker, Cassie decided to up sticks and move there. Café des Potes, a swanky basement bar, trod a fine line between elegance and ostentation, between authenticity and pastiche, between right and wrong. In a thousand other places it would have been *wrong*, but in the grandest of Georgian buildings, in the grandest of Georgian towns, it was *right*.

The place was empty except for a little old lady perched on a sofa with her knitting. She had a half-formed baby-grow on her lap and a bag of wool by her feet.

Cassie ordered a glass of Pinot Grigio and installed herself in a comfy wingback at the table furthest from the bar. She checked her phone: a load of junk, which she deleted, and another message from Angus, which she couldn't face reading but didn't delete.

The old lady with the knitting was peering at her over her reading glasses. Cassie forced a brief smile then turned back to her phone. When she looked up again, the old lady was still staring. 'Are you the Detective Inspector?' she said in a loud whisper.

Cassie grabbed her wine and went over. 'Mrs Douglas?' she asked.

The old lady nodded and waved her to the chair opposite.

Cassie offered her hand.

Mrs Douglas had surprisingly strong fingers. 'It's Céline, dear,' she said. 'Do sit down.'

Cassie arranged her coat over the back of the chair and sat down. The old lady wrapped the half-knitted baby grow around her needles and put it into the bag by her feet

'I believe you've come up from England?' Mrs Douglas said, in the sort of plummy Edinburgh accent that, for Cassie, always brought to mind Miss Jean Brodie.

'Sheffield, yes.'

'Is that where poor Gemma ended her days?' Mrs Douglas removed her reading glasses, polished them with the end of a paisley-print scarf, and looked at Cassie earnestly.

The scarf was silk, Cassie noted, as was her blouse. She wore a velvet jacket (lush, deep purple) and grey tweed skirt. All immaculate. Not just clean – new.

'Yes,' Cassie said, suddenly aware that she was staring. 'I'm afraid so.'

Mrs Douglas's hair was white, lightly permed, and, like everything else about the woman, pristine. It was difficult to divine the woman's age: her face was heavily wrinkled but bursting with energy, her hazel eyes shone clear.

'I'm ninety-two, dear,' Mrs Douglas said, waving at the barman.

'Really! Oh, no, I—'

'You were expecting a girl in her twenties or thirties. Of course you were: most of us mentors are ever so young.' A waiter was standing over them, with his order pad, before Cassie had a chance to answer. 'The usual please, Darren,' the old lady said.

Darren nodded and left them.

'Mentor?' Cassie said. 'I thought you were her social worker.'

'No, dear, I'm a volunteer. I try to help girls who've chosen the wrong path.'

It was an odd way of putting it, Cassie thought, and this old lady was certainly an odd choice of mentor for teenage prostitutes. 'Right,' she said, 'I see.'

Mrs Douglas cast a knowing look across the table. 'I'm always told that offering your body to men for financial reward is not a *choice* but an *act of desperation.* Do you think me prudish and ignorant, Detective Inspector? Or just old fashioned, perhaps?'

'Of course not,' Cassie said. 'Not at all.'

Mrs Douglas smiled, leaned over the table, and patted Cassie's hand. 'I'm teasing you, dear. You can get away with that sort of thing my age?'

'I'm investigating a murder, Mrs Douglas, I—'

Darren slid a tray onto the table. He set down a tall glass containing a small measure of pastis and a long spoon, a jug of water, a paper napkin folded into a fan, and a bowl of peanuts. He arranged all this in front of Mrs Douglas with some ceremony.

'An occasional indulgence.' Mrs Douglas smiled a *thank you* at Darren. 'Reminds me of my youth. Help yourself to the peanuts.'

Cassie shook her head, grabbed her wine, took a gulp. 'Gemma Grant?' she said, with what she hoped was some authority.

'Poor girl.' Mrs Douglas sighed, topped up her glass with water from the jug, and stirred it with the long spoon.

'Yes, I—'

'You look troubled, my dear,' Mrs Douglas said. 'You remind me of myself at your age: thoroughly hacked off with the world. But I'd been through the war. What have you been through?' She looked at Cassie mischievously and dabbed her lips with the napkin.

'Can we talk about Gemma Grant, please?' Cassie fixed on the old lady. 'I need to know something about her life in Edinburgh, and why she came to Sheffield. She seems to have slipped off the social services radar two and a half years ago. Her foster parents reported her missing at the time. But for Gemma, running away from home was a regular thing. So . . .'

'So nobody wasted any time looking for her?' Mrs Douglas sighed. 'It's not unusual. Most of them find their way to London, I think. Running away from something or somebody. London seems a world away. Streets paved with gold and all that. Are you from London, Detective Inspector?'

'Gemma Grant,' Cassie said, firmly. 'What was *her* plan?'

'I'm not sure she had one, dear. Still reeling, you see – she'd been through a lot.' Mrs Douglas scooped a handful of peanuts and began eating them, one at a time, chewing slowly.

It seemed that the old lady was enjoying the interview and had no intention of being hurried. Cassie decided to indulge her; she sank back into her chair, sipped her wine, and waited.

'An only child, poor Gemma,' Mrs Douglas said. 'Very well-to-do parents. Lived in a huge house in Barnton. Private school, ponies, wintered in St Moritz, summered in St Tropez – you know the sort of thing. When she was thirteen her father went bankrupt after some sort of hedge fund fraud. He knew he was destined for a long spell in prison, knew that his family would be destitute, so he shot his daughter, then his wife, and then himself. By some miracle Gemma survived. She had no other family, so she ended up in foster care.'

Cassie puffed out her cheeks. 'Bloody Hell!'

Mrs Douglas took the napkin and dusted her fingers. 'Gemma didn't take to her new school. The families who took her in did their best, even *she* admitted that. But they were ordinary working people and, well, you know . . .' She stirred her pastis before taking a long sip and another handful of peanuts.

Cassie waited. She was tempted by the peanuts but consoled herself with the wine.

Mrs Douglas frowned. 'I know it's not done to speak ill of the dead, but I really didn't take to the girl. There was something hard about her, and she was a terrible snob. That's why she didn't stick with any of the families she was placed with. Of course, it would have been difficult for her, adjusting to a very different way of life, on top of everything else. And she'd doted on her father. That sort of girl usually does.'

What Mrs Douglas meant by 'that sort of girl' wasn't clear, but Cassie decided not to ask. 'Isn't it a bit odd that a girl like that should turn to prostitution?'

'*Prostitution!*' Mrs Douglas sucked in her cheeks and shook her head. That's a bit strong! Girls like Gemma have used men to improve their situation for centuries. The aristocracy would have interbred themselves into oblivion if there weren't girls like Gemma to shake up the gene pool once in a while.'

'I don't think that's quite the same thing.'

The old lady smiled and picked up her glass. 'Gemma was attracted to middle aged men: men her father's age. I'm sure psychiatrists have a fancy name for it, and fancy explanations, but it was real enough to her. They had to be handsome, well spoken, and intelligent. She'd tell them she was a second-year medical student, so there could be no concern that she was under age. She was articulate, confident, beautiful, well presented, so she easily passed for nineteen or twenty.

'If they succumbed to her seduction too easily, or if they tried it on themselves, she'd drop them like a stone and move on. No, for Gemma it was all about conquest. It was about turning the tables. It was about having powerful men, who wouldn't ordinarily fall for a teenage girl – no matter how pretty, no matter how clever – fall for *her*. It was about having them eating out of her hand. Ultimately, she was hoping to find a husband – "a keeper", was how she put it.

'I told her she'd read too much Jane Austen. I told her that these days there are other ways for a clever girl to make her way in the world. She said there was no way was she going spend years slaving in an office for what a rich man could give her tomorrow. She told me she'd learned everything she needed to know about men from pornographic films on the internet.'

Cassie blew a long breath.

Mrs Douglas sighed lengthily. 'The point is, Inspector, Gemma

Grant was not a prostitute – or a pornographer, for that matter – whatever the social services reports might say. Of course, she'd spin every sort of yarn to get money out of these men afterwards. Rent arrears was the usual story: she'd claim her landlord was going to change the locks if she couldn't find £500 by the end of the day. But for her that was about testing them, and about testing her power over them. If they said no: well, at least she'd got a nice meal out of it, and champagne, and she'd got to stay in a posh hotel.'

'So . . .' Cassie was beginning to realise that things were not quite as straightforward as she'd imagined. She rolled her wine glass between her fingers before taking a sip, wondering who on earth would think Céline Douglas a suitable mentor for young girls like Gemma Grant. Well, not girls like Gemma Grant: ordinary girls from deprived backgrounds who turned tricks to pay for their next fix.

'I was terrified the first time,' the old lady said. 'A virgin, too. But it was the easiest way – the only way. Of course, they never mentioned it during training – not in so many words. But once I got out there, it was obvious what they'd expected all along. If only they'd shown *me* a few pornographic films, at least I'd have had some notion of what . . . but they didn't . . . so . . .' The old lady gazed wistfully up at the ceiling.

It was not the moment to interrupt. Cassie took another sip of wine, a small one since her glass was very nearly empty.

Mrs Douglas was watching her, looking for some sort of reaction.

Cassie didn't oblige.

'My mother tongue is French, you see,' Mrs Douglas said. 'I lived in Paris until I was fourteen, when my father took a post here, at the University in Edinburgh.' She laughed and took another sip of pastis. 'This takes me back though.' She raised her glass. 'A little taste of the old country!'

Cassie nodded and raised her own. 'To the old country, is it?'

'Good lord, no! Let's drink to bonnie Scotland, dear!'

Cassie managed a smile.

'Anyway,' Mrs Douglas put down her glass and leaned in. 'The SOE were on the lookout for French speakers to train up as agents to work in occupied France and Belgium. Philip, my fiancé, was serving in the orient so I thought I should do my bit too. I was young and naïve – not as young as Gemma, of course, I'd have been nineteen in forty-three, but back then we girls knew very little about sex. I played exactly the same game, though: act the innocent, fawn over an older man, let him buy you drinks, let him seduce you, then, in the morning, turn on the waterworks and tell him that your landlord is threatening to throw you out on the street. Gemma went for businessmen; my first mark was a German officer in the army logistics corps. And while Gemma was after money, I was after intelligence. I'd tire him out, kiss him goodnight, and spend all night copying-out whatever he had in his briefcase. Not that easy when your German isn't so good!'

Cassie didn't know what to say. 'Very brave,' was all she managed. And then, 'I don't know if I could've done that.'

'It was the war.' Mrs Douglas waved her hand dismissively. 'You can't be expected to understand. But you'd have done the same in my situation. I'm sure you would.'

Cassie raised her eyebrows. 'And if you'd been caught?'

'Oh I *did* get caught, dear! One night he woke up and caught me red-handed.'

'And?'

'I shot him, point-blank, through the heart.'

Cassie winced; she couldn't help herself.

'So yes, dear. I'm a murderer as well as a whore.'

'Not a murderer, surely,' Cassie said. 'It was war.'

'Still a whore, though, eh?'

'No. There was a cause. You . . . you made a sacrifice.'

'I made a choice, dear. Simple as that.' Mrs Douglas's sharp hazel eyes dropped for the first time during the interview. She studied her bag of knitting for a moment, then stirred her pastis and took a sip. 'The truth is, he would never have turned me in. He loved me, you see. He'd even talked about eloping to Switzerland. I think I did it out of spite.'

'You couldn't have been sure what he would do. I think you're being hard on yourself.'

'And if *he* had been a British Officer, and *I* some Mata Hari? Would you, a Detective Inspector in 1944, have seen it quite the same way?'

Cassie tried to imagine.

'Do you see, Inspector?'

Cassie knew she was being toyed with; she drained her wine glass. 'When did you last see Gemma Grant?'

'July 2011,' Mrs Douglas said, in a matter-of-fact way. 'She told me she'd be leaving Edinburgh for good.'

'Where was she going?'

'They usually go to London.'

Maybe, Cassie thought, but maybe Gemma went somewhere else. Two things pointed to Sheffield rather than London. The first was Gemma's mother, Sarah Flynn, posing as a police officer to solicit information from the local constabulary; the second was the business card found amongst Gemma's possessions when she was last arrested: David Roland Associates. But if Gemma had gone to Sheffield, where would she have stayed? Not with Sarah, surely, or Flynn would have known about her – if Flynn was telling the truth.

Of course he was telling the truth. Sarah must have organised somewhere else for her to stay. But what happened after Sarah died? Where had Gemma been for the last two years? Why hadn't she come forward? And why hadn't she claimed her trust fund? Perhaps Sarah hadn't told her about it.

So many questions. Cassie closed her notebook and stood to leave. 'Thank you, Mrs Douglas.'

The old lady fixed on her with uncommonly clear eyes. 'You, my dear, strike me as the sort of person that people trust.'

Cassie didn't know what to say. She reached for her scarf.

'Can't be easy, then,' Mrs Douglas added, 'not being able to trust them back. Is that why you haven't been entirely honest with me?'

Cassie said nothing and got on with the business of looping her scarf.

'I know you've been taken off the Gemma Grant case, Detective Inspector.' Mrs Douglas reached into her knitting bag and pulled out an iPad. 'I did my research; I made a few calls. It's always useful to have people you can call.'

'I might be on leave Mrs Douglas, but . . .' Cassie found herself unable to finish the sentence.

The old lady folded her arms and cocked her head to one side. Her eyes were wide and accusing and scornful and knowing.

It knocked the wind out of Cassie. She sat back down.

Mrs Douglas unfolded her arms, reached for her pastis, and held it under her nose for a moment. 'When I got back from France in one piece, I thought I'd escaped. But you can't escape what you've done, or what you've become. You can't escape your own history. I had survived, that was all. And surviving is such a terrible anti-climax.'

'I should go,' Cassie said.

Mrs Douglas smiled. 'Are you sure you're doing the right thing, Detective Inspector?'

'I don't know what you mean.'

'Oh, I think you do.'

Cassie got up. *Social Worker, my arse*, she thought. The old lady was marking her card, warning her off. Cassie recalled a trafficking case she'd worked at the Met a few years ago: MI5 had intervened – warned her off certain lines of enquiry. Cassie ignored them, of course, and the very next day she was reassigned.

Maybe she was just being paranoid. 'Thank you for your help, Mrs Douglas,' Cassie said briskly, and turned to leave.

The main door squeaked open. A grey-haired man in a long overcoat made his way to the bar. Cassie watched as he ordered a drink. He had his back to her now, and she'd only caught the briefest glimpse of his face, but she was sure it was her father. Same square jaw, strong nose, and soft, dark eyes. Any moment now he would realise who he had passed on the way to the bar. Any moment now he would turn around. She wondered what he would say. She didn't want him to speak. She wanted him to put his arms around her, squeeze her tight, and tell her that everything would be just fine.

He did turn around, the man in the long, old-fashioned overcoat. And he did look at her. He looked at her long and hard.

It wasn't her father.

31

AN IMAGE OF Dad, skulking in the shrubbery by the entrance to the crematorium, wouldn't shift. Cassie tried to remember the colour of his eyes, the angle of his nose, the curve of his top lip. His face – once as familiar as her own – grew more alien the harder she tried to conjure it.

Her mother's death had been a relief to everyone.

An overdose.

Not a surprise.

But the unspoken question ('accident or design?') hung in the air like a pointing finger. Cassie chose *accident*. But even if it had been suicide, as everyone assumed (she could read it in the hollow eyes that smiled condolence upon her), nobody would have blamed a seventeen-year-old girl.

Perhaps that was why she couldn't look her father in the eye that day. Perhaps that was why she hadn't spoken to him since. He had tried, but she'd rejected him.

He still sent a card on her birthday.

The phone rang. It was Stella Middlewood.

'You haven't been entirely straight with me, have you, Cassie?'

'What do you mean?'

'His picture's all over the telly. Your man Flynn is wanted for questioning about the killings at that old school. Kev recognised him straight away. He's Jamie Boreman, he's Deakin's Dandy – you knew all along!'

'No, Stella, I didn't – not before you sent the picture. And even then, I wasn't sure until—'

'So what happened to letting me know if anything interesting came up, eh?'

'I'm sorry, it's just—'

'Well, now I really do have a story! Anything to add, Detective Inspector?'

'Stella, please. Please don't print anything until we know what's really going on.'

'And when will I know that?' Stella said. 'When I see it on the ten o'clock news?'

'No, Stella, listen . . .'

Stella listened.

Cassie didn't know what to say.

'Well?' Stella said, 'I'm listening.'

'I'll come and see you, tell you everything I know. Please keep this to yourself until we've had a chance to talk it through.'

'When? When will you come and see me? I can't sit on this for very long.'

'Today. Six o'clock'

'And you'll tell me everything?'

'Everything I know.'

'And everything you *think* you know?'

Cassie hesitated. 'Yes.'

❧

She had planned to stay another night in Edinburgh. She was to have walked the Royal Mile and taken the evening air in Princes Street Gardens. She was to have nibbled on bruschetta and olives, and sipped Chianti, in a cosy Italian wine bar she'd spotted on Cockburn Street.

Detective Superintendent Greg James, who'd left the Met for

Edinburgh last year, was to have joined her there. He'd said there was a job for her here, in Edinburgh, she'd only to ask.

And she *was* going to ask. At some point on the long walk back from her meeting with Céline Douglas, she'd made the decision. It was time to start afresh.

The phone rang again. It was Angus. She picked-up before she remembered that she wasn't speaking to him.

'I've been trying to get hold of you since yesterday.'

'I know.'

'It's all blown up. Flynn's all over the news'

'I know.'

'Where are you?'

'Edinburgh.'

'Edinburgh? Oh, Gemma Grant. What did you find out?'

'Where's Flynn?'

'We're lying low for a bit. We need to . . . oh, I don't know what we need to do. We need to find out who's behind this. We need you, Cassie.'

'You're the spy, Angus.'

'I'm just a techie, I keep telling you that. And besides, GCHQ has terminated my contract.'

'I need you to find out what they have on Scott Deakin.'

'They've sacked me, I've no access.'

'You'll find a way.'

'But . . .'

'Won't you?'

Angus let out a noisy breath. 'I'll try.'

'Good,' Cassie said. 'I'll be in touch tomorrow.'

'Tomorrow! But Cassie—'

'Tomorrow.'

32

GOOGLE MAPS ESTIMATED the journey time from Edinburgh to Manchester at just under four hours, if the traffic wasn't too bad she'd be at Stella's by half past five. It would give her time to think at least. Cassie wondered if her old boss from the Met had been serious when he offered her that job in Edinburgh. She wondered what Flynn and Angus would talk about together – the cuckold and the cuckolder. Still best of friends? She wondered if she'd left it too long to be reconciled with her father. Maybe if—

The phone rang, the radio cut out, and Meg's voice filled the car. 'You were supposed to keep in touch? What's going on?'

Cassie told her everything she'd learned in Edinburgh. Meg listened in silence.

'So,' Cassie said, 'what about my hunch that Gemma came to Sheffield a couple of months before her mother died?'

'Makes sense, I suppose.' She spoke with little enthusiasm. 'Let me know when that private investigator rings you back, in the meantime I'll have someone check the local hotels and guest houses for any trace of Gemma Grant's stay. Are you sure she wouldn't have stayed with her mother?'

'Yes. Flynn didn't know anything about Gemma.'

Meg went quiet.

'He *didn't*, Meg,' Cassie said. 'He didn't know. I'm sure of it.'

'Yeah? Well Gemma definitely knew about *him*. Why else would she turn up at his house?'

There was no satisfactory answer to that. Cassie thought back to the video of Gemma stomping through the snow at the end of Flynn's lane. And then came a memory – vivid and fresh – of Gemma, naked and dead, on Flynn's bed. So young. So very, very young.

'Meg, I've just had a thought,' Cassie said. 'Sheffield's a university city: there are thousands of teenage girls living away from home. Where would you house a teenage girl so she wouldn't stand out?'

'Of course!' Meg said. 'Student digs. I'll have someone get on to the agencies.'

☙

Stella Middlewood's house was scruffier than Cassie had expected. The drive was littered with windblown chocolate wrappers and polystyrene cartons. The sash windows were in urgent need of paint. The glass in the front door was badly cracked and held together with gaffer tape. Inside was not much better. She had to wade through a sea of shoes in the hall and squeeze past coats hung five or six deep.

Somehow, Stella managed to add Cassie's coat to the rack. 'Kev's back,' she whispered, 'I took the day off to look after him. But please don't mention anything about me kneeing him in the balls, or hospital, or anything. Please.'

In the dining room, Kev was marking exercise books.

'I'll get us coffee,' Stella said. 'Jasper went out like a light when I put him down and the big ones are happy enough in front of the TV.'

Kev looked up from his books and studied Cassie for a little longer than she considered polite.

'Cassie May,' she said.

'Kevin Middlewood. Kev.'

Kev got up and squeezed past the scattered chairs and a sideboard overburdened with framed pictures of children. He scooped a pair of muddy socks and a Cinderella dressing gown from under the table. 'Please,' he said, 'have a seat.'

There was a strong smell of curry. Cassie noticed two large dollops of yellow sauce on the table and scatterings of sticky white rice. Kevin pulled a wad of sheets from a kitchen roll and began cleaning up. Cassie wondered if he might do a better job if he spent more time looking at the table and less time looking at her.

'Stella tells me you're a Detective Inspector,' he said. 'I wasn't expecting someone so young.'

'Or so pretty, eh, Kev.' Stella was at the door with a tray balanced on a box file. She turned to Cassie. 'Don't worry, he's harmless, he just doesn't get out much.'

Kevin crushed the soiled kitchen roll in his fist and stormed out.

Stella turned to Cassie. 'Oh Christ, now I've done it! He's still sulking after you know what. Listen, help yourself to coffee while I go and calm him down.'

Cassie finished the job Kevin had started – there were a few more curry smears to deal with, and the odd grain of rice. She folded up the used kitchen paper and put it on the sideboard between a collection of overstretched hair bobbles and a headless Barbie. She wondered if it would still be there next week.

Stella and Kevin came back into the dining room and sat at the table.

'Right then, Cassie,' Stella said, as if dealing with a wayward teenager. 'Tell me what you know. Kevin knows not to repeat anything that he hears through my work. Anyway he's part of this story now – I certainly wouldn't have recognised Jamie Boreman, or James Flynn, or whoever the hell he is.'

Cassie told Stella everything – not because she had too, but because she wanted to, because there was something about Stella that made you want to tell her stuff.

'So, you're in love with the man.' Stella had covered her face with her hands towards the end of Cassie's account. Now she was staring at the ceiling.

'No,' Cassie said emphatically. 'I don't think so.'

'But you're putting your career on the line for him.'

'I'm just trying to do the right thing, Stella.'

Stella rubbed her eyes. 'Look, I'm sure you're right about Flynn being framed for the Gemma Grant murder. But the three found dead at that old school – two with their throats cut, one shot through the head – that's gangland stuff. That was Jamie Boreman's life before he came to Sheffield and started calling himself Flynn. And his phone places him at the school at the time of the killings. It can't be a coincidence.'

Cassie felt the blood drain from her face. 'I know,' she said. 'But when I told him three bodies had been found he seemed genuinely surprised. And I was looking out for his reaction, really I was. I'm sure he wasn't faking. I know him. A bit.'

'A *bit!*' Stella shook her head. 'Did he *say* that he wasn't there?'

'He said he wasn't a murderer.'

'Like paedophiles say they don't "*abuse*" children? Like rapists say "*she wanted it – deep down she really wanted it?*"'

Cassie stared at the table. She spotted a smear of curry that she'd missed.

Kevin sat up and cleared his throat.

Stella got in first. 'Flynn must have been involved, you have to concede that. Did he deny being at Park Gate School?'

Cassie thought back to the conversation in the flat above the shop.

'Did he?' Stella repeated, eyes wide.

'No, but I didn't ask him that – not specifically.'

'*Not specifically!*' Stella shook her head. 'Surely, if he wasn't there, that's the first thing he would have said. Christ, even if he *was* there, you'd expect him to deny it.' She looked thoughtfully at her coffee for a moment, twisting the cup one way then the other.

Kevin leaned forward.

Stella got in first again. 'Maybe he knows who killed Gemma. Maybe he decided to dish out his own sort of justice.'

Cassie shrugged. 'He doesn't know who killed Gemma.'

'Right.' Stella rolled her eyes.

'Well, I taught Jamie Boreman in the sixth form,' Kevin said, quickly, 'and—'

The dining room door opened and a girl of five or six, in a pink onesie, appeared. 'Michael won't let me put *Horrid Henry* on. He says it's for babies. It's *not* for babies, is it?' The little girl turned and pointed at Cassie. 'Who's that?'

'This is Cassie, she's a friend from work.' Stella picked up her daughter and kissed her cheek. 'Cassie, this is Becca.'

Cassie managed a smile.

'Would you like to play on my iPad instead?' Stella asked. 'It's on the kitchen table.'

Becca's eyes lit up. She wriggled out of her mother's arms and dashed out. Stella pushed the door closed.

'You were telling us about Flynn,' Cassie said, turning back to Kevin. 'Jamie Boreman, at school . . .'

'Yes, well, it probably isn't relevant, probably doesn't mean anything.' Kevin rubbed his chin.

'Go on,' Cassie said.

Kevin pressed his palms together. 'It's just that he was a lovely lad. A bit quiet, but very bright and always well behaved. He was useful on the rugby pitch of course – took two or three to bring him down. But he played by the rules, never lashed out, never set out to hurt anyone. And the girls loved him – film star looks and all that.'

'Girlfriends?' Cassie asked, trying to sound matter-of-fact.

'No. Funny that. Some of the boys teased him about it.'

'Did you think he was gay?'

'No. I saw the way he looked at girls, you know, the way teenage boys look at girls.'

'Not *just* teenage boys,' Cassie said, under her breath, then waved Kevin to continue.

Kevin looked confused, then embarrassed. He swallowed hard then carried on. 'I only mentioned the teasing because it shows that the boys at school weren't afraid of him, which says a lot about his nature — we're talking about a first team rugby player who made Conan the Barbarian look like a wimp. He was six foot eight at least, and he'd have been big even if he didn't work out, but he did work out - two hours in the gym every morning before school. He told me that once. Can't remember why it came up. He said he didn't really enjoy it, but he was afraid of what he'd become if he stopped. I don't know what he meant by that. I wish I'd asked.'

Stella looked at her watch. 'Becca's bath time. Kev, would you get her started. I'll be up to wash her hair.'

'Okay.' Kevin squeezed past his wife, nodded a goodbye to Cassie, and shut the door behind him.

'Does he still work out, your James Flynn?' Stella asked Cassie.

'Not like that, I don't think, not hours in the gym, but he keeps himself in shape.'

Stella raised an eyebrow and leaned back in her chair. 'Sarah Flynn? The car crash? You don't think it was an accident?'

'Even if it was,' Cassie said wearily, 'there's something not right about it. That's why I came to you in the first place. I wanted to know what she was up to that day. All the evidence says she was shopping in the Trafford Centre, but we know she came to you asking about Scott Deakin.'

'What evidence puts her in the Trafford Centre?'

'Credit card spending.'

'What time?'

'I've got someone looking into that. In fact . . .' Cassie heaved her handbag on to her lap and rummaged for her phone.

'Sarah Flynn's appointment was at three o'clock,' Stella said. 'I checked my diary. And she was on time: I remember because I was ten minutes late, and she wasn't best pleased. She can't have been with me more than half an hour; I gave her a couple of names – known associates of Deakin – and that was that.'

Without looking up from her phone, Cassie said: 'These would be dangerous men, I take it.'

'Yes, but—'

'Got it,' Cassie said. 'I knew it!'

'What?'

'According to Meg, her credit card was being used in Selfridges, at the Trafford Centre, at 3:11 p.m..'

Stella slapped the table. 'Not by her, it wasn't!'

'Bloody hell. If I'd known this two years ago!' Cassie grimaced and threw back her head. 'Christ, what a mess.' Rain began to pound the french windows at the far end of the dining room. Cassie looked at her watch – it was half past six and she was dreading the drive back home. 'It's late, I really need to go. By the way, do you know anything about the Bolan bothers: Michael and Vincent. Sarah Flynn was interested in them too, apparently.'

Stella tapped her lips with an index finger as she thought. 'Local thugs. Drugs, protection, the usual. Got into a fight over a woman. Ended up shooting each other dead.'

'Any connection?'

'Happened around the same time as the Deakin disappearance, but . . .' Stella shrugged. 'I don't think anyone saw a connection at the time.'

Cassie glanced at her watch. 'I need to make tracks. Promise me you won't tell anyone about Flynn until we know exactly what we're dealing with.'

Stella nodded briskly and took a deep breath. 'Of course: Sarah Flynn, Gemma Grant, the Park Gate School massacre – they might not be connected.'

Cassie shifted awkwardly in her chair. 'Except that Flynn can be linked to all of them, one way or another.'

'Oh, yes.' Stella raised her eyebrows and made a drama out of wagging her index finger. 'Why didn't I think of that!'

'Please, Stella. Give me time to unpick all this.'

The sound of rain pummelling the french windows suddenly stopped. Stella and Cassie turned to look outside. Snow had begun to fall in Manchester.

'I'd go the long way home if I were you,' Stella said. 'I reckon they'll close the Snake Pass tonight. If it's snowing down here, imagine what it'll be like up on the tops.'

'Stella?' Cassie said, as much a plea as a question.

'Okay, I'll wait. But not for ever.'

'Thanks.' Cassie got up to go. 'By the way, have you heard of a private detective called David Roland?'

'Oh yes,' Stella said, knowingly. 'I suppose Sarah Flynn used him.'

'I think so. Why, what do you know about him?'

'Well, he has a reputation for getting results – and getting them fast. He runs quite a big outfit I hear.'

'Have you met him?' Cassie asked.

'God no! He's dodgy as they come. He'll get you what you want all right, but at a price. And I hear he'll use any means to get a result: bribery, hacks, phone taps . . .' Stella brought her palms together and rested her chin on her fingertips, '. . . even blackmail.'

'Blackmail!' Cassie's eyes narrowed. 'Who did he blackmail?'

Stella shrugged. 'The rich and the famous, I guess. Roland

started off as a bouncer, working the Manchester nightclubs. And before he became a private investigator he worked as a bodyguard for celebs. So he saw things. And, rumour has it, he took pictures.'

Cassie nodded slowly. She was thinking about the video of Angus and Sarah.

33

'NO ONE WILL find us here,' Angus said, turning the key in the lock.

Behind him, a taciturn Flynn was looking out across snow-covered pasture to the moorland beyond.

'Would have been a shepherd's cottage, I suppose,' Angus said. 'Ten years ago, when Lizzie's cousin bought it, it was just a shell,' Angus swung the door open, 'but now . . .'

Flynn, back to the door, hands deep in his pockets, didn't turn to look inside.

In late summer, the moors would have been vibrant: vast blankets of flowering heather – greens, purples and pinks – shining bright in the soft evening sun. But now, dulled by a thick covering of snow, the essence of the moors lay hidden. Angus wondered what it was that Flynn was staring at. The snow that covered everything up to the horizon? Or the heather, bracken and bilberry, hunkered down beneath?

Inside, the air was cold and stale. While Flynn got the wood burner going, Angus busied himself with the big man's laptop – 'Should run like new,' he said, 'when I've finished with it.'

Half an hour later it was warm enough to take off their coats. Flynn hung them on wooden pegs by the back door, tugging the sleeves straight and folding down collars and hoods – he hadn't spoken since they arrived.

'Flynn,' Angus said, 'are you all right?'

Flynn stretched and grunted and said, 'Computer's working now.'

'Good.' Angus folded his arms. 'I wish you'd talk to me.'

'Angus, I've told you, it's forgotten.'

'I know what you said, and I wasn't going to bring it up again, but—'

'Stop!' Flynn closed his eyes and pressed his palms together. 'Please. We agreed.'

'But—'

'If you want to be punished, Angus,' Flynn turned to face him, 'tell your wife.'

Angus went to the back door. He paused for a second then yanked his coat off its peg.

'Sorry,' Flynn said.

Angus put on his coat. 'I need some air.' The zip had jammed – he tugged at it a few times then gave up and went outside.

A cold breeze riffled the junk mail stacked on the kitchen counter, and a backdraft rattled the flu in the inglenook.

When the door slammed, the cottage shook. It took a while for all that troubled air to settle, for the creaking woodwork to fall silent, for the dust motes to sink back between the floorboards – but soon, all was calm again.

With Angus outside, Flynn could think. His head was full of words: fragments of conversations; descriptions of faces, places, buildings. It was both a curse and a blessing to think in words. Sometimes the right words gave flesh to a conceit, applied texture to the intangible, suggested paths through the impenetrable. But sometimes, of course, there were no right words. Flynn's novel was a chimera, an unremembered dream, a love no longer lived. The text was ill-conceived and flabby and, until yesterday, unfinishable.

Angus had done him a favour. A portrait of Sarah, in naked and lustful embrace with her husband's closest friend, presented a perfect ending for his story. Now, at least, he could finish it. He would print it out, bind it, and throw it onto the fire.

'It's freezing out there,' Angus said, shutting the door and rubbing his hands together.

Flynn looked up. 'Thanks for sorting my computer. Still a bit slow but it works.'

Angus hung up his coat and frowned. 'I did a clean install, and you're only working with text, so it shouldn't be slow.'

'Do you think it needs more RAM?'

'No. That was Sarah's machine, she always went for the highest spec available, she always maxed out the RAM.'

The uncomfortable silence that followed the mention of Sarah's name was broken when Angus's phone pinged. He read the message.

'Cassie's on her way,' Angus said.

Flynn snapped his laptop shut and rubbed his eyes. 'I'm not sure I'm ready to see her yet.' The fire didn't need tending but he grabbed a poker and opened the stove door.

34

'WHAT HAPPENED AT Park Gate School?' Cassie was in no mood for small talk. She dragged a chair across the room and positioned it by the wood burner directly in front of Flynn. She shushed Angus when he opened his mouth to speak.

Flynn was gazing into the dancing flames. 'They took me by surprise,' he said. 'And I'd had a few drinks.'

'Who? Where? When?' Cassie rested her elbows on her knees.

Angus put his head in his hands. 'But why—'

'Shush, Angus,' Cassie said. 'Let him talk.'

'I was going to tell you,' Flynn said, 'but . . .' He continued to stare at the fire.

Cassie waited as long as she could bear. 'It doesn't matter,' she said, 'tell me now.'

Flynn told his story:

Bag over the head. Dank sports hall. Sean Mulligan asking for photographs. The message that made Mulligan rush things. The murder of Trevor Murray. Carl taking the gun and leaving the hall. Gary Mulligan dragging Trevor's body out to the van.

Flynn had voiced the account in an uncharacteristic monotone, with nothing in the way of description, observation or dramatisation – the sort of colourless summary that reminded Cassie of a police report.

'What were the photographs that Mulligan wanted so badly?' she asked.

Flynn shrugged.

'But you told him you'd get them?'

'I was playing for time. I've no idea what he wanted.'

'And Mulligan's mobile phones, what happened to them? They weren't recovered from the scene.'

Flynn shrugged again.

'Okay, then,' Cassie said. 'What happened next?' She tried to catch Flynn's eye. He'd been staring into the fire all the while, but she thought she saw his head turn ever so slightly towards her, imagined she caught a flash of cobalt blue.

'The rope around my wrists had come loose,' he said. 'When Carl left, and Gary Mulligan was busy loading the body into the van, that was my opportunity.'

'And Carl was carrying a handgun.'

'Yes.'

'So, you were on your own with Sean Mulligan?'

'Yes.'

'But he had a *knife*, you said.' Cassie leaned in. 'No *gun?*'

'Yes,' Flynn said.

'So where did the other gun come from?'

'What other gun?'

'Carl Yates was shot, Flynn. Shot though the head. Yates's gun was found at the scene – it wasn't that gun that killed him, so there must have been another.'

The shriek of an owl cut through the night. Cassie turned to the window – it was dark outside and all she could see was a dappled reflection of the fire. When she turned back, Flynn was standing. He went over to the kitchen, took a bottle of whisky from the shelf above the microwave, and poured himself a large measure.

'You think I killed all three of them, don't you?' Flynn said.

She shook her head. 'I don't know what to think.'

Flynn drank the whisky and poured himself another. He waved the bottle — first at Cassie, then at Angus. They shook their heads.

'Actually,' Angus said, getting out of his armchair, 'I think I will.' He took the bottle from Flynn and grabbed a tumbler from the draining board.

Flynn settled himself at the table, Angus sat beside him, Cassie edged her chair round to face them.

For the first time that evening, Flynn looked her in the eye. 'You're afraid, aren't you, Cassie?'

'No, I . . .'

Flynn took a sip of whisky and rubbed his lips. 'Afraid of what you think I've done?' he said. 'Or afraid of me?'

Cassie tucked her hair behind her ears. 'Just tell me what happened.'

'Does it matter? I got out of there, that's all.'

'Of course it matters!' Cassie said. 'The police are trying to pin the whole thing on *you*. Forensics will prove that you were there – fingerprints or DNA or Christ knows what.'

Flynn pressed his palms together. 'I don't care what *they* think. I care what *you* think.'

She turned away. 'They'll prove you were there, that's what I think. And with your history . . .'

Angus drained his glass, slammed it on the table and turned to Flynn. 'So, you found yourself alone with Sean Mulligan and you saw your opportunity to escape.' He turned back to Cassie. 'Your opportunity to escape from a bunch of cold-blooded murderers. So what happened next?'

Flynn didn't respond.

'Did Mulligan's boys come back in and confront you?' Angus said. 'Did they have a gun? Did you disarm them?'

Flynn was shaking his head.

'Then what?' Angus stood up. 'Come on, Flynn. It's us you're talking to. We're on your side.'

Flynn turned to Cassie. 'You said "*with my history.*" What did you mean by that?'

'We know about Jamie Boreman,' Angus said. 'We know a little about your life before Sheffield. We understand.'

Flynn put down his glass and stared into space.

Angus sat back down. 'I read that short story of yours,' he said, '*The Wythenshawe Dandy*. I read it years ago, of course, when it won that prize, but it never occurred to me . . . Anyway, I read it again last night, and, well . . .'

'It's just a story.' Flynn said.

Cassie shifted in her chair and folded her arms. 'Wythenshawe Dandy? Deakin's Dandy?'

Flynn stared hard at her but didn't speak.

'Tell us what happened at Park Gate School,' Cassie said.

Still staring, Flynn said, 'I told you about Trevor Murray: Carl killed him. But Sean Mulligan . . . I had no choice.'

She shook her head willing it not to be true. But it was true. Flynn was a killer. Flynn had killed Sean Mulligan.

She thought back through all the killers she'd looked in the eye during her career on the force. Not one of them was the sort of murderer you come across in an Agatha Christie novel. Cassie's murderers weren't cunning or evil. Cassie's murderers were the dim-witted, pathetic sort. Men (and they had *all* been men) with little self-esteem and few prospects. She looked upon them as a zoo keeper might look upon the chimpanzees in his care: so much like us, and yet not like us at all. Not one of those killers was anything like Flynn. And that made it worse.

She was deceived.

She was betrayed.

'And Carl Yates?' Cassie said briskly. 'Did you have "no choice" with him either.'

Flynn was trying to catch her eye. She didn't let him.

'I don't know anything about Carl Yates,' he said, 'but Gary Mulligan did come back into the hall after he'd finished loading the dead lad into his van. He saw his father on the floor, and he came at me like a madman. I punched him. Just the once. And not that hard. He was unconscious but breathing. That's all. Carl Yates never came back. I grabbed my computer and my phone, and I made a run for it over the playing fields. I didn't shoot anyone, Cassie.'

'Okay,' she said. 'What then?'

'I walked to the city centre, to the railway station. I don't know why I ended up there, I just walked and walked.' Flynn shook his head. 'I didn't have enough money for a taxi home, so I went to the flat in Nether Edge.'

'And the knife? The knife that killed Mulligan wasn't at the scene.'

Flynn shrugged.

Cassie picked up her chair and joined Flynn and Angus at the table. She inspected her fingernails. 'You were kidnapped. You witnessed a murder. You stabbed one of your kidnappers in a knife fight. You escaped. But Gary Mulligan, and Carl Yates (who had a gun for Christ's sake!), were most likely still after you. And you're telling me it never occurred to you to call the police?'

Angus pushed his chair back noisily. 'I need a top up. Anyone else?'

No one answered.

'We're running low on logs,' Flynn said. 'I'll nip out to the woodshed.'

There were plenty of logs in the basket by the stove, but nobody said anything.

Flynn pulled on his boots and his coat and grabbed a large torch from the small shelf above the coat pegs. The room shook when he shut the door.

'Still trust him now do you, Angus?'

'Yes.'

'But he killed a man.'

'It was self-defence, Cassie, surely you can see that.'

'He didn't say that though, did he? He didn't say, "it was self-defence". What he said was, "I had no choice". Or did I hear him wrong?'

Angus plonked his elbows on the table and leaned forward. 'But what he meant was: "I had no choice because Sean Mulligan was intent on killing me". He'd just witnessed Trevor's murder. Do you really think Mulligan was going to let him go after that?'

'If he'd meant *self-defence*, he'd have said *self-defence*. We know how careful he is with words – how many other people do you know who correct their own grammar mid-sentence?'

'Yes, I *do* know what he's like, Cassie – and I know he's not a murderer.'

They both stared for a while at the dying embers in the stove.

'Right.' Angus got up and stretched. 'The fire needs fettling.'

'What's *The Wythenshawe Dandy* about?' Cassie asked.

Angus sighed and lifted the lid of his laptop. 'I'll email you a copy.'

'Thank you. So what's it about?'

'You'll have to read it,' Angus said.

'I will. But tell me anyway.'

'I can't explain, you'll just have to read it. And I think you might go a little easier on Flynn when you have.'

'Angus, please, just tell me.'

The lid of Angus's laptop clicked shut. 'No.'

'*The Wythenshawe Dandy*,' she said, slowly. 'A bit like *Deakin's Dandy*. So autobiographical I'd guess?'

'Just read it.' Angus said. 'It's sent, so you'll have it in a minute.'

Cassie tossed her head back and growled at the ceiling.

Angus left the table to attend to the stove. With two fresh logs the fire soon sprang back to life. He sat cross legged on the hearth mat and watched the flames. Cassie watched too.

'Angus,' she said, 'do you think he's hiding anything else from us?'

Angus turned to face her. 'No,' he said. 'He kept quiet because he didn't want us to know he'd killed a man.

'But why, if it was self-defence?'

'Because he's spent fifteen years trying to live a new life. When you've read the story, when you've read *The Wythenshawe Dandy*, you'll understand. But for now, trust me, we should leave the past alone.'

'But we can't leave the past alone, Angus. It's the key to all of this.'

Angus shook his head. 'How?'

'Think about it.' Cassie turned her chair to face him. 'For the last two years, since Sarah died, Flynn has been a virtual recluse. He's done nothing that could have led to four dead bodies. And you've known him since he came to Sheffield, when he was nineteen – can you think of anything he's done, or anyone he's been involved with, that would lead to all this?' Her eyes narrowed. 'Well, can you?'

'No, I suppose not.' Angus sighed. 'Except, maybe . . .'

'Except for Sarah?'

'Yes. No. I don't know.'

'Because Sarah made it her business to piss off the rich and the powerful, and at some point she's bound to have pissed off somebody very dangerous.'

'Well, I wouldn't put it quite like that.'

'Of course she did. And the day she died she was poking her nose into the affairs of Scott Deakin, wasn't she?'

'So *you* say, or so Stella Middlewood says. But perhaps she was just curious about her husband's past, curious about what made him the man he is. Perhaps she cared.'

Cassie screwed up her face. 'Does that sound like Sarah to you?'

Angus harrumphed. 'What about that American, Brett McRoss, I thought she was looking into his shady football dealings around the time she died?'

'That's what Flynn said, but only because he saw McRoss's Wikipedia page open on her computer – she never actually talked to Flynn about him. And anyway, Brett McRoss went back to America with his tail between his legs the day before she died. He'd wanted to buy the two Sheffield football clubs and merge them, remember? It was a non-event in the end, but it was a big local story at the time – she was probably just curious.'

'And we all know where curiosity leads us.' Angus rubbed his eyes. 'She's been dead two years, Cassie! Two years!'

'I know. But everything to do with this case points to the past. Gemma Grant points to Sarah, and while what happened at the school points to gangsters in general, Flynn's involvement points to Scott Deakin in particular. Or to Sarah, because she was looking for Deakin, or to both of them. Gemma Grant and the killings at the school *are* linked – they're linked by Flynn. He was at the scene in both cases. It can't be coincidence. Nothing has happened over the last year or two that could have led to all this, so we have to look further back: either to Sarah's death a couple of years ago, or to Flynn's old life in the nineteen nineties – perhaps we ought to take a closer look at Jamie Boreman.'

'Maybe,' Angus said. The fire was now too hot to sit by. He got up and retreated to the armchair. 'Okay, *probably*. And MI6 does have a file on Scott Deakin.'

'What! Why didn't you say?'

'Because there was very little to see, and nothing for the last fifteen years.'

'Why?'

Angus shrugged. 'Dead, probably. Or . . .' he scratched his head, then his chin.

'Or what, Angus?'

'Maybe his more recent files are locked down. Maybe you need to be at a secure terminal in the MI6 building, with top level security clearance, to get access.'

'Why?'

'I don't know, Cassie. I'm just an IT guy.'

'Ok, fine,' Cassie said. 'So what *was* there in Scott Deakin's file?'

Angus was now fidgeting like a five-year-old.

'Go on,' Cassie said. 'You know I'm not going to let this go.'

'Yes, but . . .'

'But what? Come on Angus, spit it out.'

'I will. It's just that I'm afraid you'll jump to conclusions.'

She fixed on him and folded her arms.

'Okay,' he said.

She waited.

Angus closed his eyes and took a deep breath. 'Deakin wasn't just running organised crime in Manchester,' he said, 'he was expanding into a few other cities, including Sheffield.'

'So,' Cassie massaged her temples with the heels of her hands, 'Flynn must have been involved in Deakin's Sheffield business when he moved over here!'

'I knew you'd jump to conclusions,' Angus said. 'But remember, I knew Flynn when he first came to Sheffield. I saw him nearly every day, I'd have noticed if he'd been up to anything like that.'

Cassie ran stiff fingers through her hair. 'MI6 deals with foreign intelligence, doesn't it? Why on earth would they be interested in a Mancunian gangster.'

Angus shook his head. 'I don't know, Cassie. Honestly.'

'Well,' she folded her arms afresh, 'that settles it. There's more to Scott Deakin than dealing drugs and running brothels.'

'Maybe,' Angus said. 'But he's probably long dead.'

Cassie squeezed her folded arms tighter. 'Deakin is at the bottom of all this, somehow. I'm sure of it.'

'Perhaps, but we're talking about things that happened years ago, Cassie. If you're right about there being a connection to Deakin, there must have been a trigger – something recent, something in the last few weeks. There has to be *something*.'

'Gemma Grant came back to Sheffield!'

'Came *back?*' The lines on Angus's forehead deepened. 'You mean she'd been here before?'

He'd always had lines across his forehead – but tonight they seemed longer and broader. Cassie unfolded her arms. 'I'm pretty sure she came to Sheffield to see Sarah a few months before the car crash.'

The armchair creaked as Angus got up. He put his hands into his pockets and began to pace. His socks left damp marks on the cold stone flags. 'Flynn didn't know,' he said. 'He told us he'd never met her, and he isn't lying.'

'I believe him,' Cassie said. She hadn't wanted to sound sarcastic, but that was the way it came out. 'Sarah wasn't exactly above keeping secrets from her husband, was she now?'

❧

If Flynn hadn't looked quite so contrite when he came back in with a net of logs, Cassie might have launched straight back into her interrogation. As it was, she found herself feeling sorry for him. She turned away so he wouldn't see. She tried to look past her own reflection in the window, tried to discern the silhouette of the woods beyond the yard. But all she could see was Flynn standing behind her, head bowed, pretending not to be looking at her.

Perhaps Angus was right, perhaps 'no choice' really did mean 'no choice'; perhaps she had been a little too quick to judge. In any case, it was over between her and Flynn. Cassie clapped her hands. 'So, back to business! You two, sit down and listen. I'm going to tell you what I found out in Edinburgh.'

Eyebrows were raised when Cassie told how Gemma used to pick up businessmen in posh hotels (seduce them, hit them with a hard luck story, count the cash), but they listened in silence.

'Sounds like she was playing a dangerous game,' Angus said. 'Sounds like she picked-up the wrong sort of man somewhere along the way, and . . .' he drew a long, nasally breath.

'Yes,' Cassie said.

'So this may not be about Flynn after all.'

'No, Angus. It's about Flynn: *His* flat? *His* wife's daughter? You can't think that's a coincidence.'

'No, but—'

'He might not know it, but he does know something.'

Flynn cleared his throat noisily.

Angus and Cassie turned to him, but he didn't speak – he just looked at each of them in turn.

'Food!' Angus said. 'I'm hungry.'

❧

Nine o'clock. Through the kitchen window, by the dim lights on the gate posts, Cassie watched the snow fall.

'You won't get home in this weather,' Angus said. We've room here though, there are two bedrooms upstairs, so . . .'

'So, I'm sure you and Flynn won't mind sharing.' Cassie waved her car key at Flynn. 'Would you be a love? My suitcase is in the boot.'

Angus rustled up a late supper of bread, brie, pâté and olives. Flynn opened a bottle of red and lit a few of the giant candles that were dotted about the cottage. Cassie went upstairs and laid claim to the master bedroom.

She came back down in jeans and a chunky Aran sweater. 'Whose place is this anyway?' she asked, slumping into the best armchair. She sipped her wine and looked around. It was bigger than Flynn's house, but similar in style: pretty and rustic, with exposed stone walls and ancient looking floorboards.

'Belongs to one of Lizzie's cousins,' Angus said. 'He moved to Cornwall a few years ago – rents it out as holiday cottage nowadays, but it's always empty this time of year.'

'So Lizzie knows you're here?'

Angus looked sheepish.

Cassie glared at him.

With a glass of red in one hand, and a brie baguette in the other, Flynn appeared a little more relaxed. The bottle was already empty. Angus shot him a disapproving look, removed the empty bottle, fetched a fresh one.

'Okay.' Cassie turned to Flynn. 'Are you sure you don't know anything about the photographs that Sean Mulligan thought you had?'

Flynn put down his sandwich and took a gulp of wine. 'Quite sure.'

Cassie looked from Flynn to Angus. 'Sarah then?' She knew neither of them wanted to talk about Sarah, but it couldn't be avoided.

Flynn nodded. 'Sarah had pictures that have upset people over the years: mostly of politicians and businessmen who shouldn't have been seen together. But if they were of any value she'd have already published them.'

'What if it was something she was working on just before she died?' Cassie said.

'Maybe,' Flynn said, staring into his wine glass. 'But I *don't know* what she was working on. Besides, two years have passed – why now?'

'Gemma Grant?' Angus turned to Cassie. 'You said that Gemma coming back to Sheffield was the trigger for all of this, so perhaps the photos had something to do with her, given her history, you know, with older men.'

Cassie closed her eyes, tossed her head back, and took a long breath. 'And that manila envelope she was carrying outside Flynn's place. Didn't I always say she was carrying photographs. Perhaps *they* were the photographs that Mulligan was after. Of course! Blackmail. A married man photographed with a young girl!'

'An underage girl at that,' Angus added. 'If this happened when Gemma came to Sheffield to see Sarah, she'd have been a few months short of sixteen.'

Cassie took a glug of wine. 'Shit, yes. And, according to Stella, the PI that Sarah used to use – whatshisname – he was into blackmail. There has to be a connection.'

Across the table, Angus was drumming his fingers. 'It's all speculation,' he said, 'and none of it explains why anyone would want to frame Flynn. Or why they'd have made such an effort staging the crime scene.'

'The Gemma Grant crime scene was designed to look like something it wasn't. And if—' Cassie gasped. Flynn's kidnapping suddenly made sense. She sat up and turned to Flynn, hands over her mouth.

'What?' he said. 'What is it?'

'You were supposed to have been killed.' Cassie's eyes were wide.

'I know that, Cassie. Mulligan made it perfectly clear.'

'No. I mean they'd have killed you anyway, photos or no photos. It was all planned.'

'I know they'd have killed me anyway! Why do you think I . . . ?' Flynn shook his head and drained his glass.

Angus was about to speak but Cassie held up a finger.

After a few seconds, when it became clear that Flynn had no intention of finishing his sentence, she sank back into her chair, rolling the stem of her glass between taut fingers. 'What were you going to say?' she asked.

Flynn looked puzzled. 'I don't know. I've just remembered something – Mulligan told me he'd planned to talk to me at *my* place,' Flynn said. 'He'd planned to talk to me – about the photographs, presumably – that morning, at my house. But I wasn't in, was I, because that was the day you and I were supposed to . . .' he looked at Cassie. 'It was the day I found Gemma.'

Cassie stood up, very nearly spilling her wine. 'I know which bloody day it was, Flynn! Jesus Christ, why didn't you bother to mention this before? Don't you see what it means?'

'No. What?'

'It means that both Mulligan and Gemma came to your house on the same day, and at the same time probably, and that you were supposed to be there too.'

'But why?'

'Think about it: Gemma *was* killed and you were *supposed* to be killed.'

'Mulligan mentioned something about a reunion,' Flynn said, 'which was odd because I'd never met him before.'

'Not you and him,' Cassie said, 'you and her – you and Gemma.'

'But I'd never met *her* before either.'

'He didn't know that, did he! All he knew was that Gemma was your wife's daughter?'

Angus, who had kept obediently quiet, now cleared his throat. 'But why would they want Flynn and Gemma together.'

'Leverage?' Cassie said. 'Perhaps he was planning to have one of his cronies hold a knife to the pretty little stepdaughter's throat while he waited for Flynn to come up with the photos.'

'I thought you said Gemma had the photos?' Flynn said.

Cassie waved a dismissive hand. 'But why did they kill Gemma? Why take that sort of a risk?'

'And for that matter,' Angus said, 'why had they planned to kill Flynn too. A double murder was bound to attract even more attention. Come on, Cassie, this is all speculation.'

Cassie growled. 'It's a theory, Angus. We'll probably never know what they had planned that morning at Flynn's place, because they're all dead. It's a starting point, that's all.'

Angus twisted his mouth, sceptically.

'Look,' she said, 'there's a pile of evidence implicating Flynn, and DCI Foster isn't looking for anyone else. If Flynn were found dead in a ditch tomorrow, they'd wrap things up and close the case. No trial. No defence barristers to pick holes in the investigation. Framing him wasn't enough, they had to be absolutely sure the case would be buried.'

Angus nodded. 'Okay, that makes sense. But what about Carl Yates? Who killed him.'

She put down her wine. 'That business at the school *looks* like a gangland squabble. Perhaps that's exactly what it was.'

'So,' Angus said, 'it was just a coincidence that it happened while they had Flynn?'

It was Cassie's turn to shrug. She spread both hands flat on the kitchen table, considered her ruby red nails, then clenched her fists. 'I'm going to bed.'

Cassie couldn't sleep. The name *Brett McRoss* popped into her head. She reached for her iPad and googled him.

He was a US Senator, he was a businessman, and he was very rich. McRoss came from money, had money, and appeared to be devoting his life to making even more of it. She clicked though link after link until she was woken by a 'low battery' bleep. She paused the YouTube video she'd been dozing through (a press conference McRoss had given in Sheffield a couple of years ago) and fumbled on the floor for the charging cable. It was while she was connecting her iPad to the charger that she noticed something in the top righthand corner of the screen – a familiar face. It was Sarah Flynn.

Sarah was in the video for no more than three or four seconds. It was 14 minutes and 51 seconds into a 15-minute video. After McRoss left the podium, the camera panned across the audience. And there was Sarah Flynn – standing right at the front, arms folded.

Cassie closed her eyes. She had a connection. Or did she? All she really had was a video showing a Sheffield based journalist attending a press conference in Sheffield.

But because the press conference was about football, which wasn't Sarah's thing at all, Cassie reasoned that it was McRoss himself that she'd been interested in. And if Sarah had been interested in McRoss, it could only have been because she thought he was dodgy.

Cassie watched the last few seconds of the video again. Sarah was standing stiffly, arms folded, staring at McRoss as he walked away from the podium. And while all the other journalists were holding notebooks or tape recorders or cameras, Sarah was carrying nothing at all, not even a handbag.

35

BY MORNING THE skies had cleared to an impossible blue. The snow around the cottage lay thick and smooth and even, like a hotel duvet. Cassie set to work digging out her Mini with a spade she found in the woodshed. A farmer had been out with a tractor at first light to clear the lane, so she needed to clear only the few yards to the gate. Beyond the lane moorland stretched as far as she could see. The snow up there – clumped over heather, gorse and cotton grass – lay like spikey icing on a frosted Christmas cake.

Cassie leaned against the gatepost and let the sun warm her face. Meg was coming for lunch at midday, and there was David Roland and associates after that, but first on her list were Mr and Mrs Dungworth. Cassie had a photo of their witness statement, from the Sarah Flynn file, stored on her phone. She checked the address before setting off.

❧

When the sound of Cassie's car had faded into the distance, Flynn crept out of the bedroom taking care not to wake Angus. Downstairs, it was cold. Flynn set to work on the stove: he emptied the ashpan, cleaned the glass, lit the kindling and pondered how best to structure his final chapter. A straightforward narrative would be best, he thought – nothing fancy. The prose should be simple, sharp, clean. Betrayal speaks for itself, after all. Two thousand words would do it.

❧

'One thousand and thirty-seven words,' Flynn said, 'in an hour. Just think, if I could keep up that rate, eight hours a day and five days a week, I could turn out a novel in a fortnight.'

Angus sat down and rubbed his eyes, he felt like shit. 'Why so perky?'

'A thousand words in an hour – that's a personal record.'

'I thought it was about quality, not quantity.'

Flynn closed the laptop and leaned on his elbows. 'It's about getting to the end.'

'Bacon, eggs, and fried bread,' Angus said. 'That'll sort me out. How about you?'

'Sounds good.'

The light in the fridge hurt Angus's eyes. 'I see Cassie's gone. Did you speak with her this morning?'

'No,' Flynn said, 'she was gone by the time I came down.'

Angus lit the hob under a large frying pan. 'I feel like shit,' he said. 'Hope the paracetamol kicks in soon. We polished off a whole bottle of Speyside last night, I don't know how you can get up early and write after that.'

'Practice,' Flynn said.

'Yes, well,' Angus blew a heavy breath through tight lips, 'when this business is over, I think you should—'

'I know.'

The sweet smell of bacon was doing Angus a world of good, he reckoned, or maybe it was the paracetamol. 'I must say,' he said, setting up a second frying pan for the eggs, 'you seem more yourself this morning than I've seen you in a long while.'

Flynn snapped shut his computer. 'That's why I write,' he said. 'You can lose yourself for a few hours, you can escape to another world, you can forget who you are.' He rested his chin on the heel of his hand and turned to the fire. 'You can even forget what you've done.'

'Good!'

'But it doesn't last.'

'Bloody hell, Flynn, stop whining! Like I said, you're just going to have to live with it. Mulligan got what was coming. I wouldn't lose any sleep over it.'

'*You* wouldn't have done it, though, would you?'

Angus shoved the bacon to the edge of the frying pan so that there was room for a slice of bread. 'He'd killed before, and he'd have killed again – killed you, in fact. So *yes*, I hope I would have had the guts to do it.'

Flynn grunted.

'Breakfast's ready,' Angus said, rummaging for cutlery.

Flynn moved his computer out of the way and came to help. 'I dreamed about Macbeth last night,' he said. 'I was Macbeth, and Sarah was—'

Angus dumped a pile of cutlery, as noisily as he could, on the table.

'Duncan was asleep, wasn't he,' Flynn said, 'when Macbeth—'

'Yes, yes, I know exactly where you're going with this.' Angus passed Flynn the cutlery. 'Don't.'

Flynn arranged the knives and forks, wordlessly, while Angus dished up their breakfast. Last night, softened by whisky, Flynn had confessed that Mulligan was unconscious when he cut his throat. There was a world of difference between killing a man in the heat of battle, and finishing a man off after he'd gone down – Angus couldn't imagine ever having to have to make that decision. It was rather like when Poppy had asked, on the way back from Brownies, 'Daddy, if you *had* to choose, would you rather be eaten by a tiger or a shark?'

'Toast or fried bread?' Angus asked.

Flynn shrugged. 'You decide.'

36

Mr and Mrs Dungworth lived in Lodge Moor, on the western outskirts of Sheffield. They had a neat bungalow on a finger of urban development that poked the fields, woods and valleys on the fringes of the Peak District National Park.

The place was brand new when they bought it in 1972. Mrs Dungworth would never have dreamed of living anywhere quite so posh until Mr Dungworth won £10,000 on Spot the Ball. Aside from the bungalow, Mr Dungworth treated himself to a brand-new car and a colour television (both still going strong). Mrs Dungworth got a front-loading washing machine and a teasmaid (neither of these lasted). Together, they took the whole family to the Costa Brava for a fortnight. A classy hotel, Mrs Dungworth recalled, where the waiters dressed as matadors.

Yes, 1972 was a good year for the Dungworths. Except for their Joanne getting herself pregnant, of course – she was only fifteen. But they had a grown-up granddaughter now (who'd married well – an accountant), and two great-grandchildren.

The older of the great-grandchildren, Amber, recently got herself a place at university – something to do with computers.

Mrs Dungworth's eyes shone with pride, but only briefly. Soon she was staring into her lap. 'But the younger one, Brogan, well . . .' she shook her head. 'They all have tattoos these days, don't they, but Brogan's only fourteen. They won't tell me what it is, exactly, only that it's, erm, . . .' Mrs Dungworth checked the room for eavesdroppers before mouthing the word 'obscene'. 'The doctors say they can laser it off, so that's a relief. And her school says she can still attend, provided she wears a glove. So all's well that ends well.'

Cassie offered an understanding nod.

'Oh, listen to me gabbing on!' Mrs Dungworth reached for the pot. 'More tea, love?

Cassie set her cup and saucer down on a time-ravaged lace doily. 'No thank you, Mrs Dungworth. Do you think Mr Dungworth will be long?'

Mrs Dungworth put down her tea, removed her spectacles, and polished the thick lenses with a handkerchief. The smile in her eyes had gone, but she persevered with the grin. She looked over to the open door at the far end of the lounge. 'His memory's not what it used to be.'

Cassie nodded. 'I understand.'

'No, love, I don't think you do. I mean, well, he's in the garage polishing his car at the moment, but he's not allowed to drive anymore. And I can't let him leave the house on his own because, well . . .' Mrs Dungworth reached for the tea pot again. 'Are you sure, love? Just a drop?'

'Okay then. Just a drop.'

As she poured, Mrs Dungworth mouthed a whisper: 'senile dementia'. Her pouring hand began to shake. Cassie resisted the temptation to help. When the tea was poured, and the teapot returned safely to its trivet, and milk had been offered and accepted, and sugar had been offered and declined, Mrs Dungworth shook her head lengthily. 'We don't talk about it. He's a proud man, our Bill, and it would upset him. Do you see, love? I'll fetch him right enough, but he might not be much help.'

Cassie allowed herself a sigh when Mrs Dungworth left the room. It was the Dungworths' witness statements about Sarah Flynn's crash that had raised her suspicions two years ago. They hadn't seen the car go off the road, Cassie remembered, but they were first on the scene. Mr Dungworth, who was driving them back from a family birthday party in Timperley, had stopped when he saw a dead sheep on the road – when he got out of his car he spotted Sarah's Mercedes at the bottom of the valley.

It was not the witness statements themselves that had raised Cassie's suspicion, but the discrepancy between the witness statements and what the first police constable on the scene had noted in his pocketbook. According to the pocketbook, Mrs Dungworth said she'd seen Sarah filling-up her car, at a petrol station in Glossop, half an hour before the crash. But according to the witness statements they gave the next day, neither Mr nor Mrs Dungworth had any recollection of seeing the car before they reached the crash site.

'He's just washing his hands, he'll be here in a minute.' Mrs Dungworth put a plate of garibaldis on the coffee table.

'When we spoke on the phone, when I rang you in Benidorm a week after the crash, you said that you wouldn't have noticed the car before the accident because you weren't wearing your glasses.'

'That's right, love. I'm blind as a bat without my specs, but I never wear them when we're driving because they make me car sick. Bill says it's all in my head, but it's not — wearing glasses in the car makes me car sick. I know it's true, whatever *he* says, so I always take them off.'

'So why did you tell the officer at the scene that you'd seen the driver, a woman, filling up the car that crashed, at the petrol station?'

'I don't think I did, love. It's been a couple of years though, hasn't it? Your policeman has probably seen hundreds of car crashes since then, so he's bound to get a bit mixed up.'

'But he wrote it down, Mrs Dungworth, in his notebook. He wrote it all down *at the time*.'

Mrs Dungworth removed her glasses and set to work polishing the lenses.

Cassie waited.

'Have a garibaldi,' Mrs Dungworth said. She put her glasses back on and stood up. 'I don't know what's keeping Bill, I'd best go and fetch him.'

'Mrs Dungworth, I really need to know anything either of you remembers about that day. I wouldn't be bothering you if it wasn't important.'

Mrs Dungworth sat down and brought her hands together – bony fingers, white as the hanky she was clutching. 'It was Bill who saw the woman and the car at the petrol station,' she said. He told me while we were waiting for the police to come. But by the time they arrived, he'd started to get confused. I'd known for months, if I'm honest, that he wasn't quite right. But it's easy to pretend everything's fine if that's what you want to believe. So I told the policeman that *I'd* seen what Bill told me *he'd* seen. I thought I was helping.'

'You were, Mrs Dungworth. Of course you were. But why didn't you say the same thing when you made your witness statement the next day?'

'Because the next day Bill swore blind that he'd never seen the car before it crashed, and that's what he told the policewoman. What could I do? I didn't know – not for sure. So I told her what I'd really seen, which was nothing. I thought I was doing the right thing.'

'Of course you were. But . . .'

Mrs Dungworth lifted her glasses and dabbed her eyes.

'. . . it doesn't matter,' Cassie said.

'Shall I fetch Bill now?'

'Will he be able to help, do you think?'

'Maybe. Maybe not.' Mrs Dungworth glanced wistfully around her living room. 'I'll fetch him.'

❧

William Dungworth was tall and thin, with the bearing of a military man. He wore a brown suit, patched at the elbows. What hair he had left was silver and slicked back with something shiny. Cassie stood up to greet him and offered a hand. His grip was firm, his eyes were sharp, 'Detective Inspector, is it?' he said. 'They didn't make 'em like you in my day.'

'Mr Dungworth, I'm here about the car you found crashed on the Snake Pass back in December 2012.'

'So Grace tells me.' He sat beside his wife and patted her knee. 'Bit of a shocker were that, eh, Gracie.'

Mrs Dungworth nodded.

'I know it was a while ago,' Cassie said, 'but if you remember anything at all I'd like to know about it.'

Bill Dungworth nodded earnestly. 'Mercedes, W113, 280SL, 1969 number plate. A beauty, it was: mint condition. Red – probably a respray, but beautifully done. It were so perfect, the paint job, I knew it couldn't be original. Such a shame to see it crashed down in that gorge. Mind you, them old Mercs fetch so much these days that it'd probably be worth fixing up.'

Grace elbowed her husband in the ribs. 'A woman died, Bill. It doesn't matter about the car.'

Bill's face fell. 'No, no. Of course not.'

'Mr Dungworth,' Cassie felt a surge of optimism, 'did you see who was in the car, before it crashed?'

'Aye. We were parked up beside them at that petrol station in Glossop.'

'Them?' It came out an octave too high.

'Sisters, I reckon. And a right pair of dolly birds they were.'

'Sisters?'

'Well . . . they looked so alike they had to be. The driver were older, I reckon. Late twenties, maybe. Dressed like a solicitor. She were the one filling the tank. The passenger went round to the other side of the car to speak to her sister, and then went off into the shop. She were younger, nineteen or twenty maybe, wearing those thick tights with nothing over 'em to hide her arse.'

'They call them leggings, Bill. And watch your language.' Mrs Dungworth shook her head and turned to Cassie. 'He knows, really, he's just acting the old fart.'

'I'm not complaining,' Bill said, and winked at Cassie. 'Only she'd have been had up for public indecency in my day.'

'Can you describe her, the younger one I mean? Anything at all that you remember about her.'

'I don't know?' Bill scratched his head. 'She were a tiny little thing, very slight but with . . .' Bill glanced at his wife, ' . . . well, she were flaunting it, weren't she.'

'Flaunting what,' Cassie asked.

Bill glanced at his wife again. 'Her backside. Proper peach of an arse, it were. Small, but—'

Mrs Dungworth elbowed her husband in the ribs.

He winced and closed his eyes.

'You can't talk that way in front of this nice young lass, Bill. You're forever shaming me.'

Mr Dungworth clutched his side. 'But that were her most distinguishing feature!'

Another dig in the ribs. 'You're a dirty old man, Bill Dungworth. I think the Inspector's more interested in her face.'

'Ah,' he said. 'Right pretty face she had on her, and reddish hair. Not bright ginger or anything like that, but not blond neither.'

'Auburn?' Mrs Dungworth said.

Mr Dungworth patted her arm and nodded.

Cassie rifled through her bag and dug out her iPad. 'Bear with me, please, Mr Dungworth,' she said while she ran an *'auburn hair'* search on Google Images, 'I'd like you to look at some pictures and tell me if you can identify either of the women you saw getting into that Mercedes.' She picked three images of pretty young models and showed them to Mr Dungworth, one at a time. He shook his head for each. Finally, she showed him a still of Gemma Grant outside Flynn's place.

'That's the lass,' he said immediately, 'the younger one, with the leggings and the . . .' he caught his wife glaring at him and stopped.

'Are you sure?'

'That's her.' He pointed at the screen. 'Definitely.'

Bill Dungworth looked very pleased with himself. 'Did your lot ever track down that pick-up?'

'Pick-up?' Cassie's eyes narrowed. 'What pick-up?'

'The pick-up truck that overtook us. We were right behind them lasses when we left the petrol station, and two lads in a pick-up were right behind *us*. It were like that all the way through Glossop. But soon as we got out of town and onto the Snake Pass she put her foot down – the lass in the Mercedes, I mean. The lads in the pick-up were desperate to overtake. I don't like to push my Cortina, you see. She's an old lady now. Doesn't look it though. Hard wax, that's the trick, none of that runny crap from a bottle. And elbow grease of course.'

'So, they overtook you, the two lads in the pick-up?' Cassie's hair slipped over her cheek and into her mouth, she drew it away from her face and tucked a lock behind her ear. 'And then they would have been directly behind the two women in the classic Mercedes'

'Aye, lass. Mitsubishi L200 Warrior, silver, with chrome bull bars. Seemed in a right hurry, they did. Going like the clappers! Right up her arse, they were, you know the type. They must've overtaken her, too.'

'Why do you say that?'

'Well, if they didn't overtake, they'd have stopped, wouldn't they, when they saw the Merc go over the edge.'

Mr Dungworth got up and went to the window. 'Looks like snow.'

'Thank you,' Cassie said, 'you've been really helpful.'

'*Helpful*, is it?' He spun on his heels. Bill Dungworth's eyes spat poison and his bottom lip was trembling. 'Well she's not for sale, and that's final.'

Cassie turned to Mrs Dungworth, who was standing now. Grace Dungworth held a finger to her lips and shook her head.

'Come on, Bill,' she said, grabbing her husband by the arm. She stroked his hand and ushered him towards the door. 'Hadn't you better go and check on her?'

Bill shot Cassie a last venomous look, before shaking off his wife's hand and storming out into the hall. Doors slammed. Then there was quiet.

Cassie looked around the living room. Flowery wallpaper – browns and oranges and greens. It was faded, with peeling top corners that drooped like spent tulips. The fire surround – teak-effect Formica, bubbled and chipped at the edges – was scorched ebony above the middle rank of gas burners.

Mrs Dungworth came back in, bright grey eyes all wet and puffy. 'I'm sorry, love,' she said, sounding weary. 'He doesn't mean it, he just gets confused. Now he's convinced himself that you want to take his precious Cortina away. We've had it forty years, that car, but it looks like new.'

Cassie said her thank yous and goodbyes and left the Dungworths' house. She wondered about her dad.

37

MEG PEERED THROUGH the widow of the second-hand bookshop next door while she waited for someone to answer her knock at 229 Sharrow Vale Road. She found herself remembering a brief dalliance with a History student who lived a couple of doors down during her second year at university. Meg was trying to remember his name when a young woman wearing a hooded onesie opened the door.

'DS Harper,' Meg said, fishing a warrant card from her coat pocket. 'I'm sorry, I didn't mean to get you out of bed.'

'You didn't,' the girl said, and unzipped her onesie to prove it. Underneath she was wearing jeans and a thick woolly jumper. 'The boiler's on the blink again, that's all, so it's bloody freezing in here.'

Meg kept her coat on and sat down at the kitchen table. 'Alice, is it?'

'Yes.' Alice pulled out the chair opposite and sat down. 'They said you wanted to talk to me about Gemma.'

Meg showed Alice a photo of Gemma. 'Is this her?'

Alice nodded. 'She was only here for three months, and I didn't have much to do with her, but yes, that's definitely her.'

'Good,' Meg said. 'And when did you see her last?'

'I don't know exactly. The last day of lectures before Christmas, I think. It was my very first semester, so it would have been two years ago. Zie and I went home for Christmas, but Gemma said she'd be staying here, in the house, for the holidays.'

'Zie?' Meg asked, showing Alice her attempt at the spelling in her pocketbook.

'Yes. It's short for something,' Alice scratched her head, 'but I can't remember what. She was a postgrad student from Nigeria. And she's back home in Nigeria now, as far as I know.'

'The agency says Gemma had left by the end of the Christmas vacation,' Meg said. 'Is that right?'

'Yes, when we got back in January she'd cleared out. Taken all her stuff and cleaned the whole house too – top to bottom.' Alice laughed. 'Well, that was a first! She always had some excuse when it was her turn on the rota.'

When she glanced up from her pocketbook Meg saw Alice's smile fade.

Alice covered her mouth with her hand and took a step back. 'Do you think—'

Meg interrupted: 'And did you try to contact her after she left.'

'No. Like I said, I didn't have much to do with her.' Alice seemed unable to look Meg in the eye anymore. She glanced frantically about the room for something else to fix on, eventually settling on the *Pulp Fiction* poster above the fridge. Her bottom lip began to tremble. 'I didn't have her phone number, or email, or anything. What could I have done? But I know the agency tried to get in touch with her. They phoned and they emailed, but she never replied.'

Meg put her pocketbook and pen down on the table. 'I see,' she said. 'I take it you didn't really get on with Gemma.'

'What do you mean by that?' Alice folded her arms and glared, tight lipped at the kitchen table. 'You've found her body, haven't you? And you think . . . That's why you're here, isn't it? You think that I murdered her and made it look like she'd just packed her bags and gone.'

'No,' Meg said, patting the girls folded arms. 'I know that Gemma was very much alive when she left this flat.'

Alice began to cry. 'Sorry,' she said, 'you caught me at a bad time. I've got exams coming up and I need to revise. And I should have done more over Christmas. And it's all getting on top of me.'

'Forget it,' Meg said, fishing a wad of tissues from her handbag and passing it to Alice. 'I know exactly what you're going through. What are you studying?'

Alice wiped her eyes and her nose and forced a smile. 'Chemistry,' she said.

'Me too!' Meg said, clapping her hands. 'I lived just around the corner from here when I was student. That was ten years ago, but it feels like yesterday. Sometimes. Sometimes it feels like a lifetime ago.'

Alice made no attempt to hide her surprise. 'So how did you end up in the police?'

'By accident.' Meg couldn't suppress a sigh. 'In fact—'

'Bloody hell,' Alice said, eyes wide. 'The Penthouse Murder. Was that Gemma?'

Meg picked up her pocketbook and pressed it to her chest. 'I'm afraid I can't discuss that case.'

'Oh my God.' Alice slumped back on her chair. 'Poor Gemma.'

There was no point denying it, Meg decided. But she wasn't going to confirm it either. 'Look, Alice, I'm just trying to find out everything I can about Gemma. You shared a house with her. Tell me what you know.'

'But I know nothing, honestly. She was properly posh, like one of those toffs from *Made in Chelsea*, and she was party girl – always out on the town. We made small talk in the kitchen occasionally, and that was about it.'

'What about Zie, did she socialise with Gemma?'

'God, no. Zie was a bit of a bible-thumper. She never said anything, but it was obvious what she thought of the sort of girl who stays out all night – the sort of girl who has a different man on her arm every week. And it was always older men with Gemma, most of them looked the wrong side of forty! Mind you, they were all rich, judging by the cars they turned up in. And I don't think her sister approved either.'

'Whose sister?'

'Gemma's. Older sister: late twenties, I'd say, so there must have been a good ten years between them.'

'You met Gemma's sister?'

'Not really. I saw her through the window. She'd pull up outside the house a couple of times every week, toot the horn, and Gemma would go off with her. Gemma told me she was loaded; she certainly had a nice car.'

'A Mercedes?'

Alice shrugged. 'I know nothing about cars. It was red and old fashioned, that's all I can tell you.'

Meg pulled up a photo of Sarah Flynn on her iPhone. 'Is this the sister?'

'Yes,' Alice said. 'Christ, if it wasn't for the age difference, you'd think she and Gemma were twins.'

Meg looked again at the photo of Sarah Flynn before turning back to Alice. 'So,' she said, 'what made you think she disapproved of Gemma's lifestyle?'

Alice shrugged. 'Maybe you're right. Maybe it was me who disapproved.'

Meg closed her pocketbook. 'Really, Alice, I didn't—'

'Although,' Alice continued, 'I do remember this one time . . .' she rubbed her chin ' . . . and I remember the date, too, because it was my birthday, 15th December. The sister had been tooting her horn for ages, so eventually I had to go out and tell her Gemma wasn't home. That's when she started asking all the questions. Where had Gemma gone? Who with? What time? She went on and on. She was a bit scary, actually. I told her that Gemma had gone off with some middle-aged bloke who turned up in one of those stretch limos. She even asked me if I remembered the registration number. Funnily enough I did, it was one of those silly ones where the letters and numbers read like a proper word. When I told her she went absolutely berserk. Wanted to know where they'd gone, and if Gemma had been out with him before.'

'And?' Meg said, a little more eagerly than had been her intention. 'What did you tell her?'

Alice held up her hands. 'Nothing. I didn't know anything.'

'And the registration number?'

Alice closed her eyes and twisted her mouth. She rubbed circles around her temples for a few seconds. 'Sorry,' she said at last. 'It's gone.'

38

CASSIE REREAD THE final sentence of Flynn's story one last time. She'd spent a good fifteen minutes thinking about those dozen or so words, but still couldn't decide whether they signalled hope or resignation. Her kitchen was eerily quiet now, so she turned on the radio and flicked through the stations until she found one playing an upbeat pop song. It didn't help. She couldn't stop thinking about what she'd just read.

The Wythenshawe Dandy was the most gut-wrenching account of a teenager's life she'd ever come across. Stella had painted a pretty bleak picture of what Wythenshawe was like back in the day, but Flynn's story did more than paint a picture – it took you there, it made you wince, it made you cry. It was a hard story told in gentle words: Flynn's words; Flynn's voice; Flynn's story.

Cassie turned up the volume on the radio and dabbed her eyes with kitchen paper torn carelessly from the roll.

When Meg Harper arrived, shortly after midday, the quiche Lorraine was in the oven and the kitchen table was set for lunch.

Meg told Cassie about her dad, and her mum, and her sister in Australia. Meg's sister had a husband and two children, and two Sundays ago her mum had said that it was just her luck that the daughter who'd given her grandchildren was the daughter who'd gone to live on the other side of the world. And Meg said, 'Thanks a lot, Mum.' And then her dad said Mum didn't mean it like that. And then her mum started to cry. And then Meg cried, too. And then her mum said she was very proud of her policeman daughter, and she was just upset about not having seen her grandchildren for two years. And then her dad said they were both very proud. And then they all went for a nice pub lunch.

'Graham and I talked about kids, a year or so ago,' Meg said, 'he was dead keen, actually. Christ, I'm glad it never happened, not with that bastard. What about you?'

Cassie turned away and crouched in front of the oven. She peered through the glass, watching the quiche gently bubble and brown. It shouldn't matter, she told herself. But it bloody well did matter. She got up and straightened her jumper. 'We've both moved on, haven't we, Meg?'

Meg put her hands on her hips. 'Yeah, right.'

Cassie folded her arms.

Meg looked around the kitchen. 'God, I wish my place looked as lovely as this,' she said. 'It feels like a proper grown-up's house. So neat and tidy and perfect – reminds me of my mother's kitchen. Hers is nothing like as posh, of course, but it's always clean and neat and tidy. I'd be ashamed to let you see mine. It's bad enough when Mum comes around. She never *says* anything, of course, but she always brings her Marigolds and a bucket full of cleaning stuff. Yes, this a proper kitchen, and *you*'ll make a proper mum, Cassie – a cake-baking, jam-making, clean-fingernailed mum. Not like me, I'm the sort of scummy cow who'll let her kids wallow in filth and feed them stuff from packets.'

Cassie, who was busy polishing already clean plates with a tea towel, smiled. 'My mum . . .' she began. She put the plates on the table and swallowed hard.

Meg raised her eyebrows.

Cassie hung the tea towel on a rack that slid out from under the worktop. 'Well,' she said, 'I'm sorry to shatter your illusions, but this quiche was bought ready-made from Waitrose.'

Meg feigned a look of horror.

'Mind you,' Cassie went on, 'it was baked by Heston Blumenthal, apparently.'

Meg laughed. 'I suppose it keeps him busy!'

The meal began in silence. Cassie had lots to tell and lots to ask. But it wouldn't be polite, she thought, to invite someone to lunch on her day off and then start talking shop. The reason she'd invited Meg to her house, rather than some pub or café, was, after all, to make it personal. Angus had touched a nerve: he was right, she didn't have a woman friend who she could talk to, not properly.

Meg attacked her quiche like a Labrador, refilling her mouth before she'd finished chewing the last forkful.

'It's not like you,' Cassie said, 'to take a day off in the middle of a case.'

'Foster rang me up last night and told me to take the day off in lieu of overtime – they've gone massively over budget, apparently. I'd have offered to go in for no pay, but, well, I know when I'm not wanted. Bugger the lot of them. Muxlow managed to find the money to run a second forensics sweep of Flynn's apartment, so if they think—'

'A second sweep?' Cassie's dark eyes narrowed. 'What was wrong with the first one?'

'Nothing – except that they didn't find anything.'

Cassie stared at her lunch but didn't feel hungry. Meg had started talking shop, so it would be rude not to indulge her. 'Any progress?' she asked. 'On anything?'

'Actually,' Meg said, 'yes.'

❧

Meg recounted what she'd learned from Gemma's old flatmate, Alice: Gemma's party lifestyle and her taste in wealthy older men; the visits from Gemma's putative sister (who Alice had confidently

ID'd as Sarah Flynn); Sarah's reaction on being told that Gemma had gone off with the man in the stretch limo.

Cassie wiped her mouth with a paper napkin and took a sip of water. She dabbed her lips, refolded the napkin, put it back on the table. 'How many stretch limo firms can there be in Sheffield?'

'More than you'd think!' Meg said. 'Believe me, I've checked. And besides, the limo could have been rented from anywhere in the country, or it might not be rented at all.'

'Yes, Meg, I appreciate it'll be a lot of work. But I think the man in the limo might just be the key to all this.'

'Maybe. Maybe not.' Meg shovelled the last piece of quiche into her mouth with eager fingers. 'According to Alice,' she said, pausing a moment to chew, 'Gemma went out on the town with plenty of other sugar daddies.'

'I know, but it's Sarah's reaction to this particular man that makes me think he's important. Alice says that when she told Sarah the registration number, she completely lost it. Sarah wasn't the type to lose it. She was hard and cold and calculating. If she lost her cool there had to be a bloody good reason.'

'What?' Meg said, brow furrowed. 'And finding out that your fifteen-year-old daughter has gone off with some middle-aged man isn't enough to make any mother lose it?'

Cassie pressed the flat of her hand against her forehead. 'I know. But, still, will you have someone look into it?'

'Maybe,' Meg said. She narrowed her eyes and pointed her fork at Cassie's plate. 'But only if you give me what's left of your quiche.'

Cassie smiled and pushed her plate across the table. 'And what about the killings at Parkgate School?'

'We're getting nowhere with that, to be honest,' Meg mumbled, through a mouthful of Cassie's left-over quiche. 'No one knows anything about anything – which isn't a surprise, given who we're talking about. And no one seems to know where Gary Mulligan might be – which isn't a surprise either.'

'No, I suppose not,' Cassie said. 'And the phone, the one they found in Flynn's toilet cistern? Anything concrete to link it to Flynn?'

'No. No fingerprints, no DNA, nothing.' Meg looked up at the ceiling before turning back to Cassie. 'Look, I don't think Flynn sent those texts to Gemma. I asked his phone company for a printout of the last six months of texts sent from his usual mobile. Eight text messages! Flynn doesn't do texting, does he. Flynn doesn't do *textspeak* either. He makes proper sentences, with capital letters and proper punctuation and proper spelling. Look at these . . .' Meg brought out her phone and showed Cassie a list of the text messages that Flynn was supposed to have sent from the pay-as-you-go mobile found in his toilet cistern. 'And look at the last one.'

The last text on the list read:

sent taxi 2 collect u
be w8ing in pick up zone at 9:45
blue vauxhall insignia

'Hmmm,' Cassie said.

'Of course, he may have written his texts like that deliberately, to put us off the trail.' Meg turned her attention back to the quiche.

'It's all bollocks,' Cassie said. 'That phone was planted in his cistern for us to find. How can Foster not see that?'

'The problem is, we've no other theories, no other leads.'

'Hang on though, you have a phone number for Gemma now, right?'

'Yes, but it's only a pay as you go, and its battery's probably dead, so there's not much chance of finding it.'

'Even so, the number itself might be useful. And will you send me a copy of Gemma's call history?'

'You'll get me sacked, Cassie.'

'I'll be discreet, I promise.'

'Ha! Right.' Meg smiled and shook her head. 'The phone company promised I'd have it by this afternoon, but I wouldn't hold your breath.'

Cassie was finding it difficult to look Meg in the eye, knowing what Flynn had told her about events at Parkgate school, so she changed the subject: 'I've found out some more about Gemma Grant.'

Meg listened without comment, poker faced, munching the quiche, ignoring the salad, and occasionally taking a sip of water. When Cassie had finished, Meg ruffled her gel-tousled hair and said, 'So let me get this straight: two years ago, Gemma Grant is tracked down in Edinburgh by a private investigator, David Roland. She comes to Sheffield to meet Sarah Flynn, her natural mother, for the first time since she was given up for adoption. Sarah sorts her out with digs – secretly, because your Mr Wonderful knew nothing about his own wife having a kid. Then, one day, she drives over to Manchester with Gemma and drops her off at the Trafford Centre with a credit card to play with. Meanwhile Sarah goes off to the *Manchester Evening News* to dig the dirt on some gangster called Scott Deakin. On the way back, Deakin's thugs run Sarah's car off the road. Sarah is killed, but Gemma escapes somehow. And we know she escaped because she's around to be murdered two years later. Have I got it right so far?'

'Yes. I know it's all a bit . . .' Cassie shrugged and blew out a long breath.

'Far-fetched?' Meg said, spluttering pastry crumbs.

❧

It didn't take long to clear the table, Meg tried to help but Cassie waved her away. When the dishwasher was loaded, and the olive pits thrown in the bin, and the table wiped clean, and the crumbs swept from the floor, and the kettle put on, Cassie sat down. She folded her arms and eyed Meg like a chided teenager. 'Go on then.'

'Look,' Meg put her elbows on the table and leaned in, 'your theory about Gemma being killed to shut her up about underage sex is the only credible motive that I've heard so far. Foster is saying that Flynn killed Gemma to get at her trust fund, but I'm not convinced. I've been through Flynn's finances: he might be skint now, but when the shop and the flats are bringing in rent, he'll be fine. People who murder for money are either very greedy or very desperate, and I don't think James Flynn is either.'

'But you said my theory was *far-fetched?*'

'Okay, that was unfair,' Meg said. 'But it *is* full of holes. Where did Gemma Grant disappear to after she escaped the car crash? And why did she disappear? And why didn't she get help? And why didn't she wait for the emergency services?'

Cassie unfolded her arms and lay her hands flat on the table. 'If someone had just run *you* off the road, would you wait around for them to finish you off?'

'And if Gemma did leave Sheffield, why did she come back?' Meg's tone was becoming more and more insistent. 'And why did she try to make contact with Flynn?'

The kettle clicked off and Cassie got up to make the coffee. 'I don't know,' she said. 'Maybe she wanted to get at her trust fund.'

'Did she even know about the trust fund?' Meg looked doubtful. 'That slimy solicitor, Smythe-Brown, says he never managed to track her down.'

Cassie grabbed a pair of tall white coffee cups from the shelf, set them by the cafetière, and sat down.

'Promise me you'll keep away from Flynn,' Meg said. 'I think he's dangerous.'

'He's not a murderer, Meg.'

'Maybe not. But he is involved somehow, you must see that. Gemma was killed at his flat, and his phone connects him to the Parkgate School killings. Please stay away from him, Cassie. Both our careers are on the line here. If Muxlow finds out I'm talking to you about all this, I'm finished.'

'He won't find out.'

'Will you stay away from Flynn?'

Cassie pushed down the plunger on the cafetière and poured.

'I'm not saying he's done anything wrong, Cassie.' Meg held her steaming cup under her nose a while before putting it down on the slate coaster that Cassie nudged across the table. 'Perhaps you're right. Perhaps his wife knew something dangerous and someone thinks that *he* knows it too. But if that's the case why frame him for murder? Why not just kill him?'

'They tried hard enough,' Cassie said. She was off her guard with Meg: it was like being a teenager again, like having a girlfriend you share everything with. But Flynn's abduction was something she hadn't wanted to share just yet. She was furious with herself.

'What do you mean?' Meg said. '*They tried hard enough?*'

'Nothing, I just . . .'

'Cassie,' Meg said, looking properly cross now, 'what are you talking about? Who tried to kill him?'

'Shall we go for a walk?' Cassie said. She got up and went over to the window. 'It's sunny out.'

'No!' Meg slammed down her cup, spilling coffee all over the table. 'I want you to tell me what's going on. For Christ's sake, Cassie, you're as bad as Muxlow.'

Cassie squared up to Meg: 'What do you mean by that?'

Meg didn't reply.

Cassie folded her arms. She desperately wanted to clean up the spilt coffee and put Meg's mug back on the coaster.

'Well,' Meg said, shifting in her seat, 'I just mean that you know more than you're letting on.'

Cassie didn't reply

Meg waited.

Cassie still didn't respond.

'Like I said,' Meg continued, calmly now, 'there has to be some other agency involved, and Muxlow is working with them, or *for* them. Think about it: Sarah Fitzroy-Parker, Jamie Boreman, Scott Deakin – they all disappeared off the radar about fifteen years ago. I reckon they were all on some sort of witness protection programme.'

Cassie shook her head.

'Anyway,' Meg said, 'tell me about Flynn. You said somebody tried to kill him?'

Cassie fetched a box of Chocolate Viennese Whirls from the pantry.

Meg folded her arms. 'Are you going to tell me?'

'Have a Viennese Whirl,' Cassie said, emptying the pack onto a plate. She wiped up the spilt coffee, put Meg's cup on a coaster, and put out individual plates to catch any Viennese Whirl crumbs.

'This is supposed to work both ways, Cassie.' Meg's fingers were tight around the top of the chair. 'I've kept quiet about what you're up to, I've told you things that I shouldn't, and still you won't be straight with me.'

'Come on, Meg, you don't like the way Muxlow and Foster are handling this case any more than I do.' Cassie's eyes were wide and shone amber in the cold light from the kitchen window. 'So don't go blaming all this on me!' When the sun went behind a cloud, her eyes softened to the colour of cocoa. She looked down at her box of biscuits.

'You have to tell me what you know,' Meg said. 'This isn't going to work otherwise. You have to share. You have to trust me.'

Cassie looked at the floor. 'What if we don't agree on what to do next?'

'We have to agree, don't we?' Meg said. 'We just have to.'

Chocolate Viennese Whirls reminded Cassie of picnics in Epping Forest. The smell alone sparked memories of how it had been at home before things started to go wrong. Cassie took a bite.

Meg watched her chew.

Cassie took another bite, and then another. She ate slowly, savouring every mouthful. When she had finished, she wiped up the stray crumbs that had missed her plate with a damp cloth and dried the table with a tea towel. Then she told Meg about Flynn's kidnapping, and about Trevor Murray having his finger cut off and his throat slashed, and about Mulligan's knife, and about Mulligan wanting some photographs, and about how Flynn got away, and about Mulligan having planned everything to happen at Flynn's place on the morning of the day Gemma was murdered.

Meg reached for a Viennese Whirl. She wolfed it down in three bites and grabbed another. 'Shit,' she said, brushing the crumbs from her lips with the back of her hand.

'I know.' Cassie nodded without conviction. 'But we still don't know who shot Carl Yates. And are we any closer to finding Gary Mulligan?'

'No.' Meg looked down at the table. 'Cassie, listen. Sean Mulligan's throat was cut execution style, ear to ear, while he was face down on the floor. Just like Trevor Murray. It's done from behind to avoid blood spatter. That's what Dr Latimer told me. I'd never seen anything like it.

'If Foster gets hold of Flynn,' Cassie said, 'they'll pin the whole thing on him and that'll be that.'

'Yes, but . . .' Meg swallowed the last of her second Viennese Whirl and grabbed another. 'Did you hear what I just said?'

'Trevor Murray was killed by Carl Yates,' Cassie said, ignoring the question. 'Yates is known for carrying a Stanley knife, so Flynn's story fits. And Sean Mulligan, whatever you say, was killed in self-defence. Flynn didn't have to tell me, did he? And why lie about the others but admit to killing Sean Mulligan? It makes no sense unless he's telling the truth.'

There was nothing to read in Meg's expression; Cassie chose to interpret the silent biscuit eating as tacit agreement.

When she had finished her third Viennese Whirl, and licked her lips, and wiped her fingers on her jeans, Meg considered her coffee. She picked up the cup and brought it halfway to her lips before putting it down again. 'Cassie, everything you've told me points to *Gemma* being the target of that hit and run on the Snake Pass, not her mother. If your underage sex theory is right, maybe she tried to extort money from someone and it all went wrong.'

'Maybe, but—'

Meg slapped the table. 'Maybe the photos Sean Mulligan wanted from Flynn are photos that Gemma was using for blackmail. You thought Gemma was carrying an envelope with photographs outside Flynn's place. Perhaps she was delivering them to Flynn for safe keeping. Perhaps she'd been lying low for a couple of years after the car crash but decided to try blackmail again.'

'But Flynn knew nothing about Gemma and nothing about the photographs!' Cassie sounded defensive and she knew it. She spread her fingers wide either side of her coffee cup. 'No. Mulligan expected the photos to be on a computer, that's why he went to the trouble of having it taken from Flynn's place. He wasn't expecting hard copies – Gemma turning up at Flynn's place with what look like photographs is just a coincidence. It might not have been photographs, anyway; it could have been something else.' She racked her brains. 'A copy of the deed of trust that Sarah had given her: that would have been an A4 document – a perfect fit, and too thick to fold. That's why she had it in her hand and not in that little bag she was carrying.'

'I still can't believe she'd have waited two years if she knew about the trust fund.' Meg shook her head and drew a long breath.

There was a calm in Meg's voice that Cassie found unnerving. Here was a woman able to switch her emotions on and off at will. Cassie couldn't even hide hers. If she could she'd be a Chief Inspector by now, or even a Superintendent.

'Have you checked his computer for the photographs?' Meg asked.

Cassie hesitated.

That was enough for Meg: 'Where were you last night?' she said. 'I called by. A few times, actually. Please tell me you weren't with Flynn.'

'There's nothing on his computer,' Cassie said. 'I checked it before I was taken off the case.' It was a lie, of course, but the bit about there being nothing on Flynn's computer was true enough. Angus had checked. Of course, Angus might have been lying. But she had chosen to trust him.

Meg looked sceptical. 'Wouldn't it have been better to bring it in for our techies to check out?'

'No need, I've been on a course.'

'I know. I was on that course too.' Meg twisted her mouth into an expression of unfettered scorn.

'Yes, well.' Cassie took a sip of coffee; it was tepid. She grabbed Meg's half-full cup and poured the lot down the sink. 'I'll make some fresh.'

'Okay, fine.' Meg helped herself to the last Viennese Whirl. 'But those photos, whatever they are, must be somewhere.'

The cups squeaked as Cassie went at them with her dish cloth. Halfway through drying the second cup she stopped and spun round. 'Christ Almighty, Meg, you're right. I see it now!'

'What?'

'The link. The link between Sarah Flynn and Gemma Grant and Sean Mulligan. Mulligan has to be mixed up in all of this somehow. Maybe he, or his son, or one of their cronies, botched the attack on the Snake Pass: killed Sarah but missed Gemma. It was a contract killing ordered by whoever was being blackmailed. Gemma disappears and they don't get another chance until she reappears in Sheffield two years later. Someone spots her, and Mulligan finishes the job.'

'So you agree that Gemma was the target back then, not her mother.'

Cassie grabbed a tea towel and dried her hands. 'Probably.'

'Or maybe the two attempts on her life aren't linked,' Meg said. 'Maybe she was at it again – the blackmailing, I mean. Someone else, someone new. Why does it have to be the same killer?'

'Because she'd only just come back to Sheffield. She'd only been here a few hours.'

'How do you know she ever left? How do you know she hasn't been hiding in Sheffield for the last two years?'

'Because if I'd been in her shoes, when I crawled out of the wreckage of that Mercedes, I'd have wanted to get as far away from Sheffield as I could.'

Meg conceded the point with a frown.

'And another thing,' Cassie tapped the table with her finger. 'Unlawful sex is the big deal here. After she turned sixteen the stakes wouldn't have been so high.'

'Yes,' Meg said, 'but she wouldn't be the first person murdered to cover up a run-of-the-mill affair.'

Cassie glared at her.

Meg held up her hands: 'Fair enough. But what about Flynn? Why go to the trouble of framing him?'

'To divert attention from the real killer. Think about it, Flynn is the perfect fall guy – who else can you name with a link to Gemma Grant? Who else would gain from her death? Why would the police need to look any further?'

Meg looked out of the window. 'We haven't.'

Outside, a squirrel was gnawing at the wire mesh of a bird feeder dangling from a high branch. Hanging upside down by its back legs, it was pulling the feeder to its mouth with one paw, and gripping a nearby twig with another. The twig snapped, and the squirrel tumbled into the shrubbery below. Within a few seconds it was back on the high branch, reappraising the lie of the bird feeder and considering its options. Or perhaps it was a different squirrel.

'And what about the photos?' Meg said, turning back to Cassie. 'Why not just kill Flynn and destroy the computer?'

'I don't know. But you're right. Destroying the photographs wasn't what Mulligan was about. He wanted copies for himself.'

'But why, Cassie? Unless he was planning to do a little blackmailing himself.'

Cassie nodded, slowly. 'Yes, it's the only reason I can think of.'

'Unless it was Mulligan himself, in the photos.'

Cassie shook her head. 'No, he wouldn't be Gemma's type. And besides, I can't imagine Gemma blackmailing someone like Sean Mulligan. She'd choose someone less likely to cave her head in with a baseball bat, surely.'

'Well she got *that* wrong then!'

Cassie closed her eyes and threw her head back. 'Yes. But who?'

Meg dabbed a large crumb of Viennese Whirl from the table with a wet finger, licked it off, and turned back to the window.

Cassie followed her eyes. The squirrel and the bird feeder were gone – all that remained was a small length of garden twine still attached to the branch.

'I can't help thinking we're taking too much for granted,' Meg said. She gave Cassie a schoolteacher's frown. 'We're working on hypotheses. There isn't any firm evidence.'

'I know that, Meg. We're doing the best we can with what we've got.'

Meg wasn't listening. 'Take your theory about why Flynn

was framed,' she said. 'You'd need to know everything there was to know about the target, and you'd need to be able to pull off a murder without leaving a shred of evidence.'

Meg got up and put on her coat. She ruffled her hair and slipped her hands into her pockets.

'Oh, come on, Meg, you're not still banging on about MI5 and Special Branch, surely? That's more far-fetched than any of *my* theories. And answer me this: *why?*'

'I don't know, but it's the only explanation that makes all of this hang together.'

'There *will* be another explanation, Meg. We just have to find it.'

Meg nodded, uncertainly, and made for the door. 'Can *you* think of anyone else? Anyone else with the contacts, or resources, or both, to pull off four murders, five maybe, and not leave us with so much as a lead?'

Cassie shrugged. There was Angus, of course, but that was a ridiculous notion. And besides, she had decided to trust Angus. So she said nothing, and Meg left having had the last word.

39

IT WAS EARLY afternoon, but a heavy sky made it feel like dusk. Cassie was sitting in her car outside David Roland's offices, wondering what to do. The police have rules for everything – rules that had been developed and honed over decades, rules that work. The problem with playing by your own rules, she was beginning to understand, is that sometimes you end up having to make them up as you go along.

A couple of minutes earlier, while manoeuvring her Mini into the small space between a white van and a skip, she'd seen a man leave Roland's building and get into the back of a minicab. She hadn't recognised him immediately, and by the time she did, the minicab was out of sight.

Gary Mulligan! She'd seen *Gary Mulligan* leaving Roland's building.

Too late to follow him. Perhaps she should call Meg.

As the skies above Sheffield grew heavier, so the clouds in her head grew thicker. She closed her eyes. By the time she opened them again it was too late. Too late, certainly, to ring Meg.

The offices of David Roland and Associates Ltd were in a grand Victorian house, at the end of an unadopted road, in the leafy back streets of Broomhill. Cassie had already run a few searches on David Roland's business. There was no trace of any associates, as far as she could tell, and she could find no record of a limited company by that name.

The contrast between the inside and outside of the building was remarkable; and as much as Cassie hated to be impressed, she was. The ground floor had been gutted and modernised. All the internal walls had been removed but the supporting beams were slung low enough to keep the original coving intact. Everything was white. Floor-to-ceiling glass panels separated the entrance hall from an open-plan office (sleek desks populated by sleek staff). One of the glass panels was actually a door – a young woman with a serious expression, and a serious suit, came through it and greeted Cassie with a serious handshake.

'Detective Inspector May,' she said, holding up a white envelope. 'I have the photograph you asked for: Gemma Grant – a nice head and shoulders shot. Unfortunately, we could only find a hard copy, not the original JPEG; it must have been filed before we went fully digital. But I've done you a photocopy and I've scanned it onto an SD card for you.'

'Thank you.' Cassie offered an appreciative nod.

'Pleased to help.' The young woman produced a *meeting-over* smile and went to open the front door.

Cassie opened the envelope and studied the photograph. 'Do you know who took this?'

'I'm afraid not. Like I said, it was before we went fully digital.'

'Location? Date?'

The young woman, uncomfortable in the draught coming through the half open front door, pushed it almost closed. 'I was asked to give you the photograph, that's all. And as I've already said, it was filed—'

'Before you went fully digital?'

'Yes.' She opened the door again.

'And your name is?'

'Sally Jones.'

'So, Miss Jones—'

'*Mrs*, actually.' She raised her left hand and splayed her fingers so that Cassie could better inspect her diamond engagement ring and platinum wedding band.

'So, *Sally*,' Cassie said, without acknowledging the jewellery, 'who was it that told you to give me this photograph?'

Sally pushed the front door closed and folded her arms. 'Mr Roland's PA, Mrs Davison.'

'And it was Mrs Davison who found the photograph for me?'

'Yes. It'll be from the archives, from the time before—'

'Before you went fully digital?'

Sally scowled. 'I think you're very rude, Inspector May. I can't image that's the best way to go about information gathering. It's certainly not how we go about things at David Roland and Associates.'

'I'm sorry, Sally. People have been telling me I'm *bossy* for years, and maybe they're right. They also say I'm *pushy*, and maybe they're right about that too. Of course, if I were a man they'd call me a born leader, and say I was tenacious, don't you think?' Cassie smiled when Sally gave a conciliatory nod. 'Now, would you please tell your boss I'm here to see him. I assume that's his Porsche Cayenne in the car park – private plates: *1 DR*.'

Sally Jones rolled her eyes, pointed to a white leather sofa, and scurried upstairs.

The first floor had been given the chic white treatment too, but here there were proper rooms, with proper walls. She was led into the conference room. Mrs Davison introduced herself as Mr Roland's Executive Assistant; she was a craggy woman of about sixty who wore an *I told you so* expression that Cassie suspected was permanent. David Roland was seated at the head of the table; Mrs Davison sat Cassie two chairs away before leaving the room and pulling the door shut with a little more force than was required.

'What can I do you for?' Roland spoke in a course Manchester accent.

Cassie took out the photograph of Gemma Grant. 'I believe you tracked her down in Edinburgh a couple of years ago. Gemma Grant, the daughter of your client, Sarah Flynn.'

Roland didn't react. He just stared back in a way, Cassie imagined, that would make any woman feel uncomfortable.

'She was murdered on Friday,' Cassie said.

Roland rolled his eyes. 'Yes, you explained all this to my PA over the phone. You said you wanted a photograph to help with your investigation . . . and there it is.' He nodded at the envelope that Cassie was holding. 'I always do what I can to help the police.'

'I understand that *you* handled the case, Mr Roland,' Cassie said. 'Personally, I mean, for Mrs Flynn?'

'She was a good client, and that's the way she wanted it.'

'Was Gemma difficult to track down?'

'No.'

'So . . .' Cassie placed the envelope on the table and rested her hands either side. 'You found her, you told her about her mother, and you brought her here – to Sheffield. Where did she live while she was in Sheffield?'

'Hold your horses, love. I made contact with her in Edinburgh and that was that.' Roland leaned back in his chair and folded his arms. 'Afterwards, I handed everything over to Sarah Flynn. Gemma Grant coming to Sheffield is news to me.'

'So, you never saw her in Sheffield?'

'Like I said . . .'

'And how many times did you meet with her in Edinburgh?'

'Just the once. I told her what I'd been asked to tell her, got her contact details, and that was that.'

'And what were you asked to tell her.'

Pressing beefy elbows into the armrests, Roland shifted in his chair. His stocky torso tested the seams of what looked like a very expensive suit as he moved. His shirt cuffs rose up a little, revealing part of a tattoo on the inside of his left wrist. A snake's head, in lurid green and red. He tugged his sleeve back into place and refolded his arms. 'Look, *Detective Inspector*, Sarah Flynn asked me to do a job. She wanted it done quick and discreet like. I sorted it. And that's that.'

'But you took photographs . . .' Cassie tapped the picture of Gemma Grant. 'Why?'

'My client wanted photographs. Hardly surprising, is it? She hadn't seen the girl since she was born.'

'Can I see the others.'

'I only kept the one.'

Cassie stared at him. He stared right back. Roland was lying about something, maybe everything. 'So,' she said, 'whereabouts in Edinburgh was this taken?'

As Roland affected a non-committal shrug, the door opened and Mrs Davison came in. She scurried over to her boss and placed a notepad in front of him. He tore off the top page, stuffed it into his jacket pocket, and stood up. Roland's face was impossible to read – sharp nosed and pale cheeked, it looked incapable of rendering emotion – but his body language gave him away: whatever was on that note had alarmed him.

'I have to take this call, Inspector. Mrs Davison will show you out.'

'I'll wait.'

Roland was already at the door. 'No, I . . .'

He didn't finish. Cassie heard a door slam somewhere in the building and found herself alone with Mrs Davison. Mrs Davison picked up her notebook, tucked it under her arm and nodded at the open conference room door.

'I'll wait,' Cassie said, and looked away.

Mrs Davison left without a word. Her office was directly opposite the conference room. She sat down at her desk and glared at her computer screen. Both doors had been left open, presumably so that Mrs Davison could keep an eye on things. Cassie smiled at her across the hall. Mrs Davison pretended not to notice.

There was nothing of interest in the conference room: a few abstract Ikea prints, a water cooler in the corner, a telephone on the table. Cassie didn't really know what it was she was waiting for, but she wasn't quite ready to leave. She couldn't think of anything else to ask David Roland – she had already decided not to mention seeing Gary Mulligan leave the office (instinct told her to keep that to herself) – and even if she *were* to think of something to ask Roland, it was hard to imagine him giving her a straight answer.

Sometimes, if you keep quiet for long enough, a suspect will volunteer information just to break the silence. But David Roland was not that sort of suspect. And anyway, Cassie didn't know exactly what it was that she suspected him *of*.

Five long minutes went by. She looked at her watch and found herself remembering a hospital waiting room (Mum had been admitted after collapsing in the bathroom). Dad was the only other person there. He tried to give Cassie a hug, but she stiffened in his arms. He had left, he had done them wrong, and she would never let him forget it. Never. Nobody could explain why Mum had collapsed, but Cassie knew that you can't live on green tea, digestive biscuits and sleeping pills. Telling the doctors this would probably make things worse. Only *she* could help her mother.

A phone rang in Mrs Davison's office. By the time Cassie had collected herself and looked across the hall, Mrs Davison had left the room.

Without giving it much thought, Cassie wandered across the hallway and into her office for a nose around. Other than the notebook that Mrs Davison had brought into the conference room earlier, a password-locked computer, and a chintzy mug full of half chewed biros, the desk was clear. She tore the top page from the notebook, folded it in half, and slipped it into her jacket pocket. There were a few shelves packed with ring binders on the back wall: purchase invoices, sales invoices, time sheets, expenses, VAT, PAYE. There was no time to look, and besides, what she was really interested in were the records from back in 2012, and all that was on display were the 2013/14 files. As she made to return to the conference room something caught her eye: the wastepaper basket was empty but for two squares of photographic paper with a faint *Kodak* logo printed at regular intervals on the back. Cassie picked them out of the bin and turned them over; she immediately recognised Sheffield Railway Station. There were a few figures in the background of each – people with suitcases, people with briefcases, a small child with a balloon – all out of focus. A door opened and closed up the hall; Cassie shoved the photographs into her pocket.

Mrs Davison was back.

'Ah, there you are,' Cassie said.

Without saying anything, Mrs Davison made her feelings plain. She glanced around her office and looked Cassie up and down.

Cassie produced her best smile. 'I just wanted to let you know that something has come up. Please give my apologies to Mr Roland, tell him I'll be in touch.'

40

THE CALL CAME only a minute after she'd left Cassie's house. Meg was minded not to answer but curiosity got the better of her. 'Sir, what can I do for you.'

DCI Foster cleared his throat. 'The National Crime Agency are going to raid 8 Devonshire Rise this afternoon. I need eyes on the ground.'

'Gary Mulligan's place?' Meg said. 'Everyone knows it's a posh knocking shop, but I can't see why NCA would be interested. Besides, Vic and Charlie took a team to search the place yesterday and found nothing.'

'Look, Harper, I'm in Newcastle, it's snowing, and it's gonna take hours to get back to Sheffield. So I need you at Devonshire Rise within the hour. Sooner if you can. NCA are expecting you.'

'To do what? And why me? I'm on leave, remember.'

'Because I don't want to send a fuckwit. You'll be our liaison officer.'

Meg didn't reply. She was only getting half the story, and she hated that.

'Harper!' Foster bellowed. 'Harper, can you hear me? And where are you, anyway? Can you get to Devonshire Rise in an hour or not?'

'Yes,' Meg said calmly. 'But, sir, you're going to have to tell me what's going on.' She got into her car, started the engine, and turned the heating up to max.

Foster fell silent, but Meg could hear him breathing, fast and shallow, at the other end. 'The thing is,' he said at last, 'I think Vic and Charlie might have dropped me in the shit . . .'

❧

Meg was surprised to find the whole of Devonshire Rise had been cordoned off. A uniformed constable in a bulletproof vest pointed out the officer in charge.

'You must be Detective Superintendent Baker,' she said offering her hand.

Baker accepted with a broad smile. 'That's right. Steve Baker, NCA.'

Meg smiled back. 'Meg Harper, local liaison.' The involvement of the National Crime Agency could only mean that she was right about Muxlow keeping things back from the team. Perhaps . . . Perhaps what? Meg didn't know – nothing made any sense.

Steve Baker was an athletic looking black man. He looked about her age, but you didn't make Superintendent by thirty. Older, then. Forty? Handsome bugger, she had to admit, when she found herself staring; and rather dapper: well-cut suit, slim silk tie, leather-soled brogues. But *those* shoes in *this* weather?

Meg looked down at the frayed cuffs on the very sensible woollen overcoat she'd bought from a charity shop when she was a twenty-year-old student, and felt very frumpy indeed.

Baker nodded towards the six firearms officers gathered either side the front door of number eight. 'We'll go in as soon as the Armed Response Unit give us the all clear.'

'I suppose you've been briefed on what happened to the Mulligan crew at Parkgate School.'

'Yes,' Baker said. 'But that's not why Armed Response are here. They're here because we had a report of a gunshot coming from this house.'

'What! When?' Meg, furious about not having been properly

briefed, and feeling like a fool, thrust her hands into her coat pockets like a petulant eight-year-old.

Baker looked at his watch. 'Forty-five minutes ago.'

'And we're sure it was a gunshot?' Meg asked. 'Only this isn't the sort of place . . .' She didn't finish her sentence; she already felt like an idiot so decided to stop digging.

'The guy who called it in has just come back from a tour in Afghanistan,' Baker said. 'He was walking past the house when he heard it. He reckoned it was a pistol rather than a rifle or shotgun. He seemed pretty sure.'

The sound of number eight's front door being battered down brought an end to the conversation. Meg and Baker turned back to the house and watched the armed officers pile in. There was lots of shouting, but no gunshots. Ten minutes later the whole unit was back outside taking positions around the building.

'Here comes the team leader,' Baker said, 'Sergeant Mark Heeley.' He dropped his voice to a whisper. 'I really don't know what to make of people who like guns.'

Meg couldn't help thinking that Heeley walked a little bit like John Wayne. Or maybe he was just a little bit wary of the ice underfoot. Or maybe she was just a little bit prejudiced.

'There's a body on the first floor,' Heeley said. 'Male, twenties, gunshot wound to the head, very recent. Looks like suicide, there was a pistol on the floor beside him. We found no one else in the building.'

Baker turned to Meg: 'Would you make the call please, Meg.' Then he turned back to Heeley. 'So what's with the perimeter if there's no one in there?'

With her phone pressed to her ear, and stomping her cold feet in the snow, Meg waited for someone at the office to pick up.

'You mentioned a basement in your briefing,' Heeley said, resting one hand on his holstered pistol and the other on his ammunition pouch, 'but we didn't find one. No doors or trapdoors:

nothing. And no obvious access to a basement from outside either.'

While she was waiting to get put through to the Duty Sergeant at the station, Meg found herself unable to take her eyes off Heeley's gun – he had his thumb pressed into the curve of the handle and was running a fingertip along the lip of the holster he had strapped to his thigh. Back and forth, back and forth, back and forth. Regular as a metronome. Or a ticking bomb.

Meg felt her stomach tighten and her breathing quicken. She turned away.

'Yes,' Baker said, 'all our intel points to there being a basement. Big Victorian house like that, it would have had cellars, surely.'

Heeley grunted agreement and patted his holster. 'I don't have the equipment to start taking the place apart, so I've established a perimeter. Now it's over to you.'

'Right.' Baker rubbed his hands and shivered. 'I'll make some calls. We'll rip the bloody floors up ourselves if we have to.'

Again, Meg found herself wondering. Intelligence about a basement? What intelligence? Whose intelligence? Did Muxlow know? And, if he did, why would he have held it back from Foster?

❧

'They've found it,' Baker said, plugging his phone back into a charging dock on his dashboard.

'So there *is* a basement?' Meg scanned the list of missed calls on her phone.

'Oh, yes!' he said, looking at his watch. 'Well done, by the way, for coordinating everything. We make a bloody good team, you and I, don't you think.'

Meg felt herself blush. She tried to find her reflection in the wing mirror but all she could see were swirls of exhaust fumes gleaming pink in the taillights. She knew she'd have to call Foster with an update sometime soon. Meg sensed a headache coming on. It was supposed to be her day off. She was supposed to spend the afternoon watching back-to-back rom coms on Netflix. At least it was warm and cosy in Baker's car. Maybe a little too warm and cosy.

'Tell me,' Baker went on, 'why's your DCI getting himself into such a state over all this?'

Meg turned to Baker. 'Because . . .' Her voice quavered. She felt herself blush again and turned away, refocussing on the activity outside the front door of number eight. There, uniformed officers were scurrying to and fro, carrying drills, crowbars, Stihl saws. 'Because,' Meg repeated, bullish this time, 'if your intelligence is correct, and you do find trafficked girls in there, DCI Foster will look a right prat.'

'Why?'

'Because he had that house searched yesterday, with a forensics team, and it never occurred to any of them to look for a basement.'

Baker's phone began to ring. He closed his eyes, let it ring three times, then answered.

Meg did her best to overhear, but she couldn't.

Baker lowered the phone, clenched his fist, and punched the air. 'Result! They found six girls down there. All okay, physically anyway. And no firearms.'

'Right then,' Meg said, reaching into the footwell for her handbag. 'I suppose we better get on with it.'

❧

Cocktail dresses and high heels.

Long, short, elaborate, simple, sparkly with sequins, tight with Lycra – each girl wore a different style of dress – all black though, like their shoes.

Six pretty girls – slim with Slavic features, faces numb from fear or cold or both. Elegantly turned out, Meg had to admit.

Immaculately made-up. Beautiful coiffure. Their eyes darted this way and that as they walked, hesitant and twitchy, across the drive.

At first Meg assumed that they were unnerved by the blue flashing lights and the armed officers. But it was not the cars or the uniforms they were looking at. They were looking back, at number 8 Devonshire Rise; they were looking left, to the massive leafless beech tree at the eastern boundary of the garden; they were looking ahead, past the council minibus, at the street lights and the other grand Victorian houses on the road; they were looking right, down the valley, into the fog blurred lights of the city centre. It dawned on Meg that these girls mightn't have seen any of it before. Could that be possible? The longer she watched, the more convinced she became.

The oldest, she guessed, was eighteen. The youngest was holding the eighteen-year-old's hand and struggling in her heels – twelve or thirteen, Meg reckoned. She felt a lump rise in her throat.

A social worker in a black duffle coat handed the girls blankets and ushered them to into the minibus.

The forensics team watched in silence. 'Come on, you lot,' Meg said, when the minibus's doors had slammed shut, 'there's a body waiting for us upstairs.'

A maroon Bentley cruised past, black windows reflecting amber streetlights and the frosted branches of the beech tree by the boundary wall. Meg was wondering how it had got through the police cordon when Deputy Chief Constable Muxlow appeared at the bottom of the drive.

41

IT WAS DARK when Cassie got home. The lamp by the front door wasn't working and she jumped like a spooked deer when she heard the snow crunch behind her.

'I thought you'd have had the decency to let me know before I heard it on the radio,' Stella said.

Cassie gathered herself and pushed open the door. 'Stella! I didn't expect—'

'No, I bet you didn't. Hurry up, it's freezing out here.'

Neither spoke as they stomped the snow from their boots and hung up their coats. On the floor, in front of the hall stand, lay a red towel. Cassie arranged her boots at one end and Stella's at the other. A few splashes and spots of mud found their way onto the tiles – she wiped them up with a second red towel, which she kept folded and hung on the umbrella rack for that very purpose.

'Well?' Stella said, as she sat down at the kitchen table.

Cassie shook her head and clicked the kettle on. 'Well, what?'

'I'm here for the press conference, but I'd rather hear it from you. I thought we had an understanding.'

'What press conference?'

Stella's eyes narrowed. 'Six o'clock in the lobby of Police HQ.'

'Has there been an arrest?'

'I don't know, Cassie. Why do you think I've come all the way to Sheffield? But they've confirmed that it has to do with Parkgate School and Gemma Grant. And why aren't you answering your phone?'

The doorbell rang. Cassie ran to get it in stocking feet.

It was Meg. She looked cross.

'What's happened?' Cassie said.

'Why aren't you answering your phone?' Meg closed the door behind her, taking care not to let her wet boots stray from the coir mat.

Cassie squeezed her eyes shut and shuddered. 'Just tell me, Meg. What's happened?'

'Loads.'

'What about Flynn?'

'He's in the clear . . . as far as Muxlow and Foster are concerned at any rate. Gary Mulligan killed Gemma Grant. He was the only survivor of some gangland brawl that got out of hand in the old sports hall at Parkgate School. They were probably arguing about the Gemma Grant killing.' Meg clapped her hands. 'So . . . case closed. We're off to the Sheffield Tap to celebrate. Quarter to seven, straight after the press conference. Drinks on the Deputy Chief; and I'm to make sure you know you're invited.'

The quiet in Cassie's hallway was broken by the sound of a chair sliding on the kitchen floor. Meg glanced up at the extra coat on the hall stand and down to the extra set of boots on the towel. Cassie noticed her notice; she couldn't bring herself to speak. Instead she pointed at Meg's boots, and then at the gap between her own boots and Stella's, and returned to the kitchen.

Stella was looking out of the window with one eye closed. It was obvious that she'd heard everything Meg had said.

Cassie busied herself filling the cafetière. When Meg came into the kitchen, Stella introduced herself; Meg reciprocated. Both gave only their names.

'Stella's with the *Manchester Evening News*,' Cassie said. 'She knows everything.' Then she turned to Stella: 'Meg's my sergeant, she knows everything too.'

They shook hands, awkwardly.

'Depends what you mean by *everything*,' Stella said.

Meg glanced at Cassie, who was gathering mugs. 'Yes,' she said. 'I suppose it does.'

❧

Stella tried and failed to make small talk with Meg at the kitchen table.

Cassie tried to ignore the silence while she sorted out coffee. After she'd resealed the coffee pack with an elastic band, and put it back in its place, on the bottom shelf of the top cupboard (and after she'd wiped down the worktop and the taps, and dried them off with a tea towel, and after she'd fixed the lid of the kettle that wasn't sitting straight) she put the tray of coffee things on the table and sat down.

'I've been back through my files,' Stella said, watching Cassie pour, 'and I've done a bit of digging.' Stella looked from Cassie to Meg and back again. 'A young woman, Victoria Bramley, went missing on the 21st of September 1998. The police did precious little because she was a prostitute, and because the person who reported her missing was a prostitute, and because there was no family – at least not any family that made a fuss.'

'Sounds more like the attitude of the press than the police,' Meg said, with half a chocolate digestive still in her mouth, spitting crumbs all over the table.

Cassie tore a sheet of kitchen paper off the roll and handed it to Meg. 'Calm down,' she said, 'I sure Stella wasn't trying to say—'

'Yes she bloody well was! How a journalist could have the cheek to start accusing the police of picking and choosing their cases?' Meg shook her head.

Stella held up her hands. 'Really, Meg. I didn't mean it that way. Shall I go on?'

Meg nodded without looking up.

'To cut a long story short,' Stella said, 'four *other* people died or went missing around that time: Vinny and Mike Bolan – known drug dealers who are *definitely* dead; Scott Deakin – a gangster from Wythenshawe who is definitely missing and very *probably* dead; and Jamie Boreman – AKA Deakin's Dandy, AKA James Flynn,' she glanced at Cassie, 'who is very much alive.'

'And?' Meg shot Stella a scornful look.

Stella turned to Cassie. 'There are parallels with what's been happening in Sheffield, don't you think? A dead prostitute, a bunch of dead gangsters . . . and Flynn.'

'Bollocks!' Cassie took the sheet of kitchen paper that Meg had ignored and set about cleaning up the crumbs. 'And Gemma Grant *wasn't* a prostitute.'

Meg shook her head.

Stella looked defiant. 'I want to talk to Flynn about Jamie Boreman, and the Bolan twins, and Scott Deakin, and Victoria Bramley.'

'Victoria Bramley?' Cassie screwed up the kitchen towel and threw it into the bin. 'The missing prostitute? What's she got to do with Flynn?'

'He knew her, Cassie,' Stella said, slamming her cup down on the table. Everyone watched a coffee slick form on the cup's rim before dribbling down the side. Cassie ripped another piece of kitchen towel from the roll, cleaned up the mess, and slid a coaster under Stella's cup. Stella took a deep breath before continuing. 'They both worked for Deakin at some members only club that everyone knew was an upmarket brothel – if a brothel *can* be upmarket.'

Cassie sat down and put her head in her hands.

'How well do you know this man?' Stella said gently. '*Really* know him?'

Cassie leaned back, eyes closed. 'I know he's not a murderer.'

'Maybe.' Stella folded her arms. 'But we need to talk to him.'

The kitchen window had steamed up. Cassie went to switch on the extractor fan. The noise was unbearable, so she turned it off again.

'Thanks for the coffee.' Stella got up and offered her hand to Meg. 'Nice to meet you, Detective Sergeant, but I'm afraid I'll have to run if I'm going to get to this press conference on time.'

Meg nodded a half-smile but ignored the hand.

Cassie followed Stella to the front door. 'But if you knew him . . .' She sighed and leaned heavily on the hall stand.

'He needs to give us answers,' Stella said, 'and quickly.'

'I know.' Cassie watched Stella pull on her boots, button her coat and pick her way across the icy front step.

'I can't let this go,' Stella said, turning back. 'You understand that don't you?'

Cassie nodded.

'So, will you set up a meeting for me? With Flynn?'

'I . . .' Cassie looked down at the door mat. 'I don't think he'll agree to it.'

'Right, I know where we stand then.'

'But Stella . . .'

Stella waited.

Cassie looked up into to a sea-grey sky. 'I'm going to email you a short story,' she said. 'It's one of Flynn's. He wrote it a long time ago.'

'Why?' Stella folded her arms.

'I can't explain, you need to read it for yourself. It's called *The Wythenshawe Dandy.*'

❧

'Has she gone?' Meg asked.

Cassie nodded.

'I think you're mad to have anything to do with that woman.'

Meg had found the chocolate Hobnobs and left a trail of crumbs across the worktop.

Cassie stared at the crumbs.

'Sorry,' Meg plonked herself back down at the kitchen table. 'I comfort eat when I'm pissed off. Always have. Don't know why.'

'Because you can get away with it,' Cassie snapped. 'If I ate like you, I'd be a size 20.' She grabbed the packet, returned it to its place on the top shelf, and swept up the crumbs. 'Stella forced my hand, if you must know. That's why she's involved. But she's all right, I like her.'

Meg rolled her eyes. 'Muxlow sent me a text. He wants to see you after the press conference – before he starts buying drinks for the team.'

'So why didn't he phone *me?*'

'Because your phone's been off all day, probably!'

'Right.' Cassie squeezed her eyes shut. 'So . . . what happened?'

Meg sighed. 'It all kicked off about an hour after I left you. NCA raided Gary Mulligan's house in Broomhill. We found a basement full of trafficked girls and Gary Mulligan with a bullet in his head. Suicide.'

'But . . .' Cassie saw Meg roll her eyes again. 'Sorry, go on.'

Meg went on and Cassie kept quiet: Gary Mulligan had shot himself at a quarter to three. A plastic bag containing Gemma Grant's clothes and personal effects were found in the house. The clothes had been sent off for DNA analysis but, given that they were found in Gary Mulligan's bedroom, it was likely that traces of his DNA would be present. The gun he used to kill himself was the type used in the Park Gate School massacre, and the ammunition also matched. Results of ballistic analysis were not due until tomorrow, but everyone was confident that it was just a formality. Fibres from Gary Mulligan's coat matched fibres found at the scene of Gemma's murder (missed in the first sweep; but found in the second) – again, forensic results were due tomorrow, but everyone was confident of a match.

'And her phone?' Cassie looked hopeful. 'If we knew who she'd been in contact with . . .'

Meg shook her head.

'That's that, then,' Cassie said.

'Yep.' Meg sniffed and folded her arms.

'Perfect result. No need, even, for a trial!'

'No. That'll save us a lot of work, won't it.'

Cassie put her elbows on the table and made a double fist. 'So, what's the connection between Gary Mulligan and Gemma Grant? Where's the motive?'

'Well,' Meg said, tousling her hair, 'the concierge at the Sheffield Hilton came forward and said he recognised Gemma from a couple of years ago. Apparently, she used to tout for trade in the hotel bar.'

Cassie frowned. 'Any sightings since then?'

'No, but . . .' Meg screwed up her face ' . . . the assumption is that Gary Mulligan was Gemma's pimp. Theory is, she was skimming his cut, so he made an example of her.'

'Perfect,' Cassie said.

Meg nodded. 'Yep.'

'It's bollocks, Meg. Absolute bollocks.'

'Maybe,' Meg said, staring into space. 'Maybe not.'

'I saw Gary Mulligan leaving David Roland's Offices in Broomhill at about quarter past two today,' Cassie said. 'He was in a minicab.'

Meg's jaw dropped. 'Why the hell didn't you—'

'I didn't know it was him, Meg, not straight away. He looked familiar, but I couldn't place him, not until later, and then it was too late.'

'Remind me,' Meg said, 'who's David Roland?'

'He's the private investigator who tracked down Gemma Grant in Edinburgh. He was working for Sarah Flynn. Let me show you something . . .' From her handbag, Cassie produced David Roland's photograph of Gemma and the photographs from the waste paper basket. Then she pulled out the sheet of notepaper. 'His PA wrote *this* a few hours ago,' she said, tapping the imprint of what had been written on the page above.

Meg studied the imprint. '*Scott Deakin is waiting on line 2*,' she read out loud. 'So, not dead then!'

Next, Cassie put Roland's photograph of Gemma Grant, a tightly cropped head and shoulders portrait, on the table in front of Meg. 'Roland told me he took this in Edinburgh,' she said. Then she slid the two pictures retrieved from the wastepaper basket either side. They fitted perfectly. They were the cropped sections of what had originally been a photograph of Gemma outside a railway station.

'That's Sheffield Station,' Meg said.

Cassie folded her arms.

'But . . .' Meg shook her head. 'Roland is lying, but so what? Look, the evidence against Gary Mulligan is solid. They found ten grand in Gemma's handbag.'

'And why did he leave the money in her handbag?' Cassie asked. 'And why did he kill himself?'

'Guilt?' Meg shrugged. 'Maybe he felt responsible for the death of his father.'

Cassie scoffed. 'What about Sarah Flynn and Scott Deakin? They don't fit anywhere into Foster's version of events, do they?' She turned from Meg to look out of the window. 'Those two are at the bottom of all this. We need to find Scott Deakin. Sarah Flynn was looking for him two years ago, so there must be a link. Maybe she had some dirt on him. Maybe Gemma picked him up in a hotel bar and Sarah found out. Maybe she had photos.' Cassie turned back to Meg. 'And there's definitely a link between Deakin and the Mulligans: Scott Deakin and Gary Mulligan were in contact with David Roland within minutes of each other. And then there's Flynn. Maybe there was bad blood between Deakin and Flynn – maybe that's why he had Flynn framed.'

'So,' Meg said, 'Deakin gets the Mulligans to kill Sarah because she's got some dirt on him. Two years later he gets them to kill Gemma and frame Flynn for it. Why? Because Gemma can have him charged with unlawful sex? Because Flynn annoyed him back in 1998? And then Deakin wipes out the Mulligan gang just to cover his tracks.'

'Or maybe Gemma was killed because she witnessed the car crash that killed her mother . . .' Cassie wagged a finger thoughtfully '. . . because she could name names.'

'So why didn't she name names?'

'She was terrified; she ran away.'

'Oh, Cassie!' Meg scratched her head vigorously with both hands. 'It's as far-fetched as Foster's theory, and you've no evidence for any of it.'

The ice maker in the freezer began to rumble and creak; both women sat up with a start. Cassie slumped back into her chair. 'I know, I know. I'm going to have to talk with Flynn. He knows something, even if he doesn't know it.'

'Talk to Muxlow first, though,' Meg said. 'You still have your career to worry about.'

Cassie nodded. She wished she'd talked to Gregg James about that job in Edinburgh. She wished she'd been able to stay up there a few more days to do some house hunting. She dreamed herself into a cosy Edinburgh flat with a good-sized bay window and views across Princes Street to the castle. But she couldn't see the castle because she couldn't see past Flynn. He was standing half-naked in her beautiful bay window, his back covered with scars. Flynn turned without warning. His blue eyes cut right through her.

42

'DID IT GO well, sir?' Cassie said. 'The press conference?'

Deputy Chief Constable Muxlow didn't answer. He turned away and headed for the window.

Sitting on a low sofa, cross-armed and cross-legged, Cassie hadn't the angle to see the lights of the city below.

Muxlow wasn't the type to muse over a vista – he liked to sit behind his desk, back to the window, watching others admire his view. But right now, he looked like a tourist on the Eiffel Tower. After a long half minute, he came back to his desk, hitched up his well-pressed trousers, and sat down.

'I've got you what you wanted, Cassie,' Muxlow said.

'Sir?'

'A promotion. Not the job you wanted, not Foster's job. I know he cocked up the search at Devonshire rise, but he has a good track record otherwise. No, it's a DCI position in the National Crime Agency. You'll be going after the big boys.'

'But . . .'

'You'll be based in Leeds, an easy commute.'

Cassie's eyes narrowed. 'You're very keen to get rid of me all of a sudden.'

Muxlow began to laugh (Muxlow never laughed); he laughed so much it brought tears to his eyes.

'I . . .' Cassie uncrossed her legs, did up the top button on her blouse, crossed her legs again.

'Very good,' Muxlow said. 'Think before you speak, that's the ticket. And I know exactly what you're thinking, so don't bother.'

'Sir, I don't know what you're getting at.'

'Yes, you do!' Muxlow straightened his shirt cuffs and leaned forward. 'You have no respect for authority, Cassie, or for your senior colleagues, or for anyone who isn't quite as clever as you. They can't all be as clever as you, Cassie – just remember that.'

'That's unfair, sir, I've always—'

'Sometimes, you need to keep your mouth shut. Sometimes, you have to say what you don't want to say. Sometimes, a bulldozer is not the best vehicle to get you to where you want to be. Remember that when you move up to organised crime – you'll be fighting a war there, not scrapping in the playground.'

A knock at the door prompted an agonisingly long moment of silence.

'Come in,' Muxlow said at last

Chief Inspector Foster opened the door but didn't come in. They're all waiting, sir, at the Sheffield Tap.'

'I'm on my way.' Muxlow got up and straightened his trousers. 'Tell them ten minutes.' When the door closed, Muxlow turned back to Cassie. 'Richard Walker will be in touch. He's a Commander at the Met with a good track record on e-fraud, and he'll be heading up the new unit. It's all about computers these days, isn't it? Why risk an armed robbery when you can steal millions while you're quietly sipping cocktails in Barbados?'

'And will there be an interview panel, sir? For this new DCI job?'

Muxlow stared long and hard into Cassie's eyes.

Cassie suffered it as long as she was able then looked down.

'You will say *yes*, won't you?' he said.

He was still staring at her; she could feel it. She fixed on a spot over his right shoulder. 'Yes, sir. I will.'

'Good. Now get yourself off to the pub.'

Cassie was almost through the doorway when he called her name. She stepped back into the office.

Muxlow waited for the door to swing back and click shut. 'Promise me . . .' he said, '. . . promise me you'll get the bastard.'

'Which bastard, sir?'

He considered the question a while then turned to the window. 'You'll know,' he said. 'Please, just promise me . . .'

Cassie turned to the window too. She tried to see out, tried to see if it was snowing, but all she could see was her own reflection . . . and Muxlow's. His eyes were closed; his face appeared contorted, as if in pain.

She saw in him a little boy pleading not to have to go into school, a jilted teenager begging for an explanation, a middle-aged man reading the letter he had hoped and prayed would never be delivered.

'Okay,' she said. 'I promise.'

❧

Cassie had no intention of going to the pub to celebrate with Muxlow and Foster. And neither, it turned out, did Meg. Meg was in Cassie's office, at Cassie's desk, with the Sarah Flynn files scattered about her. She was scrutinising the contents of a blue cardboard folder.

Cassie folded her arms. 'What are you looking for?'

'No idea. But if we don't find it soon, this case will be dead and buried.'

'So, you don't think it's dead and buried already?'

Meg waved a telephone log at Cassie. 'Who's this she keeps calling? It's a number in America. It looks like they spoke at least once or twice a day, for two or three weeks, right up until the day before she died.'

'It was a journalist at the *Washington Post*, if I remember rightly.' Cassie waved a finger vaguely at the files piled on her desk. 'There'll be a spreadsheet, somewhere amongst that lot, with all the details.'

After a couple of minutes shuffling through papers, Meg found the spreadsheet. 'Thelma Winters at the *Washington Post*,' she said, tapping her chin with the chewed end of a biro. 'Says here she couldn't speak to us because she was off sick. What, too sick to pick up a phone?' Meg opened up her laptop and googled Thelma Winters.

'Actually, yes,' Cassie said. 'I remember now. She'd been in a serious car accident.'

Meg held up a hand. 'Okay, I'll let her off then. But if she's recovered, it might be worth finding out what they were up to.'

'Yes,' Cassie said, slowly. She remembered thinking at the time that it was a bizarre coincidence: two journalists, thousands of miles apart, in fatal (or near fatal) car crashes on the very same day.

'Ah ha!' Meg turned the laptop so that Cassie could see. 'Look, *Thelma Winters*. Last Thursday she was alive and well and posting a story about sexual slavery under the Islamic State in Iraq. And look at this.' Meg scrolled down the list of Google hits and stopped at another Thelma Winters story, *Child Sexual Exploitation Scandal Discredits UK Child Protection Services*. 'And our very own Sarah Flynn gets a joint by-line on this one.'

Cassie looked at her watch. 'It's the middle of the afternoon in Washington. Why don't you give her a ring?'

43

FLYNN TOSSED HIS keys onto the table. 'I'll open a bottle of wine.'

'You've got to be joking,' Angus said, pulling Flynn's front door closed behind them. 'I'm still suffering after last night.' He went over to the window, pressed his forehead against the ice-cold glass, and stared out at a starless sky.

'Come on, Angus, let's get the fire going, bang a couple of pizzas in the oven, crack open a nice bottle of Chianti. You'll feel better – red wine's the best thing for a hangover.'

'Not if you've got to drive home.'

'Drive home! What for? Lizzie and the kids are still at her mother's. And besides, they're forecasting snow. Please, Angus, don't leave me on my own tonight. You can have my bed, I'll be fine on the sofa.'

'I thought you'd be sick of the sight of me by now.' Angus pressed a palm to his forehead. 'And what with—'

'I've been thinking,' Flynn said. 'I've been thinking about a new novel, and I've been thinking about a couple of short stories I never quite finished, and I've been thinking about moving back to Sheffield. I could turn this place into a holiday let, sell the flat, and buy a little house in Hunters Bar.'

'Bloody hell.' Angus turned from the window and looked at his old friend. And it *was* his old friend. For the first time since Sarah died, there was life in the big man. Angus couldn't help but smile. 'Wow, you really have been thinking!'

'Yes,' Flynn said. 'It's the first time I've been able to think about the future since, you know . . . It all started with Cassie, of course – when she and I were going to . . .' he winced. 'Then everything turned to shit. But now that I'm in the clear, I feel . . .' Flynn shook his head and shrugged.

'Relieved?' Angus offered.

'No, not that.' Flynn grabbed the bottle of Chianti and peeled off the foil. 'More like . . .' he pulled open the drawer by the sink and grabbed a corkscrew, 'I feel . . . *hopeful*. When you've spent as long as I have not being able to imagine anything worth hoping for, you forget what it's like to have hope.'

Angus nodded. But Angus was always hoping for things, all sorts of things, so it was difficult for him to image living without hope. Actually, no: he'd spent most of his life *wishing* for things. And *wishing* was different from *hoping*, wasn't it? It was the sort of question Flynn would have an answer to, but now wasn't the time. 'So,' Angus said, 'have you spoken to Cassie?'

Flynn stopped turning the corkscrew but didn't look up. 'No.'

'And you're not concerned that nothing adds up – that we know for a fact that the police are wrong about what happened at Parkgate school?'

Flynn shrugged. 'Does it matter?'

'Maybe not,' Angus said. But of course it mattered. Flynn might be off the hook as far as the police were concerned, but the police weren't the only people they'd been hiding from. 'Someone tried to have you killed, Flynn. And we can't be sure who. Doesn't that worry you?'

Flynn had uncorked the Chianti and decanted it into a chipped and time-scumbled carafe. Now he was filling the second of two oversized wine glasses. 'Of course it worries me,' he said. He passed one glass to Angus and took a big gulp from the other. 'But not much, if I'm honest.'

Angus didn't know what to make of that. 'Cheers!' he said, raising his glass. 'Just this bottle though, then an early night.'

'Fine,' Flynn said. He topped up his glass before handing the carafe to Angus. 'You're welcome to it.' He opened a cupboard by the fridge, reached in, and pulled out another bottle of red. 'I'll have the Rioja!'

Angus laughed as he hadn't laughed in ages.

❧

In truth, Flynn feared that his good spirits would flag without a bottle or two of red to sustain him, and without Angus to distract him from those darker thoughts that were already seeping into his consciousness.

Angus was bent double, sifting through the contents of the freezer. 'Maybe the police took your pizzas away as evidence,' he said, chuckling.

'What?' Flynn said, absently.

Angus reached for Flynn's car keys. 'I'll nip over to Glossop and pick up some supplies. By the way, I sent a text to Cassie to let her know where we are, so if the landline rings . . .'

'Right.' Flynn said.

'Oh, and I'll have a go at fixing that computer of yours when I get back.'

Flynn wasn't listening, he was recalling his last memory of Victoria Bramley. She was bent over one of the tables in the bar at the No. 7 Gentleman's Club.

Things hadn't gone according to plan that day, if the Bolan twins had ever *had* a plan, that is.

Flynn raised his hands immediately he saw the shotgun. Mike Bolan charged at him, all sweat and swagger, and pressed the muzzle into his neck. Flynn wasn't afraid – not really – which is not so very strange for an eighteen-year-old who, in his heart of hearts, didn't really expect to make it to nineteen.

He looked at Scotty: his stoney face was contorted by the pressure of Vinny Bolan's twin barrels pressed to his cheek. He looked at Victoria: she was standing stiffly at the bar with a champagne flute tight and awkward in her right hand. He wondered how best to extricate them all.

Mike Bolan was ranting about something or other, but, as far as Flynn could recall, Vinny had said nothing up to this point. Mike Bolan was far too close to Flynn for his own good. Flynn remembered feeling confident that he could take him: if he picked his moment, if he moved quickly. The same went for Vinny: Scotty Deakin was no slouch, Flynn had seen him disarm many an aggressor who got too close.

But, to stand a chance, Flynn knew that he and Scotty would have to make their respective moves in synchrony. It was just after Deakin mouthed 'on three', and just before he began the lip count, that Mike Bolan stepped out of reach, glanced a warning look, and trained his gun on Victoria.

Deakin had maintained a surly silence up to this point. Now he spoke: 'You can leave the girl out of this, Mike. Let her go. Then me, you and your brother can have a civilised chat. And I might just overlook you barging into my club, uninvited, and . . . err . . . how shall I put this . . . forgetting your manners?'

Bravado tended to work for Scotty Deakin. He was possessed of an uncanny ability to persuade anyone, in any situation, that he had the upper hand. Usually he did. That day, he didn't.

'Your favourite, is she, Scotty?' Mike said, edging towards Victoria at the bar. 'Give us a twirl then, luv.'

Victoria looked first to Deakin, then to Flynn. Deakin had fixed on Mike Bolan and didn't notice. Flynn gave her what he hoped was a calm and reassuring nod. Slowly, jerkily, but without spilling her champagne, Victoria turned through three hundred and sixty degrees.

'Very nice.' Mike said, sliding his fist – slowly and suggestively – up and down the barrel of his shotgun. 'Great arse, Vinny, don't you think?'

What happened next happened quickly. Mike Bolan turned the gun back on Flynn, grabbed Victoria's hair with his free hand, and steered her away from the bar. He forced her to bend over a table, twisting her head so that her left cheek was pressed against the marble.

With his finger resting on the front trigger, Bolan let go of Victoria's hair and ran his fingers slowly down the length of her cocktail dress. He yanked the dress up and over her hips, exposing the pretty lace waist band and top triangle of her G-string. Bolan squeezed then slapped her bottom, leaving a large pink hand mark.

Victoria was breathing hard and fast now, but still she clung to the champagne flute. Her hand, slick and shiny with spilt Prosecco, shook spasmodically. Eyes glazed with tears, lips tight, she looked over to Flynn.

Fifteen years later Flynn would still wake in the small hours, pillow wet with tears, belly tight with guilt. He shouldn't have reacted when Bolan slapped Victoria: he shouldn't have winced, he shouldn't have lowered his arms, he shouldn't have stepped forward.

But he did.

Bolan had the gun pointed squarely at Flynn. It should have been instinctive – Mike Bolan should have sensed Flynn's massive frame coming at him and pulled the bloody trigger. He should have taken Flynn out.

He didn't. Instead, Bolan rammed the barrels of his shotgun between Victoria's buttocks and wagged a warning finger.

Flynn stopped dead.

Bolan's trigger hand was shaking.

Flynn took a couple of steps back and raised his arms.

Bolan pulled Victoria's knickers to one side, and forced the barrels further in.

She cried out and lurched forwards. The champagne flute slipped from her fingers and shattered on the floor.

Mike Bolan didn't mean to do it, Flynn was sure of that.

The sound of breaking glass must have spooked him, or maybe he was just trying to adjust his grip on the gun.

Mike Bolan didn't mean to do it, but he did.

There was almost no noise, Flynn remembered, but for a clattering of chairs when Mike reeled backwards with the recoil and dropped the gun. And even that sound was unreal: as if warped and muffled by the tension in the room.

Flynn felled Mike Bolan with a massive overcut that smashed his nose and cracked his jaw.

Vinny Bolan's gun was now on the floor too. Scotty Deakin had Vinny in a head lock and was trying to smash his face into the counter. Vinny managed to lift Scotty off his feet and slam him into the brass rail that ran the length of the bar.

Scotty let go.

Vinny went for the gun.

Flynn stepped in. A monster right hook stopped Vinny Bolan.

With both the Bolans out cold, Scotty grabbed their shotguns and tucked them under his left arm.

Victoria's blood and guts were spattered across the floor, and the bar, and the mirror behind the bar. Flynn looked away but it was too late, the image was already etched upon his inward eye.

It was then that he experienced his first *torment* – a perfect storm of emotion: regret, guilt, self-pity, self-loathing. Flynn wept. At first he wept for Victoria, then he wept for himself. And when he realised he was weeping for himself, he hated himself all the more.

How could Flynn have known, back then, that these *torments* would never leave him – how could he have known that, all these years later, he would still wake, most mornings, hounded by dismay.

Deakin patted him on the back and told him to wait in the office. It was while he was there that he heard the muffled report of two gunshots.

Flynn's last night in Manchester was spent alone in a private room at The No. 7 Gentleman's Club. He didn't sleep. The next morning, he left for Sheffield with a brown leather suitcase and an Adidas holdall stuffed with rolled-up twenties – gifts from Scotty. The latter came with a wink: 'A little thank you from me, son. You saved my life and I'll not forget it.'

And Flynn knew that he wouldn't. Scotty Deakin didn't forget.

44

'I CAN'T BELIEVE she put the phone down on me like that!' Meg said, slumping into her chair.

Cassie plonked her elbows on the desk. 'Thelma Winters is one very frightened woman.'

'We ought to call her back,' Meg said. 'You lead this time, and let her know we're not going to give up that easily.'

'Honestly, Meg, I don't think it's worth it. We've got as much as we're going to get for the time being.'

'But we got next to nothing out of her!' Meg said.

Cassie shook her head slowly. 'She told us that she and Sarah Flynn cooperated on stories about the trafficking of girls into prostitution, she told us that they sometimes shared intelligence and sources.'

'She told us bugger all, Cassie. We barely got more than a "yes" or a "no" out of her. All she did was confirm what we guessed after a few minutes on Google.'

'And,' Cassie said, 'we know that Brett McRoss has something to do with all this. She was nervous as hell for the whole interview, but when you mentioned his name she properly flipped. That was when she put the phone down.'

'Yeah.' Meg tapped the note Cassie had passed to her during the interview. 'What made you think of Brett McRoss? Is any of that football stuff even relevant?'

'Probably not, but, oh, I don't know - just a feeling. Think about it: we know of two Americans connected to this case,

Thelma Winters and Brett McRoss. I suppose I just wanted to see if they were connected to each other. And now we know that they are.'

'Come off it,' Meg said, flicking the note back across the table. 'We don't know for sure that they're connected. We know they're both Americans, and we know that she put the phone down on me when I mentioned his name. And that's all we know.'

'Maybe.' Cassie got up and grabbed her bag. 'Anyway, it's been a long day, let's go home.'

❧

The Snake Pass Inn car park was badly lit, but Cassie could see that Flynn's Land Rover wasn't there. He must have come back with Angus to collect it. If he was in, she'd interrogate the hell out of him; if he was out, well, she still had Angus's spare key – she'd search the place. Properly this time. There had to be something, although she had no idea what.

Cassie checked her phone – still no signal. She looked up when she heard the clatter of a diesel engine. A Land Rover Defender heading towards Glossop. Flynn's? It was too dark to tell – there were lots of Land Rover Defenders in these parts.

Perhaps she should ring ahead to check – there'd be a phone in the pub. She turned to the entrance door and saw Stella Middlewood standing there in wellington boots and a long navy overcoat. She was arranging her hair under a woolly hat – awkwardly, head down, with gloved hands. Cassie marched over. 'Stella, what on earth are you doing here?'

Stella looked up briefly and thrust her hands into her pockets. 'What do *you* think?'

'I don't think he's home,' Cassie said.

Stella laughed. 'So what are *you* doing here then?'

Cassie pulled a pair of gloves from her pocket.

Stella pointed her torch towards the road and set off at pace.

Cassie went after her. 'Stella, wait!'

By the time she caught up, Stella was turning up Flynn's drive.

'He won't talk about the old days, you know,' Cassie said. 'I think he's blocked it all out somehow. Angus says—'

'Angus? Who's Angus?'

'He's Flynn's closest friend. Angus says that in all the years he's known him, Flynn's never talked about his life before Sheffield.'

Stella stopped. 'He's written about it though, hasn't he?' She cocked her head to one side. '*The Wythenshawe Dandy?*'

The moon, full and bright, appeared from behind a cloud, turning the snow the lightest shade of blue. Stella started walking again – more slowly now.

'So you read it?' Cassie said.

Stella didn't answer for a good few paces. She kicked at the freshly settled snow with every step. 'I wish I hadn't,' she said at last.

'But you can see why we need to go gently. If that story comes anywhere close to the truth, if that really was Jamie Boreman's life, then . . .'

They walked on without speaking. Eventually the sound of road traffic faded to nothing and only their footsteps broke the heavy hush. They found themselves stepping in time.

Stella adjusted her bobble hat and said, 'Most violent criminals suffered a violent childhood. You know that.' She turned and looked Cassie straight in the eye before continuing. 'There are very few abusers who've never been abused.'

'I know,' Cassie said. 'But that doesn't mean that every abused child turns into a monster, and if you knew Flynn, you'd know . . .' Only Cassie didn't know Flynn – not really. She'd fallen for the man she wanted to fall for, and for the boy who became the man. And she only knew the boy from a story. 'You've read *The*

Wythenshawe Dandy. Anyone who can live through that sort of childhood, and escape, and build a new life . . .'

'I know.' Stella said, her voice cracking.

'Stella?'

'I think . . .' Stella started. She wiped her nose on her glove. 'I don't know what I think. All I know is that I cry every time I think about that bloody story.'

Cassie took Stella's arm. They continued on up the track, perfectly in step, like an old married couple. When light from Flynn's windows began to filter through the trees, Stella let go of Cassie's arm and adjusted her gloves. 'What I find hard to believe,' she said, 'is that your Deputy Chief Constable, your DCC Bernie Muxlow, doesn't know who Flynn really is.'

'Why should he?' Cassie asked.

Stella took off her hat and scratched her head. 'Has Flynn ever mentioned him?'

Cassie glared at her.

'Once upon a time,' Stella said, 'Muxlow worked on the vice squad in South Manchester. He'd have known Deakin, and if he knew Deakin, he'd have known Deakin's Dandy . . . Jamie Boreman . . . James Flynn.'

'You can't be sure of that.'

'Oh, but I can. I have a reliable source. I've been told that Muxlow used to keep very close tabs on Deakin. Some would say "*too* close". But I suppose that's what happens when you're after someone as slippery as that.'

Cassie let go of Stella's arm. 'And what exactly do you mean by "*too close*"?'

'He used to go for drinks at that dodgy club in Sale, apparently. And there are rumours that it wasn't just the drinks he went in for. The place was a brothel, Cassie. Everyone knew it.'

'How long have you known all this?'

'Only since this morning. I managed to track down one of

my old contacts, a retired Detective Sergeant. I asked him about Deakin and he started to talk about this Detective Inspector called Bernie Muxlow. I didn't think too much of it until I turned up at the press conference. And there he was, centre stage: Deputy Chief Constable Bernie Muxlow.'

Cassie's head was spinning. 'What are you after, Stella? Why are you here?'

'I want to find out what happened to Deakin, and I want to find out if Bernie Muxlow was on the take. Do you know, the more I think about the conversation I had with Sarah Flynn two years ago, the more I think she was convinced that Deakin was still alive.'

'And if you find out what you want to know about Deakin and Muxlow – if I *help you* find out what you want to know about Deakin and Muxlow – will you leave Flynn out of this?'

'If Deakin's alive, then maybe. But if he *is* dead, and if it was Flynn who—'

'Deakin *is* alive, Stella. And if you promise to leave Flynn out of this, I'll give you everything I know.'

Stella looked jubilant for a moment, then frowned. 'You've made me promises before.'

45

'LAST OF THE coal,' Flynn said.

Cassie watched him staring at the stove, waiting for it to take. The coal smoked a bit at first, obscuring the fire – but soon the window was clear. Soon, soft flames were licking the glass and surging up the flue.

'I'll be moving back onto logs tomorrow,' he said. 'I prefer logs – they're much cleaner, and they look prettier. But they don't last long enough for an overnight burn, and it's nice to come down to a hot stove in the morning.'

Stella and Cassie were sitting at the big table, nursing cups of steaming coffee. Flynn pulled out a chair beside Cassie. He folded an old brown envelope in half, poured himself a whisky, and sat down. 'Last of the whisky, too,' he said. 'I'd been saving this bottle for a special occasion.'

He savoured the first sip and put his tumbler down on the folded envelope. A dark ring formed.

Stella turned to Flynn. 'I read your story, *The Wythenshawe Dandy*. It's very good. Simple, direct, honest prose. Beautiful prose.'

Flynn lay his big hands either side of his glass. 'Thank you.'

'Autobiographical?' Stella asked.

He stared into his whisky. 'It's a story.'

'But surely the Wythenshawe Dandy is you: a version of Deakin's Dandy, that's what they used to call you, isn't it.'

Flynn contemplated his whisky a while longer, then took another sip.

'So it *is* factual,' Stella said, 'near as damn it?'

'It's a story,' Flynn said. 'Just a story.'

'A *true* story?' Stella interlocked her fingers and squeezed a fist.

Flynn fixed soft eyes on Stella. 'If I were to write it again,' he said, turning his whisky tumbler slowly and taking the folded brown envelope with it, 'if I were to start it from scratch, today, more than a decade on, I'm sure it would end up being a very different story.'

Stella sighed, noisily, and folded her arms. 'So, Scott Deakin?' she said. 'We know he's still alive. Where is he?'

Flynn thought about this for a while, still turning his tumbler on the makeshift coaster. 'Jamaica,' he said, 'last I heard, but that was years ago – he sent me postcards when I was at university.'

Cassie had kept quiet so far. She'd promised Stella that she wouldn't interfere or interrupt, but now she couldn't help herself: 'Postcards! Saying what?'

'Oh, I can't remember. "*Nice weather*", "*wish you were here*", that sort of thing. I think he sent them to let me know that he knew where I was.'

'So he found you,' Stella said. 'You hadn't escaped. You must have been worried; I bet Scotty Deakin didn't approve of deserters.'

'You're confusing *me* with a character in a story, Stella. I didn't desert him, it wasn't like that. He understood exactly why I was leaving, and he had no problem with it. He wished me luck, he even gave me a bit of money to help me get started. No, I think he was just letting me know that he was there if I needed him. We were friends. I liked him, but I didn't want to be like him.'

If Stella was surprised, she didn't let it show. She sipped her coffee, swallowed, and wiped her mouth with one of the paper napkins that Cassie had dug out of the cupboard under the sink. 'Why did Deakin leave Manchester?' Stella asked. 'Why did he disappear?'

'He was tired of getting his hands dirty,' Flynn said, matter-of-factly, 'and he was sick of the Manchester weather. He'd done a few deals that meant he could step back from the business and manage things from the Caribbean. *Franchising*, he called it. Said he could grow the business ten times as fast, like *Pizza Hut* and *McDonalds*.'

'So,' Stella said. She refolded her paper napkin and ran a fingernail along the crease. 'It had nothing to do with the disappearance of Victoria Bramley, then?'

Flynn produced his stock expression: curious disinterest. Cassie had learned that this was something he did when he felt uncomfortable. Now *she* felt uncomfortable. She pursed her lips and tucked her hair behind her ears. 'Flynn,' she said, 'did you know Victoria Bramley?'

He rubbed his chin, and then his lips, and then his forehead.

Cassie and Stella waited.

He looked at each in turn before speaking. 'Look, I haven't seen Scott Deakin since I left Manchester. And the postcards, the ones I got when I was a student, were the last I ever heard from him. He was a good friend to me, but he's a dangerous man. You shouldn't get involved – either of you.'

'Is that what happened to Sarah?' Cassie said. 'Did she stick her nose into Deakin's business? Christ almighty, Flynn, I don't know what to think anymore!'

Somewhere outside, a fox shrieked. They all turned to the window.

'Deakin didn't kill her,' Flynn said. 'Sarah was no threat to *him*.'

'How can you be so sure?' Cassie said, calm again.

'Because Sarah was only a threat to people who made themselves out to be upright and law abiding but weren't. I can't think why she'd be interested in someone like Deakin. Not unless . . .'

Stella clapped her hands. 'Unless it was about someone Deakin had on his payroll, someone whose good reputation Deakin needed intact.' She took a camera from her bag and scrolled through a few images until she found the one she wanted. 'Recognise him?'

Flynn leaned in. 'Yes, he used to hang around the *No. 7*.'

Cassie was already peering over his shoulder. 'Are you sure?'

He nodded.

'That's Deputy Chief Constable Bernie Muxlow.' Stella said slowly, and not without a little glee.

Cassie sat back down and covered her face with her hands. 'It doesn't mean he was on Deakin's payroll.'

The fire needed poking. Or maybe not. In any case, Flynn went over to tend to it.

'Come on, Cassie . . .' Stella put the camera back in her bag and zipped it up. 'Why don't you ask Flynn if Muxlow was on the take.'

'He was,' Flynn said. 'I gave him the envelopes myself . . . a few times, anyway. Five grand, usually. No one else got that much.'

'And you'd testify to that?' Cassie said, hands on hips.

Flynn shut the stove door and got up. He turned to Cassie and shook his head. 'I don't think it will ever come to that. He'll have covered his tracks, his sort always does, so it would never get to court.'

'And if it did get to court?' It was not a fair question; Cassie knew that it would take more than testimony from Flynn to see Muxlow off.

Flynn poured himself another whisky. His eyes were so hauntingly blue, in the glow of the fire, that Cassie couldn't look away.

'Scotty Deakin didn't have Sarah killed,' he said. 'I'm sure of it.'

'And what about Victoria Bramley?' Cassie asked.

'Mike Bolan killed her. An accident, probably. But he killed her.'

Cassie looked away.

Stella clapped her hands. 'The Bolan twins! It was Deakin who killed them, wasn't it? The story about them killing each other in a fight over a woman was pure fiction, and I'd put money on Muxlow having fabricated that little tale.'

'The Bolan twins had come to kill *Scotty*,' Flynn said.

'Self-defence, then?' Stella raised her eyebrows.

Flynn didn't reply. Cassie could feel him staring at her. She wanted to turn back to him but feared she might cry if she did, and she didn't know why, and this made her angry. Why was she always so angry?

'Well?' Cassie said. She'd wanted to sound strong, but her voice cracked.

Something popped and fizzed in the stove. All three turned to look. There was nothing to see, but they gazed silently into the flames a while longer.

❧

'Bloody hell!' Angus said. He kicked the door shut and dumped a cardboard box and a large bag of groceries on the table. 'It's a nightmare out on the roads, now I really do need that drink.' Then he noticed Stella. 'Sorry, I didn't realise . . .'

'Stella Middlewood,' she said, brightly.

'Angus McDonald. You're from the *Manchester Evening News*, aren't you?'

'That's right. Just looking for a bit of background. Your friend's face was splashed all over television a couple of days ago. Perhaps someone ought to give his side of the story . . . now that he's been exonerated?'

Angus frowned. 'Least said, soonest mended, don't you think?'

Stella picked up her bag and nodded at Cassie. 'I think we'd best be off.'

Flynn stood up. 'I'll give you a lift to the carpark.'

'No, really, we can walk.'

'Not in the dark,' Flynn said. 'And not in this weather. And certainly not on your own.'

Stella looked at Cassie.

Cassie wondered why Stella was suddenly so keen to leave. Perhaps she had everything she thought she was going to get. Perhaps she sensed that Angus would not allow the interview to go much further. She looked up at Angus – he was stoney faced, arms folded. Yes, that must be it. 'You go,' Cassie said. 'I'll stay a while, I think.'

Stella yanked on her coat. She didn't look best pleased.

Flynn grabbed his car keys and showed her out.

❧

From the cardboard box on the table, Angus retrieved Flynn's laptop and a PC *World* carrier bag. 'I promised to sort out his machine,' he said. 'God knows what he's done to the thing, but it's not right.'

Cassie shrugged, took the coffee things over to the sink, started washing up. Flynn's kitchen was neatly organised, and this pleased her. She wiped down the table, wrung out the cloth, and, unsure where Flynn's dish cloth should properly be stored, hung it back over the tap where she'd found it.

There weren't many cupboards or drawers in the kitchen, but Cassie opened them all and had a good rummage through.

'What are you looking for?' Angus said.

She slammed the cutlery drawer shut and turned back to Angus, who was removing tiny screws from the back of Flynn's computer. 'I don't know,' she said. 'But there has to be something.'

There was nothing of interest downstairs, so she went up to the bedroom. Same story: a well-thumbed edition of *Crime and Punishment* on the bedside table, a few clothes in the drawers, not much else. Nothing that told the story of a life. She opened the dusty brown leather suitcase that she'd found under the bed. In it was a navy-blue suit (handmade, expensive) and a shirt – also hand-made, also expensive. The zip of the divider flap caught on something halfway round. After a little tugging and rummaging she found a burgundy cravat. His wedding suit, maybe? The jacket was certainly right for a wedding outfit: more like a frock coat than a lounge suit. She gave up on the zip (now well and truly jammed), shoved everything back under the bed, and stormed back downstairs.

While Angus busied himself taking Flynn's computer apart, Cassie wondered about Muxlow. She couldn't reconcile the stiff-necked bureaucrat she'd worked alongside for two years with the bent vice copper that Stella seemed convinced she had in her sights.

The dishcloth hanging over the tap looked untidy so she put it into an empty Tupperware box under the sink. Much better.

Perhaps Stella was right about Muxlow. But she had no hard evidence, so she wouldn't print anything. Would she? No, Stella was a pro.

Cassie decided she should forget about the whole thing. She should focus on her new job with the Special Organised Crimes Unit, decide what to do about Flynn, think about how to persuade Meg to move jobs with her.

But she couldn't forget. David Roland had the answers she needed. He was the link between the Mulligans and Gemma Grant.

'Angus . . . if you were fifteen and frightened, if your mother had been deliberately run off the road – murdered, in fact – and you thought they might be after *you* too, what would you do?'

'Go to the police!' Angus removed the last of the screws and added it to the pile accumulating on a cracked saucer. 'What else would you do?'

'Yes, but what if going to the police would mean being sent back to some children's home that you really hated?'

'If I really thought someone wanted to kill me, I'd go to the police, regardless.'

'But she didn't go to the police, Angus! She feared for her life but she *didn't* go to the police.'

Elbows on the table, cheeks cupped in the palms of her hands, Cassie stared into space.

'I can think of only one thing that would have stopped her going to the police,' Angus said. He'd put down the screwdriver and was drumming his fingers on the table.

'Me too,' she said, glaring at the offending fingers.

Angus folded his arms. 'But why would she think the police were responsible for her mother's death?'

'Maybe not *the police* per se, maybe someone *in* the police.'

'You mean Muxlow, don't you? Maybe Stella's right about him after all. But that doesn't tell us who she *did* go to for help. And she must have gone to someone.'

'I wonder if she thought that a private investigator would be the next best thing?' Cassie said. 'She knew David Roland: he worked for her mother, and her mother had chosen *him* to search for her only daughter, so she'd have thought he could be trusted. And who else would she know in Sheffield?'

'Maybe. Or maybe you're a just little obsessed with this David Roland character. I know you don't like the man, but—'

'He lied to me, Angus! He's up to his neck in this business.'

'Yes, but . . .' Angus picked up his screwdriver and twirled it between his fingers. 'Don't you think she'd go to someone she knew really well? A friend, perhaps? Or the parent of a friend? Or the friend of a parent? I'd like to think that if my daughter was in trouble, and if I wasn't around—'

'A friend!' Cassie slapped the table with both hands. 'Angus, what sort of fifteen-year-old has friends who would know what to do if the police are out to kill you?' She sprang from her chair and began pacing the room.

'What is it?' Angus said.

'I should have guessed: a ninety-two-year-old lady with a bunch of Second World War spy stories to make your hair curl. I don't know if any of it was true, but I believed her, and Gemma would have believed her too. Céline Douglas – that's who she'd have gone to.'

46

'WHAT TOOK YOU?' Angus said.

Flynn was stomping the snow from his boots. He looked over to Cassie, but she didn't look back. 'Chatty woman, Stella Middlewood. Did you know her husband taught me A-Level English?'

'No, I—'

'Shush!' Cassie was sitting at the table with her iPad propped up on its cover. 'I persuaded her to use *FaceTime*,' she said, 'rather than drive all the way up to Edinburgh.'

Flynn's brow creased.

'*FaceTime*,' Angus said. 'It's video conferencing, it's Apple's version of—'

'Angus, I know what *FaceTime* is, I'm not a complete—'

'Shush!' Cassie waved them to sit at the other end of the table, out of sight.

'It's ringing,' she said. 'And neither of you is here. Got it?'

Mrs Douglas answered, head and shoulders framed perfectly on Cassie's screen. Cassie had just spent an age trying to achieve something similar.

'Detective Inspector May,' Mrs Douglas said. 'What a lovely surprise.' She made no attempt to sound like she meant it.

Cassie was in no mood for pleasantries: 'Did Gemma Grant go back to Edinburgh after her mother died? Did she go back to Edinburgh to get help from *you*, Mrs Douglas?'

'Yes, dear, she did.'

'So you lied to me?'

Mrs Douglas held her smile. 'That's right.'

'But . . .' Cassie shook her head. 'Why?'

'At that time, and under the circumstances, it was the best course of action.'

'Lying to the police during a murder investigation, Mrs Douglas, is never the best course of action.'

The old lady huffed. 'Come, come, my dear, we both know that's complete nonsense. And besides, your investigation wasn't a *police* investigation, was it? You've gone rogue, haven't you, Detective *Chief* Inspector.'

At the other end of the table Flynn was listening intently. Angus, sitting beside him, was staring at the floor, hands clamped between his thighs.

How the hell could Céline Douglas know about her promotion to DCI? It hadn't even happened yet. Cassie folded her arms tight. 'I'll ask you again,' she said, calmly. '*Why* did you lie to me? What are you trying to hide? Who are you trying to protect?'

Mrs Douglas dropped the patronising smile. 'We both kept a few things back, did we not?'

Cassie didn't answer. She found herself looking at Angus, who was still staring at the floor.

'Is Angus with you?' Mrs Douglas asked.

Cassie glared at the old lady.

Céline Douglas raised her eyebrows. 'Then you'll know that the service kept me on long after the end of the war.'

Cassie was trying to catch Angus's eye, but he didn't look up.

'And *you*'ll be taking up a new position soon,' Mrs Douglas went on. 'So forget this business. It will resolve itself. Some battles are best left to others.'

'What do you mean?' Cassie said. '*Resolve itself?*'

Mrs Douglas's chair rolled back a few inches on its castors. An unfinished scarf, and a ball of wool with two knitting needles pushed through, sat easily on her lap. She pulled herself back towards the screen. 'Justice will be done,' she said. 'Not your way, perhaps, but it will be done.'

'*My way*,' Cassie said, 'is the only acceptable sort of justice in a civilised society.' Even before she'd finished saying it, Cassie felt very stupid indeed.

Mrs Douglas looked at her watch. 'I'll have to be going, I'm afraid.'

'I don't like secrets, Mrs Douglas.' Cassie unfolded then refolded her arms. 'And I'm not prepared to just walk away. Not on your say so.'

'Even if that puts your friends in harm's way?'

Cassie had been doing her best to maintain a poker face thus far, but she couldn't help drawing a startled breath at this last remark. She swallowed hard and composed herself. 'Is that some sort of threat?' she asked sharply.

Mrs Douglas leaned in. 'You've been asking questions about Scott Deakin. I suggest you leave Mr Deakin well alone, my dear. It is a battle you cannot win – not now at any rate.'

'And what do *you* know about Scott Deakin?'

'I know he isn't responsible for the deaths of Gemma Grant or Sarah Flynn.'

'*How* do you know?'

'I make it my business to know.'

'Right!' Cassie forced a laugh. 'And why should I believe you?'

The old lady closed her eyes for a moment and smiled.

Cassie took a deep breath. 'Are you going to tell me what's going on?'

Mrs Douglas shook her head. 'Let it go, Detective *Chief* Inspector. Let it go.'

Angus knew he was in trouble.

Cassie was staring into space. She was furious. He'd seen her furious before, of course (she was often furious), but not like this: not so furious that she couldn't speak.

He waited.

She ground the heels of her hands into her temples.

He waited some more

'Who *is* that woman?' Cassie said at last. She spoke quietly, calmly, nonchalantly, as if she were struggling to identify a familiar face by the cheese counter in Waitrose. 'And how does she know you, Angus?'

Angus took a deep breath. 'I had no idea, not until I heard the voice. I didn't know her as Céline Douglas. If I'd known it was *her* you were dealing with, I . . .' he broke off and covered his face with his hands.

'What?' Cassie's voice went up a full octave. She aped a quizzical expression. 'What would you have done?'

'I don't know, I . . .'

Flynn retreated to his stove and began to arrange, and rearrange, the companion set.

'Angus,' Cassie said, calm again. 'Will you please just tell me.'

Angus shook his head, then nodded. 'That business with Sarah, you know . . .'

'The *affair*, you mean?' Cassie put her elbows on the table and leaned in. 'Your *affair* with Sarah Flynn? *That business* about you shagging your friend's wife.'

'Yes,' Angus said. He glanced at Flynn who was pretending not to listen.

Cassie nodded. 'Go on then.'

'I don't know how they found out, or why they cared. But they did find out, and they did care.'

'Who? Who cared?'

'GCHQ, MI5, MI6? I don't know. I was only ever a contractor, only ever IT, so it never occurred to me that . . .'

'What? That you'd be under surveillance?'

'Yes.' Angus twisted his mouth. 'Or . . .'

'Or what?'

Angus shrugged. 'Forget it. Nothing. I don't know.'

'Or that *she'd* be under surveillance?' Cassie said. 'That's what you were going to say, isn't it? Your spook friends were spying on Sarah Flynn?'

'No. Yes. I don't know!'

'Right,' Cassie said. 'So *they* must know who ran Sarah's Mercedes off the road.'

'No.' Angus looked at Flynn (who was now busying himself sweeping the hearth), then turned back to face Cassie. 'I'm pretty sure they don't. It was obvious from their line of questioning that they thought it might have been me who ran her off the road.'

Cassie went quiet. She studied her fingernails for a while.

'Cassie?' Angus said quietly. 'You can't think—?'

'Tell me about Céline Douglas.'

Angus sighed and rubbed his temples. 'I knew her as *Mrs Smith*.' He pressed his palms together. 'She'd been retired from the service for fifteen years or more, apparently, but they still used her as a consultant. That's what she told me. The woman didn't seem very retired to me. She told me she specialised in debriefing honeytraps . . . and their victims. She interrogated me for three hours. She asked about every conceivable aspect of my life, so I never did find out what it really was they wanted to know.'

'And?'

'That's it. It all came to nothing in the end.'

Cassie rolled her eyes and opened her mouth to speak.

Angus got in first: 'I'm ashamed, Cassie. Please can we leave it there.'

She sniffed and brought her hands together.

'What I *do* know,' Angus went on, anxious to shift the focus back to Céline Douglas, 'is that she had top-level security clearance, so she'd have been pretty high up before she retired, if she ever did retire.'

'And how did she know you'd be here, with me?'

Angus sighed. 'Lucky guess, I expect. I've been trying to find out what they have on Scott Deakin, just as you asked me to. They notice things like that. They make connections. That's what they do.'

'Why all this fuss, then?' Cassie asked. 'If Scott Deakin is just some low-life criminal, why are the security services interested?' She fixed on Angus and waited.

He shook his head and shrugged.

Cassie got up and started pacing the room. Flynn was now sitting cross legged in front of the stove. Angus prayed for him to say something to distract her. He didn't.

Before he could think how to diffuse the situation, Cassie had rounded on him again. She slammed both hands on the table and leaned in close. 'Was Deakin on their payroll?'

'I don't know,' Angus said.

Cassie glared at him for a moment then stormed over to the sofa at the far end of the room. She didn't sit down. She just stared at the wall behind it.

When Flynn put a hand on her shoulder, she twitched but let him keep it there.

'I'm sure the old lady was telling the truth,' Flynn said, 'about Scotty Deakin I mean. He didn't order the killing of Sarah . . . or Gemma.'

Cassie threw back her head and groaned. 'So who the fuck did? It may very well have been Gary Mulligan who did the murdering, but somebody else ordered it. Who?'

Flynn took his hand off her shoulder for a moment, then put it back.

47

WHISKY WAS FLYNN'S cure for everything. Angus would talk to him about that another time, right now he was glad of his own healthy measure.

Cassie had calmed down. She'd taped together the three pieces of the photograph of Gemma Grant at Sheffield Railway Station. She was looking from her iPad (playing the video of Gemma outside Flynn's place on the day she died) to the photograph, and back again.

Angus didn't dare ask. It occurred to him that she might be trying to work out what the girl was thinking. That was certainly the sort of thing Cassie might do.

Flynn's computer lay dismantled at the other end of the table. Angus was replacing the hard drive when Cassie interrupted.

'Angus,' she said, 'do you have a copy of that video of you and Sarah Flynn? You know the one I mean? The one—'

'No,' he said without looking up.

Cassie stood over him, hands on hips, shifting her weight from one foot to the other.

Angus put down his screwdriver and drew a long breath.

'I'll go out to the shed and fetch some more logs,' Flynn said wearily.

Cassie watched Flynn get into his coat, step outside, pull the door shut behind him. She turned back to Angus. 'I know you've kept a copy,' she said. 'It's the sort of thing a man would keep a record of, like a notch on the proverbial bedpost.'

Angus hadn't the energy to argue. He set the video going on his laptop and passed it to Cassie. 'Are you going to tell me what you're looking for?'

Cassie nodded. 'When I find it, yes.'

'Find what?'

She didn't answer.

Angus pulled on his boots, grabbed his coat, and went outside.

❧

Flynn was standing by the log store, hands in pockets, staring into space.

Angus went over and stood beside him, wondering what to say.

'Do you think she'll ever mellow?' Flynn said.

'No, I think it's just who she is.'

'Maybe. Perhaps if she wasn't so angry . . .'

'But she's always angry, Flynn. Everything makes her angry.'

'*Some* things make her angry, I think, not *every*thing.'

'Other people,' Angus said. 'That's what makes her angry.'

'No,' Flynn said, 'Not people *per se*, but I think that people often *remind* her of those things that do make her angry.'

Angus had no idea what Flynn was talking about anymore. 'I've put the new hard drive in your computer,' he said. 'And I'll sort the RAM next – there are two modules in there, but only one seems to be working.'

Flynn nodded a solemn 'thank you'.

After two hours of relentless snow, the clouds had finally dissipated. Now the night was still, and clear, and so quiet that Angus could hear Flynn's every breath.

For the next five minutes the two men stared silently into the heavens.

'I'm cold,' Flynn said at last, 'let's go back inside.'

❧

'I know who took the pictures.' Cassie was sitting at the dining table, hunched over Angus's. laptop. 'They were all taken with the same camera.'

Flynn peered over her shoulder. 'What, the video *and* the photograph?'

Cassie snapped shut the computer. 'Yep. A modern SLR will do both, and with a long lens, too. And all of these were taken with a long lens.' Cassie pointed at the taped together photograph of Gemma at Sheffield Station. 'Look.'

In the bottom right-hand corner, just above Cassie's fingernail, was a blurry dot no bigger than a pinprick.

She moved her finger to her iPad, to the video of Gemma Grant at the end of Flynn's drive. 'And there, look. Same position.'

Finally, Cassie tapped the lid of Angus's laptop. 'Same goes for the other video. Identical blurry spots, in exactly the same place, in each frame, on the two videos, and on the photograph. Most likely explanation is dust on the inside of the lens – or, maybe, on the image sensor. One camera, one photographer.'

'Not necessarily . . .' Angus began.

Cassie glared at him.

He nodded. 'But probably.'

'David Roland,' Cassie said. 'We know he took the picture at the station so he must have taken the others, too.' She picked up her iPad, and the three pieces of the photograph of Gemma at Sheffield station, and slipped them into her bag. 'I'm off.'

Flynn looked her straight in the eye. 'You're not thinking of confronting him, are you?'

Cassie heaved her bag over her shoulder and pushed past him.

He slid his hands into his pockets. 'Cassie?'

She put on her coat and sat on the sofa to tackle her boots.

'The Snake Pass is closed,' Angus said. He had the Highways

Agency website up on his laptop. 'You'll never get back to Sheffield tonight; there's an overturned lorry blocking both lanes.'

Cassie scowled.

Angus looked at his watch. 'It's ten o'clock already. I don't know about anyone else, but I'm starving.'

❧

Flynn saw to the chilli con carne. Angus saw to the RAM modules. Cassie saw to the Chianti. She was onto her second glass now, and in an altogether better place. *Detective Chief Inspector* – her father would be proud.

She wondered what her mother would have said. Not much, she concluded, after thinking back through all her childhood achievements. From a lead role in the school play, to being elected chair of the school council, to getting a weekend job in the florists on Epping High Street, her mother had put all Cassie's little triumphs down to *a pretty face*. 'God knows where you got it from,' she used to say. 'Certainly not from me or your father. If I'd had your looks, I'd have . . .'

It would always be something more impressive than what Mum had ended up doing, or having, or experiencing.

And she'd have been pleased to find Cassie unattached and childless at thirty-four. Not because she wanted her daughter to become an independent career woman. Not because she wanted to see her daughter unfettered by the miserable marriage, and the far-too-pretty-for-her-own-good child, that had plagued her own life. No, it was because mental illness had made her mother jealous and selfish and spiteful.

Or perhaps mental illness had nothing to do with it. Perhaps it was in her genes – if Cassie looked long and hard inside herself, she knew what she would find. But perhaps everyone, deep down, is a little bit jealous and selfish and spiteful. She looked at Flynn.

He was opening a bottle of passata. He was browning the mince in a frying pan. He was sipping whisky from a very large tumbler.

Maybe not everyone.

❧

'Eureka!' Angus was holding up a microSD card. 'I found this taped to the back of one of the RAM modules in the big man's computer – Sarah's old computer.' He turned to Flynn: 'Not yours, is it?'

Flynn shook his head.

Cassie leapt to her feet, slopping wine over the floor, to get a better look.

'Half the RAM in this machine wasn't properly slotted in,' Angus said, 'that's why it didn't work; and this . . .' he put the tiny memory card on the table '. . . this is why it wouldn't slot in.'

Cassie held out a hand.

'Let me sort out the security, first.' Angus said. 'If this was Sarah's, and I can't imagine who else would have hidden it in here, there'll be security. We don't want it wiped clean like her hard drive, do we. Give me ten minutes.'

❧

With Flynn and Angus peering over her shoulders, Cassie scrolled through the contents of the SD card. Several dozen cryptically named folders were listed alphabetically. The first on the list – AD – turned out to be a dossier on Angela Denning, the Director of Procurement for an NHS trust in London. It contained notes, scanned documents, photographs, videos, which all pointed to Denning having been on the on the fiddle. Cassie remembered the story hitting the headlines a few years back – Denning had been forced to resign, but there'd been insufficient evidence for a criminal prosecution.

The next few dossiers contained similar material – some related to stories Cassie remembered from the newspapers, others meant nothing to her.

'I'd better check on the chilli,' Flynn said.

Angus nodded. 'Yes, this might take quite a while. I'll put your computer back together so that we can use that one too.'

It was going to take an age to go through everything alphabetically, so Cassie scanned for initials that might stand for Scott Deakin or Brett McRoss or Sean Mulligan. There was no 'SD' for Scott Deakin but--

'BM!' Cassie thumped the table. 'That's got to be Brett McRoss,' she said. 'I knew Sarah was on to him.' She clicked on the folder, scanned the contents, and then slumped back in her chair. 'Shit.'

'What?' Angus said.

'It's not Brett McRoss.' Cassie ran her fingers through her hair, slowly, and tucked it behind her ears.

'Who then?' Flynn asked. He put the lid back on the chilli pan and went over to look.

Angus got there first. '*Bernie Muxlow,*' he said. 'She had a file on Deputy Chief Constable Bernie Muxlow!'

❧

All the files in the 'BM' folder were photographs or videos. The first three photos were of a younger Muxlow, back when he was Detective Inspector, outside a building that Flynn identified as the No. 7 Gentleman's Club, with a man who Flynn said was Scott Deakin.

There were hundreds after that, all of Muxlow in places that could not easily be identified and with people who Cassie, Flynn, Angus, couldn't name. Eventually they got to the more recent images, some of which they could place because they were in

Sheffield. Muxlow on golf courses, outside bars, in restaurants, in hotel lounges. But they didn't recognise any of the people photographed *with* Muxlow until they were three quarters of the way through.

Cassie reached for her wine, took a gulp, pressed the glass to her forehead. 'Oh my god!' she said, scrolling through the pictures. 'There are dozens. Dozens and dozens.'

The pictures were of Muxlow with Gemma Grant. All taken, according to the date stamps, before the car crash that killed Gemma's mother.

There were videos too: Muxlow greeting Gemma with a kiss in a busy hotel lounge (which they all recognised as the Sheffield Hilton); Muxlow and Gemma embracing by the river at Millhouses Park; Muxlow and Gemma holding hands across a table in a dimly lit restaurant.

Cosy, content, carefree.

There were several stills of Gemma entering or leaving Muxlow's house (an uninspiring brick-built box in leafy Dore), but for the most part the pair were in very public places.

'What was he thinking?' Cassie said. 'A fifteen-year-old girl, for Christ's sake!'

Angus scratched his chin. 'Yes, but—'

'No buts: he's finished. I'll see to that. I'll never be able to prove that he had Sarah's car run off the road . . . but an affair with an underage girl, that I can prove! No, he's finished.' Cassie was scrolling through photo after photo, video clip after video clip, shaking her head. 'I still can't believe he was this stupid.'

'He thought she was older, I expect,' Angus said.

Cassie glared at him. 'Oh, so that's all right then, is it?'

'No, but . . .' Angus held up his hands.

'He's right, though,' Flynn said. 'She does look much older than fifteen in these videos. The way she walks, the way she dresses, the way she talks.'

'The way she talks?' Cassie slammed her wine glass onto the table. 'We can't hear her talking in any of these videos, Flynn! I thought you said you'd never met Gemma Grant. If you—'

'Please, Cassie,' Flynn said. 'I was thinking of Sarah. They're so alike, I couldn't *help* thinking of her. I would even—'

'Oh, I bet you *would*,' Cassie said, arms folded, fists clenched, staring at the ceiling. 'Skinny, pretty little thing like that. And she *looks* old enough, doesn't she, so that's all right!' Cassie shook her head. 'And I bet Angus *would* too!'

Flynn got up and went over to the window.

'Too far, Cassie,' Angus said, quietly. 'Sometimes you go too far.'

Cassie slumped over the table and covered her head with her arms. 'I'm sorry. I don't know why . . . you know I didn't mean it. But you were trying to defend him, the pair of you. She was fifteen, and he's a middle-aged man – it's disgusting and it's inexcusable and it's fucking illegal.' She sat up and rubbed her eyes. 'But I'm sorry, really I am.'

'We're not defending him,' Angus said. 'We're just trying to understand why a senior policeman would parade around Sheffield with a fifteen-year-old girl on his arm. It beggars belief! Look at these pictures, Cassie. He's openly romancing her, touching her, kissing her. He's showing her off. I expect he thinks she's twenty, or twenty-one, or some age that would make it . . . *okay*.'

Cassie snorted. 'Well, he should have checked, shouldn't he. How could he not have known? Come on. There's a world of difference between a fifteen-year-old girl and a twenty-one-year-old woman.'

'I bet he *thought* he knew exactly how old she was,' Angus said. 'She must have tricked him, somehow.'

'So it's her fault, is it? Is that what you're saying? Muxlow was shagging a child and yet somehow he was the victim?'

'No, Cassie!' Angus took a deep breath 'I'm not trying to make excuses for him. I'm just . . . I don't know. Honestly Cassie, look at this picture: it's a busy wine bar full of middle-aged couples. Look at this picture and tell me that what you see is a senior police officer openly fondling the arse of a girl he *knows* to be fifteen years old.'

'When Sarah was in her first year at university,' Flynn said, before Cassie could answer, 'she posed as a barrister to get an interview with an anti-capitalism protester who was in police custody. And she got away with it, she got into the police cells. She was only eighteen but she dressed the part and talked the talk and—

'Eighteen isn't the same as fifteen, Flynn. And if you can't see—'

'The point is . . .' Angus said, a little too loudly.

Cassie glared at him.

Angus help up his hands. 'The point is,' he continued, 'Muxlow must have *believed* she was an adult. That's all we're saying. What I can't comprehend is what *she* could have seen in a man three times her age. Just look at her in all these pictures – look at that smile. I know that smile. Just like her bloody . . .'

Angus stopped, but it was too late.

Flynn turned to face the fire. '*Fifteen* is just a number, Cassie,' he said quietly. 'If she'd been sixteen or seventeen, would it have been any less wrong? And if she'd been eighteen, and an adult in the eyes of the law, would that have been all right? Really? A man pushing fifty and eighteen-year-old girl?'

Nobody said anything for a while.

'One thing's for sure,' Flynn went on, 'Muxlow had fallen for Gemma. Fallen for her completely. Fallen in love with her.'

And Flynn was right, much as Cassie hated to admit it: the images were of a pretty young woman and a smitten older man. You could see it in his face, in the attitude of his body.

And he'd taken her to the places where lovers go. Places where you can be alone. Places that reflect the scale and heft of new love.

Parkland, woodland, open moorland, the heather clad banks of burgeoning valley streams, Stanage Edge. He'd even taken her to see the Christmas decorations at Chatsworth, for Christ's sake!

What was it about Sarah and Gemma that attracted men who should know better? Sensible men? Serious men? Maybe '*that smile*' was the answer. It was not the seductive smile of a femme fatale from silent movie. It was more than suggestive, more than naughty, more than wicked. Gemma's smile was Sarah Flynn's smile – it was the smile that Flynn and Angus and Muxlow had fallen for.

A clattering of metal interrupted Cassie's musings. Flynn had set a large pan of chilli on the trivet in the middle of the table.

'Let's eat,' he said.

48

CASSIE LOOKED AGAIN at her watch. She'd been lying in the dark for three hours, praying for sleep but knowing it wouldn't come. She rolled onto her side.

The sofa was comfortable, and the duvet was warm. That wasn't the problem. The problem was what they'd found on a tiny memory card long hidden amongst the silicon innards of Flynn's laptop.

Cassie tried to distract herself with matters mundane and domestic. Should she reinstate the cast iron fireplace that someone had ripped out of her bedroom back in the sixties? She'd found it in the cellar on the day she moved in – it was beautiful, with art nouveau tiles and a matching hearth. Mr Cosgrove from next door said it wouldn't cost much to have a builder put it back.

It was decided: she would do it. And she would redecorate too. No more magnolia – duck egg blue would be nice . . . in a period chalky paint.

She rolled onto her back. Yes, Flynn's sofa *was* comfortable. It was the type that became a perfectly serviceable queen-sized bed when the back and side cushions were removed. She wondered if she ought to get something like this for her house, for her living room, to accommodate overnight guests. She imagined making up a bed like this to accommodate her dad on a weekend visit. Between planning her new patio, and designing a shabby chic bookcase that would look great in her living room, she had decided that there should, one day, be a daughter-father reconciliation.

Any daughter-father reunion would, of course, be on her terms, and by her rules . . . and she had dreamed-up the perfect scenario.

It would be a snowy Christmas Eve. She would greet her dad at the front door, kissing him on the cheek for the first time in decades. She would take his coat and hang it beside a much larger coat on the hall stand. She would take his boots and set them beside a much larger pair on the towel she'd spread on the floor to protect the parquet from drips. Then she would carelessly let her cardigan fall open to reveal a pregnant belly.

And she wouldn't have warned him about the pregnant belly, or about the big man whose coat was hanging on the hall stand, and whose boots were on the towel. Her father would understand that she didn't need him. He would understand that she'd never needed him. He would understand that this reconciliation was for his benefit, and not for hers.

Cassie had revisited the scene, adjusting the decor and the dialogue, many times over the last couple of hours. The other man, of course, the man with the big coat and the big boots, was Flynn. But however many times she reimagined the episode, and however many times she adjusted the furniture and the décor and the dialogue, Flynn just didn't seem to fit. Flynn was simply too big for her little kitchen, too big for her little house.

And when he shook the big man's big hand, Dad looked so small, and so pathetic, that she felt ashamed: ashamed of herself, ashamed of her father, ashamed of Flynn.

She wished Angus hadn't found that bloody thing in Sarah's old computer. But now, at least, she had the missing piece of the jigsaw – a motive. Flynn once told her the best way to test an idea was to turn it into words, to speak it out loud. 'If it can't be expressed in simple words,' he'd said, 'or if the only way you can think to present it is through metaphor, then it's probably bullshit.' So she spent the next half hour rehearsing how she would explain it all to Meg:

Muxlow ordered a hit on Gemma Grant, two years ago, because she was blackmailing him. Sarah's Mercedes was run off the Snake Pass by a big pick-up truck with bull bars (driven by a couple of Mulligan's thugs) – Sarah died but Gemma survived and got away. Gemma, aided by Céline Douglas, went into hiding in Scotland for a couple of years but came back to Sheffield last week, probably to see Flynn about getting some money out of her trust fund. She was tracked down (we don't know how, or by whom, and probably never will), and Muxlow got the Mulligan gang to finish the job they started. Muxlow also arranged for Flynn to be framed for her murder and then killed. That way the whole case could easily be buried.

But still, Cassie couldn't rest easy. It certainly fitted, this missing piece of the jigsaw: Deputy Chief Constable Muxlow had had an affair with a fifteen-year-old girl, and she had to be silenced. Yes, it fitted all right, this grubby little piece of the jigsaw, but it didn't sit flat.

It was the blackmail theory that was the problem. In part because there was no evidence of blackmail, but also because Gemma would've had other avenues open to her if she wanted money. Her mother, for one. And Muxlow himself, for another. Muxlow, a besotted sugar daddy, would probably have given her anything she asked for. So why blackmail him?

On a more practical level, the images of Muxlow and Gemma Grant together were date stamped over a two month period, and the last of those dates was the evening before the car crash that killed Sarah. This last picture had Gemma and Muxlow walking hand in hand along the Ecclesall Road. It seemed unlikely that, within 20 hours of that picture being taken, Gemma had begun to blackmail Muxlow, Muxlow had recruited a hit squad to murder Gemma, and said hit squad had made a first attempt on her life.

No. She just couldn't believe Muxlow had ordered Gemma's murder.

Cassie found herself replaying last night's conversations in her head.

'*When you have eliminated the impossible*,' Angus had said, puffing on an imaginary pipe as he quoted Sherlock Holmes, '*then whatever remains, however improbable, must be the truth*.'

But Angus was no Sherlock Holmes. Yes, he might be good at analysing data – but in this instance he didn't have enough data to forge any sort of hypothesis. And anyway, Cassie was juggling truths, not facts. Angus struggled with this distinction, as people without imagination often do.

She kicked up the blanket, rolled onto her side, drew her knees up to her chest. If she'd thought of it at the time, she'd have told Angus another thing Sherlock Holmes once said: *We balance probabilities and choose the most likely. It is the scientific use of the imagination.*

As Cassie remembered it, Flynn had seen the problem with the Muxlow theory before she did: 'I'm not convinced Muxlow killed her,' he'd said. 'I think he was head over heels in love with her. I know she was far too young, and I know what he did was wrong, but I do feel sorry for him.'

'Your problem, Flynn,' she'd said, 'is that you feel sorry for everyone – especially yourself.'

Cassie cringed and pulled her knees tighter to her chest – she shouldn't have put him down like that.

An excruciating silence had followed.

She'd meant to hurt him, of course she had. But why? Why did she say these things? She hated herself for it.

'Not sorry for *myself*,' Flynn had said, 'I'm just . . . *sorry*.'

What did that even mean? Was he being profound or just playing with words? Flynn had a habit of saying things that meant more to him than to the person he was talking to. Ha! She'd found fault with him! She was pleased with herself. Then she wasn't, because Flynn's flaws gave him nobility — and Cassie hated *nobility.* She hated *honour* and *duty* and *heroism* and all the other romantic notions that people attach to the simple job of doing what has to be done.

She had a headache. She wished she were upstairs sharing a bed with Flynn. She wished Flynn weren't so . . . so . . . *big.* She wished she could stop thinking. She wished she could sleep.

49

CASSIE OVERSLEPT.

She was on the sofa bed, downstairs, dreaming that Stella Middlewood was telling her to get her lazy arse out of bed. Flynn and Angus were downstairs too, talking and preparing breakfast and making too much noise.

'He's only gone and killed himself!' Stella said.

Cassie opened her eyes and sat up, keeping the duvet tight to her chin. Stella was at the table staring at her phone, shaking her head. Angus was sitting opposite, nursing a cup of steaming coffee. Flynn was hunched over the kitchen sink.

'Who's killed himself?' Cassie said. 'And what are you doing back here, Stella?'

Now everyone was staring a Stella.

'Stella left her scarf.' Angus nodded at the coat pegs by the door. 'It was a Christmas present and—'

'Muxlow,' Stella said. 'Muxlow shot himself. Last night. It's all over the news. They're saying it was pressure of work, cutbacks, targets.' Stella looked hard at Cassie. 'What do *you* think?'

Cassie didn't know what to think. She suddenly felt sick and dizzy, and her temples ached. 'I need a shower,' she said. And, with the duvet wrapped about her like a cloak, she scooped her pile of clothes from the floor and made for the spiral staircase.

'You should ring that sergeant of yours,' Stella shouted after her. 'Meg Harper might know something about Muxlow?'

Cassie slammed the bathroom door.

❧

When he heard Cassie coming back downstairs, Flynn's stomach tensed. Last night he'd dreamed that he came downstairs and found her wearing nothing but the long-sleeved T-shirt he'd lent her for bed. She was sitting, cross-legged, eyes closed, in the warm glow of the stove.

He studied her fine Roman profile, her long black eyelashes, her plump red lips. He reached out, tentatively, and touched her wrist. She caressed the back of his hand, her ruby fingernails glistening in the gentle light from—

'Flynn,' Cassie was marching down the cast iron steps, dressed for the day, but barefoot, with her hair wrapped in a towel, 'have you got another towel, a dry one?'

'I . . .' He was still reliving the dream – he could feel her fingertips on the back of his hands. 'I don't think so. If you like I could—'

'Forget it.'

Perhaps that was what he should do: *forget it*. He should just accept that he'd lost her.

Cassie pulled out a chair, sharply, and joined Flynn, Angus and Stella at the table.

Flynn lowered his eyes.

'Angus,' Cassie said, 'show Stella the pictures.'

'What pictures?'

'Muxlow and Gemma Grant.'

Angus coughed and looked up, wide eyed.

Flynn didn't react.

Cassie's hands were folded neatly on her lap.

Nobody said anything for a little too long.

'Go on, Angus.' Cassie nodded at Angus's computer and placed her palms flat on the table.

She had done her nails, Flynn noticed, and the fresh varnish shimmered in the light from the window just as it had in his dream.

'We found some photographs last night,' Cassie said to Stella, 'after you left.'

'Photographs?' Stella said, plainly annoyed that they'd made the discovery without her.

'*The* photographs, I think. The photographs that Sean Mulligan was after.' Cassie turned back to Angus. 'Angus . . .'

Angus hesitated, then reached for his laptop.

Flynn left the table and went to refill the toaster. He didn't want to see those pictures of Gemma and Muxlow again. Gemma looked so much like Sarah it was too much to bear. And he couldn't think why Cassie would want to share all this with Stella Middlewood – with the press.

Angus scrolled through the images.

Stella gawped.

'I'll email you the files if you like,' Cassie said.

'If these date stamps are right . . .' Stella was scratching her head furiously. 'If these dates are right, Gemma would have been only fifteen when Muxlow—'

'Of course,' Cassie tapped the table with her index finger, 'if I give you the pictures, I'll want something in return.'

'What?' Stella said.

'Flynn . . . Jamie Boreman . . . Scott Deakin . . . the Bolan twins – I want your word that you'll forget all about it. Forever.'

'You'll have my word.' Stella said.

She said it rather too quickly, Flynn thought.

'Can I use your toilet?' Stella said, grabbing her phone.

Flynn nodded up the spiral staircase. He knew she was off to make a sneaky *hold the front page* phone call. But he also knew there was no mobile signal in the bathroom. 'Thank you,' he said, putting a hand on Cassie's shoulder. 'But do we really need to do this?'

'Yes,' Cassie said. 'I'm a Police Officer, Flynn. So I can't *not* hand this to over to the authorities.'

Flynn withdrew his hand for the briefest moment then put it back. 'Yes, but—'

'And it'll all be leaked to the press soon enough, stuff like this always ends up being leaked. This way we have Stella on side at least.'

'But they're all dead, Cassie!' Flynn drew a slow breath. 'Muxlow, Gemma, the Mulligans. Why can't we throw that SD card on the fire. Why can't we just forget about all the bad stuff?'

Cassie pulled away and looked him straight in the eye. 'Why can't *you* just forget about "all the bad stuff"?'

ꕥ

Stella had gone home. Angus had gone home. The thaw had come.

Pockets of snow lay shrivelled and translucent, shining in the low January sun. It could have been spring. The steady pitter-patter of melt water from the deep snow on Flynn's roof should have been warning enough – it had been pitter-pattering for hours. The whole lot came crashing down a few feet from where Cassie was standing. She leapt sideways, slipped, and tumbled backwards.

'Are you all right?' Flynn called from the back door, pulling on a pair of wellies.

She wished he would come over and pick her up. She wished he would stay in the house and leave her alone. She wished . . .

'I'm fine,' she said, still clutching her phone.

Flynn stomped through the avalanche and made a fuss of dusting the snow off the back of her coat.

'Leave it, Flynn, please. I'm fine.'

He put his hands in his pockets and looked up at the roof. 'Wow! If you'd been standing a few feet closer'

'Well I wasn't.' She put her hands on her hips.

Flynn turned back to Cassie. 'So, what did Meg Harper have to say about Muxlow?'

'Nothing much.'

'Was there a note? Suicides usually—'

'No.'

From the corner of her eye, she caught Flynn twisting his mouth thoughtfully.

They watched a robin land on the now snowless roof. It hopped from the ridge to the chimney cowl and then flew off into the woods.

'Cassie,' Flynn said.

'What?'

'Is it over between us?'

'Never really started, did it?'

'No, but . . .' Flynn kicked his heels in the slush that was rapidly forming around their feet. 'Would you like to try again?'

She pretended to stare at the roof but kept him in the corner of her eye. 'I don't know.'

Flynn rubbed his lips with the back of his hand. 'I'd understand, Cassie, honestly I would, if you didn't.' He shifted his weight from one leg to the other. 'But sometimes I think you might. And then, sometimes, you . . .' He cleared his throat. 'I just want to know how you really feel.'

Cassie looked from the newly exposed stone roof to the pile of icy snow beneath. When she noticed herself pouting, she bit down on her bottom lip.

Flynn waited.

'I'm too busy to think about it at the moment,' she said.

'Right.' Flynn pulled his hands out of his pockets and brought them together under his chin as if in prayer. 'But maybe if—'

'Please, Flynn. Not *now*!'

'Sorry.'

'Yes, well . . .'

They stood a while longer, Flynn staring at his roof, Cassie staring at the pile of snow.

Her phone bleeped. 'Right,' she said, glancing at the screen, 'Angus says the roads have been cleared.'

'What are you going to do?' Flynn asked, quietly.

Cassie found the strength to look at him, but the look was more like a glare. This was not what she'd intended.

'Okay.' Flynn held up his hands. 'But you're not going to see David Roland again, are you? Not on your own?'

She mustered a smile: soft and understanding and resolute.

He stared at her; he looked like he was about to say something.

Cassie got in first: 'See you later.'

'Wait.' Flynn stepped closer. 'Just so you know,' he said, 'I would like us to try again. I really would.'

Cassie didn't flinch. 'Whatever do you see in me, Flynn?'

He closed his eyes for a moment, then opened his mouth to speak.

'Actually, no,' she said. 'Please don't say anything. I've heard it all before.'

He put those big hands of his back into his pockets.

Cassie turned and walked away. She resolved not to look back.

❧

Flynn watched until she was out of sight, then stood a while longer, weighing his options, before going back inside.

Upstairs, he dragged the suitcase out from under his bed and laid its contents on the duvet. The navy suit and white shirt were made by Sam Margolies, Scotty's tailor, back in 1997. Flynn had asked Sam to make the jacket long and black, like the frock coats Colin Firth had worn when he played Darcy on television, he even furnished a picture cut out of an old edition the *Radio Times*.

Sam said it would look more like a costume than a suit.

Flynn said that was okay.

Sam said it would make him look like a funeral director.

Flynn said he didn't mind.

Sam said he should go navy rather than black.

Flynn said navy would be fine.

His cravat was a dark shade of burgundy. It came from a charity shop in Sale Moor. A thick-fingered lady behind the counter had showed him how to tie it and pin it.

Scott Deakin laughed the first time he saw the outfit. But the cut of the suit made Flynn look even bigger, so Scotty had relented.

Cassie was going to see Dave Roland, Flynn was sure of it – Roland was the only lead she had left. She'd be on foot all the way along the track, so he'd soon catch her up in the Land Rover. Dave Roland was a vicious bastard by nature. And Dave Roland, cornered, well . . .

Flynn dressed quickly. He tied his cravat in front of the bathroom mirror and brushed the dust off the lapels of his frock coat. He tried not to see his own reflection, but couldn't help looking. He wasn't quite as big as he used to be, but the suit still fitted. And if the suit fits . . .

50

THE WINDOWS HAD steamed up so Cassie couldn't see out of her car. Just now, she liked it that way. A nagging, numbing headache made it painful to think. She'd been parked up for half an hour, waiting for the paracetamol to kick in. It wasn't getting any better.

The turmoil of the last six days had turned her brain to sludge. She'd done things she ought not to have done. She'd thought things she wished she'd never thought. She'd learned things she now longed to forget. And yet, if she could spool back time and edit her part in the story of the last six days, what would she change?

Her lines, certainly. She'd have said better things: nicer things, kinder things, wiser things. She'd have held her tongue in places, and delivered wittier reposts in others. She'd have kept a poker face throughout. But the story itself was not something she could change. It was what it was. She had gone where she had to go, done what had to be done, discovered what was there to be discovered.

❧

Cassie wound down the window to let in some air. She was parked outside David Roland and Associates Ltd. The office looked closed. There were no lights on, despite the afternoon being as gloomy as dusk, and the car park was empty but for Roland's Porsche Cayenne. Odd for a Thursday.

She got out of her car and scanned the building for signs of life. Nothing. Except for the monster Porsche, of course, but that didn't guarantee he'd be in. She was tired – too tired to interview Roland – but it had to be done. David Roland held the key to understanding the facts as she knew them. He could be linked to all the protagonists: to Gemma Grant, to Sarah Flynn, to Scott Deakin, to the Mulligans, to Bernie Muxlow. And to Flynn, too, probably.

It was then that she remembered Roland's Manchester accent: perhaps Roland had known Scott Deakin back in the day. And if he'd known Deakin back then, he'd have known his minder. He'd have known Jamie Boreman. He'd have known Flynn.

And what was it Flynn had said to her an hour ago? *'But you're not going to see David Roland again are you? Not on your own?'*

Not on your own? It was the *way* he had said it that was odd. Cassie was so used to turning a deaf ear to colleagues saying that she shouldn't go here, or there, alone, just because she was a woman, that it hadn't even registered. But that wasn't the way Flynn had meant it. Now, suddenly, she understood. She had sensed it when he said it, probably, and, if she hadn't been so bloody tired, it surely would have registered.

Flynn *knew* Roland! Flynn's warning had less to do with her being a woman, than it had to do with Roland being a dangerous man. When Flynn said *not on your own* what he meant was *not without me*. And the *me* was not Flynn the writer, not Flynn the storyteller, not Flynn the suitor. The *me* was Jamie Boreman, Deakin's Dandy, Flynn the big man, Flynn the hard man, Flynn the gangland boss's minder.

Shit.

The front door buzzed open before she had a chance to press the button.

Shit.

A tinny speaker rattled and hissed. 'Come straight upstairs, love. You know the way.'

Shit.

She looked back down the road, hoping (half expecting) to see Flynn's Land Rover roaring into view.

It didn't.

She took a deep breath. She was being ridiculous! Cassie felt for her phone in her left pocket, and the pepper spray in her right. What had *she* to fear from Roland? *She* was a Police Officer, a Detective *Chief* bloody Inspector with the full weight of the South Yorkshire constabulary behind her. It was Roland who should be afraid.

She pushed open the door and charged upstairs.

David Roland was one of those men who struggles to carry off any outfit that isn't a suit: he looked as ridiculous in jeans and a T-shirt as he would have looked in a cocktail dress. And he was drunk. He was standing at the window, feet planted wide apart, swaying. He gave a stupid smile, looked Cassie up and down, and licked his lips.

'Help yourself, love.' He raised an arm to indicate the bottle of Smirnoff on the table.

'No thanks.'

'Suit yourself.' Roland pulled a plastic cup from the water cooler and poured her a large measure. 'Just in case you change your mind . . .' He slid the plastic cup towards Cassie and collapsed into the nearest chair, fumbling his own cup and spilling vodka over his jeans.

His flies were gaping, Cassie noticed. And *he* must have noticed too, when he retrieved the empty cup from his lap, but he did nothing about it.

She grabbed the chair beside Roland, turned it so that she'd be facing him, and sat down. Drunk as Roland was (he could barely stand!) Cassie felt a little more secure. And drunk as Roland was, she felt a little more optimistic about getting something out of him.

'Right,' she said, 'I want to know what you were doing filming Gemma Grant outside Flynn's house six hours before she died. I want to know what Gary Mulligan was doing here, in this building, two hours before *he* died. I want to know what business you have with Scott Deakin.' Cassie folded her arms and stared straight at him.

Roland stared back. The smile had gone. He poured himself another shot, downed it, then leaned in so close that she could smell the vodka on his breath. 'And I want to see your tits.'

He reached to grope her.

Cassie dodged his hand and aimed a punch at his throat, but as he lunged forward again, trying to grab her breasts, she missed his throat and caught him square on the chin.

Roland smirked. 'Like it rough do you, luv?'

She reached into her right pocket for the pepper spray.

Mum used to spend hours in her wicker armchair, Cassie remembered, more often than not looking at old photographs. Usually, it was the collection that grandma had left (sepia memories of a lost girlhood in the Cornish wilds, the cellophane wet with tears). But not always. Sometimes she would leaf through the stiff pages of her old wedding album, steely faced, like a penitent reflecting upon her penance. Cassie remembered chintz cushion covers and peeling white paint.

What would Mum make of her little girl now – a grown-up career woman (*Detective Chief Inspector*, no less!), trussed up, cold and naked, in a damp cellar, wrists and ankles gaffer-taped to a rattan chair?

Cassie's head ached; it throbbed with every heartbeat. An

unnaturally bright light bulb swung silently from the ceiling – she closed her eyes but she could still see it.

David Roland's hot hands were all over her breasts.

She remembered the look of amusement on his face when she punched him, remembered the raised veins on the back of his clenched fist . . . but nothing after that.

His hair was clipped short. It was thick, and the darkest shade of grey, but his pink, sweaty, spotty scalp gleamed through. What would *his* mother think of *him* now?

She knew exactly what *her* mother would say, it was what she always said when a sex crime was reported on the news: '*That's what happens to girls who think they can have it all*'. And she would say it with glee.

Cassie's mouth was taped over. She tried to breathe quietly, through her nose, so that Roland shouldn't know that she'd come round. His fingers were high on her inner thigh, now, describing warm little circles on her cold, bare skin. She shuddered – couldn't help herself – and squeezed her eyes tight shut.

Her father had always been coy about matters sexual. Surprisingly, for a nineteen-sixties teenager, he used to get quite upset when she wore a short skirt over bare legs.

He would weep if he could see her now. But he wouldn't blame her. He'd never blamed her. Never.

Roland's probing fingers were hurting now. At first she clenched, but that made it worse, so she gripped the armrests and squeezed until her hands hurt more.

Flynn would say, 'I told you so'. And he'd be right! Actually, no, he wouldn't say that. He wasn't the *I told you so* type – he made excuses for everyone except himself. Flynn was handsome and honest and clever and kind, and she was a fool to have doubted him, a fool to have ignored his advice, a fool full stop.

Cassandra Jane May, Police Officer, 34, single, from Epping, knew she was going to die.

You didn't rape a Detective Inspector (a Detective *Chief* fucking Inspector, in fact!) and then let her go. And he *was* going to rape her – she'd accepted that, and she thought she could deal with it. It was the way he would kill her that was the worry. She hoped it wouldn't be a knife – she hated the idea of being cut. Better to be shot or strangled or beaten to death.

She'd treated Dad *so* unfairly, for *so* many years. And now, thanks to her own selfish stupidity, he was going get that terrible late-night knock on the door. He'd be driven to the hospital's back gates. He'd be asked to identify a putrid corpse discovered by a pair of slavering hounds in a shallow woodland grave. He'd be made to look upon the maggot-ridden remains of a pitiful, pitiless, silly little girl – *his* pitiful, pitiless, silly little girl.

Cassie convulsed as she sobbed.

Roland's hands slid freely across her skin now. From her buttocks to her breasts to her shoulders to her chin. He was ready – she could sense it.

Her nose was congested, and with her mouth taped over she couldn't draw enough breath to fuel the crying. She tried to force open her lips to get more air but the tape was stuck fast. Thick snot gurgled into her throat with every snort. She was gagging – swallowing mucous, coughing, choking.

Light headed now.

No pain.

Much better.

The room spun like a May Day carousel. She could taste bittersweet cocoa, she could hear Dad's bedtime story voice, she could smell Mum's Chanel No 5.

The musty cellar air turned seaside fresh.

The light faded.

Faded some more.

Faded until it was gone.

❧

Flynn was still cursing when his Land Rover clipped the wing mirror of a Porsche Cayenne and came to splintery halt in the rhododendron bush beyond. He'd lost Cassie at the Manchester Road traffic lights, and it had taken half an hour to find Roland's place.

He got out and looked around. He didn't know what he was expecting, but certainly nothing so posh. What on earth was the likes of Dave Roland doing in such a large and handsome Victorian house?

Cassie's Mini was parked up on the road, and, except for the big Porsche, the car park was empty.

A house name was carved into the lintel above the main door – The Beeches. The door itself looked pretty solid. Hefty oak, probably original, but set in a modern powder coated steel frame. The locks looked new, and as hefty as the door. Flynn pressed the buzzer.

And again.

And again.

Nothing.

Sunlight broke through pewter clouds, turning The Beeches' sandstone walls a pinkish shade of magnolia.

Flynn went all round the building, testing doors. They were all locked and secure and heavy duty, not the sort of doors you could put your shoulder to – but he'd try, if he had to, as a last resort.

As quickly as it had come out, the sun disappeared. Now it was ominously dark. The midday sky was the colour of Llanberis slate. Flynn was about to try one of the windows when he spotted a dim sliver of light by his feet. He pawed away the leaves and sludge and slush to uncover a trapdoor. A narrow stairwell led steeply down. At the bottom of the stairs Flynn found a door that he *could* put his shoulder to. So he did.

Roland must have heard the grill being lifted, or heard footsteps on the stone stairs, because he was ready and waiting and swinging a rusty old golf club. Flynn caught the club in his left hand and was about to topple Roland with an uppercut when he saw Cassie slumped in a wicker chair, naked and pale and motionless. Roland let go of the golf club and landed a punch square on Flynn's cheek.

Now, Flynn was back in that bricked-up arch under the Stockport viaduct, stunned and dizzy. He wanted desperately to sit on the straw bales, but he knew he'd be in trouble if he did. A middle-aged woman, drunk and purple faced, was screaming at him: 'Hit him, you lazy fucker,' she said. 'Hit him, hit him, hit him, hit him, hit him.'

Flynn floored Roland with a right hook. He turned back to Cassie. Unconscious but alive. He knew she was alive just as certainly as he'd known that Gemma Grant was dead. With the flick knife he knew he'd find in Roland's back pocket, Flynn cut Cassie's wrists and ankles free. He dressed her in her fancy designer parka and carried her upstairs.

51

CASSIE AWOKE LYING on a sofa, head propped up awkwardly on an itchy cushion. She was wearing her parka with the buttons in the wrong holes.

Angus was sitting at a grand mahogany desk, hunched over a laptop. 'Are you all right?' he asked.

Slowly, she sat up. 'Where am I?'

'Roland's office. You've been out cold for a couple of hours, so . . .' Angus rubbed his chin nervously.

Her clothes were on a chair by the desk: hefty black knickers stuffed into the frayed left cup of a bra that used to be white; skirt, blouse and jacket arranged neatly over the chair back; thick tights and hikers socks draped over cosy winter boots. She grabbed the bra and knickers and scrunched them to her chest.

Angus got up. She didn't know what he was going to say or do, but whatever it was, she wanted him to stop.

He opened his mouth to speak.

She held up a hand.

'I just . . .' he began.

She shook her head

'But you're okay? Because when Flynn rang, he said you were okay, and then I got here and you didn't seem okay to me.'

She looked right through him.

'You were out cold for so long,' Angus said. 'I was all for calling an ambulance.'

Cassie swallowed hard. 'I'm okay.'

'I should have called an ambulance.' Angus was shaking his head and wringing his hands. 'Yes, I'll call for an ambulance right now.'

'Please, no,' Cassie said. She sat up on the sofa, pulling her coat tight over her knees.

'It's just that Flynn . . . well . . .' Angus covered his face with his hands for a moment, then shook his head. 'But I should have . . . oh, I don't know! Is there anything I can do for you? Anything?'

She shook her head.

'What about a drink? Would you like something to drink?'

Another shake of the head.

Now he was staring at her. Staring, Cassie thought, as if he wasn't quite sure who he was looking at. 'I want to get dressed,' she said.

Angus grabbed the computer and made for the door. 'Knock when you're ready. But please don't open this door. Wait until . . .' He pulled the door open an inch, peeked through and then closed it again. 'We'll be in there. Knock when you're ready. Don't open the door.'

She nodded.

'Cassie,' Angus said. 'Did Roland . . . ?' He caught her eye then looked down.

She squeezed her bundled underwear and bit her bottom lip.

He grabbed the door handle. 'It's okay, I understand.'

Angus didn't understand. The old Cassie would have bloody well told him so.

❧

Fifteen minutes later, and dead set on facing the world, Cassie opened the door she had been told not to open. David Roland was lying unconscious in the recovery position on the far side of the conference room. At the table, Angus was busy with Roland's laptop computer. Flynn, dressed in a long, navy frock coat, white shirt and burgundy cravat, was pacing the room.

Cassie couldn't help staring. He looked so different. And it wasn't just the weird undertaker's livery and the bizarre cravat – it was everything about him. The military posture, the heavy eyes, the cat-like way he turned when she came in.

Flynn was in the suit she'd found under his bed. And now she realised exactly what it was: it was the outfit he'd described so vividly in *The Wythenshawe Dandy.* Flynn *wasn't* the Wythenshawe Dandy. He wasn't the narrator, he wasn't the hero, and he certainly wasn't the noble victim of the story. Flynn was the man known only as *The Undertaker*, Flynn was the cruellest character you could imagine. Flynn was the villain of the piece.

'You shouldn't be in here,' Flynn said in a half-whisper. 'Please, Cassie, wait next door.'

She shook her head. 'Are you *The Undertaker*? Are you *The Undertaker* from that story of yours? Because I always thought, I always assumed . . .' a dry lump was forming in her throat. She swallowed awkwardly. 'You're not the Wythenshawe Dandy at all, are you? You're the fucking *Undertaker*.'

'Listen, Cassie.' Flynn tried to take her hand but she pulled it away.

'Don't touch me!'

'Please, Cassie, it's just a story.' Flynn slid his hands into his pockets and took a deep breath. 'Like I told your friend, Stella, it's a story – it isn't real.'

She closed her eyes and shook her head. There was something different about Flynn's voice, Cassie thought – calm and soft as ever, but maybe . . .

Maybe not. She turned away.

In the cellar, she'd found herself praying to a God she didn't believe in. And now she found herself delivered. But delivered by whom? By the devil himself?

Now she was seeing with new eyes, listening with fresh ears.

Perhaps it wasn't Flynn who had changed. Perhaps he wasn't a monster after all. She looked back up at him. Certainly, his eyes hadn't changed. He was still glaring, though. Or maybe he wasn't glaring at all. Maybe he was pleading. Not angry, then, but sad or sorry or solicitous. The harder Cassie stared back at him, the less certain she became.

She steeled herself. 'I don't care what you say, I'm staying in this room.'

'No,' Flynn said, in a voice she didn't recognise.

'*I'm* the Police Officer, Flynn,' she said, 'so I'm in charge.' She knew she wasn't convincing anyone, least of all herself.

'That's why I don't want you here.' Flynn whispered. 'I'm certain I can get more out of him than the police.'

Cassie scoffed. 'Is that why you're wearing that ridiculous outfit? To remind him that you know how to hurt people. Everyone's afraid of being beaten-up, Flynn – it doesn't take any special insight to know that. Which is why we have laws. Which is why we have the police.'

But he was right, of course. She wasn't going to get anywhere with Roland playing by *her* rules. And she didn't want to play by *her* rules, not really. Right now, more than anything, she wanted to watch Flynn beat Roland to a pulp, burn him with cigarettes, and piss all over his back . . . just like in the story. She wanted him to do exactly what he'd done to the Wythenshawe Dandy.

She sat at the table beside Angus, folded her arms, leaned back on her chair.

Roland came round with groan. He coughed and spat and heaved himself into a sitting position, back against the wall. The left side of his face was swollen and purple, his nose was broken and bloodied. He lay a palm against his cheek and winced. 'So you can still throw a punch, eh, Jamie. And there was me thinking you'd gone soft in your old age.'

Flynn threw a beseeching look at Cassie.

Cassie shook her head and pulled her folded arms tight against her chest.

She watched Flynn haul David Roland to his feet and sit him on a chair. Flynn lifted Roland as effortlessly as a mother might lift a toddler who'd tripped and grazed his knee in the playground.

'We need to talk,' Flynn said, 'you and me.' His tone was mild, his face expressionless.

'Easy now, Jamie!' Roland spoke with hint of a chuckle, calm and cocksure. But his hands were shaking. 'What d'you want to talk about?' he said. 'The old days, is it?'

'No.'

'Happy days, they were, till that nasty business with the Bolan twins.'

Flynn remained inscrutable. 'Let's start with Gemma Grant,' he said.

Roland shook his head. 'Can't help you there.'

'You're in a lot of trouble already, Dave.' Flynn walked around the table and sat down beside Cassie. 'Don't make it worse for yourself.'

'Trouble?' Roland opened his eyes wide and stared at Cassie. 'I can't think what you mean.'

'You've assaulted a Police Officer!' Angus said.

Roland leaned over the table, fixed on Cassie and smiled. 'Her word against mine.'

Cassie looked at Flynn.

'No, love,' Roland said. 'He's no witness. I don't think Jamie Boreman will be showing his face in a court of law any time soon. Will you Jamie? Not with your history. And besides, I've got too much dirt, on too many people, to have worry about plod like you.'

Flynn pressed his palms together and nodded towards Angus.

'My friend would like the password to your computer,' he said, calmly, as if ordering drinks from a bar.

'*Your* friend, is he?' Roland laughed, and winced, and held a hand against his bruised cheek. 'Funny that, I thought he was your *wife's* friend. Her *special* friend.'

Angus stopped typing for a moment. He looked at Cassie, who pretended not to notice, then got back to his work.

Flynn didn't react. He waited a moment longer then said, 'The password, please.'

Roland tightened his lips.

From his inside pocket, Flynn retrieved a manila envelope. From the envelope, he pulled out an airline ticket. 'Found this on your desk, Dave. Mexico City . . . tomorrow morning. Why Mexico?'

Roland shrugged. 'Nice weather this time of year.'

'And then there's this note,' Flynn said. He unfolded a sheet of A4 and laid it on the table. 'Angus tells me that these numbers are for a bank account in the Cayman Islands. Somebody wants you to deposit five million American dollars in that bank account by noon tomorrow.'

'What are you, a fucking tax inspector?' Roland thrust a hand into his back pocket and fumbled around.

Flynn drew a flick knife from his own pocket and put it on the table. 'Is this what you're looking for?'

Roland scowled.

'You know me, Dave,' Flynn said, 'I never liked knives.'

Roland looked from Flynn to the knife and then back again. 'You never *needed* knives though, did you.' He glanced at Angus then fixed on Cassie.

She held his eyes, digging her fingernails into the heels of her hands – harder and harder and harder.

'Deakin's Dandy never needed a knife,' Roland said, still staring at Cassie. 'I bet she's never seen the sort of boxing you used to do, eh, Jamie. I bet she's never seen a man killed with one punch, neither.'

'Scotty Deakin wrote that note,' Flynn said. 'I recognise the handwriting.'

Roland's heavy brow sunk low over his eyes – he looked confused, at first, then alarmed.

Flynn folded his arms.

Roland glanced at the door.

'No way out, Dave,' Flynn said. 'Do you have the five million dollars?'

Roland looked down at the table top.

'Thought not,' Flynn said. 'And I expect you've used up all your chances. And I expect you've left Scotty with no choice. He won't be asking again, will he?'

Roland clenched his fists so tight that his arms began to shake. 'I'm a dead man if you don't let me go, Jamie.'

'And how do you know I won't kill you, after what you did to DI May?'

'You're not the sort, Jamie. Deakin always knew that, that's why he let you go. He said you read too many books. You should meet your replacement. He's been with Deakin since you pissed off. He doesn't fuck about with his fists if he can avoid it. Ex-SAS, they say. And a sniper into the bargain. They say he can take you out from a mile away if the wind is right.'

Flynn didn't reply, didn't react, didn't flinch. He just waited, stony faced.

Roland shook his head. 'I wouldn't have harmed your lady copper, Jamie. Just needed to scare her off, that's all. *You* know what it's like, *you've* done that sort—'

'Start talking,' Flynn said, 'and I'll let you take your chances with the law. If you don't talk, you'll have to take your chances with Scotty Deakin.'

Roland leaned back on his chair and scratched at the day's

worth of stubble on his neck. 'Give me your word, Jamie. If you give me your word that you'll not hand me over to Deakin I'll tell you everything I know.'

'I don't need to give you my word, Dave,' Flynn said, nodding towards Cassie. It's the way *she'd* want it, you know that.'

'Shit, Jamie,' Roland said. 'Just give me your fucking word.'

'Okay then,' Flynn said, 'so long as you tell me everything, you have my word.'

Roland's shoulders relaxed a little. He was looking at Angus now, who had his own laptop open next to Roland's and a cable running between the two. 'There's nothing on that machine of any value to you,' he said.

Angus didn't look up from the screen. 'We'll see.'

'I . . .' Roland glanced at Cassie then turned back to Flynn. 'I've done nothing illegal,' he said. 'I can tell you what I know, but there's no proof of anything.'

Flynn planted his elbows on the table, tilted his massive frame forwards, and looked Roland hard in the eye.

'It was the American,' Roland said. 'He paid Mulligan to do the girl.'

Flynn brought his hands together and made a double fist. 'What American?'

'Brett McRoss,' Roland said, as if it should have been obvious.

'You're saying that Brett McRoss ordered Gemma Grant's murder? And you're sure about that?'

Roland nodded.

Flynn remained pokerfaced. 'Isn't he the venture capitalist who wanted to buy the two big Sheffield football clubs and merge them?'

Roland shrugged.

'But why?' Flynn said. 'Why would he want her dead? Why would he pay Mulligan to have her killed?'

'I don't know. But I do know that Mulligan was supposed to

have done *both of them* a couple of years ago, and he fucked it up.'

'Both of them?' Flynn pressed his fingertips to his temples. 'Sarah and Gemma? On the Snake Pass?'

Roland nodded. 'Two years ago, Mulligan paid me to keep tabs on Sarah, and to track down the daughter – but I didn't know he was planning to kill them until afterwards.'

'But I thought it was Sarah,' Flynn said, 'my Sarah, who hired you to track down Gemma.'

Another shrug. 'Her too. Just got lucky I suppose, two clients paying me to do the same job.'

Cassie found herself looking into Roland's eyes. She saw nothing: no evil, no good, no shame. Nothing. This made it worse. No, better. No, nothing. She looked again at Flynn.

He offered soft blue eyes.

She folded her arms and looked away. She hated herself.

Flynn turned back to Roland. 'So how did you track Gemma down this time? She'd managed to keep herself well below the radar for the last couple of years.'

'I didn't track her down. She phoned me up, out of the blue, a few weeks ago.' Roland turned to Cassie, a hint of a smirk on his face. 'She wanted to make contact with Jamie here. She didn't say why. Anyway, I think I played the part pretty well.'

'What do you mean – *played the part?*' Flynn said.

Roland turned back to Flynn and offered a smug smile. 'I set up a Hotmail account in your name, and a mobile number. Hardly rocket science. It was enough for her to believe it was *you* she was emailing and texting, and it was *you* who was arranging things in Sheffield, and it was *you* who sent her a bit of money to be going on with.'

'And then you gave her to Mulligan?' Flynn said.

Cassie thought she saw something in Roland's face. His cheek twitched and his eyes fell. Remorse? Maybe. Or maybe just regret. Not the same.

'And what part did Muxlow play in all of this?' Flynn said.

Roland didn't look up. 'Mulligan wanted to make sure there was somebody lined up to take the fall, and *James Flynn* had a good motive, didn't he – all that money sitting in a trust fund.'

'So Muxlow helped you and Mulligan to frame me. Had to, didn't he? Because you had those photographs of him with Gemma.'

'Sort of.'

'Sort of?'

Roland began to laugh, great bawls of gruff, choky, coughy, sweaty, stinky, nasty, wicked, evil laughter. 'I'd lost all those pictures: some cock up when we went digital and put everything on computers a couple of years ago. But he didn't know that, and I could rattle off all the wheres and whens. I showed him her birth certificate, though, and I still had one video, on my phone, from when the camera battery went dead and I had to improvise; it was a film of her at an upstairs window in his house, half naked. Not conclusive, a bit blurry like, but enough to put the fear of God in him. Should've seen his face when I showed him!'

'You knew that Sarah had copies though – copies of all the pictures you lost.'

'Oh, aye. Well, she'd paid for them, hadn't she. She knew she couldn't control the girl, back then, so she paid me to keep an eye on what she was up to. Mulligan convinced himself that if he could get hold of them photos he'd *own* Muxlow for ever. Own a Deputy Chief Constable . . . and, one day perhaps, a *Chief* Constable, or maybe even the Commissioner of the Met.'

Cassie looked at Flynn, wondering if he believed what Roland was telling him. She found it hard to believe that Muxlow would conspire to kill the girl she had seen him fawning over in all those photos – even years later, even after she'd abandoned him. But perhaps—

'And,' Roland went on, 'Mulligan thought that Jamie, here,

would have them. Did you, Jamie? Did you have them photos?'

Flynn didn't answer.

Cassie turned back to Roland, made herself do it.

He looked suddenly forlorn, suddenly afraid. Perhaps it had dawned on him that he would never make it to Mexico – somewhere, presumably, where Scott Deakin couldn't get at him.

'Of course,' Roland went on (quiet now, no more bravado), 'Muxlow had no idea who it was they were planning to off until after they'd done her. He never knew it was his little Gemma they were after. He sobbed like a baby when he found out, the pervy bastard. He'd always liked 'em young though, hadn't he, Jamie? Like your girl in Manchester, all those years ago, what was she called? The one who OD'd . . . always in a red dress . . . Maria, was it?' Roland sighed and looked wistfully out of the window. 'Still,' he said, 'even after he found out it was his girlfriend they'd killed, he did what needed to be done. He had no choice, did he?'

Cassie pictured Muxlow lifting the gun to his head. She could feel the muzzle, cold on her temple, and the trigger, warm in the cleft of her index finger. Then she remembered Muxlow's last words to her: 'Promise me you'll get the bastard'. But *which* bastard? David Roland? Brett McRoss? Both of them? Someone else entirely?

To her right, Cassie saw something flash up on Roland's laptop. Angus had appeared oblivious to everything that was being said over the last few minutes. He was tapping away on the computer with an intensity that reminded her of her mother staring at old photograph albums. She leaned in to get a look. The screen went blank, but she'd already seen it. Flynn must have seen it too.

'Why did you send me that video of Sarah and Angus?' Flynn said, still calm.

How could he be so calm?

Angus stopped typing.

'The old lady ordered it,' Roland said. 'She didn't say why. But if she'd really had it in for *him* . . .' Roland wagged a finger at Angus '. . . she'd have had me send that video to his wife, wouldn't she?'

'Which old lady?' Flynn asked.

'Which old lady?' Roland shook his head and scoffed. 'Not my fucking granny, that's for sure! The old lady you don't say "no" to, that's which old lady?' He nodded towards Cassie. '*She* went all the way to Edinburgh to see her.'

'Céline Douglas?' Flynn asked.

Roland shrugged. 'Is that what she calls herself these days?'

Flynn leaned back in his chair and studied Roland. He was trying to gauge how much Roland was holding back, or twisting, or lying about, Cassie supposed. But it seemed to her that David Roland was telling the truth. She'd seen it before – criminals who, finding themselves without any hope of getting off, resort to bragging about what they've done.

Roland was trying to look calm, cool, collected – he wore his smirk the way others wear their politest smile. But his left leg was shaking, and his fists were clenched tight and white.

'Hang on a minute!' Flynn said at last. 'How did Mulligan know about Gemma's trust fund? And how did he know it would come to me if she died?'

Roland shrugged. 'If I had to guess, I'd . . . nah, maybe not . . .'

'Dave,' Flynn clenched then unclenched his fists, 'just tell me.'

'Well,' Roland began. He glanced at Angus (who was too busy with Roland's computer to notice), hesitated, then wiped his lips with the back of his hand. 'Maybe . . .'

❧

Cassie should have been interested but she wasn't. Not anymore. She'd stopped listening. An invisible mist had descended. It was as real as it was unreal. It was a presence and an absence. It was an ache without the pain. It swallowed her whole.

She existed, and she was miserable, and that was all there was in the world. And she could think of nothing that might ever make her happy. Nothing.

The clouds broke. Light surged through the venetian blinds to form stripes on the wall. In that moment she was a little girl again – a happy and excited little girl. She was back in her bedroom in Epping, counting sunshine stripes on woodchip wallpaper, and counting the hours until tomorrow – until her first ever pony ride.

Clouds gathered anew. The sunshine stripes suddenly vanished, and Cassie woke from her reverie. All eyes were upon her now. Shame pulsed hot through her arteries. She felt her skin shine pink. They could see through her clothes. They could see the fat on her hips, the cellulite on her thighs, her heavy, saggy, never-suckled breasts. They could see through her flesh. They could see into her heart. They could see her pride, her guilt, her insecurity. They could see every mistake she'd ever made. They could see every stupid thing she'd ever thought or said. And, if the mood took them, they would laugh along with all the men who'd had her and dumped her.

And if they looked hard enough, they would see her mother. Oh yes, her mother was in there if you knew where to look. A woman who'd tried, failed, and given up. A woman who died the object of grudging pity and knowing looks.

Cassie watched Roland fold his arms and cock his head to one side. She wondered if he felt any shame for what he'd done to her. She wondered if he'd planned to kill her. She wondered *how* he would have killed her.

With the slim blade of the flick knife that Flynn had taken from him? Would he have cut her throat or stabbed her through the heart? Would he have chopped her into pieces, stuffed her into bin bags and buried her in the woods? Would, two weeks later, a giddy cocker spaniel have yapped and howled and drooled over her festering remains? Would—

Cassie was distracted by the faintest of thuds, like a pebble thrown at the window. She looked to her left. Another thud. Then came the crash of shattered glass. Now she was on the floor, flat on her back, face buried in Flynn's stupid burgundy cravat.

'For Christ's sake, Angus!' Flynn yelled. 'Get down! You both need to stay down.'

Cassie wriggled, but Flynn wasn't for moving. She twisted her head to one side to get some air. On the other side of the table, lying awkwardly on his side, was David Roland. There was a hole in the side of his head the size of a fist. A puddle of blood and brains was forming around his chin. It pooled and beaded like mercury on the polished floor. The puddle became a river. It was moving slowly, but inexorably, towards her face. Cassie tried to speak but all that came out was a moan. She writhed under Flynn's weight, but he wouldn't budge. The blood was getting closer; it had found the groove between the timbers and was accelerating, rapidly, across the floor.

Flynn held her fast. She stopped wriggling, stopped moaning, stopped clawing at Flynn's arms, and let herself cry. When she opened her eyes the river of blood had stopped coming. She looked up. Flynn's face was only inches away, so near that it took a while to focus. His eyes, close up, were bluer than she had ever seen them. The colour was constant and without grain or patina. So very blue. So very, very blue.

Was he about to kiss her? Please, no! Not now. She felt dirty and unkissable. But then she wished that he *would* kiss her. She wished he would kiss her so that she might kiss him back, so that she might kiss him as she'd kissed him that first time, standing on the coir mat, by his front door, with their coats and boots still on.

A tickle in her throat. She tried to suppress it, but the cough came, then another. Soon she was coughing like a consumptive.

Flynn rolled off.

52

THREE DAYS HAD passed since the shooting at David Roland's office and Cassie still wasn't responding to emails or phone calls. Meg Harper had told Flynn that she would have gone round to her house sooner if she hadn't been so busy at work. The truth was, if she hadn't got that phone call from him, she might have left it a few days longer.

❧

'Jesus, Cassie, you look like shit.'

'I know.'

Meg pushed passed Cassie with her shopping bags and made for the kitchen. She stopped dead at the open door. Empty wine bottles by an overflowing bin. Old takeaway containers piled on the table. Dirty plates in the sink. Half a dozen tea-stained mugs on the work top.

'Are you ill?' Meg asked.

'No.' Cassie looked at the mess around the sink. 'Not really. I just couldn't face unloading the dishwasher.'

'Then why are you in your dressing gown at half past four on a Sunday afternoon? I've been phoning and phoning.'

'I—'

'God, Cassie, it's like a Turkish bath in here. Shall we let some air in?'

The kitchen window had been painted shut years ago, apparently, so Meg opened the back door.

Same story in the living room. Screwed up tissues all over the floor. Coffee table smeared with something congealed and yellow. An empty wine glass. Several plates, littered with half eaten pieces of toast, abandoned on the side table. 'And what's that stink?' Meg said. 'It smells like a bloody kebab shop in here.' The sash window in the sitting room was stiff, but she managed to get it open a few inches.

Meg turned to the sofa. 'Well, if that isn't a sick bed I don't know what is!' She pushed aside the duvet and pillows and sat on the end. 'Are you sure you're not ill?'

'No, I'm just tired . . . and I'm on leave . . . . and I live on my own . . . so . . .' She plonked herself down beside Meg. 'So I thought: sod it, I'll watch Netflix.'

Meg smiled. '*Bridget Jones?*'

'Maybe . . .' Cassie smiled with her.

'*Pride and Prejudice?* The best one – the one with Colin Firth?'

'Well, I do like a bit of Colin Firth.'

'But who needs a Darcy,' Meg said, 'when you've got a Flynn?'

Cassie looked down into her lap. 'I thought you didn't approve.'

'I don't,' Meg said. 'But he's worried about you. He phoned me at work, said you won't take his calls.'

'I turned off my phone.'

'And he's knocked on the door a few times.'

'I know,' Cassie rubbed her eyes, 'but look at the state of me.'

Meg went into the kitchen and returned with her shopping bags. She pulled out a carton of grapes and offered.

Cassie shook her head.

Next, she offered an already open packet of chocolate Hobnobs. 'Bought them specially for you. Sorry, I ate a couple in the car . . . couldn't resist.'

'A couple?' Cassie said, snatching the packet. She pulled

out three biscuits, lay them on her lap, and handed back the empty wrapper.

Meg reached back into her shopping bag, pulled out a fresh packet, and winked. 'I'd never be without reserves.'

The eating of the first few chocolate Hobnobs passed in silence. Meg was brimming with questions, of course, but Cassie (tea-stained dressing gown, mascara-streaked cheeks, chipped nail polish) didn't look up to answering them.

Cassie had claimed that her meeting with Roland was personal business. She claimed that she was supporting Flynn, who wanted to find out a little more about Gemma Grant's relationship with his late wife. Nobody believed her, but DCI Foster accepted the story because it suited him.

Executions by rooftop snipers just didn't happen in Sheffield, neither did gangland massacres in abandoned school sports halls, or elaborately staged murder scenes with the victim laid out naked like she was part of some art installation. So for Meg, there could be no doubt that there was a link between the shooting of David Roland, the Parkgate School massacre, and the murder of Gemma Grant. Questions needed to be asked. But now was not the time.

'I've accepted the offer from the Special Organised Crime Unit,' Meg said brightly.

'Good,' Cassie said.

Meg tore open the second packet of biscuits. 'Me, a *Detective Inspector*!'

'You deserve it.' Cassie got up and looked at the mess on her coffee table. 'No, I can't bear it any longer – I'm going to have to clean this place up, then I'll have a bath, and then—'

'My cue to leave, I think,' Meg said, grabbing her shopping bags.

'I didn't mean it like that, Meg, honestly. I just . . .'

'Don't be daft. You've every right, after what you've been through!'

Cassie folded her arms. She did it briskly enough to shut Meg up.

'What's Flynn been saying?' Cassie said.

'Saying?' Meg shook her head. 'He didn't need to *say* anything. I was there, remember. First on the scene. I *saw* the blood, I *saw* the hole in Roland's head, I *saw* his brains spilt out on the floor. I can't imagine what it was like to actually see it happen, to see a man's head blown apart like that.'

'No . . . well . . . yes.' Cassie covered her face with her hands.

Meg thought Cassie was going to cry.

She didn't. She sniffed and coughed and cleared her throat. 'Meg, are you busy tomorrow?'

'Why?'

'Fancy a trip to Edinburgh?'

53

'SHIT,' MEG SAID. 'Shit. Shit. Shit.'

Cassie glanced at her then turned back to the road. They had just passed Newcastle on the A1. Halfway to Edinburgh – only 118.3 miles to go . . . 2 hours and 11 minutes . . . 2 hours 10 minutes. Meg's packet of Jelly Babies lay untouched on her lap.

'Yes,' Cassie said. 'But he's dead now, so . . .'

'Shit.' Meg wound down her window, but it was cold and noisy and she wound it up again. 'Shit. Shit. Shit.'

'Afterwards,' Cassie said, 'when Flynn had him locked in that conference room, well . . .' she swallowed, looked at Meg for a moment, then turned back to the road.

Meg nodded. 'I can't imagine; it must have been . . . I don't know. There's no word for it.'

'No. It's not that, you don't understand.'

'Sorry,' Meg said. 'I interrupted. I'm so sorry . . . really . . . I just . . .'

Silent seconds passed.

Cassie spoke without looking at her. 'I wanted to kill him. If I'd had a gun I'd have shot him over and over and over again. I'd have kept on shooting until I ran out of bullets.'

'Yes, well. He'd have deserved it.'

'So why can't I get over Flynn killing an evil shit like Mulligan.'

'Because he actually did it, didn't he. You and me, well: we say we'd do it . . . but we just wouldn't. Not really. Not in cold blood. No unless we had to do it to save ourselves, or somebody else even.'

'So maybe Flynn *had* to do it. Maybe he *really* had no choice.'

'Maybe.'

Cassie patted Meg's knee. Meg grabbed her hand and squeezed.

'Promise me, Meg, promise me you'll never tell a soul.'

'No, I . . . no, no, anyway, like you say, he's dead now, the bastard, so there's nothing . . .'

'That's why I didn't want to tell anybody – not at first. But in the end I had to talk to someone. Flynn saw what Roland had done to me, and Angus knows because . . .' Cassie shook her head. 'But I had to tell it myself, my way. And I couldn't do that with either of them.'

'I'm glad you told *me*, Cassie. But you should have told me straight away. I could have been there for you. I should have been there for you. You shouldn't have had to deal with this alone.'

Cassie remembered coming home that night. She remembered thinking that she would never again be able look anyone in the eye. She remembered not being able to bring herself to look in the mirror. 'Yes, I should have told you,' she said. 'Wish I had, now. I couldn't sleep that night. Couldn't even go to bed. And I couldn't bear the quiet. I had to have the TV on, day and night. And I was *so* cold. Even with the heating on full blast, even under the duvet, even when I was sweating like a pig . . . I felt *so* cold. I thought I'd be cold for ever.'

'God, I wish you'd called me.'

'Me too.'

'And do you feel better for having told me?'

'Yes.'

Meg opened her bag of Jelly Babies and offered them to Cassie. Cassie shook her head.

A dozen blank faces looked down on them from a National Express coach. A little girl waved. Cassie smiled back. She wasn't sure she did feel better. She'd forced herself to tell Meg because reason told her that it would be a good thing to do: because it's the storyteller, and not the protagonists, who decides how the story will end. Something like that, anyway . . . according to Flynn.

Reason told Cassie a great many things – but she was in a place where reason holds no sway, a place where she could still feel Roland's hot hands, and his thick fingers, and his eager tongue.

But she didn't feel quite so alone anymore; and, for the first time since it happened, she imagined that she might one day feel better. She had hope, at least. And that was good.

Meg screwed up the empty jelly baby packet and stuffed it into her pocket. 'Now for the Maltesers,' she said. 'Go on! You know you want to.'

54

'GLASS OF PINOT Grigio was it, Madame?'

Cassie nodded.

'And for Madame?' The barman turned to Meg with a hospitality industry smile.

'Pint of Guinness, please,' Meg said.

He raised his eyebrows, looked her up and down, nodded. 'I'll bring them over.'

Céline Douglas was on her sofa, knitting. She'd already fixed herself a pastis. She put down her needles and grabbed a fistful of peanuts from the bowl. The old lady knew they were there, Cassie was sure of it, but she hadn't yet looked in their direction.

'Mrs Douglas,' Cassie said, taking the seat opposite.

Mrs Douglas dusted her hands and bundled her knitting into the bag by her feet. She fixed on Cassie with cold eyes. 'I'm not accustomed to being summoned.'

'You didn't complain last time I was up here.'

'Last time it was *I* who summoned *you*. A different thing altogether.'

'No, I . . .' Cassie turned to Meg, who was settling into the next chair, and thought back to her last meeting with the old lady. 'Your name was in the Gemma Grant file that the local police copied for me. *I* had them call *you*.'

'My name? In a police file? How on earth did it get there.' She turned to Meg. 'What do *you* say, Detective Inspector Harper?'

Meg was reaching for the peanuts; she stopped and looked up.

'Do help yourself, dear. Don't be shy.' The old lady's hazel eyes gleamed amber in the light of the fake candle in the wall sconce.

'I'd say you don't have much time for the police, Mrs Douglas,' Meg said. 'And if you *really* didn't want to meet with Chief Inspector May, then you wouldn't have come.'

Mrs Douglas smiled, took a sip of pastis, and changed the subject. 'I'm pleased that Angus's friendship with Mr Flynn survived my little intervention. But he had to be warned off, he was poking his nose into affairs that didn't concern him.'

The barman arrived with their drinks. He took longer than necessary setting them out on the table, and took it upon himself to replenish the peanuts while he was about it.

'I think the murder of a young woman concerns everybody,' Cassie said.

'I know you do, Chief Inspector. Shall we leave it at that.'

Cassie took a large gulp of wine. 'An American, Brett McRoss, ordered the killings of Sarah Flynn and her daughter, Gemma. Why?'

If Mrs Douglas was surprised by the question, she didn't let it show. Her expression softened. 'Gemma convinced herself that Muxlow was behind the car crash that killed her mother. Did you know she always believed that she was the target, believed she was responsible for her mother's death?'

It made perfect sense of course. Cassie suspected Gemma had been afraid of the police, and now it was obvious why. 'He found out she was under age, didn't he? I bet he was furious. Is that why she thought he'd tried to kill her?'

'That was part of it, of course.' The old lady sighed. 'But Gemma had overheard things too, things that he wouldn't have wanted anyone to overhear, things that linked him to the likes of Mulligan.'

'What, and Gemma told him that she'd overheard all this stuff? Why?'

Mrs Douglas shook her head. 'It was a heat of the moment thing, the night before the car crash. Gemma was at Muxlow's house when he took a call. It was Mulligan, I suspect, or maybe Roland. Whoever it was told Muxlow that Gemma wasn't yet sixteen, told him they had evidence of his relationship with her, told him they'd would expose him if he didn't do their bidding.'

What happened next Cassie could guess. 'So,' she said, thinking it through, 'when he confronted Gemma with her secrets and lies, she told him she knew all about *his* secrets and lies.'

'So you see, Detective Chief Inspector,' Mrs Douglas said, 'sometimes it's not such a good idea to tell the police everything you know.'

Cassie scoffed. 'But it wasn't Muxlow who organised the crash that killed her mother. You knew that. Why didn't you tell Gemma.'

'Oh, I did, dear. Many times. But she didn't believe me.'

Cassie looked up at the ceiling, then back down to the old lady. 'I wonder why?'

Celine Douglas's face hardened. 'It would've made no difference in the end.'

'Back to Brett McRoss,' Cassie said, sharply. 'Brett McRoss ordered the killings of Sarah Flynn and her daughter, Gemma. Why?'

'I trust you know who Brett McRoss is?'

'Senator. Republican Party. Businessman. Rich.' Cassie folded her arms. 'Fingers in lots of pies – mining, construction, baseball teams, American football teams. And also involved in private security contracts for the US military. What some call security officers, others might call mercenaries.'

'What *would* we do without Wikipedia!' Mrs Douglas took a paper napkin and dabbed her lips, lengthily. 'Now,' she said, folding the napkin, 'allow me give you some background information you *won't* find on Wikipedia . . .

'Sir Richard Fitzroy-Parker, Sarah Flynn's father, was something big in the diplomatic service. He based himself at the British Embassy in Washington mostly, but he also worked at the UN in New York, and he occasionally provided procurement advice to the Ministry of Defence back in London.

'Sarah attended a boarding school in England during term time and stayed at Hedmere Hall in Cheshire during their July party season. But she spent Christmas, Easter and the whole of August with her parents in America. In 1990, Brett McRoss began to court Fitzroy-Parker in the hope of winning contracts with the MOD.

'In 1995 McRoss senior died leaving the family business to Brett. From that point on Brett McRoss's interest in British MOD procurement stepped up a gear. Essentially, he offered Fitzroy-Parker money to lobby on behalf of McRoss Industries. Ordinarily, Fitzroy-Parker would have given the man short shrift, but MI6 had an interest in Mr McRoss. So, being a patriot, and a gentleman, Fitzroy-Parker obliged.'

Cassie raised her eyebrows. '*Obliged?*'

Mrs Douglas topped her-up her glass with a little water. She took a sip and patted her lips dry. 'I think we understand each other.'

'You had a British Diplomat spy on an American Senator?'

'Not me, dear. It was the local boys.'

Meg downed the last of her Guinness and wiped her mouth with the back of her hand. 'Go on, Mrs Douglas, please.'

'That year, 1995, Fitzroy-Parker and his family spent a weekend at McRoss's Cape Cod beach house, which was where McRoss met Sarah. It was in that house, according to Sarah, that McRoss plied her with champagne and raped her. Sarah kept quiet about it at first. She'd been very drunk. She was ashamed. But when she got back to school in England and discovered she was pregnant, she told her father. And *he* told his handler at MI6.'

Meg glanced at Cassie, who was staring at the wall, the rim of her wine glass pressed to her lower lip.

'It was decided . . .' Mrs Douglas began. She wiped her fingers with a napkin and took a gulp of pastis, which she swallowed awkwardly. 'It was decided that the matter should be kept quiet and that Sarah should go through with the pregnancy. Her parents were devout Catholics, you see. Arrangements were made. An adoption was organised.'

Meg stared, wide eyed, at the old lady. '*Kept quiet!*' she repeated. '*It was decided?*'

Cassie said nothing – she continued to focus on the wall immediately behind Mrs Douglas, wine glass still pressed against her bottom lip.

Meg rubbed her eyes with a licked fingertip. 'Let me get this straight in my head,' she said. '*It was decided* that the rape of a fifteen-year-old girl should be *kept quiet?*'

Mrs Douglas nodded, matter-of-factly. 'Sarah never spoke to her family after that.'

'No shit!' Meg reached for her Guinness, but the glass was empty.

'And Brett McRoss,' Mrs Douglas ignored the reaction and continued, 'when he visited Sheffield two years ago, would have had no idea that Sarah lived there, or that he'd had a child by her. One can only speculate about what happened next: Sarah recognised him? Decided to break her silence? Confronted him? Told him about Gemma? Threatened to expose him? What Sarah didn't know, probably, was that McRoss is not the sort of man you should threaten.'

'But why did she never report him,' Meg said. 'I mean later, when she was old enough to make sense of things, why didn't Sarah—'

'So . . .' Cassie slammed her glass down and glared at Meg before turning back to Céline Douglas, ' . . . all of this is your doing. It was you who made her keep the baby, and you who made sure the rape was kept quiet. And this had nothing to do with saving her from a painful experience in court. Oh, no! She mightn't even have had to appear. DNA would have proved paternity, even back in 1995. And she'd have been under the age of consent: open and shut case. All this was so that MI6 could have a hold over an American Senator. And you've just told us that when McRoss came to Sheffield he knew nothing about Gemma. You never even *used* what you had on him, did you?' Cassie shook her head. 'Did Gemma ever find out?'

Celine Douglas considered this for a moment. 'I don't know,' she said.

'And why *did* she come back to Sheffield?'

'She wanted to track down Mr Flynn,' the old lady said. 'Her mother had put some silly notions in her head about your Mr Flynn.'

'Notions? Like what?'

'Sarah led Gemma to believe that her husband might one day be some sort of father to her. Gemma was frightened and alone, and imagined Mr Flynn as her knight in shining armour. She was a very silly girl, bless her.'

'Yes, well.' Cassie shook her head and took a large swig of Pinot Grigio. 'Young girls *will* be silly, won't they. That's why they need adults to look out for them.'

Mrs Douglas frowned. 'I make hard decisions, Chief Inspector, that has been my job these last seventy years - but I do take responsibility for those decisions. I did my best for Sarah . . . and Gemma. How long do you think either of them would have lasted if Sarah had gone public with an accusation of rape against McRoss in 1995? Not long, I can assure you of that. Gemma would never even have been born - she'd have had no life at all.'

'Maybe not.' Cassie downed the last of her wine. 'But that

wasn't the *reason* for the decision, was it? It's your sordid little *justification* . . . after the fact. It's a lie, Mrs Douglas.'

Céline Douglas dusted off her tweed jacket, picked up her knitting bag, and got up to leave.

'Why have you told us all this?' Meg asked. 'You didn't have to. And I get the impression you'd have preferred not to.'

The old lady grimaced. 'Your Chief Inspector is the sort who picks at scabs – I decided she'd cause even more damage if I didn't tell her.'

'And you don't even believe the rape story, do you?' Meg folded her arms. 'You think Sarah consented? You probably believe it was Sarah who seduced him. You want to believe it because that was the sort of thing you used to do. You want to believe it because it makes it easier to live with yourself.'

'We'll never know for sure, will we, Detective Inspector Harper.' Celine Douglas drained her glass in a single, rather unladylike, gulp.

Meg frowned and looked at the floor. 'I bet you're one of the "*if she dresses like a whore she's asking for it*" brigade, aren't you? One of the "*six of one and half a dozen of the other*" bunch?' She fixed on the old lady and shook her head. 'We're not taking about a naughty nurse and a dirty old man here – this isn't a *Carry On* film, this is real. She was a child, Mrs Douglas, and he was a child abuser. If you couldn't see it then, and if you still can't see it now, well . . .'

'Well what?' Mrs Douglas snapped. 'How I saw things is of no consequence. It had no bearing on how I handled the situation.'

Meg was now looking to Cassie for support.

'You know I'll go after him,' Cassie said to the old lady. 'There's nothing you can do to stop me.'

'Brett McRoss is a dead man,' Mrs Douglas said. 'The matter is closed.'

'He wasn't dead when I googled him an hour ago. He was alive and well, cutting a ribbon at a fancy new Community College somewhere in America.'

The old lady took a deep breath. 'It's only a matter of time. Mr McRoss has become a liability. He's put too many noses out of joint. These things always take care of themselves: Gary Mulligan and Carl Yates, for example . . . and David Roland.'

They watched the old lady straighten her skirt, nod at the barman, and stride – shoulders back, head high – to the door. She left the pub without looking back.

Meg turned to Cassie, brow creased, fingers peeling layer after layer off the beer mat on the table in front of her. 'I need another drink.'

'Me too,' Cassie said. 'I'll go . . .'

❧

Cassie got back with the drinks to find Meg, head in hands, staring at her phone. 'What's up?' she said, sliding Meg's pint pot across the table.

Meg slurped her Guinness and wiped the froth off her top lip with the back of her hand. 'Do you remember the story about Sarah Flynn losing her rag when she found out Gemma had gone off with some bloke in a stretch limo?'

'Yes.' Cassie took a sip of her Chianti. 'That girl at the student house where Gemma lived told you all about it.'

'That's right,' Meg said. 'I just got an email back from one of the limo firms I canvassed.' She picked up a beermat and ran her fingernail along the edge. 'It was Brett McRoss who hired that limo.'

'McRoss!' Cassie took a moment to think. This turned everything she thought she knew on its head. 'So, that's how he found out about Gemma. She must have tracked him down and told him herself. Which means Sarah must have told her who her father was.'

Meg was peeling layer after layer off her beermat. 'Maybe?' she said. 'Maybe not.'

'What do you mean?'

'I was thinking about this while you were getting our drinks.' Meg plonked her elbows on the table and leaned in. 'Remember that video you found on YouTube – the press conference where Sarah Flynn was staring at Brett McRoss like a woman possessed?'

'Yes. And now that we know that he raped her when she was a girl, we know why she'd be staring at him like that.'

'Maybe. But think about it,' Meg said, scratching her head. 'The video of the press conference was filmed the morning after Alice, from the student house, told Sarah that Gemma had gone off with a middle-aged man in a limo. And Sarah must have known it was Brett McRoss in the limo from the registration number that Alice gave her. She'd have been following him through the media while he was in Sheffield. She'd probably noticed the car before, and the reg number, E4 GLE. It scans as *EAGLE*, that's why Sarah and Alice remembered it.'

Cassie frowned. 'What you're saying is that Sarah went to confront McRoss because she discovered that he'd met with Gemma.'

'Yes. And two days later Sarah's car is run off the road with Gemma in it.'

'But that's just detail, surely, it doesn't really change anything. The way I see it, McRoss wanted them both dead so that there'd be no risk of his past, and his DNA, catching up with him.'

'I agree. But . . .' Meg was rolling a piece of peeled beer mat into an ever-tighter tube ' . . . but what if Sarah *hadn't* told Gemma who her father was?

'Why else would Gemma have met up with McRoss?'

Meg grabbed her pint and pressed the cold glass to her cheek. 'What if, as far as she was concerned, he was just another of those rich middle-aged men that she picked up in posh hotel bars?'

Cassie put a hand over her mouth and gasped.

'I know,' Meg said. 'Sarah knew full well that McRoss has a taste for teenage girls. So she confronts him, she reminds him what he did to her all those years ago, she tells him that the girl he had in his limo the previous night is his daughter.'

A long silence passed between them.

'Do you think . . .' Cassie began. Then she shook her head. 'The chances of Gemma and McRoss meeting like that were infinitesimal. It'd be like some Greek tragedy.'

'It doesn't bear thinking about,' Meg said reaching for a fresh beer mat. 'But we'll never know exactly what went on between Gemma and McRoss, so it's probably best not to speculate.'

A girl with a pierced nose and an Australian accent came to the table. She put their empty glasses (and three decimated beer mats) onto a tray and wiped the table down. 'Same again, ladies?'

Cassie nodded.

'Yes please,' Meg said.

The bar was busier now and someone cranked the music up. Lynyrd Skynyrd's "Sweet *Home Alabama*" began to play.

Cassie rubbed her hands together. 'Let's get pissed.'

55

25TH JANUARY.
ROBBIE BURNS' 255TH BIRTHDAY.
CASSANDRA JANE MAY'S 35TH BIRTHDAY.

TWO WEEKS HAD passed since David Roland had her trussed-up and naked in a cold Victorian cellar, yet the memory of it grew more vivid by the day.

Roland visited her in her sleep – sometimes with a fist-sized hole in his head, sometimes intact, always with the same intention.

Cassie woke with a start, afraid and uncertain. She doubted everything she remembered of the last few weeks. It was like this every morning. The world had moved on; she had been left behind.

It was as though Flynn had never invited her to dinner at his tenantless flat; as though Lizzie had never stormed out and taken the children to stay with her mother; as though the whole Gemma Grant saga had never happened.

Flynn had kept his distance, but they did exchange emails. In the evenings, mostly, but sometimes late at night. Sometimes far too late at night. Friendly emails, though, nothing more.

He wrote about what he was up to – a new novel, a new grate for his stove . . . oh, and a new coal shed most recently (the old one had collapsed under a ton of snow, apparently).

She wrote about her new job, her new colleagues, and Meg's romantic exploits.

They exchanged all manner of trivia.

⁂

Today was her birthday. The plan: bubble bath, Prosecco, Joni Mitchell, more Prosecco. And then there was Angus's Burns' Night party to prepare for. So, after her bath, she'd have a nice wander down the Ecclesall Road – get her hair done, get her nails done, pick-up her posh frock from the dry cleaners.

Angus would be round later with the birthday present she'd bought herself (a MacBook Pro and the various accessories that Angus said she'd probably need). It all needed setting-up, or configuring, or something or other, and she really couldn't face that sort of hassle herself . . . not on her birthday!

⁂

'Would you get the door for me, Angus, I'm doing my lashes.'

Angus had just finished configuring her new router and setting up her new printer and sorting out her new email. 'Yeah, yeah. And shall I polish the silver next?'

The man at the door was carrying a bouquet of flowers and a pink envelope. Angus had never met him before, or even seen a photo, but he knew immediately that it was Cassie's father.

They eyed each other across the threshold for a while. Angus knew the history between Cassie and her dad. He couldn't think what to say.

Eventually, Cassie's father spoke. 'These are for Cassandra, shall I leave them with *you*?'

'Actually, she's here, she's upstairs. I'll call her.'

'No, no!' Cassie's father said, thrusting the card and flowers at Angus. 'I wouldn't want to intrude.' He pursed his lips, ran his fingers through his hair, then offered Angus his hand. 'John May . . . John. I'm Cassandra's father.'

'Yes, I . . .' Angus began. 'And I'm Angus McDonald. Just a

friend. I'm not . . . we're not . . . I'm here to sort out her computer, that's all. That's what I do . . . computers.'

'Oh, right. Well, yes, of course. Computers, eh. Very good.' John smiled and nodded then scratched his chin. 'Only I've a new mobile number, you see. I've written it on the card. I wanted her to know . . . just in case.'

Angus tapped the envelope and nodded. 'I'll tell her.' He sensed Cassie behind him, or maybe he read it in John May's face.

Cassie's father swallowed and sniffed and rocked back on his heels. 'Cassandra, what a beautiful dress, you look lovely.'

She smoothed down the fabric where it had gathered just above her hips, but didn't speak.

Angus tried to retreat into the kitchen, but Cassie made a point of blocking his path.

'And *happy birthday*,' John May said. 'I can see you're dressed to go out, so I'll . . .'

Cassie took the flowers from Angus and pressed them to her chest.

'It's nothing, really.' John shook his head. 'I'm just glad to see you, my darling. And to see you so well.'

'I'm a *Detective Chief Inspector* now,' she said, in a little voice.

Tears welled in John's eyes. 'I knew you'd do well. I'm proud of you, my darling, ever so proud. I just want you to know . . .' he wiped his eyes '. . . that I'm sorry.'

Cassie smiled at her father for the first time in ages.

He ran a thumbnail along his chin and shook his head. 'I don't have the words.'

Cassie looked at her feet, and then at Angus, and then at her father. 'Would you like to come in, . . .' she caught her breath, ' . . . Dad?'

56

WHILE MEG HARPER chomped through the canapés, her new boyfriend, Steve Baker, regaled Angus's Burns' Night guests with a treatise on ancient Highland distilleries.

'What do you think of him?' Meg said.

Cassie nodded approval. 'Seems nice enough. Certainly knows a lot about whisky.'

'You don't like him. I knew you wouldn't like him.'

'Meg, don't be silly. I met him for the first time five minutes ago. We've said "*hello*" to each other and that's pretty much it. Why wouldn't I like him?'

'He's boring. That's what you think, isn't it?'

Cassie grabbed a smoked salmon and cream cheese blini from the tray on the sideboard. She'd promised herself she wouldn't eat anything except the main course tonight, but a mouthful of blini gave her an excuse not to reply.

'Anyway,' Meg went on, grabbing the last two blinis on the tray and stuffing one into her mouth, 'what did the big cheese in London have to say?'

Meg ate like a child (there was already a smear of cream cheese on the end of her nose), and she spoke with her mouth full. This annoyed Cassie immensely, but, glad of the change of subject, she resisted passing comment and wiped her lips (flamboyantly) with a tartan paper napkin. 'The big cheese in London said "*no*".'

'Shit.'

'Well, we knew it wasn't a priority – not with the Grimsby operation starting to pay dividends. Maybe in the Spring?'

'Is that what *he* said? "Maybe in the Spring"?'

'No.'

'Shit, Cassie. The Parkgate School business. David Roland. Gary Mulligan. Even the Muxlow *suicide*.' Meg described inverted commas in the air around the word "*suicide*". 'If *we* don't investigate, no one will!'

'We *will* look into it. When things have calmed down a bit.'

Meg shook her head. 'They're protecting Scott Deakin. You *know* they are. MI6 have been involved in this from the get-go, and now they're applying pressure.'

'We've no evidence of that, Meg, and my Scott Deakin theory is pure speculation. I wish I'd never mentioned it now.'

Meg finished the last of the blinis and licked her lips. 'When are we eating? I'm starving.'

❧

Angus wore the McDonald name like a kilt, though none of his ancestors had, in living memory at least, ever lived in Scotland. He delivered '*Ode to a Haggis*' in an accent that brought to mind a turban rather than bagpipes. His recital stirred the audience to hoots and howls and giggles. Cassie found herself smiling . . . and, occasionally, snorting a laugh or two. It felt good. Not so long ago, she couldn't have imagined herself ever laughing again.

Flynn, who was going easy on the whisky for once, laughed along with them. He was his usual taciturn self, but at least he was with them – part of an extended quasi-family that ranged in age from Lizzie's Lambrusco-flushed mother, Yvonne Gigglesworth, to Flynn's two-year-old godson, James McDonald. At one point during the evening Cassie watched Flynn sit cross-legged on the floor, arms outstretched, while four small children in pyjamas formed a human pyramid on top of him.

He smiled, stoically.

Cassie beamed with Prosecco-fuelled pride.

ꕥ

Lizzie McDonald clapped her hands: 'Children, get to your beds! Adults, make yourselves comfortable in the drawing room.'

Flynn and Cassie found themselves alone in the dining room. 'I've something to show you,' Flynn said. He grabbed a large manila envelope from the sideboard and passed it to her. 'You were right about Gemma trying to deliver something to me. I found this in the wreckage of my old coal shed. There's no letter flap on the door to my house, so I guess she put it in the coal shed to keep it out of the weather. She must have missed the mail box at the end of the drive . . . she wouldn't be the first.'

Cassie opened the envelope and pulled out a photobook. She'd seen this sort of thing before: people upload photos and captions to a website – the printers send them back as a glossy coffee-table book. On the front cover was a picture – a selfie – of Sarah Flynn and Gemma Grant at the Winter Gardens in Sheffield city centre. They looked happy. Gemma had one arm around a squat palm tree and the other around her beaming mother. The book had the title, in a bold white typeface: '*Gemma, my life so far . . .*'. Cassie leafed through the pages:

Pictures of Gemma as a baby and as a toddler; Gemma's first day at school; a triumphant little Gemma on a pony with a red Gymkhana rosette; Gemma's first time on skis; Gemma's tenth birthday; Gemma dressed up for the School's May Ball; Gemma on the town with her friends aged thirteen. Gemma . . .

It was hard to keep turning the pages, knowing how the story would end, but she kept going, eyes wet with tears, studying each photograph, and reading each caption. On the last page, Gemma had hand-written a note:

> Dear Mr Flynn,
>
> I put together this album in the hope that you might come to feel you know me a little. My mother hoped that one day you would be a father to me, but I know this is a lot to ask, and it's probably much too late for all that. Perhaps you could be like an uncle to me, or a godfather.
>
> She told me she fell for you because you were wise and loyal and strong. I'm afraid I have none of those qualities, but I do hope we can be friends at least.
>
> Yours sincerely,
> Gemma Grant

Flynn put a hand on Cassie's shoulder.

She closed the book and put it face down on the table. 'I can't think what to say.'

'Sometimes, there is nothing to say.' He put the book back in the manila envelope. They stared at it in silence for a while.

'Cassie,' Flynn said, taking her hand, 'do you think—'

'I don't know.'

'Right.' He let go of her hand. 'I'm sorry. I'll stop pestering you, I promise.'

'Please, Flynn . . . it's just . . .' She wiped her eyes with the corner of a napkin. 'It's too soon.'

Flynn nodded. 'I know how you feel. I understand.'

Cassie sat up in her chair and folded her arms sharply. 'How could *you* understand? What Roland did to me . . .' She covered her face. She remembered Flynn's scarred back, the cigarette burns, the dull red welts on his arms. She remembered how she cried after reading that story of his. 'I'm sorry,' she said. 'You deserve better than me.'

'No, you've every right to be angry. If only I'd . . .' Flynn closed his eyes.

Cassie's face softened. 'Have you thought about the email I sent you last night.'

'Yes.'

'And?'

'Angus said I shouldn't do it. Not tonight.'

Cassie glared at the door.

'But if it means that much to you, Cassie . . .'

'It's not for *me*, Flynn, and it certainly isn't for Angus! Angus has no right to . . . to . . . it doesn't matter.' She looked him straight in the eye. 'It's for *you*,' she said.

'Yes, but—'

'I think you *need* to do it. I think it will help.'

'I know you do, but . . .' He shook his head. 'Okay, I'll do it.'

❧

When Lizzie had finished lighting candles in the drawing room, she turned out the light and chinked an empty whisky bottle with a serving spoon until the room fell silent. All eyes were upon her. A lively fire crackled cheerfully on the grate; candlelight shed strange shadows about the room; the hush was palpable.

'I'm very excited,' Lizzie said. 'Flynn has just told me that he's going to give us a reading!'

Angus shook his head slowly.

Flynn's phone buzzed; he fished it out of his pocket.

Cassie held out her hand like a school teacher.

He yielded up.

All eyes now turned to Flynn. He was in the wingback chair by the fire with a wad of paper on his lap. Lizzie had lit the oil lamp on the mantlepiece for him to read by.

'I'm glad the children have gone to bed,' Flynn said.

Lizzie's mother, Yvonne, sat up and rubbed her hands together. 'Oooo, good,' she said, 'I like a bit of sauciness!'

Flynn glanced at Cassie. She nodded encouragement, then sneaked a glance at his phone. It was locked. She couldn't help herself – Sarah Flynn's birthday (30th March) was an easy passcode to remember: 3003.

> Your latest bill is now ready to view at Virgin Mobile. Time for an upgrade? For our latest deals, please login . . .

It was disappointing to find something quite so banal. But not surprising – Flynn was not one for text messaging if he could avoid it. She was pretty sure he'd never sent *her* a text message. She'd asked him once why he'd used email to reply to a text she'd sent him. He just held up his huge right hand and wiggled his massive fingers.

Cassie should have stopped there but she didn't. She couldn't help herself – she scrolled down. The next message on the list had been received a couple of weeks ago, the day after the . . . the . . . the business with David Roland.

> Didn't I say you'd have need of that suit one day! I'm out of the country for good now, so you'll be on your own next time. Scotty.

Deakin! Her brain buzzed. If Deakin knew Flynn was wearing that stupid suit when Roland was shot, her suspicions had to be right. Cassie turned off Flynn's phone and dropped it onto her lap. The text message said it all, really. Scotty Deakin was responsible for the shooting of David Roland. And if *that* was down to him, the shooting in the school sports hall was probably down to him too. Had Deakin been minding his minder? Was that it?

Flynn always said that Deakin was his friend. Cassie had taken it for granted that Flynn was deceived, taken it for granted that Scott Deakin was a user of people, taken it for granted that Deakin had exploited a lonely teenage boy who happened to be useful with his fists. Maybe there'd been more to it than that.

And what about Gary Mulligan and all the planted evidence that ensured Flynn was off the hook? And what about those two ever-so-convenient "suicides"? What about Bernie Muxlow and Gary Mulligan?

Deakin. Had to be. But why?

Tidying up loose ends?

She closed her eyes for a moment. Now was not the time to think about all that. Now was the time to get behind Flynn. Now was the time to support him, to support him without doubt or reservation. She must move on. She must learn to forgive. She must learn to forget what no longer mattered – or to disregard it at least. She looked up . . . looked up at Flynn. He was staring, ghost-like, at the first page of his manuscript.

Yvonne Gigglesworth, complaining that she was too far away to hear properly, abandoned the comfy armchair at the far side of the room and squeezed in between her daughter and her son-in-law on the big sofa closest to the fire. 'What is it you're going to read us, love?' she asked.

Flynn turned to Yvonne but didn't answer.

'It's a short story,' Cassie said.

Yvonne persisted: 'What's it called? And don't worry about me, I'm a woman of the world, you know. The saucier the better!'

'I don't know about *saucy*,' Flynn said. He cleared his throat, swallowed, then cleared his throat again.

Yvonne clapped her hands. 'Go on then, love.'

Flynn glanced at Cassie.

She smiled and nodded.

'Right,' Flynn said, eyes focused on the page in front of him. 'This evening I'm going to read you the first story I ever wrote.' He drew a quick breath. 'It's called *The Wythenshawe Dandy.*'

THE END

This book has been typeset by
SALT PUBLISHING LIMITED
using Neacademia, a font designed by Sergei Egorov for the Rosetta Type Foundry in Czechia. It has been manufactured using Holmen Book Cream 65gsm paper, and printed and bound by Clays Limited in Bungay, Suffolk, Great Britain.

CROMER
GREAT BRITAIN
MMXXVI